Michael Hillagrove

Child of Shadow

Book 1 of the 3 Yuriauda Saga

Child of Shadow is the first book of the *3 Yorisada* series, and it is a work of fiction. While many of the characters have historical counterparts who served as inspiration, the book does not profess to be accurate in that regard. *Child of Shadow* is a reflection of the culture of that time in the early Sengoku period, also known as the period of Warring States, and is not a history book.

First published in the United States by Yorisada Publishing in 2011
1ˢᵗ Edition

Michael Hillsgrove
Yorisada Publishing
274 Rebecca Ann Court
Millersville, Maryland 21108

Proudly printed in the United States of America
Copyright © 2012 Michael Hillsgrove
All rights reserved.
ISBN: 0984025502
ISBN 13: 9780984025503
Library of Congress Control Number: 2011942075
Yorisada Publishing, Millersville, MD

child_of_shadow@YorisadaPublishing.com

www.YorisadaPublishing.com

Dedication and Acknowledgements

This book is dedicated to Akira Kurasawa and Toshiro Mifune whose many wonderful movies inspired this book. I tried to be faithful to the their spirit and to the culture and period of history in which many of their stories were told. It is also dedicated to the culture, so very different than mine, that cherished many of the same ideals that I have come to appreciate through the eyes of an older man.

My personal thanks go to my test readers, Joe Saur, Bruce Bretthauer - himself a published author, and Sophia Smith who gave me tremendous insight with a female perspective. My thanks also go to Dan who taught me the katana as I was doing research for this book, the Emergency Room staff who sewed my finger back on before I realized that I should practice with a duller sword, and the night school writing teachers at the local community college where I trolled the halls and classrooms for opinions and advice.

So, prepare to enter a very different world, of shinobi warriors and Samurai and Buddhist monks in mountain temples. I hope you enjoy reading this book as much as I enjoyed writing it.

Table of Contents

Chapter 1 – Child of Destiny

sweet child of shadow
alone, memories of death
cold bitter winter

Icicles hanging off the bare branches of the trees added to the glare off of the fresh powdered snow as the sun peeked over the mountains to the east. Early morning in the mountains of Kumi province could be especially cold, and this late winter morning was no different. A deer, stepping carefully through the hard crust, glanced toward a noise, catching the attention of a small girl who had wandered away from the mountain village. As the deer locked eyes for a moment with the raven-haired child, little Miki had to smile as the pregnant doe turned to walk down the mountainside. As Miki stood there watching the creature bound away, the sound of a frantic woman screaming her name from the direction of the village told her that perhaps she had strayed too far from the village for her mother's comfort.

Miki's mother's panic-stricken voice grew louder as the six-year-old girl turned and crunched through the snow to head back toward the village. The scrawny child, bundled in layers of well-worn, thin, brown cloth, had learned to put her feet into the same spots that she had made on the way down the hill, a tactic she had overheard the village elders teach the children selected for training.

Ahead, little Miki could see her now-silent mother staring into the woods to her right. Something had caused her mother to freeze in fear. Crunching along, Miki moved toward her mother, certain that she was facing something dangerous.

"Miki, no, run!" The woman who had been so eager to find the little girl now so desperately wanted her child to be anywhere else. The growl told the little village girl that the danger was a wolf.

"No, mama. Miki wants to be here with you."

"Miki, PLEASE, just leave. PLEASE!" Her mother was pleading, too frightened to move and without a weapon.

"No, mama. *kunoichi*[1] don't cry. If Miki runs, mother wolf will chase Miki. See, she is with child. She is alone, and she is hungry like us."

A remarkable observation, thought the scared mother. Miki was a bright child, but she was a bit naive and was braver than a six-year-old should be. *Miki listens to the stories that the village kunoichi tell and pretends to be a brave shinobi woman, but now isn't the time for pretend.* The wolf was getting closer and could very well choose the easier target.

With the appearance of the child, the wolf hesitated. While the adult female human was terrified of her and could offer no fight, the small one was not afraid in the least. Indeed, the small one was walking toward her with neither malice nor fear.

Walking to within a few feet of the wolf, tiny Miki gazed down at the large, gray wolf while Miki's mother sank to her knees in a blind panic, fascinated by the daughter, who had come so close to the vicious animal. As the woman watched, the wolf did not strike. Miki, her little baby girl, spoke to the wolf as though she were another child, seemingly a two-sided conversation between the gentle little Miki and the pregnant wolf, who sat on the snow to listen. Little Miki reached into her torn and tattered clothing to produce the little bit of cooked and dried rabbit that her mother had given her earlier and offered it to the waiting animal, who gently accepted the offering. With no more to give, Miki bowed to the wolf, who turned and started to walk away, turning back only once before disappearing. Walking back toward her

---

1. kunoichi - Female shinobi warrior or ninja. Shinobi are mountain clans that practice ninjutsu.

mother, Miki the child held out her hand and offered it to her stunned mother. Grabbing Miki, all she could do hold her close as fear, anger, and love poured out over the child in her arms. *No one in the village will believe this. Is this a good omen, or bad? Little Miki has somehow found favor with the spirits of the mountains, but will everyone agree? Best to keep this to ourselves.*

Scolding the contrite girl, mother turned toward the village with her before the mother wolf returned with friends that weren't as friendly. As they neared the edge of the woods, Norie, Miki's mother, realized that there had been a witness to the event: the village's rabbit trapper, a foolish man named Eizo, had dropped some empty traps before the taking off for the village and likely a bottle of sake. This would certainly complicate explanations, as Eizo wasn't known for discretion.

The village itself was located in a cleared-out, fairly flat patch on the mountainside and was surrounded by a low fence to keep out wolves and other predators. That fence was also supposed to be the limit for little girls who wanted to wander, a limitation that little Miki didn't seem to understand. The village was really a group of fourteen families living in twenty-two buildings, some of which housed pigs and chickens, workshops, storehouses, and meeting places. Just a few of the wooden, single-floor huts had real wooden floors, the rest being mostly packed dirt. Asking one of the other mothers to watch Miki, Norie looked around for Eizo to see if she could talk him into silence just once.

"I tell you I saw it! Little Miki just walked up to the beast and fed it. It sat down for her, and she talked to it." The scruffy, middle-aged man's hands shook pouring the sake into his porcelain bowl. Before he could put the bottle down, his equally scruffy compatriot snatched it up. He was just a bit steadier filling his own bowl.

"Wolves don't talk to little girls. They *eat* them. You're crazy." Chugging a bowl of sake, at least a portion of which dripped down his face into his chest, the unshaven, greasy man called for food.

Soon an older woman appeared from behind a partition with a plate of pickled *yamabudo*.[2] "Stop telling tales. You're the village idiot! Instead of picking on that poor little girl, you should be skinning the rabbits you killed. It was a pretty poor catch." Dropping the plate between the two men, the gray-haired old woman snatched the now-empty bottle and turned to retreat, coming face to face with Norie, who had quietly slipped in while the men argued.

"My apologies, Iyo-san. I must speak to Eizo alone for a moment. Please." Bowing to the old woman, Norie nervously glanced at the sweaty men sitting on the mats around the rough-hewn, small table in the center of the room. Eizo shoved another pickled grape into his mouth, turning his back obnoxiously on the intruding woman.

"I apologize for my son's story telling. To pick on that poor, sweet child is awful. Feeding a wolf; how silly. I'll make him tell the truth, Norie-san, and leave poor, dear Miki alone."

"I did tell the truth! That evil wart of a girl was feeding that monster. Talking to it. Feeding it. What kind of a deal did that imp make with that demon to keep it from eating you? She isn't normal, I tell you. Something is wrong with that whelp."

"Please, Eizo-san. Please! Little Miki has enough trouble without this. I will keep her in the village from now on; just please don't tell anyone. It wasn't a monster, just a hungry, pregnant stray. Miki listens to the stories that the warriors tell and tries to be like that. Please, let her grow up. Little Miki is all I have left. Please don't give them a reason to take Miki away from me."

"So it's true? She did talk to the wolf." Old Iyo, once an *aruki miko*[3], stood incredulous at the realization that for once, her son Eizo actually had not exaggerated. "Norie-san, tell me about the wolf. How do you know the wolf was pregnant?"

"Miki said so. When she was walking toward the wolf, it was as if it was waiting for her. It was with child."

---

2. yamabudo - mountain grapes
3. aruki miko - Shinto female shaman whose gifts include speaking for the dead

"The vicious beast sat down and listened to the little imp. It sat down like a dog. It's an evil omen, I tell you. We need to send the child away before she brings a disaster on us all. You should have put the baby in the snow. You can't even feed her anyway, with no husband."

"Shut up. You don't know what this means." Casting a glance at the filthy, stupid man whose hands still shook as he poured himself another bowl of the semi-clear village sake, Iyo's mind raced with possibilities. Life was hard in the mountains and usually short. *The child is different. She is intelligent and doesn't always listen well, but is certainly not evil.* "What happened then, Norie?"

"Miki talked with the wolf and then gave it the dried rabbit that she was supposed to eat this morning. Then it let us go and walked away, as if it had gotten what it came for."

"Was the child afraid?" The gray-haired old Iyo had spoken for the mountain spirits many times in her youth and knew how they worked, how they thought. *The pregnant wolf is the mountain spirit in this province called Kumi, and this child was kind to it. The spirit sought out this child and called to the tiny girl.*

"Not at all. I was, but not little Miki. It was as if the two were friends. I'm so sorry. I should not have bothered you. Please, don't tell the village elders. I beg all of you." Norie knew that it was a waste of time getting Eizo to cooperate. At least not without old Iyo to help. Worse, the other man in the room was Goro, Eizo's favorite drinking buddy and the head of the village council.

"Bring the child here. I will speak with the little Miki alone." Iyo could not believe her luck. Her gift of speaking for the mountain spirits had deserted her when she took a husband, but she knew the meaning of what had happened. *This is a child of destiny.*

"Iyo-san, Norie-san. This is now a matter for the village council to decide. Bring the child to the meeting hut at sundown." Goro was not sure what the events meant, but he was certain what effect Eizo's story would have on the people of the village. *My friend is scared, and the other villagers will be, too. It is best to control the situation before it gets out of hand.*

Iyo hated how the men always felt the need to control everything. "Goro-san, it is a gift that we have been given. Please let me speak with little Miki so that we may understand the message of the Kami. I alone can do this."

Goro needed time, and the elders could not be called together before the evening. In a village of Koga shinobi, spies and assassins by birth, it was useless to keep secrets, anyway. "Get the child. Iyo-san, I will send for you when the council is ready."

The night was cold but clear. The events of the morning had made their rounds, and the entire village had heard one version of the story or the other. Old Iyo was nearly a legend among the Koga, and her word carried great weight among the women of the village. She had been in with the child all morning, afternoon, and now deep into the evening. The village council had been waiting and was now getting impatient, although sake did seem to make the time pass more tolerably. Now, with nearly the entire village shivering outside of Iyo's hut, the council could wait no longer. The sake had run out.

A knock at the door and shouts from a crowd stirred the old woman awake. As she opened her old eyes, the dark, round eyes of an attentive, smiling little girl sitting, waiting, watching, greeted her. There is no relationship quite like the bond between the very old and the very young, and little Miki had brightened her day. Iyo had watched her grow and play since the day of her birth, and the child never failed to bring a smile to everyone she met. This was a rare gift in the world of poverty and harsh training of the Koga shinobi. Now, foolish men in the village council stood to judge her for signs that none of them could possibly understand.

As the door opened, the old woman emerged with short, raven-haired Miki with her dark, penetrating eyes. Iyo ignored the questions and walked to the meeting hut holding the apprehensive child's hands as they were directed into the rough shack that was where the men went to train, talk, and drink. That strange mix of sweat, sake, burning wood, and filth that made even Miki's nose curl as they took their place facing the six men who would decide her fate, was the stench of men who had given up, who took no more pride in themselves. Iyo and the other women had talked about it and had no solution.

Pushed higher and higher into the forests of the mountains to avoid annihilation by Hamatsu troops, the Koga were a clan in deep trouble. When spring came, so would the Samurai with their soldiers, and they would slaughter anyone who could be identified as Koga. Keeping the village hidden was the only way to avoid death for the entire village. These were defeated men who took solace in superstition and anything they could drink. Once employed by the Yorisada who had once ruled Kumi, they had been warriors, spies, and trusted allies to all of the Daimyo and Samurai rulers in this part of Nippon. But that was before, before Lord Nobunaga betrayed the Yorisada and conquered Kumi.

"Little Miki. The council has talked about you and the wolf and has decided that you are dangerous to the village. In the spring you will be sent to the village on the north road and traded for food for the village. Wolves are bad omens, and you..."

"You fools! You drunk, cowardly, stupid fools. Not one of you is smart enough to understand that..."

"Silence, woman. We have to protect the..."

"THIS brave little girl has more courage then all the men in this village. The mountain spirits have sought out this child to save the Koga, and you would send her away? The pregnant wolf kami chose Miki. This is a child of destiny. If Miki leaves this village, this village will die. This child must be trained as kunoichi. Miki must be allowed to walk the path that the Kami has chosen for her."

As the men began to talk among themselves, Miki, who had been sitting silently, stood and walked toward Goro, locking her dark, penetrating, round eyes with his. "Mother wolf was hungry, like us. She knows pain like us. Soon the soldiers will come and destroy the village. She says we must move or we will be food for the wolf. We must move the village again." She glanced back at the gray-haired woman for just an instant, then turned to smile at the stunned, scared man who had no words for the scrawny child. She stood, waiting for Goro-san to speak, and then the girl added, "If you send Miki away, the spirits won't protect the village any more. Mother wolf said that Miki has something to do with her life."

"The child is a miko, as I was at her age. She can be trained as I was to speak for the spirits to save us all. Miki is a child of destiny, and it is well past her bedtime. Come, child; poor Norie-san must be terrified." The old woman had heard enough. *Reason never prevails with drunk men. If they don't want the child in the village, I will take her to the Shinto shrine in Yoron.* Leaving the useless men to wallow in their pathetic, self-important misery, child and old woman welcomed the clean smell of the cold outside air as they turned toward the hut at the edge of the village that Norie called home.

Chapter 2 - Banishment

old and young exiled
breaking of a mothers heart
a journey to truth

"She is a bastard child. Norie-san can't even feed herself, much less the little brat. She was out there feeding that monster again yesterday. Norie can't even watch the miserable little whelp. Two more villages were slaughtered by Hamatsu soldiers, and who knows what kind of luck that kid will bring us." Reaching for the pot of sake, Eizo had already lamented his empty traps, blaming it on the child who now was the cause of all of the world's suffering. "The worthless little wench just eats poor Norie out of house and home, and what little she has she gives away to vicious wolves. We need to drive her out of the village, I tell you. I'll just walk over there and snap the child's neck. It would be good for Norie, who could finally take a husband. A woman can't live alone. Maybe I'll take her myself. My mother is getting old, and she eats too much. Norie would keep my bed warm, at least."

Goro sipped his bowl and glanced at his dirty friend. It was spring now, and most of the six- and seven-year-old children would be joining the children from the other villages for training. Those who showed aptitude would be trained as warriors and leave their families to join their training group. This village had no warriors left and eked out a living producing poisons and tools for the other, larger villages. It was a dying village, either by starvation or by the hands of Hamatsu soldiers or their Iga allies.

As they were pushed higher and deeper into the mountains, agriculture was no longer possible. The harsh winters and meager hunting were killing them all.

"Miki is a sweet little girl. She tries so hard to be helpful. Why you are so afraid of her?" *Besides, what does it matter? Neither the little girl nor her mother can get enough food to live through the spring.*

The sun was fully up on this clear and crisp day. Most of the snow was gone, although not too much farther up the mountain, there would still be plenty. It was the day chosen for Miki and old Iyo-san to go to the shrine so that the priests could tell her what her future would be. What neither her heartbroken mother nor Iyo-san could bring themselves to tell the child, and what none of the men had the courage to tell the sprite little girl, was that she would not be returning home. Superstition and greed had gotten the better of the men, and both the old shaman woman and the child had been banished. Two fewer mouths to feed for a hungry village, two fewer non-producing people, and now a free woman for Eizo to claim for himself.

Wrapping the child in all of the clothing she had, Norie had stuffed the bag with anything edible as well as a toy top that Miki played with often. Norie handed the bag to the grateful old woman, whose own bag had been robbed of food by her own son, Eizo. The old miko Iyo bowed, thanking her friend Norie, whose heart was filled with shame, hugging the baby girl who stood smiling at the adventure that awaited her. None of the men who had decided to banish the old woman and girl had the courage to face the simple child.

As the child walked away, she turned to her quivering mother and smiled one last time. "Don't worry, mama. When I come back, I will bring you some rice. I promise."

"I know you will."

Norie stood outside the rough gate to the village watching her child, the child whose dark secret was shared by a village, disappear among the trees as she made her way toward an uncertain destiny. As she turned to return through the gate, little Miki's smile and last words stabbed at her heart as the strength left her legs and she crumbled to the ground, pouring out all the sorrow of a mother watching her child die. Hope, always so much a part of little Miki's love, was gone. She had failed.

Springtime in the mountains was a time of life in bloom. Doe nursed their clumsy young faun, and the multicolored blossoms were just beginning to paint the mountainsides between the gray rocks and trees on the often-steep slopes. Old Iyo was a woman of the mountains, yet age made the journey particularly difficult. Only the fact that she had chosen to proceed down, rather than across, the forested mountain's face made the journey possible. The child Miki steadied the old woman as they clung to branches and used boulders and trees to control their descent down the steepest portion. Despite the cuts and bruises, one especially welcome effect of going downhill was that the temperature was getting noticeably warmer.

With a well-worn but narrow dirt road before them, the exhausted, gray-haired Iyo and tired child Miki collapsed on the edge of the road under a moss bank. Reaching into the bag that Norie had given her, Iyo shared the dried meat and cooked mountain potato with her young charge. Soon Miki was refreshed enough to pull the hand of the tired and less-than-energetic old woman. West would take them to the village where the lake trail met the north road. From there, it would take another day or two to get to the Buddhist temple on the north road. East, over the mountain pass, through the gate pass to Isawa, and then to Yoron would be a large Shinto shrine. It was at the shrine in Yoron that Iyo herself had been trained. It was there that she knew she could find a place for Miki to learn the skills required of a shrine maiden, and the bright, gifted, dark-eyed little girl could start her new life.

At the highest elevation on this well-traveled road to the east was a gate between two sheer cliffs. With neither a pass nor permission, and no money to bribe a guard, east toward the temple was the easy choice. Monks, who traveled the road freely, could be persuaded to escort the very young child and the very old miko to the shrine in Yoron. It would be unlikely that they would seem much of a threat, and it was this thought that had made the shrine to the west Iyo's destination. A two- or three-day journey for a strong man, it would take longer for a six-year-old child and a woman whose years could not be easily counted.

As the pair stood to move east, really the only choice, Miki pointed to a column of men coming down the road toward them. She was fascinated by the man riding the large animal, like a gigantic deer. On his head was a hat with a big metal flower on the front, and he carried a really long sword, more curved than the straighter, shorter swords carried by the men in her village. The men walking behind carried big sticks with leather covers on the tips, and a few carried bows like the village hunters. They clanked as they walked, and with them was a man who looked as if he could be a villager. As the men came close, the little girl felt the old woman's hand pushing her head down to force her to bow low.

"Miki, bow. These men are Samurai and are very dangerous. Stay quiet or they can kill us both. Please listen."

Samurai. She had never seen a real Samurai. She had heard about them. All the men in the village were terrified of them. Here they were, on the same road. As the man on the large animal stopped, the brown-and-white animal spooked, and for a few moments the man could not control the beast. As men scattered, Miki raised her head to watch the scene. As the man fell, the men dropped their sticks and helped him stand. He took his helmet off, and she could see the scar across his face and that part of his ear was missing. He was powerful and well built with a beard—not like the thin, broken men in the village.

"What did you do?" shouted the angry man. As Miki looked into his eyes, she could see meanness, like Eizo-san's eyes from the village. The difference was that in this man's eyes, there was no fear like the constant terror in Eizo's. Old Iyo-san cringed beside her and covered the child, expecting the worst. A sword would cut through them both if he chose. Pulling the old woman off the child, the enraged, ugly, scarfaced man slapped the old woman hard, sending her sailing into the moss bank behind her. As he turned his attention to Miki, her dark, penetrating eyes met his, and he raised his hand to strike her down. Miki was kunoichi. She would not show fear. She would stare into the man's eyes to see if this might be the man whom her mother said had killed her father. He wouldn't see fear from her, just as the mother wolf had seen no fear.

He stood with his hand raised, expecting the small child to cringe, or flinch, or run. She peered into his eyes with absolute courage, with a calmness that no Samurai had ever shown him. Killing this baby would be no victory. It would not placate his anger. Lowering his hand, he signaled for a small bag from his horse. Tossing the bag at the girl's feet, he nodded, admiring her nerve as he remounted his horse. "Perhaps we shall meet again when you are a bit older."

"*Hai,*[4] Samurai-san."

So she can speak. Perhaps the horse senses something in the child that she has just showed him. As he turned and shouted orders, the men made their way into the woods as several others took control of the horse.

Iyo-san grabbed the bag and pushed the child down the road eastward, toward the lake road. They had been lucky to escape with their lives, and once again the child had demonstrated something different, something remarkable. The soldiers were looking for Koga villages, but somehow the child and old woman just didn't seem a threat. Once past the soldiers, the old woman opened the bag and nearly dropped it with excitement. The coins in this bag more than paid for the pain and bloody mouth that she had suffered. While his anger had been fierce, his apology was sufficient. She and little Miki, foolishly brave little Miki, would eat well when they reached the town. As the old miko looked down at her young charge, she was beginning to realize that the trick would be to keep the precocious child alive. "Miki-san. You must show respect for Samurai. You could have died. The horse smelled the wolf on you, and that is why she bolted. I should have realized."

---

4. hai - means yes.

"I don't like Samurai." The child had formed that opinion quickly enough.

"Little Miki, you must learn respect for those of a higher class if you want to live. We are eta, and of the lowest class." Yet, she had defeated a retainer with a glance. She had to learn her place in the world. One of many lessons to come.

The teahouse where the lake trail met the north road was a place of wonder to the child from the mountains. The floor was wooden throughout the entire large structure. It had walls inside to partition off areas used by different people. The building could hold upwards of twenty or twenty-five people, and all of the meals were hot. White rice was plentiful, and the people were all clean and well dressed in colorful clothing. For the first time in her life, Miki had a warm bath and something new to wear, and she had never been so happy. These were the very first people the wide-eyed girl had met outside of her village. Everyone was polite. Even more amazing, most of them were even happy. Behind the partition where she and Iyo-san had slept, they had thick, warm blankets and soft mats to sleep on. For the first time in her short life, Miki had gone to bed with a full belly.

The lady of the teahouse sent her daughter out to clean the rags the child had been dressed in, the remnants of clothing already worn out by adults that had been cut down for the tyke. In the meantime, Iyo-san had given her a brightly colored kimono in the child's size to wear, purchased from the lady of the teahouse. While the simple garment was used, the daughter of the owner of the teahouse had outgrown it. It was the most beautiful thing that Miki had ever seen. Never had the wide-eyed child seen or had so much, and she had never been so happy.

It was morning now, and as Iyo-san led the clean and pretty little Miki out into the bright sunlight, before the child's eyes was an astonishing sight. There were people—and not just people, but little people just like her. Not just boys, but girls like her. Up and down the street, dozens of children of all ages. Some were helping a mother or a father, but most were just playing. In her village she was the only girl who had been allowed to live. For the first time, the bright child realized just how much there was to see and do and experience in her wonderful new world.

Iyo looked at the bouncing child who wanted to play with the other children. But these children were dangerous to her little Miki. Being Koga was a crime in Kumi now, and the last thing they needed was for Miki to tell anyone what she was. Cautioning the little girl against saying anything, old Iyo decided that perhaps, just once, the curious girl could be a child, just for a day. The temple could wait for a day or two because once Miki entered training as miko, her childhood would be over.

One particular girl fascinated Miki, who asked Iyo what the girl was holding. It looked like a very small person and the brown haired girl held it close, almost like a baby. "Miki, that is a doll. Girls grow up to be mothers and they like to pretend to be mothers." Miki had never seen another girl her age before, and she watched in wonder how the boys treated her differently.

The girls spoke first to Miki, who seemed uncertain at first about leaving Iyo's side. The oldest, a ten-year-old whose name was Ai, cajoled her in their games while Iyo looked on. Would it be so terrible if poor Miki were allowed to just have a family and other children for friends, she wondered. Iyo watched Miki sing and dance and play, trying to do it all, begging for more until the evening when mothers dragged each and every other child in for the night, leaving little Miki alone in the street. That night, Miki slept well.

The rain fell hard as Miki and Iyo made their way down the narrow road. To their left was a sheer cliff wall and to the right a drop of a thousand feet into a cold mountain lake. The gray skies and downpour hid the surrounding mountains and lake below in a haze. Walking in the rain was the price they were paying for the two days that Miki had spent learning to be a child. Now she was on her way to enter a life of service to a shrine, to lose the childhood that she had been allowed only to taste, to touch, but not possess. Yet those two days were more than any other child in her village had ever had.

By the time the sun started down, both exhausted child and tired old woman were shivering hard as the day's temperature gave way to the chill of evening. The rain had ceased, but the fog remained, hiding the top of the wooden stairs that would lead to the temple gate where Iyo hoped that the kindness of the monks would save their lives. This was the woman's hope. Iyo, the old miko, had no other plan.

At the base of the steps stood a small shrine, a shrine that she had helped maintain decades ago as a traveling miko. Parents who had lost children had placed pebbles around the monument to gather favor for the spirits of their children with the mountain's Kami. Dropping her eyes, she looked for the two that she had placed herself so many years ago. The tug at her hand also tugged at her heart, for old Iyo-san had no desire to place a third pebble this night. Peering up the steps, Iyo signaled the silent child toward the steep stairs to what looked to be a path to the clouds themselves.

The painful climb up the steep steps caused both the old woman and child to slip and collapse several times. By the time the pair made the climb, darkness had taken full hold. As she stood before the large, wooden door, it took all of the old woman's remaining strength to reach the rope that would ring the bell. Ringing once in case the monks were in meditation, old woman and young girl waited, praying for enough hospitality to keep them alive for one more night. Questioning the decision to start the journey on this day, Iyo, who could hide illness no longer, coughed and sneezed. She knew this was Miki's last chance. It was unlikely that she would live long enough to make the quest to the Shinto Shrine in Yoron. Hope was running thin.

An eternity standing forlorn in the darkness was rewarded by the creak of the large, brown gate. The young monk inside stared at the pathetic sight of the gray-haired, sickly old woman who pushed forward a scrawny little girl with large, round, dark eyes, made more pathetic by the soggy clothing that hung on her. Both were shivering hard, and the silent plea for help carried by the child's penetrating stare forced him to reflect on his instructions to send visitors away. Taking only a second, the bald, young monk stepped back, motioning for the pair to come in.

Watching the two weary and wet travelers hobble along touched his heart, and no monk could ever be expected to turn away such an opportunity for an act of kindness.

Helping the obviously ill woman into the main building attracted the disapproving attention of several other monks and an *Ama* who had been meditating, until the full magnitude of the terrible need was manifest. Shouted orders sent monks on deliberate tasks as the middle-aged Ama took charge, giving orders. The pair was carried to a room on the second floor, where they were stripped of their wet clothing and wrapped in robes. The Ama, a woman they called Masako was in in her forties and as bald as the men, went to work caring for the ill Iyo while care of the little girl fell to the tall, thin, twenty-five-year-old monk who had opened the door. As the child stopped shaking, wrapped in the brown cloth of a monk's robes, she fell asleep in the gentle man's arms. Somehow, it seemed wrong to put her down. With a tear, he decided just to hold the child, whose name he did not know, in his arms—where the featherlight girl seemed to belong.

Born a high-ranking Samurai, the simple monk called Akaki reflected how much like the Buddha his life had been. As a child, sheltered by the accident of a noble birth, he had never seen suffering or understood what it was like in the world outside his castle. Since that moment when he had escaped, brought here by Lord Oto as a teenager, the boy had become a man capable of seeing the misery and suffering of others. On that first day in the temple, he was brash, arrogant, and selfish. Now, Akaki reflected on how easy it was for a small stranger to touch his heart. The man and not the boy, Akaki the Samurai had given way to Akaki the monk. The child in his arms and the misery of the woman sleeping before him were his purpose now. Their need was his, and seeing this little girl grow into a woman would be a joy worthy of a well-lived life if he could find her a home.

The old woman named Iyo had gotten worse during the night, and the Ama Masako worked hard to control Iyo's fever. Masako had come to the temple ten years earlier to escape both poverty and a drinking husband and had stayed even though the man had died. Now the principal healer in the temple, she had learned how to use the herbs and natural medicines and remedies of the mountains. This was a battle with death, with the life of the old miko named Iyo hanging in the balance. Masako's compassion for others was well known in the northern part of the Kumi province, and more than a few people made the journey to the north road temple to be healed by her hands. Akaki remembered how foolish he had thought she was to care so deeply for strangers and the lowest classes of society. As his understanding of humanity grew, what he had perceived as a foolish weakness he now saw as Masako's great strength—her endless compassion for others, no matter who they were.

The little girl named Miki sat beside the old woman, running errands for Masako or anyone else who seemed to need her. She seemed exceptionally bright and more cheerful than she had any right to be, her unusually dark expressive eyes opening a view into the child's gentle soul. It was, of course, forbidden to keep a child in the temple; eventually they would have to find her a home.

According to the old woman, she had been banished from her village and was on her way to become a miko at a Shinto shrine. One thing that the woman had said stood out, however. It was a gift that Akaki had seen in only one other person: the ability to speak with wolves.

"Masako-san, what are your feelings for how the old woman is doing?" Akaki wanted to question Iyo but didn't want to hurt her in the process.

"I apologize, Monk Akaki. She is not doing well. I do not know if I can help her. She is breathing hard, and I am concentrating on making her passing easy. The child is sweet. I am working as hard as I can, but I do not know what else I can do." Masako's compassion for others intensified as her helplessness at stopping the inevitable clearly bothered her. Instead of destroying the woman, each person, alive or dead, made Masako the healer more determined to follow her chosen path.

Something bothered Akaki. Something about the tiny girl felt familiar. "I need to speak with Iyo-san. There is something very strange about little Miki I need to discuss with her. Is she strong enough?"

"If you need to speak with the old woman, do it now. She may not last the night. Iyo-san has been asking for you by name." Masako had done all that she could. Nodding when Akaki asked to be left alone with the old woman who was resting so peacefully, Masako reached down to hold the child's hand as she stared at the old woman who had become her family. Leading the child out the room, she turned only to slide the door shut behind her.

Sitting beside the old woman, who was clearly aware of his presence, he could see the softness of her features in the flickering glow of the lanterns that surrounded the room. This was a woman who had seen death, and she was very aware that her own was waiting for her. Old Iyo had tried to speak to him before, but the child or other monks were always present. His presence now, alone, told the woman that they had given up hope. There was a secret that could not die with her. This monk who seemed to be so taken with Miki the child would need to know who she really was.

"I heard Ama Masako call you Akaki." Coughing, Iyo sipped the tea that the young monk held to her lips. Feeling better a bit, Iyo knew that she had little time for formalities. This man was probably the only one who could help Miki now. Her own time was up, and this was far too important to her clan and to Miki. "I know who you are. I was serving in the house of my Lord Oto on a task for my clan. A young woman I was serving with was favored by Lord Oto and became his lover. I was angry at Norie, who forgot why we were there and returned his love. When Nobunaga betrayed the Yorisada and Lord Oto was killed, they didn't know who we were, and we managed to escape. We were not important, so they did not hunt us down. What they didn't know was that the woman was with child."

Seven years had passed since those events. Oto's secret lover was the worst-kept secret in the Hamatsu court. The old woman had been there that terrible night when his own brother had ordered his death and she described Oto's bloody fight and his narrow escape. If it was a lie, it served no purpose.

"The man she was told was her father was killed years before she was born." Sipping more tea, the exhausted Iyo needed to make him understand. Time was short, and she would not have a second chance.

The relationship between Oto, a highborn Samurai, and his mistress was a closely guarded secret. The difference in class made that vital. Oto, his friend, would have been married to a woman approved by his clan had time allowed for it before the great betrayal. *This woman is dying. Why lie now?* He would always see to the child's future, so she had nothing to fear on behalf of the child. Still, questions remained.

"Who was the woman? What was her name? Where is she now?" Questions an impostor could not answer, not even a trained liar.

Coughing again, bringing up some blood, Iyo looked hard into his eyes. "Norie was her name, and he called her his Cherry Blossom. He would signal her by flipping the stone in the koi pond over and I would flip it back and tell her. Norie would meet him in the school where he taught the sword. Gendo-san and I would watch out for them."

Sitting back, the monk knew that this was the truth. Only one thing: Oto wasn't as dead, as Iyo believed. Akaki owed Oto his life, and the survival of his friend—and now this child—demanded that no one know that secret.

"Norie is in the Koga village hidden near the tree line. The villagers in the North village above this temple will know where it is." Thinking a bit, she added, "So will Miki. She has the best sense of direction anyone in the village has ever seen."

This changed everything. This child named Miki would never be a miko. Never would he allow her to be taken to the Shinto shrine in Yoron for training. "I understand. I will take care of the child. But for her own protection, no one must ever know."

Knowing he believed, she closed her eyes. It was time for her to rest. Softly she uttered, "The last blood of the Yorisada clan, and our last hope."

This was a day of secrets. The old miko would die having protected this one, having gotten it to the one man who could use it. Holding her hand, Akaki could not find the words to thank her. Sitting with her while she passed this night was a small repayment for her sacrifice and her gift.

Chapter 3 - Death

prophecies fulfilled
a village punished, wolves eat
path of destiny

The night was a rough one for the old woman, whose struggle
for life ended shortly before the first glint of sunlight filtered
through the drafty shutters. Monk Akaki had held her hand as
this fellow monastic had taken her last, labored breath. No one
in her world would shed a tear for this remarkable woman outside of these walls, and yet many of them would live or die by her
gift.

The man whose tears coursed down tired cheeks would have
simply dismissed the old woman as unworthy of even consideration once. A young Samurai caught in a murderous power
struggle, he had fled to this temple to hide from a brother who
would have his blood. The head monk had taken him reluctantly, and those lessons were both harsh and difficult. Praying for
old Iyo, the old Shinto shrine maiden now at peace, the monk
Akaki watched the child who could not be dragged from Iyo's
side begin to stir.

Miki, who had been sleeping beside the old miko, now
rubbed her red eyes, sitting up to see the tears in the kind young
monk's face. Death, always present in her mountain village, was
something that even this six-year-old child understood. Now,
totally alone for the very first time in her young life, with the last

link to anything that she had ever known dead by her side, she could no longer play the brave kunoichi as sorrow washed over her like a bucket of cold water. Throwing herself on top of the still, old friend with outstretched arms, Miki cried until breathing was difficult.

"No child should see death like this." Masako the Ama moved to pull the child off the old woman until Akaki stopped her.

"Let her grieve. This child has known death from the moment of her birth, and her misery is only beginning. Let Miki say good-bye to her friend now. Her life's journey will be with death by her side." Standing to leave, Akaki faced the temple's Master, whose serene expression belied what Akaki knew was a deep sense of compassion and understanding of humanity.

Peering past his young acolyte to the child whose arms encircled the dead woman who had cared for her, the wrinkled old monk had wanted to speak to Iyo, a woman he knew well. "Did she suffer much?"

"Yes. But she managed to tell me why she brought the child here."

"I have known the woman for sixty years. Her gifts were remarkable. We did not always agree, but Iyo-san was my friend. I had intended to visit her in the spring one last time. Now it is too late for apologies. Thank you, Monk Akaki, for spending time with my friend in her last moment of need." Walking down the wooden aisle toward the larger room where about thirty monks would have already started morning meditation, he stopped as he sensed that Akaki had stopped. "The child cannot remain in the temple. In a few days, we will have to find a home for her. We can care for her until then."

"Actually, no, Master. This one is different. This one needs to remain at the temple."

His young friend was not the most obedient of his acolytes but had become a kind, giving monk. Akaki was upset for good reason, and although uncharacteristic, his defiance was understandable. The girl was hauntingly beautiful. "Forgive me, my young friend, but this is a decision that I will not revisit. In a few days, you will see that finding her a home with a mother and a father is best for her. She seems to be a sweet little girl. I understand your compassion for her. It would be very difficult to not love such a gentle little child."

The decision was final, yet it could not stand. To honor Iyo's sacrifice, to keep the old woman's last hope alive, Akaki would have to make the master understand. "Forgive me my impertinence. I mean no disrespect."

"Of course."

"Master, you need to hear what your friend Iyo-san told me. Please. This is important. We must not let this girl leave. For now, she belongs here." This was the equivalent to a revolt. Monks had been dismissed from the temple for less. Akaki stared into the master's eyes and hoped for just a few minutes of explanation.

"Walk with me in the garden. I will hear this story, but then you will make arrangements for the child to find a family." Never had any monk ever been so insistent. His defiance would have to be punished, despite Akaki's station in life. Yet the look in the young monk's eyes made his patience seem justified.

The last shovelful of dirt had been thrown, and rocks were being placed over the grave of the old woman who had brought the child named Miki to the North Road temple. Miki herself had labored hard placing and carrying the rocks that she could lift and move. In the day since old Iyo's death, she had hidden her tears well. Now alone, she would have to be strong for Iyo. Masako had been given charge of the girl, and a close bond had developed between the gentle Masako and the active, remarkably self-sufficient six-year-old. Always helpful, the brutally honest child had earned her keep, and it was all the temple master could do to keep all the members of the temple focused on their assigned tasks and not playing with the child. Within the day, Miki's dark eyes and cheerful face had won over even the sternest monk.

The matter of what to do with the child had been the subject of virtually every conversation since the mountain sprite had arrived ten days earlier. Masako kept the child with her most of the time, and Miki worked very hard to please the kind Ama. One particular talent that Masako and the Master came to appreciate as the days passed, and be concerned by, was the child's detailed knowledge of mountain herbs and spices. It seemed that her village had taught her the use—and misuse—of most of the plants that grew on the mountain face. She could pick out each of the flowers and describe which were poisons and which were safe. Masako had prided herself on her knowledge of the healing herbs, but this tiny creature of the mountains showed the middle-aged Ama medicines and preparations that were new to her. Miki was far brighter than most children and remembered everything that anyone was willing to teach her. Well fed for the first extended period of her life, Miki began to fill out a bit, making her less like the skeleton that she had been on that first dark, wet night.

Master Kukai had made several inquiries on behalf of Miki, but times were hard, and young girls were difficult to find a home for when food was scarce. Several less-than-worthy offers had been made, but Master Kukai decided that this child's safety had to come first. Worse, the old monk was facing a silent revolt among the temple's monks, whose hearts had decided that the girl should stay. No family seemed good enough to satisfy the substitute fathers and mother of the temple, and no one could speak about sending her away without a crack in his voice or tear in his eye. In this mighty battle between the authority and wisdom of an old monk and the gentleness and loving heart of a child, the child had taken every engagement. Sending little Miki away was now impossible.

The old temple master had only one trick left. Miki still had a mother. This was the only way the other monks would accept the loss of the young girl's smile and infectious giggle. Finding the village was a problem best left to the Koga shinobi who protected the temple.

"Miki-san, would you like to see your mother again?" The old monk had joined Masako and little Miki in the kitchen as the morning meal was being prepared. The little girl had been assigned the task of washing the mushrooms, a task especially suited to the child as she had probably saved a life or two by recognizing the difference between the edible and poisonous variety that one of the less skilled monks had picked earlier.

"Hai." The girl's smile disappeared as she bowed quickly.

"What is wrong, Miki-san?" The girl had picked up that the question had real consequences. Master Kukai was not going to fool her.

"You want me to leave the temple." Here, Miki felt that she belonged. The thought that she would be banished again, cast out and stripped of everything that she knew yet again filled her mind. "What have I done wrong? I'm very sorry." Miki felt her world crashing around her again; the strength that she had shown her mother wasn't there this time. With the dream of being kunoichi gone, with Iyo gone, and even the idea of becoming a miko now gone, all Miki could do was shake hard as she tried to hold in the sorrow. Darting out of the room past several monks, the girl turned into the meditation room and chose a spot behind the large, golden Buddha that had become her hiding spot during meditation and classes for the younger monks.

What is wrong with me? Other girls like me have someone who loves them, who wants them. What did I do wrong? Shaking and crying, Miki buried her face in her hands, ignoring the sounds of shuffling feet and quiet questions. *Why can't anyone love me? I try so hard.*

Masako, standing behind Master Kukai, was furious but trying hard to maintain her composure. "How could you say that? What were you thinking?"

Surrounded by monks and acolytes, all of whom wore stern, disapproving expressions, the temple master felt very alone and utterly defeated, knowing that whatever the real story, this temple now had its very own little girl to raise. Still, he had to speak to Norie. For that, he needed the Koga.

Turning to the grim-faced monks whose silence screamed louder than any voice could muster, all Master Kukai could do was throw up his hands in surrender. "Please find Akaki. Tell him that he is now little Miki's teacher. Our little girl will be staying. Also send a message to the Koga. I would like to speak to the girl's mother." The temple master, who was now master of nothing, dived through the door to find solitude in his own chambers away from angry eyes.

"Come, Miki. You will be staying with me from now on. No one will be sending you away. You are home now." Masako could feel the child's suffering. This could be her gift to the old woman whose life she could not save. Giving and loving had rewards that this woman had missed. The Ama who had escaped a violent husband now had a second chance at a daughter and a family.

During the day the bright and energetic Miki worked with Masako in the kitchen and occasionally outside the temple walls gathering herbs and firewood. On this particular morning they would collect mushrooms and medicines together from the woods behind the mountain Zen temple.

"Stay close to me Miki, I do not want you lost in the woods. You have only been here about a month and I do not want the wolves to get you." Masako smiled as the cheerful child bounced about helping her choose herbs and mushrooms, even pointing out a few that she learned from her own mother.

"The wolf isn't here to hurt Miki, Masako-san. He is watching over me, protecting me."

"What?" She turned to see the smiling child face to face with the largest animal she had ever seen. Panic-stricken, all she could do is watch as the large male wolf, calmly walk away as though he had enjoyed a visit with a friend. Unnerved and in tears, Ama Masako swiftly dragged the confused child through the back gate of the temple.

"MIKI! You will never never go outside again without one of the men. Ever, do you understand. You could have been killed!" Still shaking, she knew that this is something Temple Master Kukai needed to know.

Since the monks of the temple, by silent revolt, had adopted the child, Akaki had been questioning the child to prove or disapprove Iyo's remarkable story. Since no one had shared the child's true heritage with her, all Miki could do was to confirm the story about the wolf and the village's reaction. With a visibly upset Ama demanding protection for her new charge Akaki and Temple Master Kukai now had reason to accept the story as true.

Masako now refused to go outside without an escort and requested that Miki be restricted to the temple, disappointing the child, who either saw no danger or knew no fear. Indeed, the only thing that the child seemed to be genuinely afraid of was being left alone.

The day was warm, and Masako was sitting on the porch with Miki cutting vegetables and preparing herbs. The thought of letting a child that small use a sharp knife made most members of the temple staff edgy, but she had apparently been given careful instruction and had enough experience to satisfy her guardian Masako. Akaki interrupted the productive pair to speak to Miki.

"Miki, several days ago I sent for friends from the Koga village from above the temple. The village you lived in is gone now. We could not find your mother."

"They are all dead. Iyo-san told them that if Miki went away, the mountain kami would not protect them anymore. They would die and be eaten by the wolves."

"So the wolves will kill them all?" Akaki smiled at the child's simple understanding. Old Iyo might well have said that, but wolves did not attack villages.

"No, Akaki-san. The Samurai men killed them all. The man with the cut on his face killed them. The wolves will only eat them."

How does she know about the man with the scar? The man with the scar was probably Sir Tomoe Satake. Missing part of an ear and with a large scar from an accident in a sword class, he had a fearsome appearance. It was Satake's treachery that had almost cost his and Lord Oto's life. Had it not been for the warning from the wolf that Oto had raised from a cub, they both would have been killed that terrible day seven years earlier. *Oto's wolf warned us. Oto always had a way with animals, especially dogs and wolves. Has he passed that gift to his children?* he wondered. "Miki-san, did the wolf tell you about Sir Satake—I mean the scarfaced man?"

"No, Master Akaki. Iyo-san and Miki saw him and his Samurai men on the road coming here. He beat Iyo-san because Miki made the animal that he was riding fall."

"Satake is not a forgiving man. Why did he not kill both of you?"

"Miki made him stop." Staring directly into Akaki's eyes, the little girl's cold, dark expressive eyes sent a chill down the monk's spine.

Surprised, the former Samurai found it hard to believe. "Miki, tell me the truth. You did not see the scarfaced man, did you?" Akaki had not caught her in a lie yet. The gentle child had seemed incapable of telling lies, even when scared of punishment. Yet this was too much to believe.

Reaching into folds of the robes that the monks had made for her, the child produced the small bag that contained the money that the scarfaced man had tossed to her. She handed the bag to the stunned man, who turned it over to see the fan-shaped *mon* that was the symbol of the Satake family. Any remaining doubt was gone.

The lights from the lanterns flickered, sending shadows to dance on the white walls in the small fourth-floor room of the temple. Four men sat in a circle enjoying the tea that Masako had served before retiring for the night. Nighttime in a mountain Buddhist temple is a quiet time, but this evening was even more silent than usual. The normal chirp of insects and cries of the wolves were eerily absent, as though the stars in the heavens were awaiting some momentous event. With the universe holding its breath, it was time to make certain decisions.

"You do not think the child evil, then?" The younger of the two men who had slipped into the temple after dark spoke quietly, shifting his eyes between the other three men in the room nervously.

"Most certainly not. I admit that when she arrived, I would have preferred to send her away. But the other monks would not allow it. Miki has a way of bringing joy and filling hearts. Even food and money offerings have increased since she arrived. She does tricks quite unbecoming an Ama, yet she has the best balance and is as nimble as anyone I have ever seen." The old monk sat back and smiled. "And she can make an old man laugh again. I had forgotten how. No, Miki is most certainly not evil. My friend Iyo-san was right. This is a child of destiny."

"So you believe that she is who she claims to be." For Kawachi, the Koga representative, this was a gift.

"The child Miki has never claimed anything and seems quite unaware of what was claimed for her. Koga from the north village bear out Iyo's story. Sadly, Miki was correct. The other day she told me that her village would be destroyed by what she called Samurai men. I thought it her imagination, but when Gonzo from the north village came back, he confirmed her prediction. The village was destroyed, just as Miki said it was. One of Satake's raids. She even described Satake down to his scar."

"And she was here?"

Akaki nodded his head. "Iyo-san thought that she would be a good miko. Perhaps the child should have gone to the shrine and become a *reibai*[5] after all. I cannot allow that now. Miki must be allowed to grow up."

"Gendo-san, you have heard all of the stories, and you were there at the events old Iyo described. What is your opinion? What should we do now? Does this change anything at all?" Master Kukai sipped his tea as his old acquaintance considered his words.

"Master Kukai, if this child is who you think she is, and if Iyo-san said so, then I must believe it. Lord Oto must never know. He would seek her out and try to care for her himself. He has a good, strong son who is enough for our village to care for. Lord Oto has been very busy organizing resistance to the Hamatsu. Do we want all of the last of the Yorisada clan in a single village where they can be easily captured or killed? Our purpose is to save the Koga and to return the Yorisada to rule Kumi. I hate keeping a secret from my master, but I know him well. The secret serves him better than the truth. I will offer him my life if he finds out."

---

5 Reibai is another form of miko, meaning medium or fortuneteller, or Shinto female shaman, witch or sorceress.

"Master Akaki, when you first told me who the child is, I confess that I thought it impossible. Now, with Masako-san refusing to go outside with the girl for fear of wolves and the confirmation of Iyo-san's story, I have to agree with Gendo-san and you. The child must remain here for now. Master Kawachi of the Koga, what is your view?"

"Lord Oto is a friend of my people. With the network of spies that he helped us set up, we have been able to move villages and hurt Hamatsu soldiers whenever they come into the mountain valley. Oto's son will be raised Samurai. His daughter is Koga and should be raised shinobi. But I agree that she is too young and needs a mother at this age. There is one more thing. I agree with Gendo-san. No one outside of this room should know the child's true heritage, especially little Miki herself. Some day Lord Oto will meet his daughter. By then, I want her to know who she is and who her people are. The Koga have always served the Yorisada. Now, the Yorisada clan has Koga blood in Miki." The thin, scraggly master assassin smiled at the thought.

"So it is agreed that the child Miki should remain at the temple, where we can teach her how to be a compassionate woman, and later to be a Koga kunoichi so that she might aid Lord Oto and his son in her time. But neither Lord Oto nor Miki herself must know, for the protection of both. One day, when we see what Kiyotaka becomes, maybe then we will tell the boy. But until then, no one outside of this room must know."

Chapter 4 - A New Friend

a life of service
friends, lifes destiny chosen
hearts healed, faith restored

Oversized robes covered the slight form of the energetic young girl darting about the temple garden as monks toiled in the summer sun. Carrying water to the sweating men, the cheerful child brought a smile to all who drank from the small bucket that Miki could carry. Watching the girl making herself useful, Master Kukai marveled at the joy she had brought not just to the monks, but to visitors also. No monk worked harder, learned faster, or understood the temple's teachings better than the bright, eager child he had come to love.

Once, finding the tyke a good home with a loving family had been his greatest wish; a temple was, after all, no place for a child. In the months since Miki's arrival, she had made herself more than just another of the temple's residents. She had become an attraction. Instead of becoming the crippling burden that had been his greatest nightmare, the little ray of sunshine had become the temple's greatest asset. Donations of both food and money were up, as well as the number of generous visitors. One particular visitor, important for more than money, was the governor of what once was the province of Kumi, Lord Mori no Yoshida, chief advisor to Lord Nobunaga, Daimyo of Hamatsu. Passing through on one of his frequent inspections, Lord Yoshida was quite enchanted by the attentive girl, who seemed equally fascinated by the tall, well-built, older Samurai in his colorful clothing with wide shoulders. This presented a problem, as the older Yoshida would soon return with his wife, Lady O-Sho. Should they decide to take the child, he was not sure that he could turn such a powerful man down. While it would be good for little Miki, facing thirty monks and Masako, who loved the girl as much as he did, was not a pleasant prospect. No, this was the child's home. Her life's journey toward an undefined destiny would have to begin here.

But there was one problem with raising a little girl in a monastery. Her only daily contact with a woman was the Ama Masako, and poor Miki would never see or be able to play with other children. The last thing that Master Kukai wanted was to inflict twenty-eight sullen, demanding men on the child for the rest of her life. For this, he knew he needed help. "Ama Masako, I have arranged for a Koga family in the north village to bring another child for Miki to spend some time with. It is not proper for us to isolate the child so much."

"Koga? But Master Kukai, what can little Miki learn from a Koga child? I give her everything she needs."

"Except play. Miki is Koga; she needs to have time to be a child and to learn who her people are. I see Monk Akaki coming now with them. Masako-san, the Koga have always provided protection for the temple. Why do you fear them so much?"

"Master Kukai, we have visitors." This favor would be a bit different than the normal exchange of blessings for protection.

"Thank you. Thank you very much. Please show them into the temple. I will get Miki." Walking into the garden where the girl was struggling with her too-heavy bucket of sloshing water, the old Kukai was amused and impressed with the seriousness with which the girl took her very important job. On the lookout for any of her friends who might appear to be thirsty, the girl had overfilled the bucket to the point where Kukai thought it might be as heavy as the girl. "Miki, could you come with me? You can put the bucket down there. There is someone I want you to meet."

Relieved from the toil, Miki nearly toppled over from the weight of the bucket. The self-conscious girl tried to brush away a bit of dust from her robe, but being wet from her fight with the water bucket, she merely ground it deeper into the coarse, brown fabric. Following Master Kukai into the temple, Miki lifted the robe, which dragged a bit, so that she could take the steps without tripping—equally unsuccessfully.

Guiding the child into the temple floor, Master Kukai could see a tall, thin man with Masako and another middle-aged woman. Both of the visitors were plainly dressed as mountain peasants, and both were there at the request of the village elder. Sensing that the child had stopped near the temple door, Kukai stopped, motioning the timid child forward.

"Come, Miki. I have someone you should meet."

"I don't want to leave the temple. I don't want a new family."

"That is not why these people are here. They already have a daughter. You belong at the temple. But since we will be performing a ritual later on, we have temple business now. I was wondering if you could show their daughter around the temple."

"You mean the one standing behind the door, behind me?"

Now that the eight-year-old girl had been discovered, hiding was pointless. She wasn't terribly thrilled about being dragged away from her friends and the games being played in her village to spend a week or more babysitting a special child as a favor to a monk she didn't know. The sight of this pathetic baby in oversized robes, wet and dirty, did nothing for her feelings that her life was over as she knew it.

"Impressive. Miki, how did you know Hisano was behind the door?" The tall, bearded man sitting across from Master Kukai was probably the girl's father. They had played hide and seek in Miki's village, as they did in all shinobi villages, and it was a game Miki was very good at.

"She is angry; I heard her breathing. She was curious and moved. That made the door squeak." Miki was also watching the woman's eyes. The woman whom she thought was the girl's mother had glanced at the door, holding her stare too long to be looking at just the door.

"As you can see, our little Miki is very perceptive." Curiosity made him push a bit harder. Miki had not even turned around to look at the new girl. "Without looking at her, what else can you tell me about Hisano?" Kukai could see that Hisano's mother and father were also curious.

"She is big for being eight. She is mad because she is missing her friends because of me. She wants to go home, and she is sneaking up on me."

With that prediction, Hisano stopped her slow, silent slide toward the creepy little girl. The look on the faces of her parents told Miki that she was right.

"Hisano, remember that Miki is like you. She is Koga, a child of shadow, and she has lost everything. You can help Miki remember who she is and what she is. This is all Master Kawachi has asked of you." Gunpei could see that his daughter was embarrassed by her failure to hide successfully and by how easily the tot had tracked her motion. Yet there was no denying that this little Miki was very different. "I have never seen a child with skills this developed at Miki's age."

That she was Koga was obvious. If the tiny girl was even half of what the Ama Masako had described, it was exciting. Someday she would be a very good kunoichi, if she could be persuaded to leave the temple. This had to be Miki's choice, and it was now his daughter Hisano's mission. "Miki-san. We should talk again later. Perhaps you and Hisano should get to know each other. Master Kukai and I need to talk."

Dismissed, the two children bowed and made their way into the garden.

As Miki and Hisano emerged from the temple door, every set of eyes from all over the temple grounds was pointed toward Miki, as if to ask what had happened. A wide smile from their ray of sunshine told them that all was as it should be. Soon it would be noon, and no one in the temple would eat after that, so Miki knew that it was time to help Masako-san in her duties and signaled her new but reluctant friend to follow. Life in a temple was one of work, study, and meditation, all for the purpose of service. Each resident had his task, and Miki knew hers. She and Hisano walked into the back building where food was stored and prepared to find Masako-san hard at work preparing a stew out of the pickled and fresh vegetables and mushrooms. Most meals were simple and never contained meat.

"Miki, I see that you have a friend. Maybe Hisano would like to help us feed the men. All of them worked so hard; they must be very hungry." Masako could see that the girls hadn't bonded as well as hoped, and preparing food for men wasn't the fun Hisano had been promised. Miki made herself instantly useful, as always, carrying bowls from the box where they were stored to the low table where they would eat. Not interested in the task, the somewhat taller Hisano stood helplessly by, watching this strange runt of a girl be everyone's servant. Sensing that perhaps they needed an activity more suitable for children than an Ama, Masako said, "Miki, I can take care of this today. You and Hisano eat, and then go show Hisano the temple."

"Can I go outside? Please. You haven't let me go outside for a long time."

"So you can get eaten by the wolves? I think not. Eat first. Then show Hisano the temple. I will speak to Master Kukai and Akaki-san." And speak to them she would. Having two children lost in the woods and eaten was not her idea of an appropriate activity.

With the meal finished and meditation about to begin, the girls wandered into the temple as each monk took his appointed position. Miki's position was in the back beside Masako, who wasn't there today. Rather than have Miki and Hisano, a very odd couple indeed, help with the cleanup, she had sent the two away to play and hopefully bond. Shooed away every time she got close to the busy Ama, Miki would teach Hisano to meditate.

"We're near the back; can we sneak out?" Anything would be better than staring at the back of thirty bald heads in silence for an hour. The prospect of no evening meal wasn't a happy one, either. The big, golden Buddha in the front was fascinating to the young Hisano, and the temple was the cleanest place she had ever seen. Miki had already shown her the hiding spot behind the statue, which was interesting. Now, Miki, her assigned mission, rolled out a small mat for her. *Why did her parents abandon her for this?* "What do we do? How do we meditate?"

"Clear your mind and think about something really hard. I will help you."

Just how much help do you need doing nothing? Imitating the monks, Hisano sat on her heels, just hoping that this would be over soon. Stuck inside the temple walls, she thought this promised to be the worst week of her life. All she had to do was to make the little girl like her and agree to live in her village, then she would never have to come back here again. "What do I do now?"

"Meditating isn't about nothing; it's about everything. You clear your mind to begin, but then you have to think very hard about something. First, think very hard about breathing. You don't have to control it; just feel it." Once Miki had her breathing right, she taught her friend how to reach out and touch each part of her body with her mind, allowing each part to relax. Miki sat behind her friend so that her soft voice would not disturb anyone else. Watching her friend relax, her tiny voice now directed Hisano's mind to reach out, to hear the squeak of the temple door, the wind as it made music on the chimes, the creak of the floorboards. Mindfulness at work.

As the young kunoichi did as that soft, gentle voice commanded, it was if all of her senses were heightened. The softest rustle became like thunder, the scent of the incense filled her nostrils, and she found that she could filter out everything else. It was pleasant and even useful. Hearing gentle conversation that she would have ignored, thinking about nothing, but being aware of everything. Soon—too soon it seemed—Miki's gentle voice called her back, telling her to open her eyes. As she did, she saw that they were alone. The Monks were gone. It was Mike and her, and standing behind Miki was Master Kukai. "Where did they go?" Incredulous! How could thirty men leave in perfect silence? Or was it in silence? She had listened to the gentle conversation, the rustle of the chimes, and even the creaking of the floorboards. Yet she had not detected the meaning of those sounds and sensations. Hiding behind the door the first time she met Miki, the little girl had used these same skills and sensations to detect her. Perhaps Miki did have something to teach her after all. "Where did they all go?"

That was the question Miki had asked the first time when Akaki-san had taught her to meditate. It was the question that told her that Hisano had done it right, just as it had told Akaki that she had done it right that first time. "Meditation is over, and they went back to work. I have to go back to work, too."

"Not today, my little imp. Master Akaki is waiting for you outside the back door. Hisano has seen your world. Now it is time for you to see hers. Like Hisano, you are also a child of shadow. You live in both worlds, are part of both worlds, and must learn the lessons of both worlds. Master Akaki has something both of you might enjoy."

Rolling up the mat that Hisano had used, not needing one herself, Miki smiled as she bowed at the departing temple master and motioned for Hisano to follow. Hisano's smile told Miki that the girl might end up being her friend after all.

"No, Akaki-san, please! This is a poor idea. She is too young. Miki is a child of the temple now." Masako could not believe what the man was planning to do with those two sweet children.

"Miki and Hisano were born Koga clan. They are people of the mountain, where life is difficult. Each of these children will serve her destiny. These are skills that will make them strong." The promise was to raise Miki both Koga and in the temple. Of course Akaki knew that he could never tell Masako why. Akaki leaned the *bo-staffs* against the wall. These particular staffs were a bit shorter for their intended masters.

"You are teaching children how to fight with weapons. Suppose Miki gets hurt?"

"I will also teach them balance and acrobatics and let Hisano contribute to Miki's education in other ways. They cannot be children if all they ever do is work and meditate. Let her grow up before we lock her away in this monastery. Soon little Hisano will go back to her village. Let Miki have at least one friend her age."

"Just when do you expect Miki to ever pick up a sword? What sort of education can a shinobi offer my dear Miki?" Looking at the sticks that the monk was smoothing off made her sick. Miki had become her daughter, her child. Her baby needed to be inside the temple walls, safe from all the things that could hurt her. *How dare these men, these holy men, do this to my little Miki!*

"They are both Koga clan. They are both children. And right now they need to play. I will watch them while they are outside." Akaki could see that Masako was frantic with fear for the girl. She had truly wrapped her heart around a child she could not love more if Miki were her own. "Trust me; I will watch over her." With two children making their way out the small wooden door on the mountain side of the temple, this discussion was now over.

"I will speak again to Master Kukai." Furious, the Ama wanted to grab the happy child now standing beside her and drag her back in but fought the urge. *Surely the Master will be more reasonable.* Out of patience and arguments, Masako knew that it was time to find someone new to harangue.

As the livid Masako made her way into the temple, not even able to look at her child, Akaki peered into the expectant eyes of a tiny Miki and a larger Hisano. "Hurting people is wrong, but it is also wrong to allow evil men to hurt others. Someday both of you will understand the value of peace. Now, would you like to learn how to use a staff or a sword?"

It was Hisano's last day in the temple. Gonzo, one of the young men from the Koga village, had led a small group of his students to escort the girl home. This was the meeting Masako had been dreading. As young as Little Miki was, she had a choice to make. The last ten days had been a journey of discovery for Hisano as she watched Miki choose mountain herbs and work with Masako healing the sick, and as Miki taught her how to meditate. In that time these two very different children had bonded, and now Hisano might ask Miki to return to the Koga village with her, and that thought was intensely painful to the Ama who healed.

"They will be here soon. Are you prepared?" Master Kukai watched the normally calm Masako pace uncontrollably, as though awaiting an execution. "Our little *ama-no-jaku*[6] may surprise you."

"You can't let them take her. She is mine. I mean she is my responsibility." Masako could not say what she wanted to say, what she needed to say. *Surely he can see that letting Miki leave is wrong. Wasn't it enough to teach her the use of a weapon, enough to let her play outside the walls of the temple? Now her little girl could end up in a village of assassins and eta.*

"Mine?" The old temple master knew what she meant. They slept in the same room beside each other, and they worked together around the temple and in the town where they provided medicines. This week alone Miki had helped Masako bring two babies into the world as Hisano watched, fascinated. What the Ama Masako wanted to say, the word that she wanted to use, was "daughter," for in every respect but blood, that is what they had become: mother and daughter. Yet the choice had to be Miki's. Somehow, whatever the decision, the old man knew that it would be the right one. But would his friend Masako see it that way? "This must be Miki's decision."

"Why? Since when does a child of seven decide her own future?" *That is what mothers are for.*

Should he tell his friend of the plan hatched in a smoky room with a Koga assassin, outlaw Samurai, and monks, one of whom was also an outlaw? Could he tell the woman that the child was part of a bigger plan, a conspiracy to retake two provinces, hidden even from her own father? No! Masako will accept the child's choice and her Temple Master's orders. That is the way it must be. "She is Koga. They will take care of her if Miki chooses to go with them. Trust an old man who has also come to love the little imp. I would miss her, too."

Somehow that wasn't comforting. The creak of the temple door and the swift patter of tiny, bare feet on the wooden floor told the panicking Masako that she wouldn't have to wait long for the bad news.

"Masako-san, Masako-san, they want me to go home with them!" The little girl was overjoyed. Smiling and bouncing, Miki simply could not wait to share the news with her Masako-san. Feeling the pressure of the silent, sad stare from Master Kukai,

---

6 ama-no-jaku - literally imp from heaven, also commonly used to describe someone who has a contrary nature, a diminutive.

Masako felt her heart being slowly ripped from her chest. Somehow, Masako the Ama knew that hurting the child would not help her pain. Watching the child leave would be agony.

"Miki, I am happy for you. They will be leaving soon. You need to get ready." Forcing a polite smile, the crushed woman tried to control the tears that would destroy the moment for the girl who was her beloved daughter in all but blood.

"I'm not going with them. I want to stay here with you. Besides, if I went with them, Hisano couldn't come back. She liked the temple. But they actually wanted me! They really did." Banished from one village, Miki remembered the faces of Goro and Eizo and the other men as they forced her mother to take her outside the village walls to meet old Iyo-san, herself banished. For the first time in her young life, she had a real friend and people who loved her. "I want to stay here and be just like you. I want to be an Ama like you. I want to heal people and help them. Just like you."

Miki's gentle words caught the stunned Ama off guard. Kneeling so that she could look the child in the eyes, Masako wrapped her arms around her little imp, unable to control the tears that no longer mourned a loss but celebrated a joy, and pulled the child close to hold her tightly. *The Master was right. She should have had more faith in Miki. There will be time for prayers later on.*

Feeling his own tears run down tired cheeks, Master Kukai knew that this was a moment best shared by the child who needed a mother and the woman who wanted to be one, without his interference. Turning to gaze at the golden Buddha for a moment, somehow the old man felt just a bit younger. At least he would not have to face the angry wrath of a temple full of monks who had adopted the girl, making Miki one of their own. Making his way out the back, at least this day he knew that all was right with the world.

Chapter 5 - The Healer

children growing up
hard lessons, a path chosen
friends saved, a friend lost

"Why does Master Akaki leave whenever Lady O-Sho comes?" Miki liked the old lady. The old woman was the wife of General Yoshida, the military governor of the Kumi province, now ruled by Hamatsu. General Yoshida was a mean man, feared and hated by everyone in the villages that Masako and Miki visited on their rounds midwifing and healing. Lady O-Sho always brought something for the little girl. Miki's first taste of candy, her introduction to music, and her first toy, a painted top that spun, were gifts of the aristocratic woman. Normally haughty and stiff, the Lady O-Sho seemed to relax when attended by the little girl, now nine. "She is a very nice lady. I did so want Master Akaki to meet her."

The old temple master looked into the dark, round eyes of the young girl, who was becoming more beautiful each passing year. It was as if the child could peer directly into the soul with those amazingly honest eyes. "No, Miki. Remember that no one outside this temple should ever know Master Akaki is here? That would be very bad. This is the only secret that I have ever asked you to keep. It would be terrible if you did not." Master Kukai could see that his little imp from heaven could not understand, but he knew that she would obey. She always obeyed. "Why did you not go with Masako-san? Hoping for more candy from Lady O-Sho?" Changing the subject seemed to be in order.

"No, Master. Masako-san said that there will be death in the village, and that I don't belong there. I'm not old enough, she said." Miki didn't like it when Masako tried to protect her. *She had seen death before. Nothing is permanent. Everything changes, and death is always part of life. At least that is what the Master taught.*

"Ah, yes. Wise on her part." It was not just death, but murder. Executions of criminals, followed by the obligatory testing of swords. Not the sort of thing that Miki needed to witness. Worse, at least a few of the victims were people of Hisano's village and people whom Miki knew. One, Gonzo, was the one who always brought Miki's best friend Hisano to the temple. Watching Gonzo die would have been horrific for the gentle, little imp.

"How do I learn about suffering if I don't see it? Masako-san takes me when the babies are born. I have seen babies die. I have seen sick people die. Why is this different?"

"Because this time men would be the cause. Miki, I promise you that you will see enough suffering in your life without rushing into it. For now, just trust Masako-san. She loves you very much." Master Kukai appreciated how Miki took every lesson to heart. This sort of suffering was something she did not need. "Lady O-Sho should be here today. I have been told that she intends to teach you how to dance." Indeed, Miki's balance and grace were exceptional. A traveling troupe of acrobats, street entertainers, occasionally passed this way seeking blessings, and they performed for the monks several times a year. Fearless Miki would imitate even the most complex moves nearly perfectly, without regard to height or danger, to the horror of Masako, whose remonstration was always stern and swift. Dancing, however, was done on the ground, far safer than the top of the wall, within the tree—or once, along the top of the roof. This was an activity suitable for a girl, and, finally, one that Masako could approve of.

Several times a year, Gonzo would bring Hisano to the temple, and for that ten-day period, little Miki, the imp from heaven, was free of all duties. This was a friendship made more special by its short visits. Each child would prepare from the time they left each other to the very next visit to have something interesting to show or give the other. Learning how to dance would be that special gift for Miki to give to her friend, as well as the tricks that the imp had learned from the street entertainers. This year promised to be the very best year Miki had ever had.

Standing on the steps, the old man and the small girl looked out toward the tree Miki and Hisano had planted near the gate to the temple on Hisano's last visit. "Are you and Hisano going to plant another? This one is doing so well." The hot late summer day was heading toward evening. The monks were inside doing their afternoon meditation, but this day Miki was just too fidgety in the dry heat. Excited, she waited expectantly as she had the previous day.

A ring of the gate's bell made Miki's heart jump. Master Kukai walked toward the large wooden door with Miki by his side. Lifting the latch, the old temple master pulled the heavy gate open, revealing a face that Miki had burned into her brain. The tall, well-built man carried the two swords of a Samurai, and the scar across the face and the missing ear brought the memory of that day on the road so many years ago into girl's mind. Fear shot through the normally fearless young girl, taking her breath away for the briefest of moments until her remarkably disciplined mind took over. Motioning for others to follow, the powerful man pushed his way through the door, followed by soldiers carrying a wounded man.

The dozen or so men, several of them bleeding, marched quickly toward the temple as the ugly, scarfaced man barked orders. Several of the cone-headed soldiers carried a man of great importance, one Miki also recognized. It was General Yoshida, Lady O-Sho's husband.

Following along, Miki was horrified when the soldiers sent many of the monks inside heading toward the back exit. Placing the wounded men on the clean wooden floor, several of the monks brought in blankets and water.

"I have been told that you have a good healer here. Bring her now." Scarface did not ask politely. He was not used to giving an order twice. "Lord Yoshida requires attention; where is she?"

"I am so sorry. Masako-san was in the town to minister to the people. We will do the best that we can." A bit sorry that all these duties had been left to the Ama Masako, Kukai began to wonder what they would do without her. None of the monks did this sort of work. Only Masako, and she was not here. Except for Miki, of course.

"Let me help." The tiny but confident voice caught the attention of both Master Kukai and the scarfaced General.

"Get her out of here."

"No. Masako-san is gone. I am the only one left who can do this. The arrow is near the heart. Please let me work." To tell a Samurai General "no" was usually a quick way to end up headless. Looking around into the face of a very defiant, very small girl, even Kukai had to admit that the imp was probably right.

Looking past the temple Master and the grim-faced child, Sir Tomoe Satake, aka Scarface, looked at Lady O-Sho. She was standing at the door, having just slipped in. A nod from Lady O-Sho was what Satake needed. Signaling the girl to proceed, he did not see how this child could do what no one else would attempt. "If he dies, so do you."

Moving toward the man's side, Miki knew that she would have to take charge, as Masako-san had done so many times in so many places. "Leave me. I need Masako-san's medicine box. Also, please boil some water and bring sake. Don't give it to him. Clean the tools with it. Only give him some water. I will tell you what to put in it." Kukai watched the child take command without a whisper of complaint. A child had wagered her life to perform an operation that no one else would attempt. More sure of herself than any child had a right to be, she worked swiftly, extracting the barbed head of the arrow using her own fingers to prevent the damage that the shape of the weapon was designed to do. For Kukai, it was like watching Masako work, only faster. Whatever the Ama taught the little imp, she had learned well.

Hours passed before the young healer finished the final stitch and knotted the silk on a clean chest. She used the sake again to clean the wound, as Masako had done, and now living or dying would now be up to Lord Yoshida. Washing her bloody hands one last time, Miki was exhausted.

"If he lives through the night, he will live forever." Well, maybe not forever. But at least for a long time.

The Lady O-Sho had watched as the child labored into the candlelit evening. "My dear child. I thank you. If I could have a daughter, I would want her to be just like you. I promise that I will not let Sir Satake harm you. No one could do more. No one else even tried." The child's dark, piercing eyes were on her husband. When she looked up, it was with a smile that signaled a confidence that the shaky woman needed.

"I will work here. You should sleep. He will need you tomorrow." With luck, there would be a tomorrow. Many times Miki had watched Masako do the very same thing. Watching for fever, controlling bleeding, making sure the pain was not unbearable, and hardest of all, stopping family from giving the wrong sort of help. The wound was clean, and the hardest part had been to get the barbed head out. Masako had done the same thing with the hook of a fisherman's spear earlier that summer. A stitch of silk had closed a nicked blood vessel, and tiny fingers and good eyes had done the rest. Rest and water were called for. A bit of powder made from the poppy would control pain, but never too much. Masako-san made that very clear. Now she would meditate and pray.

It would be a long night.

"My dear little Miki did it." O-Sho had come in early to check on her husband. Mori, Lord Yoshida, was awake, and although very sore, he was quite hungry. Miki, force-feeding liquids through the evening, through the night, and into the morning, as well as cleaning the wound to limit infection, had fought the demanding man most of the night. Now beyond all limits of endurance, Miki had collapsed on the floor beside her charge and could not be awakened. Monks had prepared a meal of broth and noodles for the powerful Lord Mori no Yoshida, who was now attended by his wife, O-Sho.

Now, Master Kukai motioned to the largest of the other monks, a happy, jovial man named Sanjo, who swiftly swept the little girl into his arms and carried her to the small, simple room that she and Masako shared. Walking with the large man, Kukai remembered just how hard he had tried to find his little imp a home—anywhere but the temple. Feeling ashamed at what now seemed like terrible shortsightedness, he watched as the gentle Sanjo lowered the scrawny child to the mat, covering her with a light blanket.

"We have reason to be proud of her, and grateful as well. According to Akaki, Satake, the one with the scar, has no reason, no mercy. I do believe that he would have killed Miki had Yoshida died." Kukai gazed at the slumbering young girl, no longer being able to imagine a temple without a Miki to fill it with joy. "He may have killed us all just for the feeling of vengeance."

"He is nothing more than a trained dog, more animal than man. What he was doing to the condemned men in the village was terrible. Sawing their heads off in front of their families, their children." It was hard to imagine the monk named Sanjo without a smile, yet this day the smile was absent. "There was a day when I was much like him."

"But not today." Kukai remembered the large ronin who had wandered in almost ten years earlier. A bully and a killer, the man named Sanjo had become the most fiercely peaceful man in the north road temple. Miki had particular meaning for him, as it was the death of a child much like Miki by his stupid blunder that had driven the large man with the giant heart to come to this temple.

"So what happened in town? Where is Masako?"

"In town. After the executions started, Oto, Kawachi, and the Koga from the south village attacked, and it was slaughter everywhere. Most of the Koga being executed escaped. Some of the townsfolk also were hurt. Masako is with them now. Even the little girl that Miki plays with was to be beheaded."

"Hisano? Killed?"

"No, but hurt. It was probably Hisano's arrow in Yoshida down there. Gonzo got away too, with about half the captured Koga."

How will Miki feel when she finds out that she has just saved the life of the man who nearly sawed the head off her best friend Hisano? "Maybe it would be best to not tell Miki right away. What she did was with a good heart. Amanojaku deserves not to be punished for this gift of life." *Oto's little war is out of hand. Too many innocent people are getting caught in the middle. Lord Nobunaga, Daimyo of Hamatsu and brother to his monk Master Akaki, responded to every attack, every raid, and every rescue with merciless cruelty. Satake is his dog, and Lord Yoshida and his son his Generals.* "Send a message to Oto through the north village. I need to speak to him. This must end." *For the sake of this girl sleeping before me now, the violence needs to end.*

"My husband is doing well. Miki has done Lord Yoshida and the Hori clan a great service. Master Kukai, may I speak to you about Miki's future?" Lady O-Sho looked out at the garden. A breeze had picked up in this late summer afternoon, and with the temple building itself turned into Lord Yoshida's personal domain, the monks were meditating in the garden. Soldiers had turned the temple and its grounds into a fortress, to the disgust of all of its residents. "Even you must recognize that a temple is no place for a child of Miki's obvious intelligence and wonderful gifts. I have always wanted a daughter, and Miki would be cherished in my home. If I can get my husband's consent, may I speak to the dear, sweet child?"

It was the moment the old temple master feared most. Losing Miki to Satake's mindless cruelty would be terrible. To lose her to Lady O-Sho's kindness seemed worse. Should Miki's dark secret ever become known, her death would be swift. Yet, to refuse this simple request could mean retribution. Yoshida and his animal Satake could simply take Miki if they chose. It would rip Masako's heart out, and Akaki would most certainly be moved to act. These cruel people would destroy the child. "I will not stand in the way of Miki's future, but it must be her choice. Also, you must tell Lord Yoshida the truth of her origins. She is a Koga orphan, brought here as a very small child. Please let me speak to the child first." A gamble. Perhaps the man had enough gratitude to spare the girl. At least he would wait until Lady O-Sho was gone before sending Satake to kill the child.

O-Sho took a deep breath. Mori hated everything Koga, but Master Kukai was right. It was something that would come up. Something that could not be hidden, at least for very long. "That is most wise, thank you. Thank you very much. Miki is really very wonderful."

There was no time left to spare the girl. Miki had to be told the truth, how her act of kindness had betrayed her friends—at least they would see it that way. Master Kukai asked the monk Sanjo where Miki was, and the giant of a man pointed toward the back building where Masako kept her supplies. Making his way out the small back door, Kukai saw Miki emerging from the shed with a bag slung around her shoulder. The child's red eyes told the old monk that she knew, or at least had heard a part of the story.

"Miki-san, I need to speak to you."

"Hisano is hurt. She has a broken leg. I have to go to her village."

"Miki, I understand. But you do not know where the village is."

"I will find it." The little imp seemed sure of herself. It wasn't that simple.

"Lady O-Sho would like to speak to you first."

"If Hisano's leg is not set right, it will start to heal on its own. Once it does that, she will be crippled, and I will not be able to help her. Please, I have to go now. Lord Yoshida will heal. He does not need me anymore."

"My little ama-no-jaku. I will not allow you to simply wander through the wilderness." Kukai could see determination in the child's dark eyes. Nine-year-old girls were not suited for travel in the deep mountain forests. "Tomorrow, perhaps I will take you myself, or Master Akaki will be back."

"Then it will be too late. I will not be able to help Hisano. Gonzo-san will meet me outside. He will take me." Miki could see the terrible reluctance in his eyes. The kind old man was protecting her. There were still soldiers in the temple complex, although they were preparing to leave, to the relief of everyone. "I will see Lady O-Sho before I leave. Please, Master Kukai, this is something I have to do."

"Lady O-Sho will be in the garden. Speak to her."

"Hai, Master Kukai." The man had made a promise, and Miki had the obligation to at least obey this one request. If Masako-san were here, she would go in Miki's place. For some reason nothing frightened the woman more than the thought of shinobi, or of Miki going to a shinobi village. If she were here, Miki would have already been sent to her room. They did not believe that she was old enough to think for herself yet. Even if it meant disobedience, Miki knew that she had to get to Hisano before the leg healed on its own. Heading toward the temple garden, where she would find the Lady O-Sho, she wondered what was so important. She was an Ama and a healer; thanks were unnecessary.

"My husband. Miki saved your life. She saved your life when no one else would even try." O-Sho wanted Miki. This child was an orphan who deserved a genuine life. Sweet, gentle, smart, and disciplined, she would make the most perfect daughter. Surely, even Mori could see that the girl's clan of birth was meaningless.

"And for that reason, I will let the child live. I will not destroy this temple, although it was my intention. Do you not think that we know that this temple is the center for the criminals' activities? The Koga have always protected this place. Even with my soldiers here, they slip in and out as though those walls do not exist. Where is the real healer woman? Masako-san, is it not? While a nine-year-old is left to attend to the governor of Kumi, the real healer is in town with the very bandits who put the arrow into my chest." Lord Yoshida could see how much the woman, his wife, wanted the little Koga girl. More than once during the night, the child had the temerity to give him orders, something that not even his own physician would do. She was strong and therefore a danger should she ever rediscover her Koga roots. "If you want a daughter, I will find one for you. A daughter worthy of you."

Silent tears flowed down O-Sho's face. Was there no way of touching this man's heart? What did the girl have to do to prove herself to this hard man? "My husband..."

"No more. My word is final. Go say your farewells. We are leaving."

O-Sho had never dared to disobey the man. Hard though he was, he was a good husband, selected for her by her clan when she was just seventeen. In all that time, she had never wanted for anything—until now. In the structured world of duty and obligation, a world in which a woman served her clan and family to the exclusion of desire, Lord Yoshida had treated her with respect and dignity. In return, O-Sho had labored tirelessly to help her husband, and then her son, to rise in the Hori clan and the court of Lord Nobunaga. But love was hard to come by. Compassion was excruciatingly rare in the world of Samurai, and it was something that the child named Miki could offer. To love and to be loved was the one gift that O-Sho had not known since leaving her family as a young girl. With tears silently coursing down her cheeks, she knew this simple request was one that she would revisit again. Passing through the door into the late afternoon sun, the old woman struggled to hold together the broken heart that was forbidden in her world. Looking around, she thought that at least she could find little Miki. At least she could thank the child for Mori's life, even if the man was too proud to do it himself.

Watching the old woman hide a sob as she made her way out of the temple, Lord Yoshida called for his senior officer. The scar-faced Satake hurried to his master's bedside, dropping to his knees to bow. Sitting erect on one knee, as a man does when carrying his *daisho*, the attentive Satake awaited orders.

"General Satake, as you know, I am very fond of O-Sho. She is a superior woman but does have a very soft heart. I will provide my wife a daughter, but not that Koga child. Perhaps from a *kuge*[7] family. At least from another family of our class. Certainly not that filthy little eta. Imagine Lord Nobunaga's reaction if he found out that I had adopted such a child."

"Yes, Master. Ever since the miko foresaw his death at the hands of the Yorisada and their Koga friends, he has been grow-

7 kuge - Japanese noble class composed of those related to the Emperor in some way.

ing more and more paranoid. Think about the Lord's decision to appoint your son as heir. Even Lady O-Sho must see the damage that the Koga child would do." Indeed, Satake was ashamed to admit that his and the girl's dark eyes had once before locked, on a road years ago. "The child is evil. Perhaps you should have taken the girl."

"No, O-Sho would not have let her out of her sight. When we leave, stay behind. When we are gone, take the girl into the woods and kill her. She did a great service to me, so make it swift and painless. This is not punishment. If it were not for my wife and her soft heart, I would not have cared. This is not a discussion that I will have with Lady O-Sho again. Let the monks live. I at least owe that to the little girl. The wolves can have her body."

"Understood. It will be my pleasure."

"Remember Satake, painless. It is a child, and an Ama, despite her evil nature. Kill her swiftly." Yoshida knew that Satake had a cruel streak. *Perhaps if she were not Koga, I might even feel sorry for her. Still, cruelty is unnecessary.*

"I understand, my Lord."

"Miki, I am so sorry. My husband will not allow me to purchase you. I had hoped to make you my daughter and give you the life that a sweet, gentle child like you deserves. Perhaps I will ask later, when my husband heals and can see reason again. Do not despair; there are ways of making a man do what you need." O-Sho looked into the dark eyes of a child who had obviously been crying. Holding a thin bo-staff and a small bag, the sweet child looked as if she had been hoping to go with her. But it would not be this trip. "Please accept my deepest gratitude. I will arrange for my husband to give you and the kind monks at this temple a reward worthy of your service and kindness. Farewell, my dearest child. We will see each other again. I promise this."

Time was not merciful. Long good-byes were not what Miki needed. Hisano was at a village in the mountains in pain, and if the sun set before she found the rope bridge where Gonzo-san would be waiting for her, it would be a long night lost in the woods. Not unmindful of the gift that the kind Lady O-Sho wanted to give her, it would have to wait. Hisano needed her. Bowing low, the young Ama needed to end this before something happened that would delay reaching Hisano. "Thank you, O-Sho-san. Another village needs me. Please forgive me. I must go now." Turning to walk away, Miki knew that getting away from the wonderful Lady O-Sho was only part of her problem. The real struggle was about to greet her at the gate. Master Kukai still hadn't given her permission for this most dangerous journey.

Master Kukai was standing by the small back door, shaking his head and talking to one of the other monks, the thin one named Monk Hashiba. Both Hashiba, with his grim expression that hid an amazing sense of humor, and Monk Kukai watched as the determined little girl marched up to the pair and readied her arguments. "Master Kukai. Hisano needs me. Please let me go to her. Please!"

"Yes. I have rethought my earlier objections and have decided that you are right. In fact, I think that you should leave right now. Remember that Hisano needs you, and move as swiftly as you can. Trust no one, especially soldiers. Stop for nothing, especially the man with the scar."

"And the missing ear."

Any other time, this would need an explanation. Where the young healer had expected resistance, it was as if they were kicking her out of the temple. Confused and a bit scared, Miki decided to take their advice before sanity returned to the temple. *Maybe they were scared that I would leave with Lady O-Sho. That had to be it! I would never leave the temple. Never. This is my home.*

The men opened the door for her, and the bo-staff nearly knocked the wind out of the girl as they misjudged its length and pushed her into it before she could get it pointed out the door. Outside, the startled girl turned to stare at the door being closed behind her. "Can I..."

"NO! Hurry and see Hisano. We will send for you when it is safe."

The door slammed shut, and Miki could hear the latch being locked. Standing outside the temple wall at the edge of the mountain forest gave the shocked child the feeling that she had just been ejected as ceremoniously as a slobbering deadbeat drunk might be from an inn. Nine years old, and she was now apparently on her own. *What did I do? I saved a life. Was I wrong?* As she turned to head into the forest along the path Hisano had shown her, the tears welled up in her dark eyes, and her mind twisted and turned, trying to make sense of the last few moments. *Did they want me to go with Lady O-Sho? Whom did I offend?*

It was getting dark, and as Miki trudged away from what she thought was her home, she felt angry at the situation, at Master Kukai, at Lady O-Sho, and even at herself, although the intense little girl scarcely knew why. Confused and scared with darkness falling, Miki picked up the pace to get to the rope bridge that Hisano told her about. The Koga had left marks to guide the girl, but it was getting dark, and the signs were hard to see. Feeling abandoned, Miki had the terrible sense that she was not alone. Looking around in the moonlit darkness, it seemed that she could see motion in the bushes. In the silence of the dark woods, she could hear low, deep breathing and caught the glint of the luminous green eyes of wolves. Worse, Miki had not been able to locate any of the Koga markings. She was lost.

Never in her life had the girl felt panic. She would not give in to that emotion now. Tired and drained emotionally, Miki decided to sit down and get her thoughts together. Wandering aimlessly without a plan seemed more dangerous than useful. *I am Koga. I am kunoichi. I AM a kunoichi. Now I am an Ama! Is being an Ama different?*

As she meditated with her eyes closed, her senses reached out. In the distance was the sound of men crunching through the brush. They were loud, incompetent. One occasionally shouted at the others, and it seemed that they were fighting something unseen. *I'm lost. I'm alone. They are at least men. Maybe I should go to them? Maybe they are looking for me? They can't be Koga. Shinobi rule the night and would move silently. Soldiers? What did Master Kukai and Hashiba-san say? Beware the man with a scar and the missing ear. Why? Why would men who loved her be so quick to toss her out into the night forest? And that warning...* Now it was clear! Miki's mind was now free of fear; the epiphany brought everything into sharp focus. No longer clouded by emotion, her mind had released the fear. Life or death was now her decision.

Opening her eyes brought her face to face with the largest, grayest wolf that Miki had ever seen, its eyes glowing green in the moonlight. Why had she not heard the wolf? It didn't want to hurt her; if it did, she would be dead already. The large male was at least her weight, and probably more. It was just sitting, looking at her tiny form as if attending to her. "I am lost, and I need to find my way to the rope bridge. The men on the mountain are coming to kill me. One of them is very evil, but then, you know that." Faith was something that Miki had never found herself short of. It seemed as if the Kami of the mountains had heard her silent prayers, and if she wanted to live, perhaps it was time to trust their messenger as she had so many years before.

The noise was getting closer, and Miki knew that they would be on top of her within minutes. She was not their biggest worry. Hers was not the only wolf hunting this evening, and both of the men with Satake were in raw terror. From the sound of it, it was all he could do to keep the horrified men from desertion. Sensing that the wolf wanted her to move, Miki picked up her bo-staff and bag to stand, catching the motion of an angry man in the trees within the moonlit shadows. His curses flung into the darkness told Miki that he was now alone, abandoned by his soldiers. A child of the mountains, Miki knew that separated and panicking, those men would be stalked and killed easily now.

With a shot of his eyes, the wolf indicated a path that the once-terrified girl had not seen. Within a few minutes, the sound of a mountain stream and rapidly moving water told the young Ama that she had been close to her destination all along. The rope bridge would be hidden just over the little rise, not obvious to someone not looking for it. Walking to stand beside the wolf, who was highlighted by the full moon, she could see the marks that had been left for other Koga. With luck, Gonzo-san would be somewhere on the other side and would lead her to her cherished friend. This summer's visit had been a disaster.

Suddenly, the ragged Satake emerged from the edge of the trees, wildly swinging his sword until his eyes locked on the figure of a scrawny, robed figure on the rise above the cliff.

"Where can you go now, witch? Where can you go with a cliff behind you? Come here, and I will make your death swift, as Lord Yoshida has ordered." Blinded by the moon, Satake could make out the dark figure of the young Ama in its brilliant glow. Beside the child stood the blackened figure of a wolf.

"I will go where I intended to go. To heal another person more worthy than your master. The wolves will not kill you tonight. Someday, they tell me, that will be my destiny. But if you try, they may change their minds." Miki could feel the hate in the man beaming from his terrible eyes. Loathing without reason. *What have I done?* His ugly, hairy face in the moon's glow would be the memory that Miki decided to keep locked away for that moment when they might meet again. Perhaps next time, she would not be the helpless little girl. As she turned to go to the bridge that had been hidden from the other side, the growl of the wolf was now protecting her. Maybe some day the evil man might catch her, but not this time.

"Where is Masako-san?" Gonzo was waiting at the other end of the bridge. He was just a bit upset that the temple had sent a mere child. They had a number of wounded, and it would take someone more skilled than anyone in the village to deal with the extent of the injuries. "Was that a wolf I saw you with on the other side of the bridge?"

Tripping, trying to keep up with the man, Miki could see by the glow of cooking fires that she would enter a Koga village for the first time since she and Iyo-san had been banished a lifetime ago. "Hai, Gonzo-san. I was lost and was being chased by soldiers. The wolf led me to the bridge. He protected me." The man stopped dead in his tracks, causing the girl to run into him. Picking herself up, she apologized for her clumsiness.

"A large male wolf?"

"Hai."

"How many soldiers were there?"

"I think three, but I think that the wolves ate two of them. The other one was the ugly one, Satake-san."

"Miki-san, I would not mention the wolf to the others. They might not understand."

"Hai." The last time someone in a Koga village had seen her with a wolf, she had been banished. This was a warning she would heed.

Coming to the third hut, near the center of the village, Miki could hear the scream of her dearest friend. Entering, it was clear that the older man who was in charge was preparing for an amputation. On either side of her terrified friend were the parents Miki vaguely remembered from that meeting nearly three years ago. Tears had stained the face of the girl, who was clearly in agony. One look told Miki the healer why. Hisano's leg was cocked off at a funny angle. The wrinkled old man had begun to tie the leg off for amputation.

First you must take charge. That was what Masako had taught the young Miki, and a day earlier it had worked well. "Stop, please. Let me look at the leg first."

"We have no time for children. The leg must be removed. Get her out of here."

"NOOOO!" Hisano knew that her life was over if they took her leg off. Every dream, every hope that a young woman could have would be gone. Most of the time, the old man simply killed his patient—if not during the butchery, then afterward by infection.

"I SAID LET ME SEE THE LEG. I came here to save it."

Gonzo had heard the monks talking about the child's obvious talent. At least most of her patients seemed to survive, a claim old Sato could not make. Gonzo was hard pressed to remember one who had. "Miki-san is very good, I am told. Monk Kukai would not have sent her otherwise. Let Miki-san work. I think that you can trust her. No one knows where Ama Masako is, and it could be days before we find her."

"By then it will be too late for my friend. Trust me." With a nod of consent, Miki pushed the old man aside and motioned for a lamp to see what the butcher had started. She cut off the rag that the man had tried to use to cut off the blood flow. The flow of blood would increase the pain to intolerable levels. Pulling a little bottle out of her bag, she handed it to Hisano's father. "Mix it in some clean water and make her drink half of it. It will help with pain. We will use the other half later." It was from the

Chinese poppy plant, and it would at least calm Hisano down enough to work on her.

She ran her hand down the lower leg, and the break was easy to identify with so little muscle in the way. It would have to be set properly very soon. This would require all of her strength. She gave orders for the wood that she would need to hold the leg in place when she was done. Saying a silent prayer that wasn't as silent as perhaps it should have been, Miki waited for the medicine to have its effect. "Wrap the wood in cloth or it will hurt Hisano. This will hurt very much, and I am very, very sorry, but it can't be helped. Hold her down hard."

"NO! I'm afraid. Don't hold me down, Please. I can take it. Please!" the tall child begged.

"No one can take it. No one. Hold her down now." As hands reached around the child, Miki waited for Gonzo's nod before gently grabbing the thin leg of her friend and pulling to separate the bone and move it back into its original shape. A feeble cry told the young Miki that Hisano was beginning to succumb to the painkiller, and the pop as she let off of her grip told her that the bones had found their proper place. That would most certainly lessen the pain once the drug wore off. "Let her sleep. When she wakes up, give her the other half of that. Boil water and make tea with this when that wears off. Help me get the leg tied up. We will be tying both legs together because she must not move for at least ten days. Then we can let her up some." Miki could see that the pain had subsided, both because the leg was now set and because of the medicine. It could have been much worse.

The previous evening and night had been very long. There had been three patients after Hisano, one a sucking chest wound that had been improperly bound by old Sato the Slayer (as the villagers were now calling him) and who nearly didn't make it. The others were less serious, although one might have developed an infection had Miki not scrubbed it clean and used tree moss to cover the wound.

A few hours of sleep after checking in on Hisano again made Miki feel more like her happy self. Over the last three days, the young Ama had gone from being a child looking forward to dancing lessons and playtime with her friend to a young woman working endless hours saving lives. Nothing would ever be the same again. Now evening was falling again, and there was still one thing that had to be done, and that was more frightening than the wolf or even being pursued by Satake. It was now time to face her friend Hisano.

As she made her way past the grateful people of the village, her people, it seemed as though somehow the air became thicker, holding her back from the house where Hisano lay. Standing at the crude wooden door, she listened for the sound of her friend, now much happier. Before she could raise her hand to knock, the door swung open, and the happy hands of Hisano's mother pulled Miki inside.

"Thank you. Thank you. Hisano is feeling much better, but she wants to know when she can walk normally."

"In ten days we can use a different splint, and she will be able to move around. It will be about forty before everything is fully healed. Don't put too much weight on it, and let it get strong before doing anything dangerous. Even sixty days is better. By next spring Hisano won't remember which leg was broken."

"And to think that we were going to let Sato the Slayer cut her leg off. Miki-san, would you be willing to teach the girls of the village to do what you do?"

"Hai, but it requires much work and study. Perhaps we can teach them at the temple?" Miki's presence had not gone unnoticed by a tall twelve-year-old who chafed at Miki's decision to splint both legs.

"Miki, Miki, Miki. Thank you! But why can't I use my left leg? It wasn't broken."

"Because you would want to move too much. It is too soon. I want to be able to play with you when you heal. What happened? How did you get hurt?"

"It was awful. I thought that I was going to die. Gonzo took us to the town to teach us stuff. Somehow, someone found out that we were Koga and told the soldiers for a reward. When they took us, Lord Yoshida ordered them to kill us. His dog Satake tortured some of us. Anyone who helped us was going to die. They kept us tied up in a single room for three days. It smelled horribly. Two old people died while waiting. I was the youngest, so they didn't question me. A few of us had gotten away." Hisano was having trouble with the explanation. Some of those who died had been friends, even family.

"How did you get away?"

Speaking was now very difficult. Hisano was quivering a bit and often looked away. It was a tone that Miki had never heard in her friend's voice. "They dug holes and put us in them. They used boards and held our heads up." Looking away, this was clearly painful. "They were going to saw our heads off. The people watched and some threw stuff. They started with Goeman. It was slow and painful, and he screamed for a little while, until they cut through his throat."

Hisano was shaking hard and crying. This was ripping Miki's heart out. It would not make the truth easy.

"I couldn't look anymore. They did one more, and then it was my turn. I felt the blade against my neck, and I was really scared. Then there were a lot of people moving, and I saw the man holding the saw blade fall with an arrow through his chest. We couldn't move. There were lots of arrows everywhere, coming from all over. A man with a sword pulled me out of the hole and broke the boards. Some of the men were Koga from the south village, but this man was leading them all, and he was a Samurai. Some of us died getting away, but many soldiers died also." Hisano's face hardened. "I wanted to kill Yoshida. When one of the other Koga was killed, I took his bow. It was very hard to use, but old Lord Yoshida was very close. I shot an arrow into his heart, and his horse kicked my leg and broke it. At least I killed Lord Yoshida."

Miki detected the satisfaction her friend was taking in the elder Lord Yoshida's death. This was not making it easy. "My friend. I am very sorry. I did not know."

"The Samurai who was in charge pulled me away and carried me to the village. He was the kindest man I ever saw, and he was very good to me. He is the only Samurai that I like. They call him the mountain wolf because he had a wolf with him, helping him. He had dark eyes, like yours." Hisano could see that her story had upset her gentle friend Miki. Poor Miki stared at the ground, almost as if she had done something wrong. "I wish that I could have seen Yoshida take his last breath. I am glad that I killed him."

"Lord Mori no Yoshida is not dead." Miki's tiny voice was barely audible.

"I put an arrow into his heart."

"No. You missed the heart. You missed the lungs. The arrow didn't go in very far."

"NO! You can't know that. There is no way you can know that." Her friend had to be lying. She saw the shame on Miki's face. *How could Miki know that! How can she say that awful thing?*

"They brought him to the temple. He was dying, and no one wanted to help him. Masako-san was away, in the town. So I took the arrow out and fixed the damage."

"NO! NO! No one is going to let a nine-year-old baby cut arrows out of a Samurai General. You are lying! The monster is dead, and I killed him!" All the shouting wasn't going to change the truth, and the truth was that Miki never lied. She was incapable of it. This was devastating. *Why did she do this? How could Miki betray her people like this? Why did she betray me like this?*

Muttered apologies were ignored. The truth was out, and it had hurt her friend more than anything Miki could have imagined. She rose to leave the house, and Gonzo blocked her path.

"Maybe it's time to understand what it means to be shinobi. What do you think would have happened to the monks and the temple if you had not saved Yoshida's life? What would Satake have done to the monks and the temple? You saved more than Yoshida's life by your actions. Masako-san tells me that she is very proud of her little imp. Hisano will come to understand. I will take you home now."

Chapter 6 - Little Brother

a child of shadow
destiny redirected
sacrifices made

It had been warm in the mountains of Kumi. The late summer afternoon breeze rustled the branches on the cherry tree that Miki and Hisano had planted six years earlier. Enjoying the cooling breeze and momentary solitude, Miki, now thirteen, reflected on the life that could have been. Satisfied, she knew that hers was a life that now mattered. Dozens of children were alive because of her efforts. Indeed, she was in such demand as a healer that she had been relieved of many of the other mundane tasks that she and Masako normally performed. Sitting on her favorite perch near the temple door, Miki knew that hers was the perfect life.

Sensing a presence, Miki opened her eyes and smiled. Both Master Kukai and Master Akaki had quietly slipped beside her. These men, and all of the other monks, had been her father. They were patient, kind, and wise, some serious and some funny, and there was nothing that the dark-eyed young beauty wanted for. Loved, cherished, respected, and valued, the little imp had grown into a strong, beautiful, young woman who knew who she was and what her future would be.

"My little imp, will you miss your hair when it is gone?"

"This has been my dream since I can remember, Master." Being the only one in the temple with hair made her a bit uncomfortable at times. For years she had pleaded to be made a full member of the temple, and now Master Kukai had finally agreed. Soon her long, straight, midnight black hair that ended at her waist would be gone forever. Even Masako-san had hoped that Miki would choose to keep her hair, even though the middle-aged Ama had none of her own. "No, Master. I have looked forward to this. The temple is where I belong. It is where I can do the most good. "

The temple had never been richer. Their tiny Ama had made it so. The sick and lame sought her out, and rich and poor sought her kindness and comfort. Her popularity meant donations and gifts to the North Road Temple. Neither Akaki nor old Kukai wanted to remember a time when this seemingly delicate child had not graced this holy place, or their hearts.

Reading voraciously, the exceptionally intelligent young woman had even added a few scrolls of her own, usually of medicines and mountain herbs, to temple's library. Gifted, the girl was a gift. Wiser than a thirteen-year-old girl should be, Miki had even been allowed to teach in the village and the homes, where she was always an honored guest.

Highlighted against the garden with its pink cherry trees and setting sun, the temple's beautiful daughter had made a choice. In a few weeks, she would be an Ama with all of the duties and privileges that any other adult had. But then, Miki had already shared in all the labors and duties the temple demanded. Nothing would change except the hair and the recognition that little Miki, the imp from heaven, was no longer the child but the young woman.

Sensing that the two most important men in her life, Master Kukai, the old temple master, and Akaki, the man who was for all purposes her father, had something to say, Miki turned to face them as a mountain breeze caught her hair and sent it whipping in the wind. "Please, Master. This is what I want. Please let me serve."

"Master Akaki and I cannot deny you what you have earned. My little imp, you have made an old man proud. You have taught an old man what it is to love." The old temple master was trying to say something. His words were slow and deliberate. "Master Akaki and I have decided that perhaps there are things that you should know before you take this step. Important things about who you are."

"Master, I know who I am. I know that I am Koga, and I remember my mother, and my village." *What is he trying to tell me?* Her life was no secret. Yoshida's dog Satake had nearly killed her for her past. "And I know that to be an Ama is all that I ever wanted to be."

"Miki, What Master Kukai is trying to say is that you may not have been told everything. For your own protection, I fear that we may not have been entirely honest with you." Watching their gentle spirit close her eyes and breathe deeply, both men could see that their little Miki misunderstood their intent. Neither Akaki nor Kukai doubted what path their temple's daughter would take. Still, the truth demanded its due. Their child had grown up living a lie designed by suspicious men in a dark, smoky room seven years earlier. *Perhaps our dark-eyed beauty should meet her family first. Miki's secret has waited thirteen years. It can wait another ten days.*

"Miki-san. A Samurai whom you have never met will be leaving his son here for instruction soon. For the next ten days or so, I need for you to teach and take care of him. This is a special young man, a bit younger than you. Masako-san will go to town for you, so you have no other duty." Kukai could see that his little imp welcomed the change in subject. Only after she knew everything, once Miki had forgiven their hidden truth, would her decision to shave her head be an honest one.

Early morning rains meant that the day would be gray and cooler than normal on this late summer morning. Two men had come through the back gate, normally reserved for Koga and monks looking for firewood. One, a tall, well-built man who carried the two swords of a Samurai and whose face was hidden by the large, round, straw hat, escorted a scrawny boy of about twelve, who also carried both katana and the short sword of a Samurai. This was unusual, as the child was still too young for this honor. But then, Master Akaki had indicated that the child was special in some way.

Watching Master Akaki show the strange pair across the moist grass of the back courtyard behind the main temple, Miki wondered what was so important that for ten days, she would have no other duties. The small, scruffy boy was plainly dressed in a brown *hakama* as a ronin might be, his dark eyes much like hers. *Maybe that is how it is for all children who have to grow up too fast. What do they expect of this boy that a simple Ama could give him?* She was no larger and not really any older than he was. Master Akaki spoke to the tall, muscular Samurai like a friend. These people knew each other.

Bowing to the pair of Samurai standing before her, Miki marveled at how straight and powerful the Samurai looked as he nodded his reply. As he gazed into her eyes, Miki felt as though the man were staring into her very soul. Feeling very small, the young Ama lowered her eyes, wondering what she should do next.

"I am told that your name is Miki-san. I have heard of you. You are even prettier than I was led to believe. We have a common friend. A girl I once rescued had her leg repaired by you. Hisano was her name, I believe." The Samurai's deep voice was not threatening. Indeed, the man sounded kind, respectful even. "The people in the local villages speak of your kindness and intelligence. Miki-san, I have a great favor to ask of you. My son Kiyotaka requires instruction of a kind that I cannot give. I am told that you would be ideal for this task. It would honor me if you would consent."

He was asking her, not ordering her. This was the Samurai Hisano had spoken of so many years ago, the kind man who had carried her friend with the broken leg home. Miki had seen Hisano maybe a dozen times in the intervening years, with few words actually spoken. Miki missed her friend, who had seemingly outgrown her. "Hai. My friend Hisano is angry with me. But her leg did heal well."

"Please look at me. You look so very much like a woman I once knew. So very much. Little Miki, I think they call you among the Koga. They hold you in very high esteem, especially your friend Hisano. She speaks of you whenever I see her. I do not believe that it is anger." The man was being kind. The little boy with the dirty hair just stared at her. *What is Kiyotaka thinking?* she wondered. "Miki-san, speak to Hisano. You may find that she misses you as much as you miss her." *This man actually cares about people.* The boy was lucky to have such a father. A bit ashamed of herself for her jealousy, Miki wondered what it would have been like to have such a man as father.

"Master, I would be honored to teach your son. Thank you for your great kindness." Miki bowed again as the Samurai nodded. Saying good-bye to the boy, the man walked with impressive dignity as Master Akaki escorted him to the back gate. She turned her attention to the boy, and his unblinking stare unnerved her. The seriousness on the boy's face, and his hand on a katana resting in his obi, left the young Ama puzzled. *Is this boy here against his will? Does he not trust me?*

"So you are Kiyotaka? Welcome to our temple. Would you like to clean up after your journey?" *If he would only stop staring.* Maybe she could get him to open up. He was a bit scary with that long stare with those dark eyes.

"No. I'm hungry. Can we eat something?" At least the boy was following her toward the eating area. The other monks gazed disapprovingly as the boy simply ignored them all.

"Normally we do not eat after midday in the temple, but I think that I can make something. We have plenty of vegetables." At least he blinked once. Wiping his face with his sleeve, the boy was no model of sophistication. Not what Miki expected of a Samurai.

"Any meat?"

"We do not eat meat in the temple, Kiyotaka. I am afraid that we only have vegetables and some pickled fish." This promised to be a very long ten days. This boy was nothing like any of the boys in the towns and villages. His voice was soft but firm. The scruffy kid did not ask; he simply made decisions and expected the world to comply with his will.

"No problem. I'll go kill something."

That announcement stopped several of the monks in their tracks. Apologizing to her friends, Miki moved to get in front of the boy. "No. Kiyotaka, please! We cannot kill here. We do not kill anything."

"Anything?"

"Anything. Life is precious. All life. Everywhere." Miki looked into the boy's dark eyes, hoping, praying, that the heart beyond was not just as dark. *What kind of life has this child led?* "I will make a meal. Trust me." Turning the boy around, she got him to sit down while she prepared a stew of vegetables and salted fish. "Tell me about your mother, Kiyotaka." There had to be a way to get beyond the emotionless wall the boy was hiding behind.

Shoving a chunk of potato into his mouth, Kiyotaka wiped his hands across his *keikogi*. Miki knew that basic table manners were going to be first on her list of lessons. "My mother died when I was a baby. The other women in the village took care of me." Picking the bowl up, the hungry boy started to slurp, and Miki could take no more. Seizing the bowl, a now-thoroughly disgusted young Ama slapped the wooden spoon onto the table.

"This is a spoon! We use it when we eat food. These are the utensils we use to pick up food." Apparently, this was news to the boy. His blank stare when she handed him the sticks told Miki that he was not used to being spoken to like this by a girl. Using one of the sticks to spear another chunk of potato was at least some progress, Miki supposed. She would have to work on technique later. Miki was guessing that he was not raised among high-class Samurai, who were always immaculate, wondering instead if he was raised by people at all. This was going to be a long ten days. "When we are done here, Kiyotaka, we will work on getting you a bath. I need to wash your clothing."

Miki rose as usual before first light. It was going to be a warm day, and the young Ama had a full day planned for her student, starting with cleanliness and table manners. A quick search of the room assigned to Kiyotaka irked the girl, who had expected that at least he could stay put. As the frantic search proceeded quietly, Miki felt a growing panic and shame at having lost her charge. Having searched the entire complex several times, the teary-eyed Miki knew that she could not hide the loss of a twelve-year-old boy any longer.

Miki, spotting Master Akaki in the back courtyard near the back wall gate, wiped her tears and prepared for the inevitable recriminations. "Master Akaki? I cannot find Kiyotaka anywhere. It is nearly midmorning, and he has not eaten. I wanted to feed him separately."

The monk seemed unconcerned. "Why separately?"

"I needed a chance to teach him how to eat."

"I think that Kiyotaka probably knows how to eat. I imagine that he has been eating most of his life." His smile told Miki that he was playing with her.

"I apologize. I mean how to eat properly. He is not very... well...I mean polite. Washing is also something I was going to help him with."

"I remember a little imp who also needed to learn those things, so many years ago. But I can help you in your search. You might consider that the boy is not the child that you think he is. Treat him like your little brother, and you will find that you have as much to learn from Kiyotaka as he does from you." Walking out the back gate, monk and little Ama proceeded up the trail into the forest. In a small clearing was a lean-to and a small campfire, complete with roasted rabbit on sticks. The boy was drilling with drawn sword, precise movements like sort of a dance. Reaching the end of the drill, Kiyotaka deftly flicked off imaginary blood and smoothly drew the katana down the mouth of the *saya*, slipping it slowly into its home. "Is this the young man you seek?"

"Hai," she said, not sure if she should be grateful at finding him, embarrassed by losing the boy, or angry at him. For that matter, Master Akaki must have known that the boy was here, and he had seen her increasingly frantic search of the small temple's grounds. "Master Akaki, why did you not tell me that you knew where he was?"

"Why did you not ask for my help, young one?"

Master Akaki was going to make it one of those little lessons in life that he was good at. "I was embarrassed. I apologize."

Kiyotaka kicked out the fire as he shoved what was some form of animal meat that he had roasted over the fire into his mouth.

He held out one of the meat-laden sticks, and Miki shook her head no. Unfazed, the boy simply ate the offered meat. "Nothing lives until something dies. I have some grapes and potatoes, too. You look hungry."

She was. Miki had spent the morning looking for an unkempt boy who needed to be cared for. Here he was in his element, more than capable of handling just about anything. "Hai. We do not eat meat. Potatoes are just fine."

Master Akaki nodded and headed down the lush green path, leaving two unique youngsters to sort out their affairs. So very different, so very much the same. Both self-reliant, courageous, and exceptionally intelligent. One a creature of peace, incapable of violence, the other born to it. It was time to let them experience each other's world before they found out just how much alike they really were.

"So you did not really know your mother?" The last several days had been revealing. The boy was the last surviving male of the Yorisada line. Destined to either rule Kumi or die quickly at Hamatsu hands, he had been taught the katana and combat from the moment of his birth. Raised a Samurai in a village of mountain peasants, the boy was dedicated to protecting his village. Quiet and modest, he was surprisingly friendly and kind, much like his father.

"I almost remember her. Sometimes I hear her voice, but it's going away. I think she loved me, but I don't know. Everyone treats me differently. It's hard to have friends. There isn't any other Samurai my age in my village, and the boys are afraid of me. I'm the only one who has to carry a katana, even though we make them in our village."

This was a problem that Miki understood. Except for Masako-san, she was the only girl. With no exception, she was the only child, and the only one with hair. The certain knowledge that the hair problem would soon disappear made her smile. Kiyotaka was lonely, facing great expectations, never allowed a mistake or a day of rest. Behind the dark eyes was the longing for a friend, someone who understood. *This is why he is here. This must be why his father brought him here.*

"My friends used to call me Taka, when none of the adults were listening. Now I can't even have friends. Not now." Kiyotaka looked at the girl sitting on the boulder. Her smile was bright and genuine. Small, she was light and fast, with amazing balance. Miki was the most beautiful girl he had ever seen, and the only one who would really talk to him. Drawing his katana again, he started his exercise of the eight deadly cuts again.

"I'm your friend." He was sweet and gentle, if a bit on the rough side. Miki noted that he never lost sight of that sword. It was always with him, as if his heart would stop beating if it left his hands or was ever out of reach. He was always listening, always aware. Never did his guard go down, not even for a moment. *What would cause anyone, especially a child, to live like this?* "Why not now? What changed?"

Finishing up, Kiyotaka snapped the katana smartly, flipping it up so that he could respectfully replace his soul in its saya. Would she really understand? "A group of ronin came into my village when my father was away. He's away a lot. I was supposed to protect the village while he was away. They came to steal weapons and food."

"You are just a kid. What could you have done?" Miki could see that the boy was ashamed, as if he could stop an adult warrior.

"My cousin found me in the woods with my wolves. She was scared. By the time I got back, the ronin had killed my friend's father, who tried to stop him. Everyone in the village expected me to save them all. He was big and mean and strong, and I was afraid."

"Oh Taka, there was nothing you could have done. He would have killed you." Expectations. Why do adults always expect so much? Reaching out, she offered her hand to the boy, who seemed to need it so much.

"He thought I was a child. He called me a peasant with a sword. He yelled, and then he tried to kill me. I was faster, and I opened his belly. He still tried to fight from his knees, so I cut his head off. I hated him. He hurt my friends and my village, and it was my fault." The boy stared right through her, as if he were watching it in his mind. Miki dropped her hand, unsure how to handle this new knowledge that the boy had beheaded a human being. Like her friend Hisano, the boy had been faced with horrific decisions and no real options. Was this how it was everywhere outside her temple?

Taking a step toward the boy whose stone face and cold dark eyes were betrayed by a single tear, Miki wrapped her arms around Kiyotaka. Boys did not cry. They kept their pain inside. Miki had always wondered what price men paid for their pride. Now she knew. The scruffy boy stiffened, as if no one had ever touched him before. Unsure at first as to this gentle girl's intention, it was a gesture that even Miki knew that he could not return. He was Samurai. This was how it was.

"Do you have a family in your village?" Releasing the boy, the young Ama reached down to hold Kiyotaka's hands.

"No. Not really. A pesky little cousin."

"You have family here. From now on, you are my little brother. Let me help you." She was an Ama, the relief of suffering her chosen path in life. Like her, he was alone. For the next few days at least, both would have family. "Can you show me the exercise you do with your sword? I used to be Koga. Maybe I can still hold a sword." In fact, holding the instrument of death was frightening, even painful. But it was a way into the young man's world, a way to see through his eyes. It was a way to let the boy named Kiyotaka be in charge, to let him lead rather than follow. Somehow, Miki knew that this boy really was different. What they were preparing him for she did not know. Somehow, Miki knew that she wanted to be part of it all.

"The last eleven days have been wonderful. Soon I will have to go back to my work, and you will go home." Indeed, they had been. Miki had learned as much as the boy had. She now understood the war her people fought, the role of the Iga in her people's misery. It was all suffering hidden from her, injustice they would not let her see. Perhaps, just maybe, this was the secret that Masters Akaki and Kukai wanted to tell her about later. They had even asked Kiyotaka to be present.

"And the day after, you'll be bald." The boy reached over and gave the girl's hair a quick tug before jumping off the boulder overlooking the temple. He dashed down the wooded hill to his camp near the small clearing, a giggling Miki in close pursuit. He slowed down just enough to keep the girl close.

The boy also had learned much. Miki had a magnificent spirit. He had a friend he could talk to, and family, even if for just a week. Someday, maybe she could be his wife. Miki the little Ama would always be his friend.

Catching the boy at the edge of the clearing, Miki grabbed the naughty Kiyotaka by his scruffy hair, nearly pulling him off of his feet. Turning, Kiyotaka grabbed the still-giggling Miki around the waist and hoisted the wiggling girl to his shoulder. Protesting, Miki struggled against the boy's surprising strength.

"Is this the way for an Ama to behave? And with a Samurai. How disgraceful!" Standing at the other edge of the camp was Master Akaki. "And what are your intentions with my young acolyte, Sir Kiyotaka?" For the last few days, his little imp had behaved dreadfully, as though for the first time in her life she felt like a child. Amused, Akaki loosed a stern stare at the boy, who was still holding the girl. "You may put Miki-san down now."

The two young people standing before him had transformed each other. Now, as they stood there together, Akaki could see the similarities. Kiyotaka looked directly at him, and his sweet little imp Miki stared down at the ground, biting her lip, terrified at what penalty Master Kukai might exact. "Perhaps it would be best not to mention this to Master Kukai. This will be our little secret. Miki-san, please go back to the temple. Kiyotaka and I will join you shortly."

Watching the girl shuffle off down the trail as piously as possible, Kiyotaka turned to face Master Akaki. "Miki did nothing wrong. We were just having fun."

"No. Miki did nothing wrong. I am very proud of her, and I thank you for all that you have given her. Before we join Miki and your father, there is something that I need for you to know."

"About Miki?"

"About Miki-san, and you."

"I like her very much. She's my friend."

"She is more than that, my young Samurai. What I am about to tell you, only Master Kukai, Kawachi of the Koga, Gendo, and I know. Even Miki-san herself does not know. I tell you because I believe that you are a man of honor. I believe that you have a destiny, but it is a destiny that Miki will share if you let her."

So this is why they wanted me here. Even my father did not understand their urgency. "Why didn't you tell my father?"

So the boy had figured it out. Oto was a man of exceptional intelligence. It made sense that his children would be also. "For Miki's protection. You and your father are hunted criminals. If they know of her, how long will she live? She already has powerful enemies. If they catch you and Lord Oto, she will be the last."

They're right. Miki wouldn't stand a chance. Do I want my life to be hers? "I'll keep your secret, even from my father. But I want the whole story." It wasn't a request. It was a demand that even the monk named Akaki understood.

"Very well. Like so many tragic stories, it started on a dark and stormy night..."

What have I done wrong? For eleven days I taught Kiyotaka about my life. I taught him meditation and the words of the Buddha and medicines. For eleven days I learned also. This was a boy who had been taught how to kill as soon as he could walk. He had seen death and created death to save others. They were opposites, alike in no way but their shared concern for justice.

Reaching the back gate to the temple, Miki grabbed the rope that would ring the bell inside. She hesitated for a moment, almost expecting Kiyotaka and Master Akaki to catch up. Deep voices drifting over the walls were not from monks. Soldiers! This was something that both Master Akaki and Kiyotaka needed to know. Both were wanted outlaws, although it was difficult to imagine anything Master Akaki could possibly have done that should make the gentle wise man, for all practical purposes her father, a criminal. Kiyotaka, however, was a Yorisada, and for that reason alone would die. Kiyotaka had not told her this, but Miki was not stupid. Stories and news from the many people who had passed through the temple over the years spoke of the great Mountain Samurai fighting for justice against the evil Hamatsu and their Daimyo Lord Nobunaga.

Looking at the rope in her right hand, Miki realized that if she let go, it would give its characteristic little tinkle. Perhaps if she let it go ever so slowly, maybe!

The sudden silence from over the wall, followed by the opening of the gate, told the now-terrified girl that it had not worked. Turning to run brought the surprised girl face to face with several soldiers moving around the wall's corner. Even if she managed to dash up the path away from the wall, she would only be leading them directly to Master Akaki and the boy she had adopted as a brother. Helpless, all she could do was to await her fate.

Rough hands seized her hair and robes as two armed soldiers dragged the girl through the open temple doorway. This was an ambush planned for someone else that she had sprung prematurely. Screams of innocence brought several hard slaps across her face as they pushed the terrified Miki through the door. Miki, praying as hard as she could that Kiyotaka had heard her and would not come, tried to keep up but could not, finding herself dragged more than led into the main temple chamber with all of the other monks.

"Look what we caught." Afraid to look up, Miki stared at the rough wooden floor as the guard presented his prize. *How courageous. He captured a thirteen-year-old Ama who was not even armed with a violent thought.*

"Take the girl to see General Satake. He'll want to question her." Miki wanted to never hear that name again. Even if she were not guilty of teaching a fugitive, or trying to warn him to stay away, there was still his pursuit of her several years earlier. Maybe he would not remember.

"We caught this sneaking in the back gate. She tried to warn someone." Dropping the girl into a heap of robes and hair in front of the scarfaced man, the brutal soldier went to one knee, lowering his head in salute before being casually dismissed by the wave of a hand.

"I lost two good men the last time I saw you. They were hunted down and killed by wolves. But you knew that, did you not?" Satake said. "Sneaking in? What was it that you said to me then? Something about your destiny to kill me, as I recall."

He remembered. *Why had I thought that he would not?*

"I did not sneak in. I live here. I did not know about your friends." *What is he going to do with me now?* Masako-san was kneeling with the other monks. She didn't know about Miki's little encounter with Satake three years earlier. Neither Master Akaki nor Kukai thought that she would handle the news well. They were correct.

"Honorable Sir, little Miki is a child, a little girl. Miki is no killer! I am sure that you must have misunderstood her. How can my little Miki be a threat to such a powerful Samurai as yourself?" The soldiers were reluctant to silence the Ama, who had turned to face the smirking, scarfaced man. It was clear that no one wanted to abuse the monks.

"That is what the wolf told me."

"MIKI! Please, Kind Sir, my little Miki thinks that she can speak with the wolves. Please, let her go. I assigned her the task of teaching the boy." A lie. Kukai and Akaki had given her the task over Masako-san's objections. She was protecting them.

"SILENCE! Let the witch speak. What were you doing when you came back? Who were you warning?" Satake expected an answer. Never had she uttered a lie. Miki could not do so now.

"I was teaching the sutras and meditation to a child, a young boy."

"Who?"

"A boy named Kiyotaka."

"And that is who you were warning?"

"Hai." He already knew the answer. Lying would solve nothing. Either Master Akaki had gotten the boy away or he had not. Either way, that was whom the ambush was for. There would already be men hunting in the woods. Kiyotaka's camp would be found quickly. "But if you find him, you will lose many soldiers."

"Miki. Tell them the truth. Tell them that you do not know who he is." A quick slap from a reluctant soldier silenced Masako.

"He is the son of Lord Oto, the man you want to kill."

"I am impressed. No lies. No hesitation. Not even any fear. Spoken like a Samurai. But you are no Samurai, are you? You are a stupid Koga girl."

"I am an Ama. I am a teacher and a healer. I have never harmed anyone or anything. If you were hurt even now, I would heal you. I was trying to teach Kiyotaka that killing was unnecessary. I even made him my brother." *He's going to kill me anyway.* Miki was scared, but the boy had taught her to hide it. As long as she was alive, there were at least possibilities—another lesson from the boy.

"Lord Oto is outside. We will track down his son soon enough. He was under the assumption that we already had his son. Lord Yoshida no Mori will kill him personally. For once, I need you alive, to serve as witness. You will watch the fight. You will tell the Koga that their hero is dead." Grabbing her by the arm, the evil man marched the scared but defiant little Ama out the front door to the main garden outside. On one side stood the fine, gentle Samurai, now in bloodied brown clothing, who had left the boy in her charge, and on the other side the man, Lord Yoshida no Mori, whose chest she had repaired three years earlier.

The noble Samurai turned his head to face the captive girl, and Miki could see that he had taken a terrible beating. With an eye swollen nearly shut and a pronounced limp as he hobbled a few steps toward the horrified girl, he asked, "Kiyotaka?"

"When I left him, he was safe." Miki could see that this was not to be a fair fight, but little more than an execution. This was to be a show fight, so that Lord Yoshida could claim that he had killed the mighty Mountain Samurai in personal combat. Yet, to kill this man without Kiyotaka, his son, would be a much smaller victory.

"Thank you. I apologize for involving you. A child so beautiful should never have to see what you now will be forced to witness." Turning back to face Lord Yoshida, this noble Samurai stood straight, as though his pain did not exist. He was regal, his dignity and bearing impressive. "This child is innocent. Little Miki-san had no idea who my son was."

"I will spare her life, as Miki-san once saved mine. She is nothing. Your son cannot be spared." This, of course, was obvious. Kiyotaka was the prize, the last Yorisada and the last legitimate heir to the province of Kumi. Maybe a dozen soldiers formed a circle around the two combatants as Satake released Miki and took up a position across the garden to get a better view to command the spear-armed guards. Lord Yoshida no Mori drew his sword, a slight smirk below his cold, focused eyes.

"My son cannot be caught. We may begin at your command." The noble Samurai raised his left hand to the saya of the katana resting in his worn black obi. Closing his eyes, he breathed deep, as Miki had seen Kiyotaka do as the boy prepared to draw his sword. *Why doesn't he draw his sword? What is he waiting for?* Every set of eyes focused on two men standing in the garden, awaiting the inevitable conflict.

Yoshida struck downward quickly as the nearly blind Samurai's sword flew from its saya so fast that eyes could not follow its path, blocking Yoshida's blade. Surprised by the Samurai's speed and power, as wounded as he was, Yoshida backed off into the guard position. Near the gate, Satake drew his sword and motioned the soldiers forward.

"NO! Oto is mine. Do not interfere." Yoshida's fierce stare at the Samurai, whose calm demeanor seemed so out of place, belied a hint of fear. "You cannot win."

"You have already lost."

A clash of steel rang out as Yoshida's blade once again slid down the slanted blade of the swift Samurai, whose blade buried deeply into Yoshida's neck, cutting into his chest. As the Lord Yoshida no Mori sank to the ground spurting blood, the horror of their Master's death froze each soldier in place.

Flicking the blood from his blade, the Samurai flipped his blade over, slowly drawing the blade down the mouth of the saya, letting it drop into the saya slowly. Turning to face Satake standing in front of the closed gate, he waited for the ugly, scarred man to move, but clearly not expecting it.

"You murdered Lord Yoshida, my Master." Satake signaled his four closest men, and as they started to advance, Miki could see motion on the walls and hear motion from the inside of the temple. An unseen hand grabbed her from behind and pulled her into the wide wooden door of the temple.

"Wait here. Stay safe." Kiyotaka pushed the girl into the waiting arms of Masako-san, whose gentle arms wrapped around her little Miki, holding tight to prevent the child from leaving the safety of the temple. Miki glanced around and watched in horror as her savior, a scrawny boy of twelve, smiled at her before turning and signaling the three grown men, probably Koga whom she did not know, to follow him out the door into the garden. As he disappeared, the monks who loved her surrounded her to prevent her escape.

Screams. The clash of metal. The sound of battle lasted for just a few minutes. Shouted orders, then silence. No one in the room dared to look outside as loving arms held back a crying, screaming little Miki, who needed to know that the kind Samurai and her adopted little brother had survived.

Finally, after what seemed like ages, Master Kukai rose and opened the temple door that had been shut by the last Koga out. As monks filtered out of the door and drifted outside into the courtyard, they were greeted with a scene of unimaginable horror. Bodies everywhere. Blood leaking out of severed limbs, the groans of the dying. Arrows standing out of men lying so still that they could be sleeping. Most were soldiers; a few were Koga. Miki pulled away from Masako to search for a young boy whom she prayed she would not find. A quick check brought her relief until she realized that some of the men on the ground were not dead and might still be saved. Asking one of the older monks to get the supplies she and Masako would need, Miki turned her attention to the man groaning at her feet.

"How many did we save?" Kukai had watched Masako and Miki work into the evening and through the night. Both were exhausted.

"We have three. The only Koga was sent with Master Akaki to the north village. Thanks to little Miki over there, he will live. When the soldiers come back, they would kill him. Miki's skills have grown well beyond mine. Last night I watched her repair wounds that I thought meant certain death. I am so very proud of her." Masako watched the girl tend to the men lying together on the other side of the room. She was changing a bandage on the one whose heart had taken the arrow. By all rights, the young man should have died. "So very proud."

Miki tossed the bloody patch of bandage into the bowl before checking the silk bindings that kept the wound together. The boy was in pain, but she had managed to get a smile from him. "Do you have a wife? Children?"

"Only if you want me. Soldiers aren't allowed to get married." The boy was in good spirits.

"I'm only thirteen. Besides, I was going to have my head shaved today." Miki helped the boy drink. It was important to replace the lost blood. "There was a boy, younger than I, who fought you. Did you see what happened to him?"

The young man did not have the chance to answer before the temple door opened. Sanjo the funny monk wasn't smiling. "General Satake has arrived. Lord Yoshida's son is with him. "

Kukai turned toward the door as the scarfaced Satake shoved Sanjo out of the way.

"YOU! How did Koga shinobi get into this temple? Search this temple. Find the tunnel." Soldiers moved swiftly around the monks gathered in the temple. "How many men did we lose? How many did that boy kill?" His Lord was dead by Oto's despised hand, and soon he would have to answer to Lord Nobunaga for his failure to protect his master. But for now, Satake wanted revenge.

"Sir, there are ten being prepared outside. The monks have three others being cared for." The older soldier pointed to Miki, on her knees with a cup in her hand, helping her patients drink.

"The healer. Choose ten monks, including the temple Master, to pay for this crime. Include the Koga witch over there. I want that girl dead IN PUBLIC. Take them to town, now." The one they called Little Miki would not escape this time. This girl's destiny was now his to command.

As the pronouncement sank in, eyes dropped to the temple floor. Masako could not believe the terrible injustice and for a few seconds could not move. As soldiers seized the tiny girl and dragged everyone's little imp from heaven toward the front door, a dozen arms encircled the devastated Masako as the woman fought to reach her little girl. As Miki disappeared through the temple doors, the Ama named Masako sank to her knees in rage, pounding the floor in agony. As individual monks were pointed out, each walked to the front door with dignity and acceptance of what was now an inevitable fate.

Chapter 1 - Execution

life interrupted
agony, a mothers love
shared experiences

The cramped, filthy room stank of urine and sweat. Outside, the taunts and sobs of town women were muffled by the cloth barriers hung over the barred windows, allowing no air to circulate on the hot summer day. Each monk, arms tightly bound, sat as still as possible, most with eyes closed in prayer to conserve what little energy remained. No food or water had been allowed, and without hope, there seemed to be little to say. The monks could hear the sound of soldiers, or townspeople forced to work, digging holes in which poles being carried in by craftsmen would be placed. Satake had announced that the monks and the little witch would be hung by the wrists until the criminals could no longer breathe.

"Master, do you think that the Mountain Samurai or the Koga will come for us?" Miki's arms hurt, and she could no longer feel her hands. Lightheaded from dehydration and hunger, she shook in fear from the anticipation of another night in this hell. Hope. Any hope at all, even false hope, would help.

Opening his eyes, the old temple master smiled. Serene, it was as if he were back in his temple. "No, my little imp. There will be no one coming for us." Closing his eyes, it was as if he were walking back into his temple.

Master Kukai had not helped. Tears welled up as Miki thought about those who would die with her, and whom she would leave behind. "Will Masako-san be there?"

"Do you want her there?" Kukai kept his eyes closed. *How can he be so calm?*

Do I? "I don't think so. Hai, I want her, but I do not want to see her sad. No. Masako-san should not be there. I miss her." Her dry throat seemed to close up. Miki could feel tears that she had no way to wipe off stream down the path that so many tears had already traveled. *Why is he smiling?* "Why won't they rescue us?"

"Because I asked them not to."

What? Why? Master Kukai cannot be serious! "Master, why would you not want to be rescued?" *They rescued Hisano. Why would they not come for us?* The newest monk, a young man named Shibata, had joined the temple only last year. He had spent the night begging, at least until the guards beat him in the darkness. Now he just lay on the floor whimpering.

"Because, my little one, they have waited two days to execute us to draw Kiyotaka and his father into a trap. Because if we escape, who would you choose to take your place? The pregnant mother who tried to give you water? Perhaps the boy Kiyotaka?"

"I apologize. I should not be selfish. No one, Master. I am sorry." Time meant nothing. The heat and stench made Miki want to vomit. Listening to the workmen outside, she could tell that they were almost finished. "Master, why do you smile?"

It was as if the question were amusing somehow. "Because I have enjoyed my life. I think now on those times that were best. All of them were with you, because of you. Thank you, little one, for the life that you have given me. I can ask nothing more."

He never called her by name. It was as if he did not know it. It was always Imp from Heaven or Little One or something cute. She always thought that he considered her a pest or an annoyance. There were tears in the eyes of her friends. Nods from other monks tugged at her heart. "I am sorry for the pain that I have brought all of you. It was General Satake's hatred for me that caused this. This is my fault."

Kukai's eyes popped open. The smile was gone. "It is your fault that Hisano can walk, that many sick and injured people are alive. It is your fault that the child held by that mother who cried for you was born to take a breath. The lessons that you have taught, the joy that you have given all who have lived in or visited our temple, THESE ARE ALL YOUR FAULT! The actions of an evil man and the fact that you were an innocent part of a larger game of power that you do not understand, these are not your fault. They are mine. Miki, you have a life that matters. Old men pray in halls begging for food and thinking themselves holy while they hide from the sins of their past. From the moment of your first breath, you have harmed no one. Yours is a life of peace and one that I envy. Tomorrow, nine guilty men will die, and the only shame is that they could not protect one innocent child. I will hear no more." Kukai glared at the scared child, whose eyes pointed toward the floor. "I apologize, my little imp."

"I did so want to be an Ama."

"You have always been an Ama. Tomorrow you will die an Ama."

"Please inform Lady O-Sho that I have an urgent matter that needs her attention." Masako-san was exhausted. The trip from the temple following the soldiers who escorted her friends to the post town along the North Road had been fast. Two days of begging for an audience, of gathering food for her friends, and arguing that monks dead of thirst would make for a poor show. Getting permission to get this close to the Lady O-Sho had required a bribe. Ten tall poles had been erected to murder her friends and awaited their victims, who were spending another uncomfortable night bound in that stinking, terrible, crowded room. At least they were given water and rice, a concession to prevent premature death before the next day's planned spectacle. If a spectacle was what they wanted, perhaps she could give them one.

"I am very sorry. My Lady is very tired and quite upset. Perhaps tomorrow." The young servant woman was the last barrier to her plan; tomorrow was just not good enough.

"I am here to save little Miki. This is what your Lady wants. Please tell her that I need to speak to her now. This cannot wait." There was no time for the expected humility. Politeness would have to wait, a casualty of need. This was her last chance.

"Lady O-Sho was insistent. I am sorry. You must go."

Before Masako could open her mouth, the Lady O-Sho stepped through the door. The makeup on her face had been ruined by the tears that she had shed. "That is enough; you are dismissed. I will speak to this woman. You must be the Ama Masako."

"Hai."

"I have already spoken with my son. He will not spare the monks, criminals who murdered his father, and my husband. Not even the girl Miki. I have already tried."

"If this is what General Satake told you, than he dishonors your husband with his self-serving lies. Lord Mori Yoshida died in a fair duel fought at his own request. Lord Mori no Yoshida died a proud Samurai, as he wished. His orders to release Oto, the man they call the Mountain Samurai, were ignored by a man who knows no honor. It was then that Oto's son, a boy of twelve, led Koga shinobi to force the General's hand. Miki was never involved. None of the monks were."

"He died in a duel?"

"Hai."

"Satake is a snake. But he has Lord Nobunaga's ear. My son must be seen as strong, or he will lose to Satake, and that would be worse for Kumi. I am sorry, but this is how it must be. I will grieve with you tomorrow."

"My Lady, I would not have come if I had nothing to offer. Miki is very popular with the people, and her death on the new Lord Yoshida's orders would make him as hated as General Satake."

"Tomorrow, ten criminals will die. My son cannot stop that."

"Tomorrow, ten criminals will die as your son requires. Little Miki must not be among them. The new Lord Yoshida needs help with the people. I offer him that." Masako hoped that she would understand.

"I understand. We will see my son now. Come with me."

"It is a beautiful morning. I will enjoy the sun on my face." Miki was surrounded by her family, men who had loved her since she was a small child. She had served their meals, bandaged their blisters, and tried to keep them happy. Duty. She had one last duty, and that was to make the passing of her friends, her loved ones, easy. She had held the hands of the dying in order to give the last bit of comfort before. This would be no different. Today they would see her smile. What they needed was their little imp from heaven. Today there would be no tears.

The room still stank. Everyone was still filthy, although by some miracle they had been fed by local women. Sanjo the jolly had smiled and joked, although Miki was not sure that it was very funny, something about being much taller soon. Still the men laughed, and that was good to hear. A door opened, and two guards dragged the still-crying Shibata out first. Even the guards were tired of his begging.

Standing on shaky legs, Miki did not want to be carried. The only one small enough to actually walk through the door, she wanted to be next, hoping that her example would give her men courage. Fear would find no home in her heart this day. It was important that all of them see this, especially Master Kukai. The crowd outside seemed stunned by her appearance.

"Look at how brave she is."

"How can they kill such a beautiful child?"

An unruly, angry mob had assembled to watch the execution. Nervous soldiers kept sobbing women, curious children, and angry men at bay, soldiers no less unhappy then those that they had to control. The sun felt good on her face, and Miki needed to do this right. As the guards dumped poor Shibata in front of the last pole, they turned to return to collect the rest of their victims. Miki, unwilling to be led to slaughter, marched out to meet them.

Stopping to bow to the officer in charge of the execution, Miki politely asked where she was to stand. Motioning to the first pole, the armored man watched this child step to her position and face a crowd now silent, in awe of the child's bravery. As her friends walked past her, Miki offered a smile and a kind farewell to each. This was a duty that Miki understood. None of them was afraid for himself; all, except for poor miserable Shibata, were terrified for her.

Miki stood watching the tension in the mob rise, seething at the crime of killing monks. Shouts calling for the death of Lord Nobunaga—itself a crime worthy of death—rippled through the crowd. Scared soldiers poked and pushed with their spears, occasionally finding a slow-moving peasant. Blood was being spilled. This would not do on this special day. If holy men were to die, it should be done respectfully. *I have to stop the violence.* Turning to the officer in charge, Miki asked politely if she might address the people before someone was hurt.

Nothing permitted a prisoner to speak, yet after a brief consideration, the tall, straight, older man nodded his consent. Her noble behavior had earned this privilege. Thanking the officer, Miki stepped forward to speak.

"Please listen to me. Please. The men behind me are men of peace. They have chosen to die to avoid bloodshed. Your blood. Out of respect for our act, I beg that all of you accept what must be, as we have. Do not poison our sacrifice with your blood. Let us die knowing that we are alone in death." The crowd was listening, hanging on her words, whispering them to those in the back. "Let no act of violence happen today. These soldiers have no more choice than we do. Today I will feel the sun in my face for the last time. I recognize so many of you as people I have treated, and you are all people I care about. Please!" Silence. Turning to return to her pole, Miki waited for her fate.

Executing criminals was the officer's duty, but this felt wrong to him. Grateful for the child's remarks, he knew that her light weight would work against her, prolonging the agony. Perhaps an arrow to be merciful once the crowd thinned. Jeers and insults attracted the officers' attention to a hated figure arriving from behind. "Lord Yoshida, I was told that you would not be in attendance." The officer in black armor bowed at the approaching man, who was flanked by two equally well-dressed attendants. "Where is General Satake? Will he be coming?"

"The General is in pursuit of the Mountain Samurai. I am in charge now."

"Hai."

Turning toward the crowd, Yoshida could see that the crowd could easily overwhelm the soldiers if they ever figured it out. The girl's words were remarkable, her effect stunning. That would make this next little drama so perfect. "Several days ago, Lord Yoshida was killed by one of the finest swordsmen I have ever known in a fair duel. Afterward, monks allowed men loyal to the Mountain Samurai into the temple. For that crime, ten monks were chosen at random to die. But I now know that this girl had nothing to do with this crime. If someone will take her place, I will allow her to go free. She has already demonstrated her courage. Is there anyone willing to die to save this child?"

"No! NO!" *What's happening? This isn't how it needs to be!* Yoshida's attendants now stood at her side, holding her still.

"I will." As Masako-san made her way through the crowd, Miki could see what she was planning.

"NOOOOO!!!! PLEASE NOOOO! This is my duty, my place! Not her, please not Masako-san." Her own death she had accepted. Miki could see that this was theater, planned for the crowd's behalf. Trading her Masako-san for her was worse than death. "No one must die for me."

Standing in front of Lord Yoshida, Masako turned to face the crowd. "I was the one who let the men into the temple. Miki is innocent. I stand here to pay for my crime."

"Get the innocent child out of here." Yoshida motioned to the attendants. They picked up a struggling but still-bound little girl and hustled her through the crowd, which was eager to let them through.

Masako-san's words were lies. She had been in the temple the whole time. Even the peasants and townspeople knew it, but it served a purpose. It allowed for the tiniest bit of mercy and justified the unjustifiable. Miki's wonderful courage, her speech to the crowd, had made it all that much better. This was the leverage Yoshida needed in his struggle with his cunning but vicious General. Smiling, Lord Yoshida ordered that the executions proceed. Soldiers cut ropes and tied hands. They lifted the nine monks and one Ama by the wrists to the top of the poles, to the jeers of the mob.

Reaching the waiting monk on the other side of town, the struggling, screaming Miki was handed over as the two Samurai attendants disappeared as quickly as possible, not wanting to face the mob without the protection of the little girl. Looking around, Miki could see her friends dangling on those ten terrible poles over the top of the crowd.

"Cut her ropes."

"Not yet. We have to get Miki out of here first."

The girl stank in her soiled robes, made worse by the warmth of this summer day. Tears soaked her face, and her hair had matted with sweat, vomit, and the rice that kind people had dropped while trying to feed the poor girl.

Miki was not out of danger yet. As soon as Satake returned, the vicious man would not wait for the executioner. He would simply behead the child himself. At the inn, a knife swiftly disposed of the ropes encircling the limp girl's wrists and arms. Two well-dressed women went to work stripping the now-worthless robes off the shivering little Miki. The girl could not, or would not, respond to requests. It was as if she had retreated into a world within her own mind, hiding from the agony of the world outside. Only the pain of blood flowing back into cut and bruised arms seemed to get the girl's attention.

A quick bath and new clothing made the girl presentable, without any involvement from Miki herself.

"Miki, we will have to go soon. Can you walk?" Akaki waited for the response that did not come. "Before we leave, someone wants to speak to you. Someone who helped you today. Please listen to her. Miki?"

The girl whose cheerfulness had filled so many hearts with joy was not there. As if she had already died, she stared at the floor in front of her, no longer a participant in this world. Since the last of her screams, Miki had said nothing, moving only when pushed.

"Master Akaki, may I be alone with the girl?" If Miki recognized the voice, she did not show it.

"As you wish." Akaki nodded to the Lady O-Sho and stepped out into the street with the two women who had bathed Miki. Perhaps a woman could reach his child.

O-Sho could feel the hopelessness in the girl, whom she had seen only in happier times. Sitting in front of the girl, she looked into the still-dark but now-empty eyes of Little Miki, the child who might have been her daughter.

"Last evening a woman came to see me. She was quite desperate, and if she had not been an Ama, the guards might have killed her for her impertinence. I recognized her, although I thought that there was nothing that I could do for her since I myself had already begged for your life and the life of the others. Not even my own son would hear me." O-Sho searched the young woman's eyes for any spark of life. Miki lifted her eyes to meet the old woman's, still silent.

"I apologized but told her that there was nothing I could do, but what your Masako-san offered was a plan that might reach my son. The sacrifice she offered would save only one, the one we both loved most."

"I should have died. Not Masako-san. It was my place. It was my fault."

"Your fault? No, it was mine."

"Satake hated me. It was to hurt me that he ordered our deaths."

"No. The last time I saw you, when you saved my husband's life, I asked my husband that I might take you as my daughter. In my arrogance and greed, I believed that I would be a superior mother. I thought that your life in the temple would be wasted begging for food and praying for peasants. But last night, your Masako-san taught me what it meant to be a mother. And this morning, you taught me that your life was not wasted in the temple."

"Why does Satake hate me?"

"In order to punish me for wanting a girl of Koga birth, my husband Lord Yoshida no Mori ordered that Satake kill you once I left. Never did I think that to love you would mean your death. I am very sorry, little one."

"He failed."

"He was humiliated. My husband was a brutal man. General Satake paid a high price for being defeated by a nine-year-old girl. Until my husband's death, he was forbidden to harm you. Now he competes with my son Kondo for control of Kumi. To spare the monks would make my son seem weak to our Lord Nobunaga. Masako-san's sacrifice made mercy possible for you and my son popular with the peasants. What do you think will happen if Satake becomes governor of Kumi? Your Masako-san and your friends will not die for nothing. Please forgive me."

"It would have been better if I had died then, three years ago."

"Ama Masako did not think so. Please, my little Miki. Live. Honor Masako-san and the men she dies with today with your life. I will never see you again." With that, all that could be said, had been. O-Sho could see that the child still blamed herself. Time would heal this, but only if she lived long enough. Neither Miki nor Akaki could be taken by Satake. The child had to go now.

Stepping out the door, O-Sho touched Akaki's shoulder. Several peasants had gathered with cloth and supplies. "My dear friend. The child still blames herself. I wonder what we have done, what I have done. Thank you. I will give you some time. Please use it well."

Motioning to the men, Akaki entered the inn to gather Miki, the girl who would never again be an Ama.

"This is not the way to the temple. I want to go with Masako-san. I want to go with Monk Kukai." They had been traveling in the woods all afternoon. Now it was night, and she could barely walk. Miki did not want to be carried, but she could no longer keep up with the three men. Miki did not know the other two, probably Koga from one of the villages to the south. Monk Akaki was a surprise. He had gone to the town, the first time that Miki had ever seen the man off of temple grounds.

"We are not going to the temple. You must never enter the temple again. Satake will look there first." Akaki had not spoken to Miki about her future. Surely she would have figured this out.

Miki could go no farther. Only the thought of being home, surrounded by the trappings of her temple, had kept her moving at all. She dropped to her knees, and the world swirled around her. "I want to go home. I want to be there for Sanjo, and Masako and the Master." The mental toll added to the physical stress had drained tiny Miki. The press of leaves and dirt on her exhausted cheeks felt good. Perhaps just a few seconds to rest.

"I will carry her. She needs to sleep. Help me with her." Akaki directed the men to place the collapsed young woman on his back, soft rope substituting for the girl's inability to even hold on.

The crunch of leaves, soft-spoken voices, the shifting of her body that she had no control over, made the passing of time irrelevant and welcome.

Light leaked around her eyelids, and the smell of stew with the sound of motion brought Miki to full alertness. The blanket and sounds of life told her that she was no longer in the woods. Looking around, she saw an old woman working on the other side of the dirt-floored room, weaving. What time it was, what day it was, a mystery. *How long have I been here? Where is here?*

"Excuse me. Where am I?" She repeated her question a bit louder when it became obvious that the old woman either could not hear, or did not want to hear her. Trying to sit up was difficult when her slight arms simply would not hold even her light weight. Even her fingers were difficult to move, as her arms ached badly. *Is this some sort of dream?*

Turning to look at her, the old woman dropped her needle, rushed to the rag that served as a door, and excitedly shouted for people to come. Like most huts in the mountains, half the floor was rough wood and the other half packed dirt. Level ground was tough to find in the mountains, and this one-room hut was not quite as level as it could be.

Gonzo, followed by Hisano and several other younger men, quickly entered the hut as Miki struggled to sit up.

"How long have I been here?"

"Two days. You must be hungry."

She was. Now that Gonzo mentioned it, her thoughts drifted to that stew that she had smelled when she woke up. "Hai. Thank you for your kindness. I need to get back to the temple. But I want to eat first and drink something. Do you have water?"

Hisano swiftly handed Miki a cup that her hands could not hold. Catching the cup, as though anticipating Miki's difficulty, the tall girl held it to Miki's lips. "Your arms will feel better in a few days. The more you move them, the faster you will heal. You probably know that already." Miki had not spoken to her friend in years, at least not more than a few words or a polite greeting.

Gonzo waited until Miki had gone through her second cup before addressing her. "Miki-san, I watched you in the town. Your courage was most impressive. I was there to kill you to spare you the pain of a long and terrible death because you are one of us. Through the years of your short life, you have sewn up our cuts, set our bones, and cured our illness. Hisano speaks of you so often that I think that you are sisters. But you must understand that you don't live in the temple anymore. Even now the scarred one, Satake, has twenty men surrounding the temple to trap you. If you are caught in the temple, he will kill more than you. Your life as an Ama is over. These people are now your family. You are now kunoichi, and your training begins tomorrow. "

"But the temple is where I belong." Miki wasn't taking it well.

"Not anymore. Hisano will protect you and be your body-guard until you can protect yourself. Don't try to leave. We don't forgive disobedience."

"I am an Ama." *They have to understand. Home is a temple, and Masako-san, but Masako-san is dead, because of me.*

"You are a Koga kunoichi. Miki the Ama died with ten other monks three days ago."

"But I am Ama."

"Not anymore."

Chapter 8 - Kunoichi

healing, decisions
life reborn, transformations
new friends, a new life

In the temple, rising early to begin the day was normal. They had let her sleep a bit late for the last several days, but they had never left her alone, not even for the briefest of moments. It wasn't as if she had anywhere to go. The temple would not take her back. The woman who had raised her, who had become her mother, had died in her place. Monk Kukai, her mentor, was dead. It was her fault. What she had done to cause it Miki did not know. All she knew was that it was her fault.

"Are your arms feeling better, little one?" The old woman seldom left the hut. Ancient by any definition, she walked with a hunch and could barely see. Still, old Yodo seemed to have a sharp mind and a sharper tongue.

"Hai, Yodo-san."

"Good. Then come with me and carry the pails. We need water." Old Yodo shouted more than spoke and seemed to hear only what she liked. Still, helping the old woman made Miki feel less useless, less out of place.

It still hurt, and the full pails would be difficult, but at least Miki would see the sun and smell the fresh mountain air. Yodo shuffled slowly into the center of the tiny village toward the common well near the lower end, near the path that Miki knew would eventually lead to a rope bridge and temple. The other women and residents stopped to bow or offer greetings or help. There was respect here. Perhaps they weren't aware of what she had done, Miki thought. She was ashamed that she was alive, no one but her seemed to care.

Struggling with the well's bucket, Miki lost her grip trying to fill the smaller pails and spilled much of her first attempt on the ground and herself, the pain in her still-bruised arms making an otherwise easy task quite cumbersome. Apologizing for her clumsiness, Miki lowered the bucket again for a second attempt.

"I see that you are feeling better. Are you ready to start your training, or would you prefer to carry water for old women for the rest of your life?" Appearing from apparently nowhere, Gonzo and a few young men and women, a crowd that included Hisano, faced her as she struggled in her second attempt to fill the small pails.

"Leave the girl alone. I need her more than you do." Old Yodo wasn't letting go of a willing servant without a fight.

"Well, be Yodo-san's maid or learn to be kunoichi? What is it?" Gonzo seemed to see it as an obvious choice. They had spoken to her before, but Miki hadn't seemed interested.

"I do not mind helping Yodo-san. She has been most kind." Actually, not. Yodo was a woman with no sympathy and very little patience. Miki supposed that at her age, patience was a luxury. More than once she had been poked by the old woman's surprisingly well-aimed cane.

"Gonji, carry the water. Fusa, please help old Yodo home. Don't let her wander off. Hisano, you stay here with me. The rest of you, continue to train. And you, don't move." Gonzo could see that this was going to be difficult. Either the girl was openly defying him or she was truly incapable of standing up for herself. Miki was a pathetic sight, soaked from her fight with the well, eyes glued to the ground in front of her feet. What was he going to do with this girl?

"Miki, you are Koga. Your destiny is to be kunoichi like Hisano, like Fusa. Here you are going to be useful, or you will be dead. Hisano tells me that you are a good acrobat. She tells me that you can read and write. What else can you do?"

"I am a healer."

"Is that it? Is that all you can do? Did they teach you how to use a weapon in the temple? What else can you do?"

"I do not know." Miki's soft, uncertain voice was barely audible.

"LOOK AT ME! Get your eyes off of the ground. Don't you want to get revenge for your friends? Ama Masako died for you. You can't live for her? Are you going to let that demon Satake kill the rest of your monk friends? What kind of coward are you?"

Looking up for just a moment, Miki dropped her eyes again. "Revenge would dishonor my friends. I cannot give in to hate."

This was too much. Gonzo knocked the timid girl to the ground with the back of his hand. "Stand up." Watching the miserable young woman stand, Gonzo raised his hand again. Miki merely closed her eyes and tearfully waited for the blow. What would he have to do to make the girl stand up for herself? *Run, cry out, raise her hands to defend herself—anything, anything at all would be better than this!* Deciding that just slapping the defenseless, or rather undefended, girl served no purpose, or rather just taught the wrong lesson, the frustrated Gonzo lowered his hand, to the great relief of Hisano, who was watching nearby.

"Hisano. You are Miki's keeper. Take her to the training ground. Her arms are still weak. Just make her watch today." Gonzo watched the tall Hisano lead the still-shaking Miki away. Nothing had gone as planned, and now he didn't know if he was guarding a friend turned prisoner or a student. If the girl would not fight, she was useless, unreliable, and a danger to herself and others.

"What did you expect?" The older, gray-haired man stroked his scraggly beard as he stared down the path toward the training ground. Ryuzoji was the village's *jonin* as well as the head of the council of elders.

"I thought that I could get her to protect herself. I called her a coward, and she didn't care."

"Why should she? Maybe we are appealing to the wrong girl. I think that she is still Miki the Ama. She hasn't had time to become one of us. Let us do a test to see just how strong her will is. Let us see if we can find a reason for her to want to be here. Right now she feels like a captive. We can't guard her forever."

"Understood. I'll send Hisano back so that you can tell her what we are going to do. She is my best girl, and I think that she is ready to work on her own. Making Miki her responsibility is a good first mission."

"One she will not like. I wish that I could tell her why the girl is so important, but for now, neither of them can know. I see that hurting Miki is bothering you, too."

The men walked toward the training ground, the sound of adolescents exercising their talents and cajoling one another growing stronger with each step.

"I remember the night that Miki made her way to fix Hisano and the others. So much compassion. So brave. Miki was also by my mother's side when she died. Not a family in the village does not owe a debt to the girl, and being so harsh to her seems wrong. Am I making an enemy or a companion? We may have to accept that the girl simply isn't kunoichi. Would it be so terrible to have her just be the village's healer? We could do worse." Ever since that night when the nine-year-old Miki had treated the injured Hisano, Sato the Slayer had been relegated to preparing poisons. During a period of illness in the village, Sato had been foolish enough to take his own medicines, and in the mind of many Koga, he had performed his greatest service to the Koga clan by killing his last patient.

"This girl has a destiny that she does not understand. The old woman Iyo saw it. You don't remember her. Iyo was an Aruko Miko of Koga birth, but she never lost her gift, even as she got very old. Trust me. This girl is very important to the Koga clan."

"But what do I do with Miki if she will not kill?"

"What if that is her destiny, and she never kills? I don't know. Give her time. Let her heal. Use Hisano if you can. Miki seems to trust her."

Gonzo considered the problem as he walked to the training ground with the village head. The other young men and women had, against his instructions, gotten Miki onto the obstacle course. The most difficult obstacle was two parallel long logs sloping up at a frightening angle. It took considerable practice, and more than one student had been injured in falls. The logs were both rough and shaky, and to stay on them was a test of timing and judgment. In his absence, the other young people had goaded the delicate-looking Miki into giving it a try.

"It's too soon. I'll stop this."

"No. Let us see how she handles this. We need her to have friends, and they seem to be helping her."

With weak arms, how she would keep her balance? Gonzo wondered. A fall could certainly kill the girl. Like it or not, the only one capable of providing any real medical help was on those long logs. Surprisingly, Miki had asked for a bo-staff. Foolish, he thought, to try to carry a weapon. Miki hadn't even learned balance yet. Still, she seemed comfortable with the height and the balancing act. Indeed, her purpose in asking for the staff became clear as she shifted it back and forth to keep her footing.

Most young shinobi tried to get up the logs as quickly as they could to get it over with, but not Miki. Using the staff, it was almost as if she were dancing. With perfect balance, the young girl frequently tested her own skill by standing on one foot and raising the other leg as though performing for a crowd, elegantly swinging the staff in a graceful arc as she continued her journey. Hisano and the others who had conned Miki into the stunt stood and watched, spellbound by the dance. Gonzo realized that none of those young people had even gotten halfway in their first attempt. As Miki reached the top, she turned and bowed as though she expected donations to be thrown into a bowl.

"Impressive."

Gonzo realized that his own jaw was hanging open. "I see that learning balance isn't a problem. Maybe we have found the girl's best identity also." All Koga learned an honest trade as well as the skills of a shinobi. Not only did the village benefit, it allowed a shinobi to blend in easily. As a street acrobat, Miki could travel freely as she performed her missions. Best, thought Gonzo, was that street acrobats traveled in groups. They would not have to trust the girl to be alone.

———— ✸ ————

"This lesson is about estimation. It is important to the Generals of Samurai to know how many men they must fight. Being able to get close enough to see the enemy is one thing. To remain hidden long enough to count the enemy soldiers is quite another. You mission requires you to return alive. Over there we have laid out stones to represent enemy soldiers in their formations. Those blocks represent enemy horses. Just as no one can count all the leaves in the forest, no one can count all of the soldiers in the army. It is easier to guess based on the number of groups and report that. Everyone, take a good look. I will have a special treat for the one who gives me the best report." This was one of those important exercises that all shinobi must master. In a time of war, shinobi served as the eyes and ears for the army, for which the clan was well paid. Ikido, Hamatsu, Kai, and most of the Northern Daimyo employed Koga from time to time in their incessant wars of conquest to serve as scouts. "Gonji, care to take a guess?"

The boy looked out at the pattern of stones and blocks from the boulder. "One thousand soldiers in ten groups. One hundred horsemen in two groups" Looking back at the disapproving stares of his comrades, the thin thirteen-year-old realized that he hadn't done well. Worse, the new girl Miki was stifling a laugh.

"You don't seem to approve of Gonji's estimate, Miki. Do you think that you can do better?"

"No, Gonzo-san. It was unkind of me. I apologize."

"That wasn't an invitation. All of your companions have done this many times. What makes you think that you know more than they do? We will be kinder to you on your first guess than you were to Gonji. Now take a few minutes and tell me what you would tell the General who employed you."

"6506 enemy soldiers composed of 6332 on foot and 134 on horse, plus another group of forty horse that are not part of the Hoshi (Arrowhead) formation. The enemy plans to attack without delay, and he should counter with the Kakuyoku (craneswing) formation."

Stunned, Gonzo could not believe the nearly instant estimate. In fact, it wasn't an estimate at all. It was the correct answer. "How did you arrive at your estimate, Miki?"

"Twelve groups in a forty-eight-by-ten array are 5760. Those two groups are fifty but only five rows deep for five hundred, and that one group is twelve across the front and six deep; that adds up to seventy-two. That is 6332 total stones. The blocks have three groups, two of which are fifteen wide and three deep. The other is eleven by four, for a total of 134 blocks. That group behind the bush is eight wide by five deep, so that is forty more horses." Staring down at the ground in a false modesty, Miki knew that she was right. One of the advantages of being trusted with keeping the books at the temple was plenty of practice with numbers. Calculations were easy. The monks had taught her to do the abacus with her fingers.

"You also presumed to identify the formation and give a Daimyo advice. Where did you learn these things?"

"Monk Akaki taught me. I think he may have been a Samurai or something. I also read Sun Tzu and the commentaries. He made me read all of the scrolls."

"You read all of the scrolls at the temple? You can read Chinese and Japanese?"

"Hai. I remember everything. Can I go back and help Yodo-san now? She will need my help harvesting the potatoes."

Once more Miki had surprised him. Once more, the girl had disappointed him. "Potatoes. Pulling potatoes is more important to you than the training I give you? Is this what you think?" For the last month, the girl had performed brilliantly in every task. Nothing escaped the girl's sharp eye and sharper mind. Yet, Miki had shown not the slightest bit of interest in the life they offered her. She would sit and stare into nothingness whenever not actively engaged and only speak when spoken to. None of the other adolescents in the group had been able to penetrate the wall around her that Miki guarded jealously. Even now, the disapproving stares and disgusted faces of the other kids told Gonzo that no one wanted her here. Even Hisano, who was now fifteen and an adult, was tired of the girl she once thought of as a friend sucking the life out of every enjoyable moment. Training Miki was a waste of time. Her comrades neither trusted nor liked the insufferable show-off.

"Hisano, take Miki back to the village. Make sure she collects her potatoes."

"Me? Again? Why do I have to babysit her?" The next game was hide and seek, followed by weapons practice. This was her favorite activity, and the thought of missing another opportunity to spend it with her companions sickened the tall girl. Yet, to question an order was forbidden. This act of defiance would have consequences.

"Please, we need Hisano. Let Miki go by herself. Who cares if she runs away?" Fusa was the other girl in the group. Miki would find no sympathy here.

"Let her run away. It'll be fun to hunt her down." Gonji had once been fascinated by the pretty Miki. Now, tired by the tiny girl's total indifference toward him, the boy had developed a special dislike for her.

"Enough! Hisano, leave Miki with Yodo-san and then get Master Ryuzoji. Tell him that I need to see him. Miki, I will waste no more time training you. You are incapable of being one of us."

Hisano grabbed Miki's arm and shoved the girl up the path. She could feel the sympathy from her friends and hear the open relief as they digested the announcement that Miki's days as a kunoichi were over.

Not a word was spoken as Miki willingly accepted her banishment. As they neared the village, Miki's silence started to bother the tall kunoichi, as if the girl wanted to die. Her bubbly, always-cheerful companion had no more smiles, no more interest in anything. Miki went only where they dragged her, did only what she was instructed, and never spoke first to anyone. The bright, happy girl whom Hisano had known was gone. This thing was a shell with all of the knowledge, but none of the life, none of the special wisdom. This was no longer her friend.

Shoving the prisoner Miki through the rags guarding the door of Yodo-san's hut, Hisano marched over to the larger, rough wooden building occupied by the village jonin. Knocking twice on the door, she was met by a gray-haired old woman named Sakai, Master Ryuzoji's wife.

"Oh, Hisano. Ryuzoji has been expecting you. Where is Miki? I think that he wanted to speak to both of you. I so enjoy the girl."

"My apologies. I left Miki in Yodo-san's hut. Gonzo-san sent me to get Master Ryuzoji. He needs to speak with him about Miki."

Sakai could see that things had not gone well. Gonzo and Ryuzoji had spoken many times since the girl's arrival, and Hisano's face told the perceptive Sakai that the exercise had gone very poorly. "Estimates are difficult, especially for girls, and this was her first time. Gonzo should not have expected her to be good at it."

"That wasn't the problem. Miki was perfect. In less than a second she gave him the exact number. Exact. She laughed at Gonji, who was way off. And then she asked to leave to help Yodo-san pull potatoes. That's when Gonzo and everyone got mad at her. Gonzo sent her home. He doesn't want to train her anymore." Hisano wanted to get back to her friends. This had grown tiresome, and now she wanted to be rid of the burden of Miki. *Let someone else guard her.* "That made everyone happy."

"Oh my! Come on in. Ryuzoji needs to know this. I'll go and speak to Miki."

"That won't be necessary. Hisano, walk back with me. Gonzo is very pleased with you and feels that you can be trusted with an important task. Sakai, please see to Miki. This will not go on." Ryuzoji had been listening, and now the gray-haired man ducked through the door, pushing past his wife and the girl. "Come. This involves you also."

It had been a long day. The sun was now below the horizon, and the cool breeze sent a chill down the sweaty girl's body. Soon it would be dark, and the wolves would be on the hunt. Wolves did not scare Miki. Throughout the journey of her life, it seemed as though they had watched over her, checking on her from a distance, even talking to her. That was silly, of course, but still, they represented the kami of the mountains, and she was an Ama. Other monks seemed to have special relationships with other creatures like birds or insects, but none of them had her love of the wolves whose howls graced the nights in the mountains of Kumi. Masako-san had been terrified of them, tensing up at the first howl or sight of them. Masako-san had always seemed upset that Miki was not afraid also. No, she liked the wolves. Perhaps that presence that she felt watching her was a wolf. At least she hoped so.

The baskets were full of potatoes, mountain grapes, and other herbs and roots that would be useful as spices. Even shinobi had to eat. Surely even Gonzo could see that. Old Yodo, of course, had come out to oversee her, without providing any actual help. Still, the old woman at least appreciated her in an odd, cantankerous sort of way. But that was hours ago, and Miki had labored alone, outside the confines of a village, gathering the vital foodstuffs. Yodo would be pleased, if that were even possible. Best of all, she had been alone for hours, shunned by everyone, and it felt good.

Now the problem was how to get it all home. Being alone was great, but a bit of help would be nice about now. She was filthy, but it felt good, like working the garden back at temple with Masako and the others. Of course, now there were fewer mouths to feed in the temple. Eleven fewer. For a few hours that thought had not crossed her mind. Now it crashed down around her. The village was just over the rise and beyond the line of boulders down the well-worn trail, at least well worn by the standards of the shinobi, who were always careful to cover their tracks. This would take at least five trips, and it was getting dark now. It would have been smarter to take the baskets back as she filled them, but then, it really wasn't about the potatoes, was it?

Wiping the tears off, Miki knew that it was not smart to wait until darkness settled through the trees. Maybe she could get one basket home before total darkness. Strangely, she felt more at home here in the forest than back in a village that never felt like home. As she picked up the largest of the baskets, it became obvious that this one was a bit too ambitious. Grabbing a smaller one, Miki started to shiver harder as she made her way up the trail.

Someone was watching her. Like a chill blowing through a crack in the wall, Miki could feel the eyes. What difference did it make who it was? She would be feeding either the wolves or the people in the village. Someone would eat, a thought that made Miki giggle.

Whoever was watching her was human. The smell was distinctive. Definitely male. The fact that she could smell him at all told her that he was down the hill, as the breeze was coming off the lake. If he wanted to kill her, what was he waiting for? If he wasn't going to hurt her, he needed to go back and get the big basket. It would take her half the night to get all five baskets home, and she was pretty certain that no one was going to offer help.

"All day for one basket of potatoes?" The voice came from ahead. It was Master Ryuzoji. Not the one she was smelling.

Ryuzoji was obviously expecting something, and Miki's reaction was less dramatic than he had hoped. "I have four more down the hill. The big one is too heavy. "

Miki wasn't even startled. The girl knew she was being watched. She didn't even look up at him as she struggled forward with her load. Impressive, actually. Miki had not allowed her fear to take over. Did she even feel fear? "You didn't try to run away as I expected. Most girls would be afraid, being alone in the woods in the dark."

Who is he kidding? Where can I go? To the town, where Hamatsu soldiers would execute me? To the temple, where my very presence endangers the monks I love? This world has no place where I would be welcomed. "The wolves protect me in the forest. I am safe here. At least from the wolves." As she reached him, she dropped the heavy basket on the ground. Master Ryuzoji was not a man you wanted to show disrespect to.

"When did you know you were being watched?"

"When I smelled Gonji. The breeze off the lake told me that he was there." Actually, Miki had no way of knowing that it was Gonji. He was just the only one dumb enough to track someone while upwind. Just standing there made her shiver. Whether it was the chilly breeze against the sweaty rags they made her wear or the cold, unblinking stare of the gray-haired master assassin she was not sure.

The girl stood before him shivering, probably expecting punishment of some type. The nights in the mountains of Kumi were getting cold, and the child had labored hard. It seemed brutal to stand in her way now. "Gonji. It seems that you have failed in your attempt to remain hidden. Take the basket to the village. Come with me, Miki."

"I have four more."

"They will be taken care of. You said the wolves protect you in the forest. I heard that from a boy who came through our village once. He was very smart, just like you."

"Kiyotaka?"

This startled Ryuzoji, who wasn't aware that the two children had ever met. "Hai, Kiyotaka." Even in rags, the girl was pretty. Born under different circumstances, she would have made a perfect Princess. The tired, shivering Miki struggled to keep up with the old but fit man as he led her through the trees and rocks in the growing darkness. "And how do you know of this Kiyotaka?"

"He was brought to me for religious instruction. I spent eleven days with him. It was when Kiyotaka rescued his father that General Satake had me and the other Monks taken for execution. The soldiers accused me of helping Kiyotaka escape."

"And did you?"

"Hai. I liked him very much, once I got to know him. I even told him that he could be my little brother. That was silly."

The tired girl was having trouble keeping up. Still, for a month Miki had not put three words together except to answer a question. Did she know? Ryuzoji wondered. "Did you meet his father?"

"Hai. He was kind to me."

Could she not see the resemblance? The dark, haunting eyes, the calm demeanor, the intelligence? The intelligence. The intelligence behind those dark, penetrating eyes saw so much, understood everything, and yet Miki could not recognize her own value, or the truths staring her in the face, the old man wondered.

Coming to the rocky but open training ground where the young practiced their art, Miki could see Hisano on her knees staring at the ground, Gonzo standing beside her, sword in hand. Sakai, Master Ryuzoji's wife, sat close to the fire holding something in her lap. There were lanterns forming a lighted circle around the fire. Whatever they were planning involved her, and it would not end well. For the first time, the normally fearless girl felt real fear. Facing death surrounded by her temple family had been easy. Here, Miki stood alone.

"Oh, child, come here, come here. I have something you want to see." Sakai always called her child. She was a nice lady but had never gotten involved in training or spoken to her, not just in passing. *What is Sakai's role here?* Sitting beside the old woman, Miki was confused. What was happening with Hisano? *This is very wrong.*

"Look here! Isn't this beautiful?" Smiling, old Sakie handed Miki a small blanket. Inside the folds of blanket was a small bird, still in the brown fuzz of a hatchling. "It came from that tree over there. It must have fallen out of the nest." If she was confused before, Miki was now utterly lost in their purpose. Still, it was life, and it felt good to hold. Watching it squirm in her hands brought a smile to a heart that had not known joy. Cupping the bird in her hands, she held the creature up in the light to inspect. It was hungry and would need care, but Miki knew that she could do this.

"Touching. Do you like it?" Ryuzoji moved to the other side of the fire to stand beside Gonzo.

"Hai. Hai. Very much. Thank you, thank you very much." Miki's mind raced at how to feed it, how to teach it to fly. Was it a songbird? She would need a cage. How to explain it to old Yodo?

"Excellent. I was hoping that you would. Now kill the bird."

The enormity of what Master Ryuzoji asked closed in on her. Holding the creature to her chest, Miki looked up at the stern-faced, gray old man, the shadows of the fire giving his face a demonic appearance. "What?"

"Kill the bird. Snap its neck. Crush it if you like. You heard me. Kill the bird."

"No."

Such defiance usually earned a swift death. Ryuzoji looked down into the eyes of the devastated young woman. Surely Miki had to know that. What he needed to know was how far Miki would push it. "Does your life mean that little to you?"

"If I pay with my life, may I put the bird back in the nest first?"

"Just snap the neck. I've done it many times. It is quite pain-less, really." The smiling old Sakai was in on it. She was part of this abomination.

"And what do you think I would do with a dead Miki? We were assured by your friend Hisano that you were one of us. I see that she failed in her task. Gonzo, behead Hisano."

"NO! WHY? She did nothing wrong! Kill me instead."

"I can't do that. The head of the clan has forbidden it. You have been a friend to the Koga. It isn't your fault that you have chosen not to join us. The fault is Hisano's. We don't tolerate failure. Gonzo, please."

"NO! WAIT! It can't be her fault. Please, please. Not this!"

"I would have thought that you would have grown used to others dying in your place by now. When you were six, Hisano was given her very first mission: to become your friend and to keep you close to your clan. You have a destiny, you see. Old Iyo saw it. All of us placed our hopes in you. Now you disappoint us again. Gonzo, if a dead bird is not in my hand, kill the failure Hisano."

So there it was, their purpose. Looking over at Hisano kneeling in the dirt head down, Miki saw Gonzo's raised sword above her. Her choice: the life of her only friend or the life in her hands.

Ryuzoji watched the quaking girl struggle to her feet and make her way around the fire, past the still-smiling Sakie. Miki closed her tear filled eyes as she squeezed her thin fingers together, silencing the innocent life in her shaking hands. Holding the lifeless bird out for Ryuzoji, Miki fixed her gaze directly into the evil man's eyes, her hatred for what he had forced her to do evident.

If any other man or woman dared look at him in such a way, he or she would be dead before another heartbeat. Miki, this evening, would be the exception. Ryuzoji had learned what he needed to know. There would be time later to correct the girl's attitude. "You now have blood on your hands, like us. You may now live in my village and serve your clan. No one will stop you should you try to leave, but as long as you are with us, you will obey my orders and learn the village rules. Release Hisano. Hisano, your friend will not kill to protect her own life, but will to protect yours. Since we need a healer, I give you the task to protect the life that Miki herself will not when outside the village. Do you understand? Both of you?"

"Hai."

"Hai."

Sakai was still smiling as she touched Miki's still shaking arm. "See. It wasn't so bad. Only the first life is hard. After this it will get much easier. Yodo said that you collected many things to eat. Come, join us for a meal. You will feel much better once you've eaten. These things always make me hungry." As the lanterns were extinguished and fire kicked out, Miki stood silently as the last of the participants, Sakai leading the way, made their way toward the huts of the village.

With the fire out, darkness had once again made itself Miki's only companion. Never in her life had she felt more alone, so cold, and so dirty.

"I didn't think that she would do it. Poor Hisano was wondering what we were going to do if Miki hadn't." Gonzo shoved another chunk of potato into his mouth, dripping a bit of the broth down his chin. He swallowed, his sleeve serving to clean his face.

"You can't expect Miki to abandon everything that she learned in the temple. She will get better." Sakai carefully spooned out another load of seasoned potato stew, as well as a pickled fish head from the lake into Gonzo's bowl. "Hisano's performance was especially convincing. You should reward the girl."

"Hai. But Miki will never willingly kill. Her other talents more that make up for that. She is far too small to ever use a sword well. It remains to be seen if Miki can ever pleasure a man. That may be one more thing that isn't in her nature. Her size will help her pass as a child for some time. And she is very nimble."

"Her mind is everything. Miki's intelligence and memory would serve us well. It's too bad that she won't use it to help us. At least she is better than Sato the Slayer ever was. And Miki can make poisons and explosives. Still..."

Sakai rose to answer the knock on the door, reveling a concerned Hisano. Making her way into the room, the tall girl stooped to avoid the beam holding the ceiling up. "Master, Miki never came back from the field. She isn't in the village. I checked the training ground, and she isn't there, either. Should I get the others to track her down?"

"No. Monk Akaki will not take her back. She has nowhere to go. Miki knows this. She cares about the Monks, so she won't go there."

"She has no weapon. She won't survive the night in the forest."

"She feels safer in the forest than in this village. She is protected by the wolves, like Kiyotaka, like Oto. I don't think that she is running away. I don't think that Miki ever ran away from anything. She's certainly no coward. If she comes back, she will be our sister in whatever role she chooses. If not..."

Sakai could see that the food had lost its flavor. This was not a task the men wanted. "If not, bring her to me. It will bother the men. I did so much enjoy the child."

Hisano could see where the conversation was going, and it wasn't pleasant. The evening's events had destroyed her friend. It had been the girl's last chance, and she hadn't taken it. There would be no more chances. *The bridge. Perhaps I can head Miki off.* Bowing before leaving, Hisano bumped her head on the beam that she hated so much before ducking through the door. Heading toward the bridge at a dead run, she was certainly not silent. Tripping once on a vine that had crawled across the path, Hisano cursed her size as the branches smacked into her face near the rope bridge that served as Miki's assigned limit. Coming to the clearing ending in the sheer cliff leading to the river below, the tall kunoichi walked toward the bridge, catching her breath.

A growl told the girl that she wasn't alone. It wasn't coming from the bridge, but from the edge of the cliff to her left, near the rock that jutted out over the fast-running stream below. Two black figures, one probably human, the other most certainly wolf, sat at the edge.

"Miki? Is that you? Don't move. There is a wolf near you." Even the slightest misstep that close to the edge would mean a long fall to a certain death.

"Hai. He is here to protect me. Leave me alone."

"You didn't cross the bridge."

"I have nowhere to go."

"Come back to the village with me."

"No."

Not wanting to tangle with Miki's new bodyguard, who was keenly interested in maintaining Miki's privacy, Hisano could see that this was going to be a long distance conversation. "If you fall, you will die."

"Hai."

"So you came here to kill yourself."

"Hai."

"Why?"

What a silly question. Why indeed. "I cannot kill. I will not kill."

"You don't have to. Master Ryuzoji has decided to let you work in the village. Tonight you made them realize that this is something you can't do. You can be the village healer. There are so many things that you can do. Please, come home with me."

"They don't want me. I cannot live with what I have done. I cannot live with this pain."

"I never thought that you could be so selfish. How dare you. HOW DARE YOU! Do you think that you are the only one who has been hurt? Fusa was with me when I was going to be executed. Goeman-san, the man executed before me, was Gonji's father. Gonji watched him die from the rocks that overlook the town. His mother died in childbirth because we didn't have someone like you around. We are a dying clan, Miki! We used to live in hundreds of villages. The Koga were farmers. Now we are starving to death in these high mountain villages to avoid being exterminated by Hamatsu troops."

"What can I do?"

"You are so lucky! I was so jealous of you. You were surrounded by people who loved you. Ama Masako even took your place to save your life. No one would do that for me. The crowds begged for your life; the mobs threw rocks at me. You can read. You are smarter than any of us. You know about so much stuff that we don't. You have a destiny that I don't understand. All of our hopes are in you. We don't need you as a prisoner, but as one of us. You are so lucky and are too stupid and selfish to see it. Go ahead and jump. We can live without you, at least until Satake shows up and slaughters our village just as he did yours. But what do you care? The life of a stupid bird is worth more than hundreds of Koga lives to you." Hisano was angry and crying. *How dare that selfish little girl wrap herself in pain and suffering. My companions have already seen more pain and suffering than this spoiled child ever will.*

As Miki watched Hisano stomp off, she realized she had much to consider. *Am I being selfish? Have I ignored the suffering of others? Am I so convinced that I am right that I have considered no other possibility? It will be a long, cold night.*

It was a clear, cool morning, with the wind whipping off of the lake below. Gonzo had decided on a late start, given activities of the night before. No one had seen Miki since Hisano had, but then no one had looked on the rocks below. No one in the village believed Hisano's tale of the wolf until he had admitted seeing the very same thing the night she came to the village for the first time.

Hisano and Fusa arrived first, followed by Gonji, Benzo, Koan, and Toko. Usually the mood was lighthearted, but the events of the evening had leaked out, and Miki's absence was hard felt. No one had wanted to dislike her. She was one of them, just a bit confused. Hisano, the de facto ringleader, was normally efficient and enthusiastic. This morning the mood was somber and serious.

"Today we will study intrusion and climbing."

"Guess where we will be climbing." Gonji couldn't leave it alone. The effect on Hisano was immediate. Everyone, it seemed, was blaming her.

"Enough! Enough. Benzo, Toko, get the claws and the ropes. Hisano, you have done this exercise many times. You should rest today."

"That won't be necessary, Gonzo-san." Hisano could not believe her eyes. Everyone turned toward the figure emerging from the edge of the forest. It was as if a spirit were gliding across the ground. Stopping in front of Gonzo, for the first time Miki looked into his eyes.

"Miki?"

"Master Gonzo. I apologize for my behavior. I was thoughtless and rude. I ask to be allowed to be part of your group. I will work hard and take your lessons seriously. I need to be kunoichi. Everything now depends on this."

"I need you here on time tomorrow."

"Hai. I apologize. I was lost in meditation. It will not happen again."

"Work with Fusa and Hisano today. And don't eat or drink anything Sakai gives you until I've had a chance to speak with her." That last warning was important. Miki joined the other two girls.

"My friend Hisano. Please forgive me. You were right. I was selfish."

Miki's smile told her that her friend was back. "This will be fun today. Maybe some hide and seek later on, the kunoichi way." Hisano knew that her friend had a way to go. But Miki had at least started the journey.

Chapter 9 – First Mission

new friends, a new life
old habits are hard to break
miki, the honest thief

"Where did you learn how to do the handstands and flips, Miki?" Gonzo had watched Hisano, Miki, and Fusa practice their new art. It was perfect! Not only could acrobats travel freely without suspicion everywhere, but the very arts they practiced were useful for shinobi purposes. Except for Miko, who maintained the roadside Shinto shrines, it was rare for women to travel far.

"Acrobats pray for success at the temple in early spring. They would teach me tricks. Ama Masako disapproved, but Monk Akaki allowed it. She did not approve of him teaching me the staff or the sword, either." It had been a fun summer. Life in the shinobi village was very different from the beloved temple, but life in the temple was no longer possible. The ugly, scarfaced Satake frequently made the temple his base when in the northern part of the mountain valley, from which he would collect taxes and search for criminals. Of course the criminal that occupied Satake the most was the man identified only as the Mountain Samurai. Catching Miki, the little Ama, would be a major source of pleasure for the man as well.

"Monk Akaki taught you the sword? Show me."

"Hai, Gonzo-san." Being the smallest and lightest one in the group, Miki was always on top of the pyramid or leaping into the arms of one of the boys. Fourteen now, her small stature allowed the slight girl to easily pass for a younger child. Picking up a suitable stick, the girl carefully placed her hands at the appropriate distance, left hand at the bottom, the right about a finger's width under where the guard would be. Kiyotaka and Monk Akaki had always emphasized that the right provided the power, and the left hand the control. Assuming the guard position, Miki went through the movements of the Dance of Death that the boy Kiyotaka had taught her in what seemed nearly a lifetime ago. Getting to the end, which finished with a flip of the sword, a stab upward to the rear, and a snapping motion forward designed to cut through a target's belly, Miki flicked off the imaginary blood and slowly returned the wooden blade to its pretend saya, Samurai style. Giving Gonzo a bow, she smiled her wide Miki smile that nearly connected the ears as her performance met with everyone's approval.

"Brilliant. That was in the style of a Samurai. Monk Akaki taught you that?" All of the girl's movements had been precise, perfect, and complex. Miki learned everything fast, and whoever had taught this to her was a master in his own right.

"The Dance of Death was taught to me by a boy named Kiyotaka."

"Hisano, lend Miki your sword. I want to see it with steel. Have you ever touched a real sword before, Miki?" The girl had already demonstrated her skill with the staff, a common weapon with monks because of its non-lethal nature.

"Only Kiyotaka's. Even Monk Akaki only let me touch a wooden *bokken*." Miki took the offered *ninto*, a straight sword unlike the curved katana Kiyotaka carried. The ninto was a multipurpose tool as much as a weapon. The steel was poor, but the saya had a breathing tube for underwater work, and the square guard was like a stool.

"Proceed."

Another perfect performance, just a bit slower because of the extra weight. Miki would never be able to defend herself against a trained swordsman, skill not withstanding. Weight and muscle counted for something, and Miki had neither. Still, just as with the staff and acrobatics and even lock picking, the bright girl could teach those who could. Another use for Miki.

"Gonji, go get Miki a sword of her own. The smallest we have. Miki, the purpose of a sword is to escape to fight again another day, not to fight to the death. You are a Koga kunoichi, not a Samurai; remember this. Now, teach us all this Dance of Death."

Hours of drilling later, while all could get through the most of the motions, none could do it with Little Miki's grace and precision. Still, it was a way to practice basic and some very advanced moves. No one but Miki could quite get that last little flip of the sword and slashing motion.

"Gather round, all of you. Master Ryuzoji has decided that the time has come for all of you to attempt your first mission. This is rather simple, but your lives will depend on your skills and the faith you have in one another. Since both Miki and Hisano's last performance in the North Road village was unpleasant, we will go to Isawa and then Yoron. Maybe even to Kumi Castle."

Unpleasant was an uncharacteristic understatement for Gonzo. Miki had nearly been crucified on a pole, and poor Hisano was to have her head sawed off. Not a young adult in the group didn't lose a family member that day when Hisano nearly died. Getting through the high pass gate would be the problem. Both Miki and Hisano were hard to hide, Miki for her haunting dark eyes and Hisano for her uncharacteristic height. These two girls together stood out. Many of the soldiers who had tried to execute both children were stationed at the wall in the high mountain pass. It connected two sheer cliffs; there was simply no way around it.

Four young men, aged fifteen through seventeen, and three young women, fourteen through sixteen, would become a troop of acrobats and street entertainers. They would have to keep their weapons hidden as well as the tools of the trade. Hisano, although sixteen, was the most skilled, so she would be in charge. Their first contact would be at the inn in Isawa. From there, they would receive their orders.

Tomorrow, the adventure would start.

"Gonji, Benzo, take care of Miki. She likes to wander, and she is far too well known." It was midmorning, and all was in readiness. The weapons were hidden in the packs, except for Toko's blades. They were used for the act and were short enough to pass inspection.

"I can take care of myself."

"Unlikely. Miki is never alone, does everyone understand me? Koan, Fusa?"

"I can take care of myself. I used to go to all of the villages and treat their injuries. Helped them with their babies."

"Exactly. No helping anyone. Nobody at all! If anyone sees Miki being Miki, beat her up; stop her." A cover story was only as good as how well it was acted. Hisano knew that all of their lives depended on secrecy, and Miki being recognized would be a disaster. Worse, Miki seemed incapable of telling a lie, a very dangerous personal flaw in the world of the shinobi.

Gonji held up the rope they used for the balancing act. "Gladly. I'll tie her up at the first sign of kindness."

"You would enjoy that. Let's go. Miki, wear that large hat and keep your face covered."

"They were going to execute you, too."

"That was five years ago. Thank you for reminding me." The trail down the mountain was a bit rough. They could go around the post town where the trail along the west side of the lake met the North Road, but that was something Koga would do. No group of acrobats or street entertainers would ever travel in the woods, particularly one with three young women. In this case, they would need to hide in plain sight, get through the post town quickly, and go up the North Road to the gate at the pass at the top. With luck, they might make the shelters travelers shared outside the gate by nightfall and then go through the gate in the morning. "Miki, lose the bo-staff. You look too much like an Ama. People might remember you."

Reaching the North Road put them on the road with other travelers. Fortunately the temple was to the east, and they were traveling west, one less distraction for Miki. Hisano grabbed the girl, who was having trouble seeing past the ridiculously large woven straw hat, and pointed her in the right direction. Almost a basket, the hat hid the girl's face well enough, but it required two of the boys to steer Miki down the road. Gonji was perhaps having a bit too much fun with the overloaded, nearly blind former Ama.

"We have no money, so we can't stay in the town. If we can steal some food, do it. Not enough to notice, though. "

Toko dangerously juggled his two straight blades as he walked, occasionally tossing one to Koan, who deftly tossed it back. "Hey Hisano, we can't call Miki Miki. How about a different name?"

"I like my name. STOP, I can't see. Get out of my way. Give me my staff back!"

"Gonji, leave her alone. You gave poor Miki too much to carry. She is stumbling as if she's had too much sake. I think Toko is right. Miki needs another name."

"We all have the same size load."

"Miki is half your size. All of you boys need to be ashamed. Fusa, redistribute Miki's load. Miki, pick another name." Being the smallest one in the group and an outsider as far as the boys were concerned, Miki always ended up being teased mercilessly. Boys do not like being shown up by pretty girls.

Benzo and Koan, both sixteen, were the tallest and strongest of the boys. Born nearly the same day, these two young men were inseparable. Benzo's brownish hair and lanky walk made him easy to recognize even with the *oni* mask on. Koan, with his thin, jet black hair and large nose, was the best fighter in the clan. Physically very strong, he was also fast and was deadly with the empty hand. The two boys typically walked ahead so that they could talk and wrestle in play.

"What are those?" Koan pointed to ten poles on a small mound in the open area outside several of the outlying buildings. The mound was covered in flowers, small containers of rice, and sake cups around the base of each pole. "Let's check it out. Maybe there's stuff we can use or eat."

THWACK! Miki's staff found its mark, leaving a serious gash on Koan's straw hat and the tall boy on his knees.

"OUCH! What was that for?" A shocked Koan held his head as Benzo moved between him and his attacker. Miki had never even uttered so much as a mild insult, much less attacked anyone. Not even willing to eat meat, the girl's peaceful nature had bothered her companions. Now, stunned, all of them wondered what had set their little Miki off.

"Leave him alone." Benzo's plea was unnecessary, as Miki ignored all of them and glided toward a woman tending the flowers and gifts at the base of the first pole. For some reason, this post seemed to have received the most attention. Small toys, hair combs in a pleasing pattern, and wooden bowls that had once contained offerings surrounded the pole.

Miki pushed her hat back to watch the old woman fuss over the flowers and offerings, cleaning the now-empty bowls.

"Why?"

"I saw you coming. Travelers see the poles and they come to see. I want everything to be pleasing for them. So that they remember what happened here." The old woman continued with her work on her knees. "Hamatsu soldiers murdered ten monks here about a year ago."

Each pole had a sign with a monk's name on it. Three of the signs simply said UNKNOWN. Beside Ama Masako's pole was Monk Kukai's.

"This pole was supposed to be for a little girl named Miki. She was so brave when they brought her out to die. I remember what she said to all of us. Her gentle words stopped us from fighting the soldiers. Killing monks was so evil. They would have killed many townspeople that day." The old woman sat up and closed her eyes. "I still see the little girl offering courage to each of her friends as they were brought out."

By now Koan, Benzo, and all of the others were standing behind the small girl with her large, floppy hat. Koan, still rubbing the lump on his head, had to know. "What happened to the little girl named Miki?"

"I don't know. One of the Hamatsu soldiers offered the girl's life if someone would take her place. That is when Ama Masako offered hers. They carried the tied-up girl away screaming. They say that Ama Masako was the girl's mother. That is why all of the women who want to be mothers offer gifts here." Opening her eyes, the old woman bent back over and started her labors again. "I would like to think that little Miki the Ama found another family and lived. Another group of soldiers went looking for her, but I don't think that they found her. The scarfaced man is still looking for her."

"Toko. May I borrow your knife?"

"Why?"

"Because the dead should have a name." Miki went to each of the signs saying unknown and carved a name into each. Hashiba, the thin, serious one whose face had hidden a secret sense of humor. Sanjo and Shibata also could be remembered now.

"How do you know them? Who are you?"

"A little girl named Miki told me. She was taken to a village in the mountain where she found a new family."

"So she still lives?"

"Miki the Ama died in that village. I am Masako, the acrobat."

Hisano felt a pang of panic as it was clear that the old woman understood. They hadn't even gotten to the high pass before the stupidly honest little girl had given everything away. Still, the old woman seemed to be no danger.

"Masako the acrobat. I will ask the men to make new signs for your friends. Should I add Miki's name to this pole?"

"No. Miki is not worthy. Miki helped the Mountain Samurai escape, and that is why her friends were made to suffer. Miki was the only one who should have been put to death that day. It was all my fault." The hat could not hide the sorrow in the voice, or Miki's shaking body. This was ripping the girl apart, and Hisano knew that it was time to leave.

"I always wondered why the Mountain Samurai didn't rescue the monks as he did the Koga a few years ago."

"He was badly hurt killing Lord Yoshida in a duel in the temple. General Satake was chasing him and his son."

"If I were to meet this Miki the Ama, I suppose I should tell her that not all of her friends died that day. The soldiers were afraid of the Mountain Samurai, and they left the town before darkness. They shot arrows into the monks who still looked alive, but still a few lived. I don't know their names."

"Time to go. We have a performance to give, and we will be late." This information was deadly, and the old woman was now dangerous. Hisano didn't want to take the risk. This was a public place, and the innocent old woman's death would attract attention. Motioning to Toko, who sheathed his knives to take control of Miki, Hisano decided to remain behind just a bit longer. Watching her friends guide the reluctant girl along until all were out of sight, Hisano faced the old woman who had finished her work.

"I will have the men put Miki's name on this sign. Your secret is safe with me."

"Hai. It will be."

The North Pass Gate was built at the highest part of the mountain pass between two sheer rock faces. Designed to stop any invading army from Ikido, its thick door was open only during daylight hours to prevent either shinobi infiltration or smuggling. Over the years, travelers had constructed a number of small shelters as well as a few actual inns just outside of the gate for those unfortunate enough to arrive after the gates had closed for the evening. There seemed to be an informal brotherhood among travelers that put aside rank, class, or clan and allowed for conversation and entertainment that under ordinary circumstances would not be allowed.

The gates opened at first light, and perhaps two dozen travelers had spent the evening singing around the campfires as they entertained one another. Miki and the boys had put on quite a show, leaping and throwing knives while Hisano stood by the target. Miki, with her balance and agility, walked the rope and easily put on the best show, earning the most money, nearly thirty *zeni*.

"Miki, you can hold onto your coins. If I can't trust you, who could I trust?"

"You can't trust the rest of us? I'm hurt."

"No, she's just afraid Miki will bash her in the head like she did yours."

"Miki never hurt anyone."

"Except Koan. Miki got him good!" Indeed, it was the very first time anyone could remember even the briefest bit of hostility from the girl who was always the gentlest Ama at heart.

"They tortured Miki and killed her family on those poles. You were going to rob their graves. I would have bashed in your head, too." The only one not a part of this discussion was Miki herself, who had avoided everyone when not performing. Hisano couldn't tell if it was the shame of attacking Koan or reliving the horror of that day. Indeed, her own stomach turned a few times when passing the ground where her own execution had nearly happened five years ago. Only Gonji seemed to understand both Miki's and her personal agony.

The troop assembled behind some merchants and a small wedding party. The night had been chilly because of the altitude, but by midday, they would be in Isawa, halfway down the mountain, and it would be warmer as winter lost its grip to the spring. The downhill trek should be easy going, but they were running a bit short of food. But now, the problem was getting past the guards, who did not seem too trusting.

"And where are you coming from?" The guard finished poking through the box of wedding gifts as the bride sat astride a horse being led by an older man, whom they knew to be the young woman's father. Her brothers carried the boxes containing clothing and small gifts.

Hisano signaled Fusa, who pushed Miki, hidden under her over sized hat, into the center of the group. This day, the girl was to carry nothing but her staff. Without baggage, the guards should have no interest in the child.

"From our village on the lake. We are acrobats." Koan juggled and Gonji donned his Oni mask as he performed his routine designed to scare children.

Pushing past Hisano and Fusa, the green-and-red-clad guard in his red cone hat lifted Miki's hat. The apprehensive girl glanced up before fixing her gaze on her sandals. "I know you. Wait here."

There were at least a hundred guards assigned to this wall. At least a dozen were on duty and armed as well as armored. Hisano looked for a way out, and the playful banter between the boys had ceased as suddenly Miki seemed expendable if the guards couldn't be fooled by a lie. Trouble was, would Miki back their lie? With no way out, what could she do?

"Miki, how do you know that guard?"

"I treated him after the fight in the temple. He was one of the young men I saved that day. I held his hand so that he would not be alone when he died."

That ended any chance of mistaken identity.

Hisano looked into Fuso's face and noticed the tear. Gonji was in a state of near panic. This boy had witnessed his father's beheading. Toko fingered his blades nervously, and Benzo and Koan were getting a bit of space to make a break for freedom through the still-open gate behind them. "Let me speak. All of our lives are at stake here. Miki, please don't contradict me. For once, let me tell a lie."

"It won't matter. That officer that he spoke to, the one who is coming, is the man in charge of my execution."

More good news.

"Sir, if I may explain."

"You may not." The tall, straight, older man, resplendent in his black-and-red armor minus the helmet, towered over the girl. "I wondered what had happened to you. You should have stayed hidden. General Satake is obsessed with finding you. You are fortunate that I am under the command of Lord Yoshida, and he has released you. I cannot express my gratitude for what you did for my son in the temple, or my sorrow for the loss of your friends. You must not stay in Kumi. It will never be safe for you or your companions should General Satake ever find you."

"Sir, these kind people took me in. They have done nothing wrong. We are acrobats. Please let them go."

Motioning to the young soldier, who rushed off to get something, the old soldier quickly glanced at each of the nervous young acrobats. "Take good care of this young woman with the heart of Samurai." Taking a round disk from the returning soldier, he handed it to the astonished Miki. "This is a pass that will get you through the border north into Yugumi Province. There is a road that turns north just beyond Isawa. Leave Kumi and Hamatsu, and never come back. You will never be safe here, little one." With a wave of his hand, Miki's executioner motioned them forward, and breathing resumed.

Hisano kept a fast pace on the road down the mountain. No one felt like talking until midmorning, with Isawa in sight. Leaving their evening's companions in the dust, the group was now alone on the empty dirt road.

"I thought we were dead!" Toko voiced the sentiments of all.

Even Gonji had lost his compassion. "Is there any place they won't recognize Miki? She attracts trouble like meat attracts wolves." That was a question begging for an answer, thought Hisano.

Fusa wasn't going to give Miki a break, either. "Miki attracts wolves, too. I've seen her talk to them." Hisano remembered that time at the edge of the cliff, and the story Gonzo told of meeting her at the bridge. Miki, her friend, was very strange indeed.

Fear was driving the discussion now, and Miki bore the brunt of their anger. How one little Ama could attract so many vicious, powerful enemies in such a short, peaceful life was beyond anyone's comprehension, and Hisano knew that Miki was feeling the pressure from people she had thought of as family. The poor, silent girl, the youngest of the troupe, was having trouble keeping up, pulling away when Fusa tried to push her shoulder. This wasn't much fun for anyone anymore.

"Stop it, all of you," Hisano said. "It wasn't Miki's fault. She did try to protect us. It's time to perform. And now we have a pass that gets us past the borders of Kumi." Maybe something good came of it, after all. Unhappy performers make for lousy profits. Hisano knew it was time to put it all together.

"Maybe cute little Miki can do us all a favor by using the pass to go north to Yugumi Province while the rest of us go west to Yoron."

Koan should have known better, thought Hisano. This was the worst sort of betrayal, and it penetrated deep into Miki's heart. She stood silently under the large hat, unable or unwilling to move, shaking while hiding her face. Shinobi were not known for kindness, and the vulnerable girl attracted attack like a dying deer attracted wolves.

This had to end. Hisano moved beside the quaking girl. Even some of the townspeople were taking notice at this motley crew picking on this apparent child. "STOP! Miki is one of us!"

"You always protect Miki! What would she do without you? When is she gonna grow up? I don't want to die for Miki just because she saved your life! What makes her so special?" Toko mouthed the words, but it was evident to Hisano that it was what all of them felt. Truthfully, she herself was tired of the burden. The bigger problem was that this was a direct challenge to her leadership. Her team was coming apart.

They had an audience. The very last thing shinobi needed was attention, and the small crowd at the edge of town was getting very attentive. Hisano needed to have this fight elsewhere. "Toko, meet me at the inn. Your participation with this troupe has ended. I will pay you then. The rest of you prepare for a show, NOW!"

"Hisano, no one wants..."

"Leave now. You've failed us all and have no place with us. We protect one another, and you didn't do that. All of the rest of you, get ready. Toko, I never want to see you again. Leave us now." Why had she sacrificed the most experienced member of the group? The boy hesitated before walking off, Hisano's glare offering no reprieve. Benzo's eye's followed his friend, glancing back to plead with Hisano. Fusa stared at the ground, her interest in the handsome boy a poorly kept secret. The rest of the boys seemed torn by Hisano's harshness. She was the leader, her word carrying the weight of life and death. This was their evaluation, their chance to become fully accepted into shinobi adulthood. Toko would have to pay the price for failure on his own.

"Does anyone else have a problem with Miki?"

Silence told Hisano that her point had been made. The boy's future with the clan was now in jeopardy. This was his third mission and his third failure. He would not have a fourth chance.

"Miki, wipe off those silly tears. Acrobats never cry." Hisano's solution seemed to satisfy the townspeople, who filtered off to their daily routines expecting a show as this strange new troupe of street entertainers prepared to enter town. As much as she hated to admit it, Toko was right. Miki could easily get them all killed.

It had been a busy day. The other groups of entertainers demonstrated more skill and perhaps more maturity, but the team, minus its knife thrower and juggler, had done respectably its first official time out. With the sun now gone, outdoors was a bit chilly, and without an audience, Hisano knew that it was time to finally resolve the issues. The inn was a Koga safe house and had a private room on the second floor reserved for clan business. Toko had dropped off his baggage but was not present when the group arrived.

By keeping them very busy, Hisano hoped to work off the tension and restore a little bit of the trust and goodwill that had been lost. Indeed, the successful day had helped, and each member of the group enjoyed a share of the coins that had been tossed their way. Only Miki seemed reluctant to rejoin the group, even with the invitation of Koan and Gonji.

"Miki, why are you just staring out of the window? It's getting cold. I have a task for you."

"Hai, Hisano-san. I was praying for Toko."

"He said terrible things to you. You should hate him."

"Oh no. I could never hate anyone. Toko was just afraid. Toko is my friend. He teases me. Please Hisano-san. Please let him back in. He is part of my family now. He did not mean what he said."

"We can discuss this later. But now all of us are very hungry. Miki, I need for you to steal some food. Three buildings over is another inn. The second floor is a storage area for the inn below. I want you to go across the roofs and enter the small window. Once inside, bring back what you can. Don't be seen, and if you are, leave no witnesses."

"But Hisano-san, we have money. We can buy food."

"MIKI! Is that what I asked you to do? This is a training exercise. You are the best at opening locks and the only one small enough to get through the window. Gonji, give Miki her sword."

"I should go with her." Koan was much too large and far too heavy for the tiles on the rooftops.

"No. I want Miki to do this on her own. I want her to know that we trust her. Also if she is caught, we will need to get her out if we can. All of us stick together, always. You can do this, Miki." Hisano needed to talk to the group without the girl. Soon Gonzo would be back, and Miki didn't need to hear what had to be said. It was also time for Miki to start acting like a kunoichi. "Gonji, watch Miki go across the rooftops and learn. Come back when she enters the warehouse."

Watching the two youngest disappear into the adjacent room, the storage room leading to the window out to the single-story rooftops, Hisano turned to Benzo, Koan, and Fusa. "Master Gonzo will be back soon. Toko won't be."

"Why? We all feel the same way. Nobody wants to die for that little demon!"

"All of us like Miki; she just isn't one of us. She does everything better. She remembers everything. Miki is just like that Samurai we fight for, and what do we get out of it? We aren't Samurai. When we die, it should be for a reason."

"And her eyes. Everyone remembers her eyes. Just like that Kiyotaka. Just like his father. She talks to wolves, just as they do."

"So you don't like her because she is pretty, smarter than you, and good with animals?"

"Hai. We didn't think of it that way. But horses hate her."

Every hand went to a weapon as a knock at the door disturbed the intense mood.

"Gonji?" This wasn't possible. He had gone into the other room. Banging the floor twice produced the proper two-then-one response Hisano expected. Gonzo slipped into the room, to the relief of everyone.

"Where are the others?"

"I sent Miki to steal food. Gonji is watching her in the next room. Toko...well, I need to explain that."

"There is nothing to explain. You were right in dismissing him." Gonzo's pronouncement sucked the air out of the room.

Fusa seemed to have the most problem with their jonin's judgment.

"Gonzo-san, Hisano was wrong. Toko was just saying what all of us thought."

"Hisano needed to keep control. Toko challenged her. Toko's crime was against all of you. Do you believe that the townspeople needed to hear our business? That isn't how we survive. Toko nearly killed all of you. His stupidity has to be punished. Hisano was following her orders. Are you following yours?" There would be no further discussion. "Now, get Gonji. Let's wait for Miki. Tomorrow you have a real mission. You need to depend on each other. You need to trust each other, or you will not survive."

"How did you get so much food? This is prepared, not raw."

"Tasty, too!" The boys weren't questioning the source. Koan inhaled another bowl while Gonji sat back against the wall and belched. "This was worth waiting for." It was well past midnight, and everyone, especially Hisano, had been worried.

"Miki. You didn't find prepared food in the warehouse." Miki's eyes dropped to the floor before her. The girl was never happier than when she was caring for someone else, and feeding the boys was a strange source of satisfaction for the former Ama. Now she was biting her lip like a child caught in a lie.

"No, Hisano-san. I prepared it in the kitchen."

"After which you killed the witnesses?" Not a likely event. Hisano glanced over to Gonzo, who stared at the trapped little girl, hanging on every word.

"No Hisano-san." The quiver in Miki's nearly inaudible soft voice told Hisano that Miki knew how much trouble she was in.

"Then what took you most of the evening? Gonji said you had no problem getting through the window."

"I was cooking for the people in the inn. The man who owns the inn wasn't there. His two daughters were trying to run the inn but didn't know how to cook very well. Their mother died a few days ago in childbirth. I taught them to cook in exchange for the meals." The boys were finding Miki's plight more entertaining than Gonzo, who closed his eyes in stone-faced silence.

"Does that sound like 'steal food and kill witnesses' to you?"

"No, Hisano-san." Tears dripped silently as Miki lowered her face to the floor. Deeply ashamed, Miki was not expecting mercy.

"You won't lie, you won't steal, and you can't kill. Just how can we trust you, Miki?" Hisano watched the girl hug the floor, waiting for either the order or the blow that she knew was coming. Koan had taken the bowl that Miki had been holding to protect its precious

and tasty contents. Fusa glared at the worthless whelp groveling like
a beaten dog, angry that Toko had been sacrificed for this thing.
"Do you still have your money? You worked for the stew."

"No Hisano-san."

"And where is it?"

"I gave it to Kai and Narumi for their mother's funeral." Miki
could barely get the words out. Fusa stamped her foot, clenching
her fists. Even fear of Gonzo's wrath could not silence the howls
from Benzo and Koan. Only Gonji fully realized the repercus-
sions Miki now faced.

"Master Gonzo. I will take care of this. Miki, please get up.
It's time for us to go now." The world of shinobi was one of harsh
rules and harsher expectations. Hisano was the leader, and Miki
her problem. The room was silent now. Everyone now understood
Hisano's duty. The tiny girl moved back on her heels and shook
her head in compliance. Standing up, Miki wiped her face dry and
stepped toward the waiting Hisano beside the open door.

"Enough." A tired Gonzo opened his eyes and signaled for
Hisano to slide the door closed. "No one in our village or this
room hasn't received Miki's kindness when we needed it. All of
us have grown up to become what we are, shinobi. Miki grew up
in a temple, away from our world for far too long. We need to
stop expecting Miki to be what she can never be."

The boys relaxed a bit as Master Gonzo let the steam out of
the room with his pronouncement. Hisano took a deep breath
as Miki dropped to her knees as the stress and fear took its toll
on her fragile feelings. Fusa was not as relieved, or as happy, for
Miki.

"Master Gonzo. Miki was the reason Hisano made Toko leave.
Why did you send Toko away? Toko is one of us! Why Toko? We
need him, not the little servant girl here!"

Normally this would have earned Fusa a quick death. Now,
when feelings were on edge, was not the time. "Toko is performing a mission on my orders. As far as Miki is concerned, none of
us can read Chinese and Japanese as Miki can. Getting Miki here
alive was your mission. She is very important now. Without her
knowledge, we will be blind. Protect her."

Chapter 10 – Hisano's Little Burden

purpose redeemed
hisano's little burden
the power of cute

"We've been here four days, and you spend your days performing for us and then your evenings working in the kitchen at the inn. How do you do it?" Hisano gazed out the window in anticipation. Girls were hawking their wares in the lantern-lit darkness to passing men of any description, arguing with one another when potential customers were not around. Occasionally armed men would wander down the street, Samurai and ronin looking for a good time.

"It's what you do for others that matters." Miki concentrated on the papers placed before her. With ink and quill she wrote a series of numbers before rearranging a few characters. "Besides, I like Kai and Narumi. They are nice to me."

Koan shoveled another fish head into his mouth as Gonji sat back with a belch. "For shinobi it's what you do TO others that matters. But the stew is really good."

"What were you doing yesterday? You were gone for most of the morning."

"I performed a funeral ritual for Kai and Narumi's mother. They couldn't find a monk or a priest to do it. Normally one of the older monks takes care of funerals and blessings at the temple, but I do know the prayers."

Hisano winced as she realized just what little Miki had done. How anyone could be so smart and so stupid at the same time was astounding. "MIKI! How could you be so stupid? They are looking for a girl just like you who was an Ama. You're WANTED! A cute little criminal with a price on your pathetic head. The last thing we needed was your bringing attention to yourself—and us, too! Master Gonzo?"

The man who had been sleeping near the opposite wall opened an eye. "I was listening. Miki, it would have been better if you had not done what you did. We have already stayed here too long. How is your work coming? Toko took great risk in intercepting these. If I don't have to take the risk, I would rather recall him."

"This was an Iga code, not a Samurai one. It is in four parts, of which we have two."

"So you can't figure it out?"

"I did figure it out. Tell Toko to stop. I have it all. They broke each character into four parts and rearranged them according to a set order. The order repeats, so once I figured it out, it was simple. After that it was just completing the character. The handwriting was done by a woman."

Gonzo sat up and shuffled over to sit beside the tireless girl working by lantern, pages of numbers and chicken-scratched paper surrounding the girl. "Interesting. What does it say?"

"Lady Teruko of the Suwa clan from the Yugumi province is on her way to Hamatsu to serve in the court of Lord Nobunaga. The Iga plan is to substitute one of their own for her to have a spy in the Hamatsu court. Lord Nobunaga is desperate to have an heir. Several women have already been executed for failing him. Lord Yoshida has been adopted as heir at the clan's insistence, and a plan that they don't go into is already underway to find him an appropriate wife."

"And that is why Miki is here. None of us could have done this."

Hisano stepped back from the shuttered windows. "It may not matter, Gonzo-san. That man outside has been watching this building for hours. He has just been joined by two other men with *sasumata*[8] and *jutte*.[9] They must be officers, and they intend to capture someone."

"I'll give you three guesses who." Gonji put his bowl down to fondle his ninto. He had seen an execution and didn't want to become the executed. *Better dead here.*

"It's likely that they just want Miki. Miki, can you crawl across the roof and get to the other inn?"

"No, Gonzo-san."

"Why not? You've done it before."

"I redesigned the lock so that it would be impossible to break. We weren't the only ones stealing from the Koi and Crane Inn. I was trying to be helpful."

"Nice job, stupid. At least one of us could have made it out, even if it was you."

"The officer has been joined by the father, who is pushing one of the girls. The oldest one, Kai I think. Maybe they want to lure Miki out and take her in the street. Kai doesn't seem to want to do something. She is pleading with the officer and her father." Hisano reached down for her ninto, checking its draw as she kept watch from the corner of the window.

"I have an idea. We need a diversion."

"Another brilliant little Miki plan. Maybe we can offer to sharpen the executioner's sword for him. That would be helpful." Koan's cynicism wasn't lost on Hisano and Gonji. Nor was his imitation of a sword sharpener at work.

"Master Gonzo, they don't know that you are with us. Leave now and warn Benzo and Fusa to not come back. Act as if you are drunk and delay them for a bit. Meet us on the road to Yugumi Province. Also tell Toko to not waste time getting any more messages; I already know everything. Hisano, leave and go to the Koi and Crane. Tell them that you are looking for me. When the officer notices the window open, tell them that is probably me. These devices make smoke. Just drop and step on them. It will make it seem that the Koi and Crane is on fire. Escape in the confusion. Koan, go open the window in a few minutes when you hear the disturbance in the street. Gonji, take our stuff down-

---

8 sasumata - a pole with hooks at the end used by Japanese police officers in a form even today to help restrain a prisoner they intend to capture.
9 jutte - a weapon symbolic of officers of the law for restraining enemy weapons.

stairs. Then when Kai tries to go upstairs for me, go out and get the officers."

"You are leaving through the window?"

"No, the front door with Kai. I am Narumi's size. Everyone needs to be downstairs now so that I can prepare a few surprises. Don't join up, don't wait for me, and don't come upstairs. Leave me only my staff. I will need it. Move now." All eyes moved to Gonzo, the chunin in charge.

"You heard Miki. We brought her because she's smart. Now we find out how smart."

It was a scene of confusion in the darkness as smoke billowed from both the Koi and Crane and the second floor windows of the storehouse that the traveling troupe of acrobats had thought of as their home in Isawa. Two officers shouted at each other across the roof between the two buildings, gasping for breath. The dark, narrow alley between the brewery and pleasure house opposite the Koi and Crane provided a perfect view of the comical scene.

"Their eyes will burn for a while. Wash them with water, and in a few days they will be fine if they don't rub them. Also, thank you for your friendship. Your kindness was most appreciated." Miki smiled at the overwhelmed innkeeper's daughter, who was trying to understand what had just happened. She looked back toward the Koi and Crane, as well as the second floor of the safe house, both with windows open to clear out the smoke.

"I am sorry. You have been so kind. Father let his greed get in the way. I did not want to..."

"I know. The acrobats that I was with will not want me back, so I will head toward either Kumi Castle or Yugumi. I have a pass that will get me past the north border. Maybe I can join a temple in Yugumi." The smoke bombs had done the trick. The flash device that triggered when the officers broke into the second floor room also burned an oil made from mountain herbs and onions that burned the eyes and throat. In the confusion Miki had pushed the coughing Kai out the door standing behind her. "Maybe I'll see if the shrine in Yoron will accept me. Farewell, my friend."

Miki grabbed her small bag of tricks and her staff and turned down the dark alley that led to the south side of town. Once outside, she would need to go north before skirting around Isawa and heading south again. This would keep her away from her friends, but at the moment Miki was certain that her friends were not particularly pleased with her. There was so much that she needed to tell Gonzo, so much contained in those messages that he needed to know.

North would put her into the woods, and with the woods, the wolves and the bears. Wolves were no problem; they did not scare her. Wolves had always protected her. Bears, on the other hand, lived in the trees, and in the dark were difficult to see. The ninto would have been nice, but since she had forgotten the ninto that first night at the inn when she taught Kai how to cook, Hisano had refused to let her have it back. The thin bamboo staff, barely taller than she was, probably wasn't very impressive to the black bears in these mountains.

At least they were officers and not soldiers. That meant their numbers would be few, and they would not have horses. Officers would be skilled at capture rather than killing, a small comfort if Hisano or Gonji were caught. The problem was, would any of her friends actually allow themselves to be caught? Perhaps they should have all left the swords and the tricks back in the village.

Owls hooted as the breeze rustled the leaves. A bit higher, the trees would be evergreen. Looking at the stars on this clear night, Miki picked out the pattern that pointed to the star that pointed north. She would have to go north for a while until she was past the road down from the high pass before turning west again, and then go around Isawa. The forest was comforting for Miki. For most young women, this would be terrifying, but for a child brought up in the mountains, whose entire life was spent surrounded by trees and mountains, this felt like home.

She enjoyed the smells of the woods, the decaying leaves being turned into the food that fed the trees and bushes, the crisp air and the smell of the animals. Inside Isawa, it was impossible to smell anything because of the stench of people everywhere. The stench of a man was the clue that she was not alone now.

Whoever was tracking her was silent. He knew what he was doing. It was the silence that bothered her. An officer or a soldier would be out of place in the darkness, atrociously incompetent in the forest, and very, very noisy. Learning how to walk, what to avoid, was a shinobi skill derived from the heritage of a mountain life. Whoever was tracking her had to be shinobi.

Dropping to one knee, Miki listened for a bit before swinging to stand behind a tree. Patience was a virtue, and in this case, life or death. After what seemed half the night, the smell of a man and the crunch of a leaf told her that it was time.

WHAP! A thin bamboo staff across the stomach sent the dark figure to his knees with an "umfff." Stepping out, Miki raised the staff to bring a blow down through the figure's head as he raised his right hand and tumbled backward, gasping for breath. "Miki, stop."

"Gonzo-san?"

It took more than a few moments for Gonzo to catch his breath. His ribs were going to hurt for a good long time. "I forgot how good you are at ambush and stealth. I also forgot how good you are with that stick."

"I'm very sorry. I didn't know."

"Why? You were good. Everyone got away, but Isawa is one more place that we can't go, at least with you. Miki, I won't risk their lives anymore. You are just too dangerous. From now on, you stay with me. Understand? Now let's find the others. We will meet them south of Isawa at the old shrine. I'm sure you know what a shrine looks like."

"We need to stay off the roads for a couple of days. This shrine is good for a while, but the Iga use these shrines the way we use the North Road Temple. Look for anything hidden. Koan, Fusa, take positions near the road and warn us if anyone is coming."

"Hai, Hisano. Do you think Miki got away?" The lanky Koan stretched his legs. The nap after a night on the run had felt good. Now, a cool, late summer midmorning promised a bright and comfortable day for travel. Grabbing his ninto, he signaled Fusa to follow.

"Who cares? She is more trouble than she's worth. Let's find Toko." More than once during the night's narrow escape, Fusa had expressed that shared sentiment.

"She was my responsibility. Gonzo will be furious." Everything had happened so fast that no one had picked up on the part of the plan that Miki would be alone. "Miki has a talent for getting into and out of trouble. I'm sure that the little imp is wandering around somewhere doing someone a favor."

Benzo took another bite of his rice ball. "As long as it's not us."

Gonji looked out the door, as if he expected the girl to bounce up the stairs. "I did like her, sort of, when she wasn't being, well, so much like Miki."

Hisano weighed her options. "If Gonzo doesn't get here by tonight, we will leave without him. I don't think Miki will be along. I never told her the meeting point." *What do I do now? I don't know what Miki knows. They are depending on me.*

"Thanks. Why didn't I think of that?" Benzo took a swig of water from his flask. "Empty. I'll get more. There's a well out back."

"Check on Fusa and Koan. They haven't signaled. See what they are doing." *They know the procedure. Hoot twice in position. It is as if everyone has forgotten how to be shinobi. We are failing, and it's my fault. The only success was the escape, and Miki did that.*

"Hai, I'll go with Benzo." Gonji seemed to miss the girl. "Maybe I should watch the road. The stupid little imp might find her way here. You never know with her."

Hisano looked back to face the little statue of Kan Shojo, a falsely exiled government official hundreds of years ago. The shrine had been built to placate his vengeful spirit. It seemed fitting now. Gonzo would be very angry at Miki's loss.

Turning toward the door brought Hisano face to face with a large, well-proportioned, stern-faced officer holding a jute to her throat. She had been so preoccupied with her next move that she had allowed an officer to walk up right behind her. Behind the man, standing in the door with rope in hand, was a taller, thinner man with a crooked nose. She remembered him from the street the night before when the officers came for Miki.

"Where is the little one? She is the one we want."

It is Miki that they are after. "We don't know. Little Miki told us to leave, and we haven't seen her since. She was always trouble. All of us are glad she's gone. We never told her that we were coming here."

"That is unfortunate for you. She matches the description of a girl that General Satake is looking for. There might even have been a reward."

"Do you think that they are shinobi, Boss?"

"No. No shinobi would be stupid enough to think that they could hide at popular shrine near a road, or to come directly here if they were being chased. General Satake will still want to question them, though. Tie her up and put her with the others."

The noonday sun beat down hard on the five prisoners. Arms tied behind the back ached and sweat rolled down dirty faces as they marched down the road, enduring the occasional verbal taunt.

"At least Miki got away."

"SILENCE!" A swift crack of the officer's cane sent Gonji to his knees, nearly causing the others to topple because of the rope that linked them by the neck. It had taken only three officers to capture the five of them. Apparently they hadn't been as clever as Hisano had thought. The officers had given up the chase because they had already figured out where they were going. Another foolish move on her part.

Hisano bit her lip as the magnitude of her failure as leader was made manifest by the sound of heavy breathing of her friends facing an uncertain future. She had let them all down. Their best chance was to be seen as unknowing participants in Miki's crimes, whatever those crimes were. How had Miki escaped? They had all made fun of the girl, but no one had ever been able to ambush Miki. Not even Gonzo, the best tracker in the village. Remembering the very first time she ever met her friend, she knew that no one ever could take the dark-eyed beauty by surprise. Three officers had taken five Koga shinobi without so much as a fight. Miki would have at least given them a fighting chance, just as she had done in Isawa.

Benzo stopped suddenly, causing Hisano to walk into his back. "What the...What is she doing?" The two officers up front walked ahead as the crooked-nosed one pushed all of them to their knees. Ahead, in the middle of the narrow road, between a large boulder and forest on both sides, stood the small, dark-eyed girl wielding her bo-staff.

The officer in charge motioned to his crooked-nosed assistant to move. "You go left. I can't believe our luck. Hey, little girl, we aren't here to hurt you. What are you, ten years old?"

"Let my friends go." Miki held her staff out to her side, moving back a step as she moved it into a forward attack position.

Hisano could not believe what she was seeing. "MIKI, RUN! YOU CAN'T DO THIS!" The stupid little Ama was facing off against two full-grown officers. The older, good-looking one was probably a low-ranking Samurai. A solid whap along the upper arm sent the kneeling Hisano to the ground along with Benzo. The officers would work to opposite sides of Miki and use the *jutes* and *torinawa*[10] to tangle her staff. The stupid young girl stood no chance.

"Wait. This kid knows how to use that thing. This is the one who set all the traps in town. She wants you to step off the road. Go really wide." The crooked-nosed, skinny one darted off into the woods that lined the road. In a few minutes he would make his way behind the graceful Miki swinging her staff as though it were a dance and work together with the Samurai to make the child a prisoner.

---

10 torinawa - arresting rope, used to snare the prisoner's weapon and person during the arrest.

Silently Miki's dark eyes fixed on the movements of her adversary as she matched the motions of the wary man. A crack of a bush and the cry of pain told them both that something had happened to the crooked-nosed officer.

"Subai, they are tied together. Knock them over and go right. They can't get away. It's this one Satake wants." With the staff, the petite girl commanded the width of the road. The officer tried to catch the end of the staff with the hook on the jute, but Miki was just a bit faster, catching the back of his hand and sending the short, hooked weapon to the ground. The girl raised the staff for a downward motion, and he stepped back rather than receive the blow. There was no fear in this child's dark eyes. Focused and disciplined, the child silently ignored his taunts. Those dark eyes that seemed to suck in all of the light around them were familiar. This was a fight he had had before. "Your father taught you how to use the staff well. He taught me how to use this katana."

"Monk Akaki taught me the staff." Her time was up. Behind her both of this officer's assistants were finding their way out of the woods, although one could barely walk. "My brother taught me the katana."

"Make this easy. You are surrounded. It is a shame I did not see your sword technique. You have already lost. Do not make me kill you."

"I have already won. My friends have escaped."

"No matter. Why does Satake want you, a child? Who is your brother?"

He was delaying, giving his partner time to get in position. "Kiyotaka. Son of Lord Oto. I was the one who helped Lord Oto escape." The crooked-nosed one was nearly in range behind her. Miki could hear his heavy breath, smell his sweat, feel his position. Just a moment longer. There! She shoved the staff directly behind her under her arm, catching the man in the chest and knocking him back, gasping for breath. She swung around, and a well-placed strike to the head put him on his back. A swift stroke of the officer's katana neatly cut the bamboo staff in half as Miki, discarding the now-useless pole, grabbed the shorter sword protruding from the obi of the now-unconscious assistant. She was no match for this Samurai, but at least she could ensure her own death. Anything to avoid Satake.

"Excellent. Now we get to see your skill with a sword. You were the tenth monk. Excellent stance. Your teacher would be proud. So General Satake is afraid of you?"

Backing up put the younger, wounded man closer. The stakes had no doubt penetrated the sandal. The large bruise at the knee meant that he wasn't going to be running after her any time soon. *Maybe there is still a chance.*

Katana sang as two blades met with a clang of metal. The officer kept his distance as Miki flipped the blade and shoved it into the thigh of the young man behind her. She snapped the blade forward as she stepped forward, her blade met steel, and a hand shoved her head forward into the ground, someone kicked her sword away, and Miki could feel steel at her throat as strong hands picked her up and spun her around, lifting her off the ground. This fight was over.

"Please kill me quickly." Miki's feet dangled as the powerful man considered his tiny conquest. This man was Samurai, an officer charged with justice. Perhaps, just maybe, a tiny bit of mercy from the man. "General Satake will torture me. Please kill me quickly. Please."

"That last move was Oto's favorite. If you were larger and stronger, you might have won. You said Oto had a son. You were the little Ama, the tenth monk I've heard about. Before I kill you, you have a story to tell. You are not what I expected in a criminal."

Gonji stared out the shutters into the darkness. The rain beat against the leaky roof as the wind whipped through the openings in the rotting walls. "It's been three days. Miki isn't coming."

Gonzo had cut the ropes and helped them escape while Miki was supposed to run, leading the officers into the traps that they had set. "No. Miki said that she had a plan, and I believed her. Now I think that her plan was always to sacrifice herself."

"I miss her. She was a good cook. Miki was very brave."

"Gonji, get some sleep. Tomorrow the Iga will attack Lady Teruko's escort. We have no way of knowing how many Iga there will be or what their intention is. Whatever it is, they need to fail."

"Hisano is coming. I see her signaling."

The wooden door slid open briefly as the straw-coated tall girl ducked into the dark room. She was soaked to the bone, and Gonzo handed her a cloth to dry off with. "Gonzo-san, We don't need to worry about Miki anymore. The word in Yoron is that she injured two officers but was executed by the third after treating their wounds."

"Sounds like Miki. I wonder if the imp sharpened the sword and cooked them a meal first." Koan tossed a bit of straw on the embers of the cooking fire.

Benzo tossed a pebble across the room. "Miki saved us. She saved us all, and all we did was run and leave her. Twice she saved us."

"And twice we left her."

"She took on three full-grown men. One of them a real Samurai. Miki was really brave. She was better than any of us." Gonji was the most upset. At least until now there had seemed room for hope.

It didn't take a map to see where this was going. "Enough. There is enough blame to go around. All of us treated her badly. None of us watched her as we should have. Hisano, is Fusa in position?" Loss was part of a shinobi's life. This was also a lesson that these students had to learn.

"Hai. I left her in Yoron. Toko will track the escort. We will meet him on the road near the border. Miki was my responsibility. I failed."

A soft tap at the door filled every hand with a weapon. Hand signals positioned Benzo and Koan to either side of the rough wooden door. A second set of taps, and the door was pushed aside, revealing a small, dark figure highlighted by lightning and the clap of thunder.

The soft, shaky voice came from a trembling, shivering young girl. "Master Gonzo? Hisano-san? Can I come in?"

Unbelievable! There she stood, a pathetic, dripping ghost of a figure in the dark. "Miki? You can't be here! They killed you."

"I apologize. I was going to wait until morning, but I was cold and wet, and I hate lightning and thunder, and I was really lonely. Please can I spend the night with you? I'll leave in the morning if you want. Please?"

"Get in here! Were you followed? How did you get away? You're really shivering. Get those clothes off now. We heard that you were dead."

"Where is your staff, and where did you get that sword?"

"I'm sorry. The officer cut my staff in half, so he let me keep Officer Shinbo's sword instead. Officer Uhkita was actually very nice to me. He let me help the other two officers. I asked him to kill me, but he said that he owed Lord Oto a debt. I don't know what that means, but he made me tell him about the monks and General Satake and Monk Akaki and Kiyotaka and Lord Oto, and he gave me the sword, and he told me to leave, and I'm so cold now."

Wrapping the soggy, scrawny, shivering little Miki, now naked, in one of Benzo's larger kimonos, Hisano pushed the girl down beside the cooking fire. Shoving a rice ball in Miki's hand, she wrapped her arm around her shoulders to warm Miki up. Koan was already at work on the fire.

For the longest time, the scraggly Miki just stared at the flames. "I know I'm a burden. I don't want to be. I know you don't want me. Officer Uhkita said that if everyone thought I was dead, it would be easier to move. I'll go north to the temple in Yugumi tomorrow." Hisano pulled her closer so that Miki could rest her head on her lap.

"No, you won't. You're one of us, Miki."

"I'm just a burden on all of you."

"You're my little burden and my very best friend. You didn't fail us. I failed you. But not anymore. Sleep now. We will need you tomorrow." Everyone had gathered around the small cooking fire, watching over their little Ama as she drifted in and out of sleep until all but Gonzo and Hisano had succumbed to fatigue.

Gonzo stared at the sleeping girl as Hisano stroked her matted hair. Once more she had surprised them all. "Monk Akaki told me that she had a destiny. I wonder who she really is."

"You know who she is. The only one who hasn't figured it out is Miki. I don't think that they want her to know."

"I don't want her in the fight tomorrow. She won't kill."

"She won't stay away. Miki will try to take care of us. Maybe we should send her north to the temple. It would be safer for her. Little Miki will never really be kunoichi."

"No. In her heart Miki will always be the Ama."

"In her heart, I think that Miki is Samurai. I'll take care of her tomorrow."

Chapter 11 – Assassination and Reflection

kunoichi princess
disobedience and lies
loving enemies

"Why do I have to stay behind? I've fought before. I'm not afraid!"

"We're not questioning your courage or skill. You're just too small. You stay with me until Fusa gets here to protect you." Hisano smiled at her eager little charge. "Besides, you are still the only one of us who can read. There may be too many of them to even give it a try."

"I fought three men a couple of days ago."

Koan reached over and messed up the resolute girl's hair. "And lost, you little imp. We don't need you in the way. Being cute doesn't work on shinobi."

Gonzo checked his equipment before signaling the party forward through the trees. "Obedience is a lesson you need to learn first. I remember how well you did with estimates, and your skill with stealth and scouting is excellent. Take the lead and make sure we're not walking into a trap. Keep your distance and remember that you must stay alive with your report. Hisano, take her weapon. Let her keep her stick."

"Master Gonzo-san, why?" It was a sword she had earned.

"Remember, obedience! Weapons mark you as kunoichi. Your best weapon is looking harmless, like a peasant child. You aren't big enough to use the sword well. Maybe Koan is wrong; looking cute might work on shinobi if you do it right. We don't kill unarmed peasants."

"Only Samurai."

"And one another."

"Hai, Gonzo-san. I won't fail you."

"And when you get back, stay out of the fight. Some of us will be wounded, and you are the only healer we have." Gonzo watched the small girl dart into the woods ahead, full of serious excitement that it was Miki whom Gonzo-san trusted with this most vital of tasks.

"Suppose she gets lost?"

"Would that be a bad thing?"

"Stop it. Miki is trying."

"The stupid imp is always trying. Trying to get herself killed."

"Us, too."

"You have short memories."

Gonzo motioned for silence as they proceeded to the pass where the ambush would take place, if Miki was right. "All of you can learn from the girl. If I'm right, you won't even be able to track Miki."

Fifteen men with *naginata*[11] on foot carried a Suwa clan banner and led a very beautiful young woman dressed in a flowing red kimono with wonderful designs and gold threads on a horse. She was young—maybe sixteen, maybe eighteen at the oldest. The woman's hat was shaped like a little silk boat, and fancy combs and sticks or something came out of her well-groomed hair. Miki scratched her head. Fleas. It was so hard to not pick up fleas with her long, dark, straight hair in the woods and villages. If she had stayed in the temple, she wouldn't even have hair. Lady Teruko probably didn't have to worry about fleas, thought Miki. She wondered what it would be like to be led on a horse, to serve in

---

11 naginata - essentially a sword blade on a pole, commonly used by foot soldiers, ashigaru, and retainers

a castle as this woman would soon do. *What can the Iga possibly be planning for her?*

An older Samurai leading his horse, very senior and in expensive black armor, led the procession as it made its way toward the pass between the two large hills. Miki was watching from her perch in the tree on the larger of the hills. Trees were scattered about, not dense enough to provide cover and much thinner than the evergreens that marked the start of the forest behind her. This wasn't ideal for an ambush, so why did the coded letters describe this place? More disturbing was that the Iga were nowhere around. No disturbed earth that might indicate holes, no one else in the trees, seemingly no one in the tall grass at the edge of the forest. Had she been wrong about the message? Worse, it hadn't occurred to her that she may have been reading the only copy, and the ambush might not occur at all.

Reaching the small shrine at the start of the pass, just past the border of Kumi and Yugumi, the procession stopped, and the older Samurai helped the pretty girl dismount. It seemed that this would be a meeting rather than an ambush. The young woman didn't seem happy about something, earning a stern rebuke from the senior Samurai. What would it be like, Miki wondered, to wear such fine silk clothing, to ride on a horse, and to be cared for by others? Miki fingered the coarse brown *hakama* with its holes and many repairs. Even the robes she had worn at the temple had been plain and a bit itchy, although always cleaner than anything the Koga had given her. If we could just switch places, even for just a day, for just a moment, she dreamed.

The lazy late summer sun and the cool breeze felt good as noon turned into mid afternoon. Miki closed her eyes, imagining her life as a Samurai-class woman with servants and suitors and never having to sleep outdoors again. Voices from below woke her up, and her mind struggled to become fully alert. A second set of soldiers had arrived whom she had not noticed during her unintended nap. A pair of the new ones in the red-and-black armor of a Hamatsu soldier were using the tree to relieve themselves.

"And what is this?" A rock thrown in her general direction told Miki that she was no longer unobserved. "YOU, child, get down here NOW!"

Unarmed, trapped in a tree, and now surrounded, it was time to test Gonzo-san's belief. Crawling down the tree brought her face to face with a group of soldiers as ugly as she had ever seen. Why send soldiers who looked like this to meet an important person? Some of the armor had tears and holes in it, and old bloodstains even. Was something wrong?

"And what were you doing up there?"

"Sleeping."

"We have a monkey girl here. Sleeping in trees and spying on us. What did you hear, monkey girl?"

"Nothing. I was looking at the beautiful woman over there." The soldiers who escorted Lady Teruko were departing, leaving behind their charge. A second woman, plainly dressed in a yellow kimono, was bowing to the Lady. "Can I go home now?"

"I don't think so. How old are you?"

"Fourteen."

"Maybe in four years. I think monkey girl has fleas. You're a liar, too. What's the stick for, monkey girl? If you were fourteen, I might have a bit more fun with you. Maybe we would all have fun with you." This soldier was the ugliest, hairiest thing that Miki had ever seen. The scars and pockmarks covered every piece of exposed skin, including his bare feet.

The soldiers were being cruel, but they didn't consider her a threat. Gonzo-san was right. A sword would have gotten her killed. Many of these soldiers were barefooted. Very odd indeed. The weapons were mismatched, also. These couldn't be soldiers! These were Iga shinobi in stripped uniforms. *Why fight for Lady Teruko when you can simply take her with a false escort? A change of clothing means that when they do turn Lady Teruko over, it will be the wrong Lady Teruko. Why didn't I figure this out before?*

The woman in the yellow kimono looked down at Miki, who was trying hard to look as small, scared, harmless, and pathetic as possible. Yellow kimono lady was in charge. She was young and sweet looking and smiled as she discussed the situation with the soldier holding her by the arm. *Is Gonzo-san watching from the forest?*

Miki knew that with the departure of her escort, the need to be nice to Lady Teruko was gone. Now the poor woman was a liability, her clothing and baggage representing more value than the woman to whom they belonged.

"Remove Lady Teruko's clothing, but do not damage it. All of it. Have her put this on." Yellow kimono lady glanced down at Miki and swiftly slid her thumbnail across her throat, a gesture that would be missed by anyone not shinobi. "Take the little one into the forest and let her go. Be kind."

Letting her go wasn't going to happen. Miki would be an unfortunate accident in the forest. They would probably keep Lady Teruko alive long enough to ask her some questions. That meant a safe house, probably in Isawa or Yoron. Either way, if she lived long enough, she could follow them. "Can I keep my stick? I need it in the woods to get home."

The ugly, hairy one who wanted to have fun with her when she was older her was directed to take her out of sight. Lady Teruko would go with a few others. Meanwhile, Teruko's clothing would no doubt find a new back to cover.

Feigning a limp, Miki tried to delay enough to see what direction the tied and terrified Teruko would be taken, but ugly hairy-san would have none of it. Dragging her to the edge of the forest, he tossed her in, almost as if he thought it might swallow her up so that he might be done with her. "Sorry, brat. Just a little farther. Make this easy and don't cry. I will make this painless."

Miki had heard those words before, and she hadn't believed them then, either. "I apologize. This won't be painless." The stick wasn't as nice as her bo-staff, but catching the unwary man between his legs sent his hands away from his head, where Miki's second blow sent him all the way to the ground. This was not the sort of a trick that would work twice, so leaving fast seemed the only viable option. No one had ever been able to track her in the forest, not even Gonzo-san, so a few moments were all she would need. The question was, would Monk Akaki be proud of her skill with the staff or ashamed by her act of violence? That was a meditation for another day as distance gave her the option of choosing stealth over speed as her tactic.

By late afternoon it was clear that either there was no pursuit or they had given it up—most likely the former, as peasant girls seldom posed much of a real threat. Ugly, hairy one probably would face the wrath of yellow kimono lady—most likely now dressing in Teruko's red silk finery—for losing to a mere child, and a girl at that. The real question was where were Hisano and the group now.

Moving southwest would put her beside the road on the other side of the pass. Miki knew that she would certainly miss the Iga and the new Lady Teruko unless they were crawling on their bellies, but it would certainly put her into a position where she could track them west to Yoron or east to Isawa.

As Miki neared the edge of the thick woods, she could hear the familiar sound of squabbling. Not wanting to be ambushed by her own party, two quick wolf calls followed by a long would identify her if they were paying attention.

"Miki? Is that you?"

"Hai, Hisano-san."

"Were you lost, too?"

A quick reunion was followed by a longer report of the day's activities. It seemed that not being able to track Miki, the group had gone too far north and missed the pass completely.

"So the woman being led by the soldiers was the real Lady Teruko. They went east. We were too late to stop the Iga from passing off their Teruko as the real thing. At least a dozen of Teruko's guards and at least fifteen more Hamatsu cavalry went west with her. Now the Hamatsu will have a dozen Iga shinobi inside their castle. Interesting. Hisano, what will you do now?"

"Go west to Yoron and kill the impostor, Master Gonzo."

"Miki, your opinion?"

"Forgive me, Master Gonzo. I have no right to..."

"This is a training exercise. Your opinion?"

"Go east to Isawa and find the real Lady Teruko. She only had two guards, and if we save her, their whole plan will fall apart. All of the Iga will be executed, Master Gonzo. Forgive me, Hisano-san."

Koan groaned a bit. "Another lame little Miki plan. They don't like us in Isawa, or don't you remember? Let's follow Hisano's plan."

"Hisano, you are the jonin. What are you going to do?" Gonzo watched the tall girl fidget a bit. He knew that Hisano knew the right answer; the question was, would she admit it?

Swallowing hard, the tall kunoichi glanced in each direction. Would she let her pride get in the way? Pride would get them killed. This time, Hisano knew that her pride had to be put aside. "Miki is correct, Master Gonzo. But Miki can't go back to Isawa. Let her go to Yoron with Toko. It will be safer for her there."

"I'm sorry."

"Why? You just saved us all again. I would have had us facing thirty guards, half of them shinobi. Lay low in Yoron and do nothing. You don't have to prove anything, Miki. You've already proven enough."

This was going to be a hot summer day. Miki could feel the mid-morning sun on her back, drying the sweat before it could even soak the worn, oversized hakama and *keikogi* she wore that made her look even smaller than she was. Yoron was huge! So many people, so much activity. The farmers on the outskirts of town were collecting the night waste that filthy men carried out in the large wooden buckets to spread over their paddies. Miki had to curl up her nose at the stench—not just of the night waste, but of the walled collection of so many people in one place. Buildings as high as three or four floors were visible just beyond the walls, and through the open gates Miki watched women haggle with shopkeepers as children played in the wide street.

It was the play of the children that attracted Miki the most. From the very first moment she could remember, in the village with her mother and then in the temple, play had always been forbidden to her. There was always work to be done, always meditation, lessons, and chores. Never once, not even once, had she ever been allowed to own a toy beyond the simple wooden top that she had left in the temple, or simply waste time with other children. The temple had no other children and only one other girl. Even in Hisano's village, play was little more than training for an adult life that started early and so often ended too soon. At the age of fourteen, she had already fought for her life several times, having been nearly executed a year earlier. But these children were smiling and laughing. They were playing games and doing nothing useful. Fun for the sake of joy, and it looked wonderful.

"Why are crying, you little imp?"

"I am sorry, Toko-san. I have just never seen such a wonderful place."

"This is the marketplace, and that tall building is where they make sake. Over there they store the dried fish, and that is the physician's house. But he won't work on people like us."

"People like us?"

"Yeah. People like us. You do know what we are, don't you? To them we really aren't even people at all." Toko gave the curious Miki a bit of a tug to keep her walking. All of the children were dressed in simple but immaculate kimonos and brightly colored clothing, like many of the adults who carried on business in the market square.

"What is wrong with us, Toko-san?" She felt like a person. In the temple she had always been treated with respect and dignity. Now people were ignoring them. Mothers occasionally shooed children back as she and Toko passed quietly by.

"Do you think real people collect people's poop and sell it to the farmers? We are just like those guys, and all the other eta. We don't belong in this part of town. That's why we are going over by the river. When we were street entertainers, we were better. Bow low and don't talk smart like you do. Act like me; they expect it. Especially to the Samurai. They can cut your head off."

The concept that she was somehow this different, this inferior, had never occurred to Miki. She was smart, nimble, and could read and write and use numbers better than just about anyone. Yet because she was dressed poorly, the doctor would not treat her? Children could not play with her? Miki remembered the babies she had helped into the world, the wounds and sicknesses she had treated, never once caring about who or what class of people she was helping. Somehow the world seemed less wondrous, less fair. The fine shops gave way to plainer, colorless buildings and narrower streets, and people dressed more plainly. Still there were children, but except for a few young ones, they worked alongside their parents in the workshops and streets, carrying what they could and doing what they were told. Are these people like me? That wasn't so bad.

"We belong with the river district people. Eta, like us. They live on the boats and make leather and bury the dead. Samurai don't go there, except for the pleasure district. We are lucky because we can pretend to be anyone. Not like the others." Toko pushed Miki into the alleyway that ran between the crudely made buildings and the wide, slow river. Piers jutted out into the water, each with six or eight boats attached, maybe thirty boats in all. "Watch yourself and stay close or you will find yourself collecting poop or making the men happy."

This was a dismal place. The few children were occupied with chores or staring out at her from behind walls with empty eyes, closely guarded by wary mothers. Men argued and women squabbled as mothers kept their children busy with work. Miki wondered if these children ever played like the ones in the market district. All were dressed in heavily patched rags, even worse than in Hisano's village.

"Stay quiet and don't wander. That warehouse down there has a room we can use." Toko dragged little Miki into the creaky, gray warehouse, being careful to step over the broken, rotted floorboards. Lining the walls and on poles were fish being dried, and barrels were stacked in the far corner. "Go up that ladder over there. That's where the room is. Wait there."

Suffering. All of her training in the temple was about suffering and how to end it. It was about how things don't matter but compassion for others did. But here, in this terrible place, things did matter. Simple things like the colorless rags they wore and the rotting wood that would shelter them when winter came. Simple things that meant life or death, tools for their trade and the most basic of necessities. So much wealth, and so little of it shared here in this terrible corner of Yoron, the happiest and most miserable place on earth, in Miki's mind. Curling up in the corner, all Miki could do was weep.

The patter of the rain on the roof was barely louder than the patter of the rain in the buckets around the small room that had become a home to Miki and Toko. Miki emptied the nearly full bucket out the window, struggling not to spill it. "We've been here nearly thirty days. Can we go home soon? I smell like a fish."

"I'll trade you for jobs. I've been collecting night waste. But it gets me into General Yoshida's mansion, where I found out that the Iga fake Teruko is going to leave for Hamatsu castle in three days. She is being taught by a Lady O-Sho, who is getting her ready for Lord Nobunaga. Her son is off trying to track down the Mountain Samurai."

"Lady O-Sho?" That was a name she hadn't heard for a while. If Lady O-Sho had been allowed to take her, she would be living in that wonderful fortified mansion instead of here, in a fish warehouse.

"Yea. Didn't her son try to crucify you or something? I sent Fusa back to Master Gonzo with the news. If I don't hear from Gonzo we will have to kill them both. I'll let you take O-Sho."

"Kill Lady O-Sho?"

"You say that like it's a bad thing. That is who we are. We kill enemies, like Samurai."

"It will take two days for Fusa to reach them. They can't get here in time. By then Teruko will be gone, and we don't need to hurt Lady O-Sho."

"I didn't think of that. Then we should do it tonight. There is a tree that overhangs the wall. The wall is low, so even you can get over it. There is nowhere to hide around the mansion, so we have to move quickly." Toko pulled the floorboards in the corner to reveal the compartment below. "We keep this stuff here just in case. The rest of our clothing is on the boat with the Minori family. They are Koga, too. You know, the family with the pregnant girl."

"Hagi is my age, only fourteen. How did she get pregnant?"

"The woman who runs the inn in the pleasure district is the boss. Hagi was sold to her to cook and clean, but one of the Samurai liked her, so Meiko the innkeeper made her entertain the man. When Hagi got pregnant, boss Meiko tossed her out like rotting garbage. She even wanted her money back from the

Minori because her contract was for two years. Gonzo took care of that last spring."

"So what will happen when the baby is born?"

"If it's a girl, it gets tossed into the river. If it's a boy, the Minori family will take it back to their village, and he will be Koga shinobi like us. Another family will take over their boat."

Life and death, poverty or wealth, accidents of birth. If the child was a boy, he would live; a girl, she would die. He would live to kill because that was his family's occupation. When the time came, he might take a wife if there were sufficient girls allowed to live. Only the need to appear normal allowed Hagi to stay pregnant at all.

Making their way down the ladder into the warehouse and across the street, Miki and Toko climbed aboard the second boat. It was a bit larger than the others, designed not just to be the home of the Minori family, but to be a working fishing boat also.

"Hagi-san, would you please tell your father that we need to go tonight? I know that it is upstream, but it will really help us. We can't walk through town."

"Hai, Toko-san. Father isn't here. He's away selling fish. Mother and I can't move the boat without him. Can you use the small boat? Miki, the baby is kicking harder. I think it will be soon. I hope that it's a boy. I really want to keep it."

"You should keep it even if it is a girl."

"We need a shinobi warrior to fight. Father says that we need a strong boy to fish."

"Hisano is a warrior. Fusa is a warrior. I am a warrior. Please don't kill your baby."

"It isn't Hagi's decision. Her family will decide. That means we have to go through town. I'll go in to collect the night waste. You go over the wall. That means that we can't take the swords. Take your bag and the dagger."

"There is another way, Toko-san. We can tell Lady O-Sho. She will believe me."

"Gonzo said that you have to learn obedience. There's no other way. You have to kill the old woman. An officer let you live, reported you dead. You would condemn him to death for his lie?

You have to stay dead. Get a bit of sleep now. We will move in the early morning."

"Hai, Toko-san. I just need to write a letter."

Even in the early hours, the town of Yoron was alive. Drunk Samurai stumbled home from their dealings with the girls in the one-street, walled pleasure district while officers patrolled the streets. There were a few gambling dens and more than a few places to drink sake that occasionally ejected a customer. The shops were boarded, and the only legitimate tradesmen still awake were collecting night waste.

Slipping from shadow to shadow, Miki followed Toko through the streets as he slipped under each house and emptied its container into his bucket. As he came to each walled mansion, a ring of the bell brought the guard, who would allow Toko in to carry out his necessary but smelly task. This was one of those activities that no one wanted to see in the light of day, yet it provided a shinobi assassin the perfect access if he was discreet.

The Yoshida mansion was the largest in all of Yoron. Formerly the home of a high-ranking member of the Yorisada clan, it now was the home of the governor of Kumi province and the Hamatsu heir. Well kept, it was easily defended. What was curious was how a tree was allowed to hang a branch over the wall with a simple drop to the roof of the stable inside. This was the route that Toko had chosen for Miki this night, yet somehow it seemed wrong, too obvious.

Toko's silent signal sent Miki across the street to work her way through the moonless shadows to the back, where the tree would be. It seemed too easy, far to simple, and far too stupid a mistake to make. Creeping along the wall, Miki stopped to listen. Out of sight, she adjusted her hood as she became part of the ground, part of the wall itself. Carefully, she reviewed every shadow and each and every sound and smell. Something was just not right.

Easy entrance or not, the tree would not work. Backing up along the wall, Miki made her way back to the street. She would find another way in.

Across the street from the door where Toko had rung the door and was granted access, Miki watched for any clue. The wall had a short wooden decorative wall on the lower half with poles supporting the tile roof. The tiles were a problem. Breaking tiles would be noisy and leave behind a clue. A distraction would be possible but unlikely to be helpful. The corner of the large door and the wall was perhaps the best possibility, she thought. The wooden beam and the wall would make the climb possible, and the molding along the top of the wall would protect the tiles. So that was it. Once on top, Miki knew that any mistake would be lethal.

A simple enough climb. The unarmored guard turned to return to his route along the wall as Miki dropped inside. Shadow to shadow, the beam and wooden porch roof made getting to the second floor window easy for the nimble acrobat. Since it was a hot day, the shutters were open. Miki felt her heart pound. Her very first act as a real Koga, and her last if this did not go as planned. Toko's task was harder, as his target was kunoichi. That was the only target that mattered. Problem was, where was Lady O-Sho? Searching each room seemed a tedious and impractical solution, sure to wake someone armed and more than capable of fending off a fourteen-year-old girl with a dagger. Samurai slept with their weapons, as did shinobi.

The new Lady Teruko would most certainly be the yellow kimono lady from the pass, and she would just as certainly recognize the short, flea-bitten little girl, not that mercy was ever a possibility. Creeping around the wall put the time near first light— suicide if she delayed. Miki would have to work fast, but how?

The alarm bell solved that problem. Ducking back into the room with the window, Miki considered her options, none of them good. Toko must have been caught, or at least his actions discovered. Shouted orders, questions, the patter of feet. It was one voice that caught Miki's attention, worried but soft and familiar. Closing her eyes, she dreamed for just a moment of what her life might have been like, here, as O-Sho's daughter. A smile drifted across Miki's face under the cloth hiding her face as the idea that at this moment that she herself would be hiding in a corner, hiding from a terrible shinobi assassin.

Finding a screen to hide behind until the shouts subsided, Miki winced as the door flew open and was shut moments later. At least they weren't thorough. From the sound, Lady O-Sho would be just down the hall in an inside room. Problem was, was she still there, and was she alone?

Time had run out. A light, faint glow told Miki that if she stood any chance, it had to be now. Waiting for one of the servant girls to pass, the small kunoichi slipped down the hall and, taking a chance, slid open the most likely door, committing herself.

Turning to face the intruder now no more than an arm's length away, the old woman nearly dropped the lantern she was holding. The dagger pointed against her throat stunned O-Sho as her intruder signaled for silence.

"Why me? Why kill me?" Surprise turned to horror as Lady O-Sho's eyes met her assassin's. As horror turned to anger, her tiny killer reached into her keikogi, producing a letter, which the dark, hooded figure held out. Unsure as to the assassin's intention, although now certain of her identity, O-Sho accepted the offering. "What is the point of giving me this if you plan to kill me?"

The small figure rotated the dagger away from her throat as she backed away with a slight bow. Discarding the blade, she quickly departed the room, leaving a relieved but puzzled O-Sho to wonder what had just happened.

Putting the lantern down, O-Sho's shaking hands carefully opened the neatly folded paper. As her eyes read the well-formed characters, handwriting so beautiful and precise that it was clear who the author was, puzzlement became gratitude as the risk her little girl had taken to bring this message sank in.

Lady O-Sho

A friend respectfully asks that you forgive her for scaring you. I was told to kill you, but I would never hurt you. The woman calling herself Lady Teruko is an Iga impostor. The real Lady Teruko has been taken to Isawa by the Iga. Her bodyguards are Iga also. Your life is in great danger. You should leave Kumi at once.

A friend

Folding the letter around the dagger, old hands carefully put the pair in a box containing the clothes that she would wear this day. This letter explained so very much: the poor knowledge of protocol, language unsuitable for a woman of the Samurai class, no talents like dancing or singing. She had been preparing an assassin for her mission rather than a worthy bride for her husband. This would not do. There was perhaps another way, perhaps a bride more worthy.

It was midmorning of what promised to be a very hot day, and the troops were assembled for departure. A large, white horse waited patiently for the beautiful woman in her bright red kimono, who would most certainly become the latest wife of the Hamatsu Daimyo, Lord Nobunaga. There was just one last detail to attend to.

"Before my men kill you, where is the other one? The one who came into town with you? Where is the child?" The young man on his knees in front of her had almost succeeded. The cut on her breast might have been fatal had the smelly young man not already not been wounded. "We had a trap set up for her in the back, but she didn't appear. Maybe she ran away, or maybe you didn't bring the little witch at all. It would be stupid to bring an Ama on a mission. Still, I have to admire her resourcefulness in the pass. Too bad that I didn't know what she was then."

Blood dripped into the sand from his soaked, soiled clothing. Despite his smell, he had gotten past the Hamatsu guards, although that seemed a minor achievement given their lack of alertness. The boy before her, barely an adult, had even killed one of her Iga clansman before reaching her. He would get no older because if she didn't kill him, infection and blood loss would. "How did you think that you could steal two messages and kill two of us and not have us figure it out? The question is, who deciphered the messages?"

Toko closed his eyes in anticipation of another beating. Missing teeth with a bloody mouth, he knew that the woman really didn't expect an answer. Mumbling an indecipherable insult, he knew his life was over. The only bright spot was that Miki had gotten away.

"Was it the Ama Miki? Do you know who Miki really is? Does Miki know who she really is?"

The game was over. Time for her to leave. A quick signal as she walked away sent a katana through the air, sending the boy's head into the dirt. A soldier helped her onto the horse, and the procession started to the gate before a soldier stopped the horse holder. "Lady Teruko, the girl was here. Several tiles were broken on the north wall. We have no idea how she got in or what she did. She didn't kill anyone, and no one saw her."

"I'll take these twelve men to escort me. The rest of you can go home. Rande, you stay in town to find and kill the little Ama. She was the only one who could have figured out the code, and that makes her very dangerous. If she spoke to O-Sho, arrange for an accident."

"Hai."

Chapter 12 – A New Bride

a worthy bride
consequences of mercy
unhappy princess

"Sir Junkai, you look well on this fine, sunny day. You have never been so cheerful. I see that Doctor Anenokoji's medicine has finally worked. Last week you could not even walk without pain." O-Sho admired the garden. The days had been turning cooler as summer had burned itself out, but winter had not yet arrived. It had been more than a month since Lady Teruko's departure and that night's encounter. Ichi's garden reminded her of the one the monks had kept and Miki had tended.

"Lady O-Sho, how kind of you. It is always a joy to see you. Alas, that quack put me through hell for months. It always got worse and never better. Ichi the gardener told me about a healer down in the river district he said could work miracles. I was in so much pain, so I had him show me this healer who works on a fishing boat. Even that quack Anenokoji has been in, complaining to the magistrate that his business is drying up because of the competition." The bald, pudgy, middle-aged Junkai was the administrator for the town of Yoron. Today, though, he was a man without pain for the first time in a season, and his uncustomary cheerfulness caught O-Sho by surprise.

"Perhaps we should invite the man to come here. I know that General Satake has been having trouble with his shoulder since he fell off his horse. He refuses to see the doctor."

"I should mention it to him. But to my surprise, it was not a man at all. It was a small, young woman with very dark eyes. Like the eyes on Oto; you remember him."

"A girl?"

"Young and very intelligent, too. She had read all of the Chinese classics on war and could recite them all from memory. She must have come from a Samurai or Kuge family. She was certainly no fisherman's daughter. Where would anyone in the river district learn so much about medicines? She was very polite, very sweet. If I did not already have two daughters, I would have brought her home."

"Sir Junkai. I would be very grateful if you did not mention this to General Satake. Please let me handle this. You said that she was on a fishing boat?"

"Hai."

"Miki, don't you understand the words 'lay low?' There must be ten people waiting to see you! Who's screaming in the next room?" Hisano could not believe what her little Miki had done. News of Toko's death had spread fast, even reaching her and the group in Isawa. Finding out that Miki had set up shop as a doctor was just too much.

"Hagi is having her baby." Pouring sake over the fisherman's wound, Miki tugged and tied the knot on the stitch holding the nasty cut on the greasy man's arm closed. Wrapping a bandage around the wound, Miki gave careful guidance on changing the bandage and keeping it clean.

"Gonzo is furious! We've heard a dozen stories about what happened, and he doesn't know what to believe. Fusa is blaming you for everything."

"Please send in the next one. Hisano, could you help them in while I take care of Hagi real quick?" Darting into the next room, Miki could see the head crowning. This would take more than a few minutes. Two other women from the boats were helping Hagi along, but Miki was a bit concerned about Hagi's young age. Her body was just not developed enough to be a mother yet. Still, things were going normally, although the poor girl had been in labor since well before first light. It was now mid-afternoon, and poor Hagi was near the end of endurance. Feeling around the pelvis and then guiding the shoulder through, Miki knew it would be only seconds now. With other women getting ready to receive the baby, the question was would it be a boy or girl. Normally not a concern, here it was the difference between life as a Koga and being raised by another family for whom a girl would be an asset. Miki knew that she could never let death be the only option. Life was far too precious.

She caught the boy as he squirted out, a slimy, wiggling, crying bundle. Helpful hands took over for Miki's, allowing the exhausted mother and doctor a few moments of rest. Miki plopped down on a box near the hull and closed her eyes for just a second as she leaned back on the boat's side. Perhaps just a minute of rest.

"Let her sleep. The poor girl has been up most of the night with Hagi. I don't know how she does it." Hisano stared at her friend. Day after day, sunrise to sunset, her little Miki labored for others. On this day, the stupid little imp hadn't even had a chance to eat, although there had been no shortage of offerings.

"I don't know why she does it. Who are these people to her, anyway?"

"Gonji, tell the people outside to come back and let Miki rest. She can't even move." In a place with so much misery, Miki had brought hope. It was in the eyes and voices and faces of those who waited for her touch, who surrounded this boat, and it was where her friend belonged.

Turning to check on Gonji, Hisano's eyes met those of an older woman, very well dressed and very out of place. "I'm sorry, but the healer needs to rest. Please, she's been up all night and…"

"That is quite all right. I have been watching my little imp from heaven from the door. I just needed to see her again. I need to give her a message."

"You can tell me and…"

"Are you Koga like my Miki? Are you one of her friends?"

"My Miki." She called her "my little imp from heaven." This woman isn't a stranger. "Are you Lady O-Sho?"

"Hai. My little girl is in terrible danger. One of the men Miki treated knows General Satake, and if he tells him about the healer in the river district, even a man as stupid as General Tomoe Satake will figure it out. My Miki must not be here when he does. My Little Miki has done Hamatsu a great service, but Miki and all of you must now leave. Please give my Miki this letter."

Once again, her friend's kindness was being repaid, this time by the very woman whom Miki had been ordered to kill. Taking the letter, Hisano could see the pride in the old woman's face as she took one last long look at the snoozing girl in the other room. "I should walk with you out of the river district. It isn't safe for you here."

Walking off the boat with the regal woman, Hisano felt the eyes of every fishmonger, leather worker, and undertaker on them. Polite bows couldn't hide the surprise and resentment that a woman of her class would cause, coming to see their little Miki in this, their world.

"Miki said that she was ordered to kill me." O-Sho stared ahead as they walked. Soon they would pass the dilapidated but open wooden gate that marked the exit from this grim place.

"The boy they executed was supposed to protect Miki. He had no orders to do what he did. He walked into a trap that Miki saw through. Miki did the right thing. Miki always does the right thing. How did you know it was her?" Taking note of everything, from the women arguing about children, the leather man scraping a hide, or the two odd men sitting alone near the gate, the only ones who didn't seem busy with a trade, Hisano knew that Miki's actions had attracted the wrong kind of attention, and caution was called for.

"No one has eyes like my Miki. What happened to the real Lady Teruko, I wonder?"

"We rescued her. But she killed herself rather than be married to Lord Nobunaga. We would have let her go once we exposed the Iga plan. Without the real Lady Teruko, we had no proof." Sharing information with an enemy wasn't going to make Gonzo happy, but Miki's plan was the only one that seemed plausible now. Hisano noted that no one who ever saw her friend could forget those dark eyes, and being remembered was a very bad, very dangerous trait for any shinobi. Getting the girl home alive would now require a miracle.

Passing the gate, Hisano tucked her dagger up her sleeve and faced Lady O-Sho with a bow. Enemy or not, this woman had come to warn one of her own in spite of the danger, and for that reason had earned real respect. "We will take Miki home through Isawa and the north road pass tomorrow. You shouldn't worry about her. We won't let anything happen to Miki."

"Thank you. Did you notice that man? The one who followed me here. I think he was one of Lady Teruko's guards. Is he one of you, also?"

A sharp shiver went down her spine as Hisano realized that O-Sho had been followed. The two men by the warehouse near the gate weren't familiar, but then, no one was in Yoron. "Are you sure?"

"Hai. The man beside him was also. I think that his name was Rande. It was odd that Lady Teruko should call her guards by name. I told her that she must not do this in the Hamatsu court. It would be quite unseemly."

"It's because they probably grew up together. Go home and don't stop for anything. Don't go anywhere without a guard anymore. It's not safe if they think Miki talked to you." It would have been nice to know this before they left Miki on the boat. Gonji, Gonzo, and Benzo had no clue that Miki was now being stalked. The choice was whom to protect: O-Sho or Miki? The mission now rested with O-Sho and the knowledge that Miki had given her. O-Sho had to live, or Toko's sacrifice was for nothing. O-Sho it was, then; Miki would have to be sacrificed.

Slipping behind a few barrels as the street became more crowded, the tall Hisano went to her knees to blend in with the brown wooden wall behind her. If both men were following O-Sho, she might have a chance to save Miki. If neither followed O-Sho, Miki would most certainly be dead already. The question was, would either of the Iga men know her as Koga? If so, their tactic would be different. One would follow at a distance to prevent her from doing what she was about to do.

The shorter of the two men strolled past Hisano, just staying within sight of the slow-moving O-Sho, who shuffled along on her tall *geta*. He was good, thought Hisano. There was no sign of the other man, so perhaps she was in luck. Standing up, she needed to get close enough to use the blade low, out of sight, between the second and third ribs to eliminate the bleeding, to give her time to get away.

At least O-Sho was shuffling along, her nervousness obvious to another woman. That was making it difficult for her assassin to catch her without being obvious. Hisano knew that would give her a chance to get ahead without being seen. Cutting around several of the stalls and jumping over a short fence, Hisano could see Lady O-Sho in tears moving toward her. It was clear that the old woman knew she was being followed and was terrified.

Hisano positioned herself facing the wall to avoid being recognized by old O-Sho as she passed; the scent of cherry blossoms and the heavy breathing of fear as O-Sho passed was the cue. Flipping the thin blade out of her sleeve, the tall kunoichi turned, shoving the blade upward into the man's ribs to the handle. Without turning to check, Hisano walked away, flipping the blade into a box as she walked by. Best not to be caught with the murder weapon if anyone figured it out too quickly. If she hit her target right, the man would bleed out inside, unable to breathe as the blade should have penetrated the lower lung. The delay as he stood, unsure of what had happened, gave Hisano time to disappear into the crowd that would move past the man unconcerned. O-Sho would live today, probably without realizing what had happened, saved by one of the Koga that her son was trying to hunt down and exterminate.

"Gonzo-san, where is Miki?"

"Her last patient just went inside. What happened to you?"

Reaching inside Gonzo's sleeve, the kunoichi quickly extracted his knife, and without losing a step hopped onto the boat and slipped inside the cabin. The taller man of the two by the gate was reaching inside the back collar of his keikogi, as if to show an attentive and smiling Miki where his pain was.

"I can help you with that pain." Slipping quickly behind the man, Hisano flipped Gonzo's sharp, thin blade into her hand

and pressed it across the Iga shinobi's jugular, quickly drawing the knife through the throat to the bone. She heard the sickening gurgle of air as blood shot in every direction. The nearly headless man spun off the box, landing on the floor in front of a horrified Miki.

"HISANO! HISANO! NO!" Miki fell to her knees and reached down in a blind panic. Her mind seemed to be looking for a way to undo her friend's grisly deed and put the head back where it belonged. The boys, sensing Hisano's urgency, had followed her in.

"Benzo, grab Miki and hold her, tight. Koan, you and Gonji wrap this thing up in a mat. We'll toss the body into the center of the river. Master Gonzo, we need to get Miki out of here now." Hisano wiped the blade clean on Miki's last patient before handing it back to its owner. "Lady O-Sho is alive. She knows the truth about Lady Teruko. His friend is dead, too. Satake is in Yoron."

"Good job. I'll tell Hagi's father that we need to leave right away. This boat moves slowly, and this isn't a very wide river. They will catch us."

"I told O-Sho that I would take Miki overland through Isawa and the North Road pass. She will try to protect Miki, so when they do force it out of the old woman, they should believe it." Hisano watched Benzo try to control the sobbing, squirming girl. It was hard to tell if Miki was more shocked, horrified, or angry. "Koan, help Benzo and make sure that Miki can't get to a weapon. Take her below, and then both of you help with the boat. I'll take care of my friend."

"I don't see why the imp is this upset. I hear all doctors lose patients now and then."

"Yea, that was a pretty nasty cut. He should have been more careful shaving."

"My dear Lady O-Sho. It seems that you were very lucky today. The officer tells me that the man was carrying several weapons in use by shinobi, some of them poisoned. He was probably going to kill you. Who killed him is the mystery. It was most certainly a professional assassin. Strange that no one saw anything. My question is why one assassin would kill another to save you. Where were you coming from?" It had been a busy day for the officers in the town of Yoron, with a dead man just outside the Governor's mansion and a nearly decapitated body washing up on the river's shore. It would be a cool evening in the moonlight, and yet the old woman insisted on speaking in the garden.

"Sir Junkai, I went to see that healer you told me about. She was very nice. I had been having pain since last spring. My heart feels better now. Perhaps the men were just ordinary criminals."

"Perhaps, but your son has arrived, and he is quite upset. Two assassination attempts in less than a month. He is arranging a guard to escort you back to Hamatsu." Junkai had known O-Sho since she had arrived in the castle, a mere girl nearly thirty years earlier. She was not telling him everything, nor would she. A woman of duty, O-Sho could be as hard as stone when she needed to be. "For a woman who walked so close to death, you seem remarkably happy."

"Do I? I am merely enjoying the good health my little healer has given me. Thank you, Sir Junkai, for telling me about the girl." O-Sho could hear her son Kondo giving orders in the background. Soon he would be demanding explanations. Turning to face the footsteps, she knew that he suspected something.

"Mother, Junkai, was this healer girl short, almost childlike, with very dark eyes?"

"Lord Yoshida, it is pleasant to see you again. Why yes, how did you know? Dark, haunting eyes, like Oto, if you remember him." Even in the light of the garden's lanterns, Junkai could see the lines in Lord Kondo no Yoshida's brow.

"Junkai, I will explain everything later. If I could have a word alone with my mother." Watching the bald Junkai disappear, the young Lord Yoshida turned to his mother. "How dare you. How DARE you. What were you thinking? Contacting that girl."

"You should be grateful. In truth, my Little Miki came to me that night before Lady Teruko left. My little girl held a knife at my throat and gave me a letter. She then disappeared into the night, and in so doing has done Hamatsu a great service."

"A letter?"

"In it she explained that Lady Teruko was not who she claimed to be. The woman's ignorance and poor conduct proves my Miki's words. It seems that we have an Iga spy in the Hamatsu court. The men she brings are also Iga spies."

"That is absurd! Madness! You want me to trust the word of a Koga girl? Even if I were to believe this, we have no proof. She is an assassin, nothing more."

"But we do have an opportunity. An opportunity for you, my son. When Junkai told me of the healer in the river district, I could not believe it and had to see for myself what my Miki had become. How many assassins heal the sick? My imp was mid-wifing a child from one of the girls who live on the boats. She is a poor assassin indeed to have me under her blade and then simply deliver a message. Who killed the man who was trying to kill me? I recognized that man as one of Lady Teruko's guards."

Yoshida considered the old woman's words. "Then we should expose them immediately. Lord Nobunaga would be grateful. We must act before she can kill our Lord."

"No. That is not her plan. A simple assassination would be easy. No. She wants her child as heir to Hamatsu and the Hori clan. We have time to act, but we need a plan. We need a more worthy bride for our Lord, and a worthy bride for you. I have an idea."

"Waiting is a risk. Should she kill our Lord..."

"Then you would become Daimyo of Hamatsu and execute them all. But if you wait, if you are patient, you can secede to head of the clan in your own time without opposition."

"What is your idea, Mother?"

"Lord Nobunaga always favored the woman whom Prince Shigenori of the Yorisada clan married. As I understand it, General Shigenori and his army serves the Lord Yamamoto no Torii by guarding the middle road pass into Ikido. Lady O-Kin was quite beautiful. As I understand it, she had a daughter. The girl is still too young, but by next spring she should be ready. Perhaps this would be the perfect task for General Satake."

"A raid might be attempted. But it would be dangerous."

"Which is why you should not lead it. If Satake is killed, then you are rid of him. If he succeeds, then we expose the Teruko woman and provide Lord Nobunaga with a bride who gives him a legitimate claim to Kumi that the Emperor will recognize with General Shigenori dead. Since Lady O-Kin is past child bearing age, she poses no threat to your position as heir."

"Bold. A dangerous plan. It would mean our heads if anyone should learn of it."

"The silk merchant told me about O-Kin's daughter. The girl is named Yumi, and she is educated and quite pretty. With training she would be a suitable wife."

"But Teruko? She may not wait until next spring."

"That will be my task. I must leave for Hamatsu tomorrow."

"There is one more thing to take care of. The Koga girl who gave you this information needs to be protected. She is our only witness. I will send officers to bring her here so that we can use her at the appropriate moment. You said that, what was her name, Miki, was in the River District?"

"No. My little Miki and her friends are on their way home. By the time I reach Hamatsu Castle, Miki will be through Isawa and the North Road pass. Her friends will protect my little girl as they protected me."

"I will see that no one interferes with her." Watching his mother glide into the mansion, Yoshida called for General Satake, waiting inside.

"My Lord. We lost many men in the mountains. We need additional men on foot if we are ever to catch this Mountain Samurai. I have also removed the execution posts. They were becoming a symbol."

"Forget Oto for now. I have a task for you. This is one you must not fail, but one I think you will enjoy. The little girl named Miki is traveling east to Isawa. She and her companions were responsible for the assassination attempt on my mother. Miki and her companions must not reach the mountains alive. Kill them instantly. Once inside the mountains, they will be impossible to catch. Take as many men as necessary. This whole experience has been very upsetting to my mother, so under no circumstance mention this to her."

"The little Ama? I thought that the little witch was dead. Hai, my Lord. How do you know this?"

"Let us just say that it comes indirectly from Junkai. Bring me the girl's head; she has a habit of surviving. And when you finish, we need to plan a raid into Ikido for next spring."

"We're past the border now. This river leads to the sea. I figure that we can move through Yugumi and go over the pass into Kumi and home. It's getting cool in the evening, so we need to be home before first snow closes the passes." Gonzo was watching the shore for activity, but aside from other fishermen and the occasional woman carrying a bucket, it was quiet. "I can't believe they didn't come after us."

"They did. I watched Satake lead cavalry out of the mansion going east toward Isawa when we passed Yoron. There's a town ahead. I think we need to be off the boat before we get there. We can sleep on shore." Hisano smiled. Either O-Sho had let it slip or by trickery they had forced it out of the old lady. It did not matter because for once the escape had been easy. "Miki is a problem. She hasn't said a word, and she won't even look at me. I'm afraid to leave her alone."

"That is going to end now." Gonzo took one last look at the dark river ahead before signaling the boat's owner to move to shore. A night in a town would be welcome, but Hisano was right. There would be spies in a town, and getting Miki home would be challenging enough. For some extraordinary reason, the Iga considered the girl important enough to kill. For that reason alone, it was important to keep her alive. "Help him with the boat. I'll take care of Miki."

There she was, curled up in a corner of the small, dark lower deck that served as cargo hold and sleeping quarters for Hagi and her family, head buried in arms. Hagi was across the room breastfeeding her new son. Grabbing Miki by the hair, Gonzo dragged the surprised girl to the deck and dropped her before the equally surprised Hisano, who was helping with the ropes. "Hisano saved your life. She saved your precious O-Sho, too. You owe Hisano your thanks. If you had just stayed out of sight, you wouldn't have endangered Hisano. You wouldn't have endangered the mission that you yourself decided on."

It hurt. Gonzo had nearly pulled the hair out of her head. Sobbing, Miki had wallowed in anger and helplessness for the better part of the night. "SHE KILLED HIM. HE CAME TO ME FOR HELP!" A swift hand sent the girl to the deck. Looking up, Miki stared at the stern Gonzo, who was ready to strike her again. "I was helping those people. Nobody needed to die anymore! Not for me. Please, let me go back to where I belong."

So smart, and so stupid. She stared up with those defiant, bloodshot, dark eyes, blood running down the corner of her mouth. "And when Satake shows up and slaughters all those people you care about just because they are with you, are you helping them then? Do they have to die like your village, like your fellow monks? How many people have to die for you before you are happy? It was Hisano's lie that kept us safe. Your precious O-Sho sent Satake after us—after YOU." Reaching into his keikogi, Gonzo held up a dagger. "This is poisoned. It was the knife that your patient was going to kill you with. To save the rest of these people, I considered killing you with it myself, but I have a problem. You see, the Iga want you dead. I don't know why. Our orders from the clan are to keep you alive, but I don't know why. Who are you? WHO ARE YOU?"

They are all looking at me. Are they afraid of me? "I don't know." A child from a doomed village. An orphan, an Ama, a healer, an assassin who has killed no one. A mother she could barely remember, a father she never knew. "I'm just like you. I'm Koga, just like you."

"No, Miki, you aren't like the rest of us. You will never be like us. I want Gonji and Benzo and Koan to make it home alive. If I leave Fusa with you, she'll slit your throat as soon as we are out of sight. There is a large temple to the east in Yugumi. Hisano will take you and show you where it is. Go make soup and clean the clothes for the men who live there. You'll never be kunoichi." Gonzo signaled for the others to follow him off the boat. One by one they said farewell until it was just her and Hisano on the lonely deck, the only sounds the crying of a baby in the cabin below and the lapping of the water on the side of the boat.

"Come, Miki. You need to sleep. You can barely stand. You still haven't eaten. We can travel by day in Yugumi."

"You're going to kill me."

"If I were going to kill you Miki, you would be dead already. My mission is to keep you alive."

"Why?"

"I don't know."

Chapter 13 – The Temple

a little monkey
her spring, an old mans winter
home for the first time

It was a cool, gray day as the two very different young women made their way through and around the fields. The taller Hisano, with the brownish-black hair, walked in front to see over the tall autumn grasses, stopping every now and then to let the smaller, dark-eyed, raven-haired Miki catch up. The need to stay off the trails and roads had pushed the journey into the late afternoon. "It should be just over the next hill, I think."

"Why does Master Gonzo hate me?" The sticker bushes were drawing blood, and Miki was tired of fighting the rocks and bushes as well as hunger. "We're in Yugumi, not Kumi. Why can't we use the road over there?"

"Master Gonzo doesn't hate you. None of us do. The Iga still have spies."

"Fusa does. She wants to kill me. She said so. So does Gonzo-san."

"Fusa liked Toko very much, and she blames you for getting him caught. Gonji likes you very much. Master Gonzo ordered me to protect you. He likes you, too. Next spring we'll try to get home again. By then they won't be looking for you as hard."

Miki could still feel the burning of her scalp where Gonzo had grabbed her. In her memory none of the boys had ever been nice to her, especially Gonji, who especially enjoyed embarrassing her in front of everyone. Now they had abandoned her. But, there was always Hisano. "I don't want to go home. If the temple will take me, I want to stay there forever. You can go home."

"You wouldn't like what the boys are doing now. They're learning how to kill. Samurai, I expect. You don't seem to approve of that. All warriors have to kill, Miki, if they want to pass their test. It's easier for us girls because we can get closer to our targets. But you're too young, anyway. Maybe next year."

Looking down at the temple complex from the nearly bare hill, Miki stood in stunned wonder. Yugumi was a much richer province, and this temple was nothing like the simple wooden temple where she had grown up. The Fujiwara Ikko temple was much larger than the relatively tiny mountain North Road Zen temple in Kumi. Its massive, six-story pagoda commanded the valley. Protected by thick walls, it even had its own little army of *sohei*.[12] The glint of the gold ornaments at the corners of the green-tiled roof gables and immaculate white walls housed what seemed to be hundreds of monks in a variety of colored robes—nothing like the simple brown robes of her poor Zen temple.

"Why are you crying? I thought you would be happy."

"It is so beautiful. I never thought that any place could be so beautiful." It was beyond anything a mountain girl could imagine. The fatigue of the day was gone, and Miki felt that she could float the rest of the way. Surely this was a place that would want her; this was the place she needed to be. This was the home that she dreamed of every night. A place without death or fear.

"No. Go away. We have no time for little liars." The monk was a well-built warrior in his late twenties, wearing the dull orange robes and white cowl of an Ikko sohei. Miki had never seen a monk carry a katana, much less the naginata that he had handed to another man in similar robes before picking her up and tossing her out the large wooden gate. Miki looked up at the stern man from the dirt.

12 Sohei – A Warrior Monk

"If you come back to this temple," the monk said, "I will beat you. Now go home to your family. We don't need helpless children here."

Compassion was the basis of her faith. No monk at the North Road Temple had ever touched her, much less in an act of violence. Getting up, Miki picked up her staff and twirled it before slanting it in the attack position to indicate that she was offering battle. "I NEVER LIE, AND I'M NOT HELPLESS!" Turning, unconcerned, the monk signaled for a weapon from his companions, who quickly produced a bo-staff at least half higher than Miki's. *No matter; now it's about skill.*

This was a fight that was attracting attention. A group of the sohei monk's friends was gathering as the sohei twirled his staff with precision, taking a practiced defensive posture with a smile on his face. The other monks formed a ring around the mismatched pair, the tiny peasant girl and the strong, experienced, professional warrior. Bringing the staff back to launch the first attack, Miki felt someone grab the tip of the staff from behind, and suddenly her feet were no longer under her as she felt her backside slam into the dirt. Struggling to get up, Miki felt a pair of familiar hands pushing her down. Swinging her knee over the infuriated little girl, Hisano sat on Miki's chest to control the squirming bundle of rage. The laughter and derision of the sohei monks did nothing to calm her friend.

"MIKI, STOP IT! He's a full-grown Samurai, and he'll kill you. Please, sir, please. Please forgive us. Miki is an orphan my village takes care of. She is a little different. All of her hopes and dreams were in this temple. MIKI! She can't go home. We need the money. Please, I'll do anything." Between the tears and dirt, Miki wasn't the smiling, pretty little girl who had walked into the temple minutes earlier.

"Get her out of here before I teach your friend a lesson in respect."

"I'LL TEACH YOU A LESSON IN RESPECT!"

"MIKI, stop it!" Choosing one's enemies and one's battles was not the small girl's forte, thought Hisano. The idea that discretion was not cowardice was a lesson that Miki simply would not learn. This made the fearless imp far too dangerous to ever trust as a fellow kunoichi. Either as an act of kindness to give her a chance to get control over Miki or because of simple boredom, the sohei retreated into the temple compound, closing the large wooden door, no doubt to fend off Miki's impending assault. By all rights, these men had every right to execute Miki, but they were monks as well as warriors, and taking a life was no doubt distasteful, more so a young girl, however undisciplined.

With the audience gone, a very unhappy Miki relaxed a bit. Standing up, the larger, stronger girl dragged her against the wall to keep her from running away. Any chance that Miki would ever choose the life her clan offered was gone. Despite Miki's skills, regardless of her intelligence, she would never have the heart of a shinobi. The defeated girl sat on the ground, face buried in her knees, back up against the temple's stone wall.

"What did you think that would accomplish? You almost made that monk kill you. What did you think that would do to him? We need to find a place to stay. It'll get cold tonight." It was getting dark, and the town was an hour away. Even there, what would they do? Miki was in no condition to travel. The little imp was devastated, her world collapsing around her. Plopping down beside her friend, Hisano wrapped her arm around the shivering girl. At least the wall would stop the wind. Maybe they could keep each other warm.

"You should have seen her! This tiny girl no bigger than a dog wanted to fight Rennyo with a bo-staff, master instructor of the Fujiwara Ikko order of sohei, like a fierce little monkey. I never laughed so hard! There stood Rennyo, quaking with fear of this tiny demon." Shaking his hands in the air, the middle-aged, bald warrior responded to the laughter of his fellow warriors with facial expressions of horror. The story of the mad little girl had spread rapidly among the temple's residents, to the disgust of the peace-loving monks but to the delight of the armed sohei. "The dumb brat thought that walking in with a stick would make us think that she was an Ama."

One man was not finding it funny. Rennyo shook his head and gazed out of the shutters on the barracks window. "I am not so sure now. Did you see how she handled that staff? Someone taught her well. How many peasants have you ever seen with that kind of spirit? She showed no fear. Impressive."

"Her sister showed more sense. We could use the tall one in the stables."

"And how many peasant women can take down another person like that? That one was shinobi, I bet. The small one had to be from a Samurai family. The tall one said that the small one was an orphan that her village cared for. I would like to speak to them again."

The yellow-robed old monk in the corner had been silent, listening to the sohei make fun of the little girl. "The two of them are out by the front gate, trying to sleep by the wall. As cold as it is, both of them will be dead by morning. We should at least bring them inside."

Rennyo nodded and made his way down the steep, narrow staircase and out the door on the way to the gatehouse. By morning there would be a frost that could easily kill. At the wave of his hand, two orange-robed sohei monks opened the door.

The girls blended into the darkness, lying on the ground a dozen yards away, the taller one on the outside protecting the small one next to the wall. The loyalty and the compassion of the larger girl was a profound act of beauty. How much had these girls been through together? he wondered as he walk up to the pair. The tall one scrambled to her feet, bowing, while the other one slept, shivering.

Picking up the small girl, Rennyo was surprised by her lightness. He walked back into the temple to be met at the door of the dimly lit barracks by several of the monks, led by old Arikuni, who had suggested bringing in the girls. Handing his package to one of yellow-robed monks, Rennyo motioned for Hisano to follow him up the narrow stairs.

"Sit. You care about that girl. Who is she? What is she?"

Hisano glanced at the men sitting around the room. *This is Miki's last chance for happiness. If I bring her back to the village, Miki will be allowed to leave again. These are monks, like Miki. No lie can serve as well as the truth at this moment.* "I first met Miki when she was only six. The monks at the North Road temple adopted her when the old miko who brought her to the temple in a thunderstorm died of illness the next day. The warriors from my village protect the temple, and Monk Kukai wanted Miki to have another child to play with. An Ama named Masako took care of my friend and taught her how to be a healer. Miki was very smart and learned very fast. It's a long story."

"We have all night. I want to hear everything."

"Hai. They tell me that Miki has a destiny. Over the years..."

It had been a long night for the exhausted girl, and the monks had allowed her to sleep past midday. Waking up within the walls of the temple building surprised the clueless Miki, who enjoyed her first real meal in days, followed by a bath and a change of clothing. The Ama in the temple, many of whom had joined to escape bad husbands, took interest in this strange, dark-eyed child, and they decided that she would wear the white dress of a novice Ama for now. In this order, women did not shave their hair, nor did they rely on meditation, as had Miki's Zen temple, but instead read the sutras that the temple masters taught.

Miki's ability to read well was astonishing enough, but her ability to recite long sutras from memory earned her a place of honor in the front of the evening's class, removing any doubt that she had been raised in a temple.

"Master Arikuni, where is my friend? I haven't been able to find her all afternoon. I want to show Hisano my new robes. I owe Hisano for all of this. I have never been so happy."

The old man smiled as he stood up and motioned for Miki to walk with him. As they entered the temple's main hall, he stopped before the large gold statue. "My child, today you came home to where you belong. Do you know the second noble truth?"

"Hai, Master Arikuni. Desire and attachment are the causes of unhappiness and suffering. But Hisano..."

"Has gone home to her village. She wanted to leave before you woke up. She knew that you would not want her to go. But your friend does not belong here any more than you belong in her village."

Desire and attachment. She had wanted to share this joy with her very best friend. Hisano had always been there for her. Her friend, her teacher, and her protector—there had never a time when Hisano had not been nearby, within reach. The thought that she might never see her friend again had not occurred to her.

"We made sure she had warm clothing and food. Your friend left with our gratitude. She gave me a message to give to you. Would you like to hear it?" Arikuni watched as silent tears made their way past quivering lips. How many times, he thought, had this girl been punished for simply showing an honest feeling? He pulled the girl toward him, letting her bury her face in his robe to give his little Ama the chance to cry freely, perhaps for the first time in her life. How many times had this child had to say good-bye to someone she loved? The old man could feel his own tears as the quaking child poured out the accumulated sorrow of her short life. "You are home now. I will take care of you."

The early winter snow had forced most activity indoors on this bright but cold afternoon. Even after more than a month in the Ikko Temple, Miki marveled at its beauty and size. The day started early, as it always had at the North Road Temple, but everything was on a much larger scale, from food preparation to the cleaning and repair of robes. They even had a forge for weapons and tools. The Ikko temple was a small town and community that included not just monks and warriors, but craftsmen and merchants as well. Within the walls of the temple there was even a Shinto shrine, complete with priests and *mikos*. This morning's labors had been with women making robes.

Arikuni had led the morning prayers and asked Miki to recite one of his favorite sutras. Afterward she prepared his meal and administered medicines. She had hoped to spend the afternoon reading scrolls from the massive library that the temple maintained, but on this day her teacher Arikuni thought otherwise. Today she would clean the training hall, the school attached to the sohei barracks. Bucket and rags in hand, Miki pushed her way into the large, wooden-floored hall.

Three rows of monks led by Rennyo were going through their drills with perfect precision, shouting with each strike, stomping a foot at the conclusion of the form. With a bow the class was dismissed, and the nine men took their positions lining the training floor. Turning to face the little intruder, Rennyo offered a slight bow. "It is good of you to come. Monk Arikuni has been selfish in keeping you to himself. I hear that you are even helping to teach the younger monks how to read."

Putting the heavy bucket down, Miki bowed, respectfully looking at the floor. "Master Rennyo, I apologize for my behavior before. I was being disrespectful. Master Arikuni told me that you brought me into the temple, and I am very grateful. Please forgive me."

"As I recall, I called you a liar. I now ask for your forgiveness. You have more than proven your worth. All of us are grateful for what you have done for Master Arikuni."

"I should clean, then." Miki watched him turn and walk to the other side of the floor, and one of the other monks handed her a thin bamboo bo-staff. It was light, like the one she had used with the officers from Isawa.

"Do you think that I asked for you so that we could watch you scrub a floor? As I also recall, you offered me a battle. Your friend told me that you even took on three Samurai to save her life once. I can believe that. I have seen your courage. Now show me your skill."

Is he serious? There was nowhere to go; they had moved her bucket. It was strange to be worrying about the bucket at this moment. *What choice do I have?* Walking onto the floor, Miki could feel all eyes on her. Arikuni had told her to do her best, although she had thought that he meant clean the floor well. *Rennyo would not hurt me, would he?*

Twirling the bo-staff to feel its weight and balance, she could feel that this was a superior staff that had been chosen with her in mind. Miki bowed as she dipped the staff to indicate that she was ready.

There is no feeling like standing across from an opponent when life was on the line. Every muscle tensed in anticipation, every sense focused on a single point: the weapon that her opponent would use to kill her. Bamboo clacked, and Miki dropped to the floor, swinging the staff for the ankles, nearly catching the man as he jumped back. Master Akaki had taught her to never give up in the attack, and Rennyo caught her downward blow as she thrust with the other end. Backed up to the wall, he signaled for the match to stop, and the customary exchange of bows followed.

"Excellent! Did everyone see how all of her motions flowed? She continued her attack until she had an advantage. Would anyone else like to try our little monkey?"

It was a long afternoon but a fun one. The bruises hurt as some of the men had forgotten to pull their blows. Still, she had done well in their eyes, and she had earned their respect. She had even won the two-on-one match, as much for her acrobatic skill as for her talent with the staff.

"Your friend also said that you taught the men in her village the use of a sword. She mentioned the Dance of Death. I would like to see that, also." Miki wondered what else Hisano had told Rennyo.

"But Master, I do not have a katana." The practice with the staffs had been enjoyable. They were not generally lethal, which was the reason monks carried them. The katana was nearly always deadly, and that scared her.

"We have katanas. Give her the small one. It is not sharp. We use it for *iaijutsu* practice."

Taking the blade, she held it by her side, as her dress had no suitable obi to take it. Standing at the far end of the hall, Miki swiftly drew the loose blade, dropping the saya, and moved through each cut attack and defense until the last sequence, which required letting go of the handle to reverse the grip so that the strike could thrust upward to the rear. She followed this with the end cut across the middle and walked through the imaginary opponent. In practice she was only able to do it half the time, but the one time she needed it for real, it worked perfectly. This was not practice. While the opponent was imaginary, the eyes of men whose respect she needed made this as real as the fight on the road. Cut, block, flip, thrust backward, stand while cutting, and walk through. As she stood, blade in hand, Miki realized that she had no saya, so she flicked off the imaginary blood and lowered the katana.

"Magnificent. Impressive, particularly for one of your size. Your father taught you that?" Taking the blade, Rennyo put it in the saya and handed it to another monk.

"No, Master. A twelve-year-old boy whose father was Samurai. The boy was brought to me for instruction in religion. The Koga call his father the Mountain Samurai."

"And did you ever meet this Samurai?"

"Hai. Only once. It was when the Mountain Samurai came with his son. I saw him again when he fought and killed Lord Mori no Yoshida in our temple garden. General Satake came and took ten monks to be killed in revenge. It was my fault. I helped Kiyotaka get away, so it was all my fault."

"Your fault for saving the life of a child placed in your care? You were one of those chosen for execution?"

"Hai."

"Your twelve-year-old Kiyotaka led the Koga attack to rescue that Mountain Samurai. And what were you doing when General Satake came?"

"Treating the wounded."

"All of the wounded, from both sides?"

"Hai."

"And yet you stand there ashamed, blaming yourself for acts of compassion, responsibility, and courage. Kindness remembered in gratitude by one of those soldiers a year later. Courage remembered by the man who was to be your executioner. Is that why you work so hard? Is that why you are so reckless with your life, little one?"

"I have no right to be alive. Masako-san died in my place. It should have been me!" A sword through her heart would hurt less than the gaze of so many men, unacknowledged tears rolling down her face.

"So you would deny the woman who raised you the right to a favorable rebirth? This is how you treat her gift to you? How arrogant to believe that any of this could possibly be the fault of you, a thirteen-year-old Ama. Your friend told me that your bravery was well known to her people, but so was your inability to choose your battles, and that is why you needed a bodyguard. Here, I will teach you when and how not to fight. An old man for whom I have great respect is fond of you. You fill his heart in a way I did not think possible. You will walk the way of peace with Arikuni. You have nothing to prove here, nothing to be ashamed of anymore."

"Hai, Master Rennyo. That is all I ever wanted."

Rennyo sipped his tea by the light of the lantern, watching his mentor dip his brush into the small pot of ink. Old Arikuni was proud of his poetry and liked to converse with his students in the evenings, winding useful lessons for each into his poems. Some students dreaded these encounters with the stern master, but Rennyo remembered each of those special evenings over the years with gratitude. Wisdom was a precious gift, and wisdom was the old monk's specialty. It was through Old Arikuni's eyes that he had been forced to look within his own soul, the gift that had freed him to choose a different path. This evening Arikuni had asked for his company.

"What did you say to Little Monkey? She has been a changed girl these past months. I actually heard her laugh this morning, although she tried to hide it. All this week she has been sneaking out to play with the children and to tell them stories when she did not go into town. That dagger she used to keep hidden in her sleeve—she was using it to cut vegetables this morning. She leaves it in the kitchen now." The old man smiled as his brush glided across the parchment.

"Master Arikuni. I need to speak with you about Miki. I believe that I know who she is."

"She is my Little Monkey. A very dear, sweet girl who is the best of my students."

"When I watched her perform with the sword, Miki showed me a form that she could have learned from only one man. My father was a Samurai of the Yorisada clan. He died fighting with Lord Oto. I believed that Lord Oto was also killed in that battle. It seems that I was wrong."

"Little Monkey never knew her father. She grew up in a temple. Surely you do not doubt that."

"No. Lord Oto also had Miki's very dark eyes. It was as if he could see into your heart. He scared me as a child, although he was known to be a kind and fair man. I believe that Oto had a son whom he taught a sword form, the Dance of Death. That son then taught a young Ama in the mountain temple on the north road. Oto was very smart, just like Miki. I believe that Miki was hidden in that temple for her own protection. I believe that Miki is the daughter of the Mountain Samurai whom we have heard news of. I believe that the Mountain Samurai is Lord Oto."

"All conjecture."

"True. But Koga never accept strangers into their villages. They not only protected her, but taught her their art. Why would the Hamatsu execute an Ama, much less a child with ten unarmed monks? Why would the son of Lord Oto teach a strange Ama a secret move that only Oto himself could perform? Indeed, why would Oto seek out that very same girl to teach the words of Buddha to his son? Surely one of the monks would have served better."

"So you are saying that my Little Monkey is a warrior Princess of some kind. Nonsense! Little Monkey is a wonderful child becoming a compassionate and useful woman. And why would that matter to us? She is ours now."

"Why? Because Miki's blood matters. How many fourteen-year-old girls are being pursued by Hamatsu Generals and Iga assassins? I think that they know Miki's secret, a secret that Miki herself does not. Oto and the monks were wise to keep it from her. I am certain that the Koga know also."

"If you are correct, and I do not believe it, then I give the task of protecting my Little Monkey to you. Perhaps it would be safer if the girl does not travel alone. The people in town are quite taken with her, and offerings are up. I have even had a request for Little Monkey's exclusive services from the governor. I had to say no, of course. Little Monkey insists on treating the neediest first."

"Hiding the girl may be impossible. Miki is very pretty and becoming more so each day. No one who has ever looked into those dark eyes can forget them. Worse, travelers speak of the Ama from the mountains. She apparently caused quite a stir in Isawa, and in Yoron, Miki worked as a physician to the poor. That is why her friend could not take her home. The Koga live in the shadows, and Miki cast far too bright a light."

"It sounds as if her friend brought her home, to us."

"I am fond of Miki also, but I believe that there will be a price to pay."

"Then I will pay the price."

Arikuni cleaned his brush, laying it aside as he picked up the parchment to dry it.

> *a little monkey*
> *her spring, an old man's winter*
> *home for the first time*
> *a child of shadow*
> *assassin of death, life giver*
> *drawn to Buddha's light*
> *girl of destiny*
> *walking along karma's path*
> *suffering no more*

Chapter 14 – Choices and Consequences

choices, decisions
inescapable karma
two women, one fate

It was a beautiful early morning on this late spring day in the mountains of Kumi. The fresh, clean smell of water from the nearby lake mixed with the brightly colored blossoms and foliage was magical. The group of acrobats readied their gear for the boat trip to the middle road. The lake was at a high point thanks to the runoff from the mountain snows. For once, thought Hisano, they wouldn't have to walk.

"I wish we had Miki now. The ugly, little, dark-eyed imp is really good at this sort of stuff." Gonji had grown a bit over the rough cold winter and now towered over Hisano, as did the other boys. "Are we going to pick her up when we go through Yugumi?"

He wasn't fooling anyone. Miki was all he had talked about since last fall, when Hisano had left her friend at the temple. "Why would we go through Yugumi? Our mission is to find out why Hamatsu raided the Middle Gate into Ikido. That doesn't take us anywhere near Yugumi or the Ikki Temple. Keep in mind that Satake will be with the soldiers, and he knows Miki all too well."

"Yea, what could the imp have done to make him hate her that much?"

"The brat lived when he wanted her dead." Koan pointed toward the landing where the boat waited.

"Surviving is what Miki is good at. How she got away from those officers was amazing. Why did we leave her in a temple, anyway? Whose idea was that?" Benzo was the oldest now. He also had grown a bit and was now the swordsman of the group. Lean and lanky, he and Koan had trained hard to become not just acrobats, but cold-blooded assassins as well.

"Gonzo knew we couldn't get home with her. Half of Kumi was after her. Did you think that Miki could stop being Miki long enough to get home? Besides, she's better off with the monks. I'm tired of protecting her. I have a life, too, you know." Hisano remembered watching Miki wake up in the temple. For the first time, her friend was truly happy, in a place she belonged, safe from Hamatsu soldiers. Getting Miki was the last thing she wanted to do.

Watching the boatman push off, the boys helping with the poles, Hisano considered their next move. The Hamatsu soldiers probably had Iga help, and there would no doubt be an Iga jonin with Satake, coordinating with his team, making sure they got paid and not sacrificed. Killing him, if done right, might drive a wedge between the Iga and their employers.

The boat ride took most of the morning, cruising slowly down the shore with poles and oars when the water became too deep. There was no reason to hurry, and while walking might have been faster, their target probably had not used this route, anyway. The south road would have been faster and closer to Iga territory. Satake hated these mountains and the dangers they held. No, they would go south or even through the northern pass before crossing the lake and traveling through the forest between the mountains. On this mission, Hisano knew that she and her young team were the afterthought backup. More experienced, more capable teams of tested shinobi handled the northern and southern routes.

The town of Hino was hardly a town at all. It had maybe a dozen or two buildings, and only a few with a second floor. The principal occupation was fishing in the lake, followed by working the ferry and running the two little inns that catered to travelers trading with the mountain villages. It was in one of those inns where Fusa would meet them. Normally quiet, on this day the town was very busy. Hamatsu soldiers were on horseback, and men were everywhere, weapons in full display. This was exactly where she did not want to lead her team. Perhaps she had been wrong. Maybe in spite of the logic of it all, Satake had chosen the middle road.

"Hisano, I don't like this at all. Way too many people, all of them armed and none of them friendly."

"Koan, get our stuff. Gonji, Benzo, help the boatman go back. They haven't noticed us yet, and I think we would do better on the opposite shore. There must be a hundred men."

"About that many on the opposite shore, too. If Fusa is there, she's trapped."

"Fusa will be fine. They seem to have prisoners. We have to know who those prisoners are. I'll go over the side here and go into Hino. The rest of you go to the opposite bank and lay low until tonight. Don't cross until you see my signal. If you don't get the clear signal, return to the village."

"You'll be alone. Why you, anyway?"

"Girls aren't as suspicious. It will be easier for me to find Fusa. Make sure they don't see you get off the boat." Grabbing her bag, Hisano crawled to the fore of the boat, away from the view of the pier ahead. Slipping over the side, she could feel her feet touch the soft, rocky bottom, as the cold water was only waist deep this close to shore. The mission was to find out the purpose of the attack into Ikido, nothing more. Nothing that made the loss of even a single shinobi life worth the risk. The last thing she needed was male heroics.

Slipping and sloshing onto the rocky shoreline, Hisano climbed into the woods to change out of the wet clothing that would make even the stupidest soldier suspicious. Her sword would also have to remain behind, as would the signal lamp. The dagger she would keep, as well as the cord for strangling. Both of those could be explained as something innocuous. The trail ahead would take her into Hino and its two inns. One of the pleasure girls in the smaller inn was Koga, a fact unknown to the rest of the team. Kimiko was from one of the southern villages, and Hisano had occasionally met her to get her report. She had hoped to tell the girl to go home to her village on this trip.

Walking into town, as much of a town as it was, was made difficult by the presence of so many horses and soldiers. Horses were rare in the mountains and nearly useless off the narrow, packed dirt roads that turned to rocky mud when it rained. The military strategy was lost on the trained kunoichi, as the amount of time lost in transporting the beasts across the lake and the multitude of canyons and streams would have made walking preferable. The middle road was a road in name only, and the number of ambush points was beyond measure. Traveling south was impossible from this side of the lake; they would have stayed on the opposite shore had that been their intention. No, the only possibility was the lake road through the North Road pass.

Why so many soldiers? What was so important? The ferry could handle only four horses at a time, and with what she estimated were two hundred horses, getting everyone across could take a day or more. With the force split between the two sides of the lake, this was clearly not going the way Satake had planned it, if indeed anyone had planned it at all. Ahead by the single pier, the ferry—really just a wide barge that had a platform on top for horses and ox-driven carts—was being poled into position. This trip had brought a single horse, apparently Satake's, and a couple of interesting prisoners. This she would have to investigate further.

One of the guards had taken interest in her arrival. "What are you looking at? GET MOVING!" The spear emphasized his concern. Looking around, she saw that all of the town's residents had been herded indoors. She was the only non-soldier on the street. Bowing, Hisano moved toward the inn Kimiko worked at, one of the few multistory buildings.

Several officers were in the building, as well as the middle-aged, bald owner, a particularly greedy man named Ichi; his businesslike wife, whose name she didn't know; and Kimiko with a couple of other girls, all taken no doubt to pay their families' debts. All were standing in line, and all seemed scared.

"Who are you, and why are you here?"

Kimiko spoke first. "That is Hisano. Her father is a fisherman, and Hisano buys sake here."

"Fine, over there."

The officers spoke softly as the inn staff stood silently for what seemed an hour. Finally two prisoners were pushed through the door, hands tied in front, bags covering their heads. The first was a normal-sized woman, the second a child. Both were in beautiful green matching kimonos, all silk, both from Samurai families. The small one was weeping, nearly hysterically so. A normal prisoner would have hands tied behind the back with ropes around the arms. They cared about both the comfort and anonymity of these women.

The officer leading them in pointed to Kimiko, who understood. Kimiko led the pair plus guards upstairs to one of the private rooms where deals were made, and for the girls, deals were consummated. Orders sent each of the girls on one mission or another. Hisano was to bring food upstairs to the prisoners, but not go in. Only Kimiko was to see or speak to the women. This could mean only one thing: that whoever was chosen would either be taken to serve the women or would be killed to keep the secret. Kimiko had been handed a death sentence, a fact that she must have figured out.

Putting the tray on the floor, Hisano called softly through the door for her friend. Through the thin paper walls, Hisano listened to the older woman comforting the girl, probably fifteen and terrified. Mother and daughter, both valuable, from the quality of the language, were most certainly high-born Samurai class. Kimiko took the tray, and as Hisano looked into her eyes, she could see that her friend indeed did understand. She would be isolated from the others. The bastard Ichi had probably traded Kimiko's life for a few ryo. Gold from one monster to another in payment for the life of the woman whose services they would use for the evening. Kinder, perhaps, than killing everyone in the inn.

The inn had built-in sound channels, places to listen to private conversations from other rooms. They were useful for an innkeeper intent on blackmail, a girl anticipating a client's needs, or a shinobi wanting to spy on Samurai plans. Making her way to the kitchen, Hisano sat in the corner, near the tube that Kimiko had installed for this purpose. The others sat in the main area, occasionally running an errand at the request of one of the Samurai officers. The mood changed for the darker as Satake made his way into the main area and accompanied several other officers upstairs. Now she would find out what was going on.

Hisano leaned against the beam, closing her eyes and pretending to nap. The usual greetings were followed by the obligatory call for sake, which one of the other girls answered, and some revealing chitchat. Apparently Yoshida had ordered the raid at the request of his mother. Interesting. Satake didn't know why, but it did present a unique opportunity as he saw it.

"You will leave this evening with Lady O-Kin and her daughter Yumi. Take twenty men and ride hard. Get through the north pass as rapidly as possible and deliver the women to Lady O-Sho at Yoshida's mansion. She has arranged transport to Hamatsu castle. The rest of the men will leave with me tomorrow with the two girls, as I discussed, dressed as O-Kin and Yumi. These I will lead into the middle road pass at a more leisurely pace. My spy within the Koga will arrange for word to reach the Mountain Samurai that these were the two women taken during our raid. What he does not know is that I have positioned nearly a thousand infantry along the road to trap him and his Koga allies. He will not let an opportunity to attack so much horse on such perfect ground go to waste."

"A perfect plan, but why such an effort for Oto? He is only one man."

"The Emperor will not recognize our conquest of Kumi as long as Shigenori is still alive with his army and Oto still fights within its borders. O-Sho has convinced our Lord that taking O-Kin as wife and giving the girl Yumi to Lord Yoshida will strengthen our argument that we are the rightful rulers of Kumi. Shigenori and his sons have to die. I personally killed his younger boy and have his head. I missed the chance for Katsu. Oto would also present a claim if he lives, as would his son."

"And Shigenori? Katsu? I hear that he is now quite a swordsman."

"The Iga will take care of them both and make sure that the blame goes to the Koga."

"And Oto's daughter, the little Ama?"

"According to our spy, Oto is not even aware that he has a daughter. The Koga have hidden that fact from him. When we find her, the Iga will perform that task for us as well. Oto's son is the problem. It seems that he is every bit the leader and swordsman his father is. The Iga are afraid of him. They believe that he speaks to the mountain Kami."

Noise from outside, followed by a soldier storming up the stairs, interrupted the meeting. *Oto's daughter, the little Ama? A spy within the Koga? Who were O-Kin and Yumi? Worse, which two women does he intend to take as decoys? So Miki does have a destiny. This is why Miki is being protected, why her friend was taken into the temple.* No spy is worth anything dead. Now Hisano had to get away. She opened her eyes to the confusion as Satake and several other officers stormed down the stairs and out the door. A guard shoved one of the girls whose name she hadn't learned yet through the door.

"What happened?"

"The boat sank in the middle of the lake. It looks as if they killed a couple of shinobi."

Male heroics; she had left them to their own devices too long. Also, where was Fusa? The other inn? Was she caught? Was Fusa the spy, or was she operating under a separate set of orders? "How, who? Where are the other girls?"

"Kimiko is still upstairs. Suni is getting clothing for the prisoner girls. I feel sorry for them, especially the young one. All she does is cry. They made them take their clothes off. Good for us though; that ugly Samurai general man gave their kimonos to Suni and me." Twirling her hair around a finger, it was clear that the simple peasant girl was unaware that the kimono came with a price. That left Kimiko and her as expendable and possibly compromised if indeed they had a spy. Kimiko's quick explanation of Hisano would have worked against her.

The guard was joined by one of his officers, who motioned to Suni and Kimiko. They made their way down the stairs to join the others. "Go to sleep, all of you. Tomorrow will be a long day for some of you."

What wasn't said was more important.

Peace lasted only a few hours. No one was going to sleep through the crying and complaining of the young girl as they brought the pair down the steps and out the door into the darkness, minus the ropes and bags. Horses galloping away in the darkness confirmed their departure. Getting away was now imperative, for both survival and to save the lives of many of her clansmen.

Not all Koga were shinobi warriors, and very few of the women were kunoichi. Hisano was proud to be one of the few warriors and jonin of her very own team as well, assuming that her team was still alive. Kimiko was neither a warrior nor a kunoichi. She was trained to be a plant, specializing in listening and fitting in. Kunoichi don't cry, a rule that Kimiko didn't have to follow. Sobbing quietly in the darkness sent Hisano the message that she would be on her own when the guards came for them in the morning. Perhaps they would have to make breakfast for the officers first.

First light brought activity to the inn. No one had seen Ichisan and his wife since they had taken payment and left the inn the previous evening. Normally both would be here to give orders and assign tasks to the girls locked in the back room for the night, but this morning they had new masters. The Samurai officers were demanding yet polite. Tea followed the morning meal as it became clear that the army outside was preparing to move out.

"You two, help these two get into those kimonos. You will be coming with us."

Protests and pleading could not delay the inevitable. None of the girls really understood how to properly put on the complex kimonos, so assistance came in the form of officers giving direction. Bags and ropes to bind their hands completed the outfit for the terrified girls, who were then dragged into the street for a public viewing before being placed on horses for transport. If she was going to make a move, Hisano knew it would have to be now.

"Sir? My father sent me for sake. May I take my sake and leave?" Maybe the soldier would simply let her go.

"No. You stay here."

"But he must be worried. I've been here for more than a day. Please can I go home? Please!" She had his sympathy; unfortunately the officer behind him had his fear and obedience.

Kimiko must have figured out that Hisano could do nothing for her as a prisoner. "Sir, Hisano doesn't work here and never saw the Samurai ladies. I promise that I won't remember what they look like also. I really don't know who they are. Really!"

The officer signaled to the remaining soldiers to report for departure with the column, and now they were alone with a single Samurai. As he watched the column leave town, somewhat short of its intended numbers because of the accident with the ferry, he nodded to each commander as they passed, including General Satake. Only one horse remained in town, a fine brown mare in blue-and-yellow livery. Hisano felt the kunai blade hidden in her sleeve. He wasn't in armor; that would make it easier. Her mind raced with possibilities, with tactical solutions. One man, one knife, one chance if it came to that. Two lives depended on her skill.

"Get your sake. I will escort you home and make an apology to your father. What is your name, Kimiko? You will come also."

It was a lie. The sake was a ruse to keep her calm, to make her think that there was hope, to keep her hands busy. He would walk behind and draw his weapon while they were engaged in conversation. It was his way, Hisano thought, of being kind, being merciful.

As they walked along the road north out of town, along the mountain lake to their right, Hisano waited for the moment. The sound of steel sliding along wood, imperceptible, perhaps too imperceptible. If she dropped the jar of sake he would move instantly. Kimiko was silent but frantic. Useless. The man had insisted on the large, heavy ceramic jar for a reason: to keep both hands busy and in sight. She would get one chance, and it would be a poor one.

The road ahead had a short, steep drop to the right into the woods and thick woods to the right. This was the place to make a move. Hisano stumbled a bit closer to the panic-stricken Kimiko on the right, who was struggling hard not to whimper, and pushed the girl off the road and down the embankment. Spinning around and hurling the heavy jar, she managed to catch the sword just clearing its saya. Dropping to avoid the blow, the nimble kunoichi grabbed the kunai—the light throwing blade from her sleeve—and hurled it toward her target, catching him in the left shoulder.

She was defenseless and on the ground. Had her blade found the heart, had it penetrated the gut or someplace vital, she would have a chance. As he raised his blade, she prepared to dodge without any plan better than running away if he missed. For a moment the man held his blade, waiting for her to commit to a direction. Hisano waited for him to start the downward blow so she could dodge.

A blade pushed through her opponent's chest, and blood filled his mouth. Backing away like a crab, Hisano watched as the Samurai officer took one step forward and collapsed, blade handle protruding out of his back.

"Hey, Hisano, you should have aimed for his chest. What were you thinking?"

"Koan, what are you doing here? You weren't supposed to cross."

"Sorry, I didn't know you wanted to die. I can find you another guy to kill you if you want. Hey, great, the sake jar didn't break."

There they were, Koan and Benzo, obnoxious as always. Gonji pushed Kimiko up the embankment. She was still holding the sake jar.

"I heard that you were killed. Did you sink the boat?"

"No...well, kind of. Gonji used that stuff that Miki made last year that burns when it gets wet. It burned through the bottom, and there was nothing they could do about it. What do you want to do with this one? She was trying to run away with the sake. I mean it! If you want to run away, why keep the sake?"

"Kimiko is one of us, from the south village. We need to get ahead of the column and warn Master Kawachi that he is walking into a trap. The real prisoners went north. It's too late to catch them."

"Now what?"

"We have to find Master Kawachi. We have to find the Mountain Samurai and stop them from walking into a trap. The girls they have are just *baishun*, eta like us." Because of an accident of birth, they didn't matter. Two lives that amounted to nothing for either side. Hisano watched Gonji unceremoniously dump the body down the embankment. His sinking the boat would take at least seventy-five soldiers out of the coming battle. Perhaps it was time to reward him.

Never one to waste good sake, Benzo helped himself. "Dressed nice, though. Pleasure girls? We have the sake. Kimiko, why didn't you drop the jar and run faster?"

"Ichi-san will beat me if I break the jar."

"We'll have a talk with him for you." Koan helpfully lightened her load. Hisano wondered how much good these boys would be to her if they drank much more.

"Oh no, Ichi-san is good to us."

"When he's not beating you, you mean."

Hisano could not believe her friend's naïveté. Left as a servant girl for so long, she was useless as a Koga, worthless as shinobi. "Forget Ichi-san. You're going home. Take us to your village. Koan, Benzo, drop the sake and help her. Gonji, his katana is yours now. We have an ambush to stop. I mean drop the sake jar before you empty it."

"Little Monkey has had a hard day. I am going to make her sleep late tomorrow." The old man held his brush in a shaky hand, and for the very first time in Rennyo's memory, his mentor seemed empty of advice for his poem of the evening. Incense cast a smoky cloud around the man, whose mind seemed in as much of a haze.

"What happened? She is usually happy after a day of doctoring."

"A baby was stillborn. Nothing that she could do. The mother was unhappy, but already has three living children, but Little Monkey was devastated. She just held the child for the longest time until the father took it from her. She could not even speak."

"Unfortunate. Your Little Monkey has been here a year, and I still don't understand the girl. In practice she is fearless and skilled, but it is her compassion that conquers all. I fear that it is her compassion that will get her killed."

Turning to face the monk knocking at the door, old Arikuni motioned for the nervous young man to come in.

"Forgive me, Master. There is a man at the gate holding a child. He is begging to see Little Monkey. I told him that she was very tired, but the child, a boy, is very ill, burning with fever."

"Rennyo?"

"I will get her."

"Bring the man in. Also get Monk Ikiro. He has more experience than Little Monkey. "

Within minutes the worried father stood beside the weeping nine-year-old as the older Monk named Ikiro pressed the boy's abdomen, sending the boy into a screaming fit. "I am sorry. There is nothing that can be done. Let me make the boy comfortable, at least."

"No. Please! Let Little Monkey see my Benyo. He's all I have left. Little Monkey can help him. Little Monkey will help him. Please!" *How does one argue with blind hope?* The scrawny farmer had carried the boy for hours to find the person villagers called Little Monkey. Stories had built a legend that no person could live up to, much less the slight, fifteen-year-old woman. Nodding to Arikuni, the old healer reached for the powder that would at least bring the boy some relief as he died.

"Monk Ikiro, may I look at the boy?"

"Ah, Little Monkey. I am afraid that it is too late, even for you."

"Please?" Miki placed her bag on the table. The terror in the farmer's face told her what she was most afraid of.

"There is nothing to be done. Master Arikuni, please let the boy die in peace."

They never believe me. Because I am young, and a girl, they never believe me. For a year, all of then had watched her treat the villagers, always deferring to Monk Ikiro for their own. All except the Temple Master. "Master Arikuni, please let me try. Please!"

"If, as you say, there is nothing to be done, then I must ask that we honor the request of the boy's father. Our agreement was to let Little Monkey treat the villagers, and they seem quite pleased with her. It is up to the father." Arikuni could see that the decision was not sitting well with his old friend.

"Hai. There is a scroll in the library that describes this procedure. A healer woman in the North Temple did this years ago. Perhaps this might help?"

"The healer woman was Masako-san, the Ama who raised me. I wrote the scroll, and Master Kukai had it copied for all the temples. I helped Masako-san, and I know what to do. Please trust me!"

With a father's consent, Miki prepared her tools. The resources of the temple and the gifts from her patients had filled her bag with tools and medicines that Masako-san had never dreamed of. Cleanliness was most important. As she started, Miki could feel all eyes on her every move. Sake to wash her hands and blades, a medicine from China to make the terrified boy numb, and most important of all, a prayer that her skills might find favor with the Kami. She pricked the boy's abdomen to be sure the drug had done its job, and it was time to cut the toxic organ out. With luck, perhaps it had not burst on its own.

"Look at how swiftly her fingers move. I would have expected much more blood, but I see almost none." Rennyo wondered how many times the girl had done this procedure. No hesitation at all. The boy's father stood by his son's head, finding comfort in the girl's gentle smile. He heard the squishy sound of the purplish bit of flesh being dropped into the bowl that might ordinarily be full of rice and watched Little Monkey pick up the silk and needle for the second time and work with her tiny fingers inside the small slit that she had cut. Glancing over at Arikuni, Rennyo watched the old Temple Master glow with pride as Ikiro, the temple's healer, hung on Miki's every move.

"I will spend the night with Benyo. We need to change the bandage often, and I need to get his fever down. We were very lucky today. He needs to stay here for several days."

The old man smiled as he watched Ikiro swallow his pride and offer help to the tired but satisfied girl. Facing Rennyo, he chided his former student: "This was the child you threw out of my temple a year ago."

"An act for which I have asked forgiveness many times. It seems that Little Monkey has an admirer in Monk Ikiro."

"And more than a little gratitude from a farmer. Do you still think that there is a price to pay?"

"Hai. When this farmer tells this story in town, hai. Hiding Little Monkey is not possible. I suggest that we give your favorite student a stronger escort in the future."

"As you see fit."

"Oh come on, Kimiko. You're lost, admit it." It was getting close to nightfall, and they had been traveling all day. Koan had helped the confused, struggling girl keep pace all day. Terrified of her new companions, it was all she could do to hide her tears.

"I'm sorry. All of the trees look the same now. I'm sorry."

Her friend was in a blind panic. Sensing her uselessness, poor Kimiko clearly believed that they would abandon her, a fear not helped by the usual attitude of her boys. Hisano had to keep Kimiko focused on survival. "How long has it been since they brought you to Hino?"

"Five years, Hisano-san."

"Then you have remarkable skills. The village is just beyond that rise. Thank you, my friend." Well, it was certainly a village; Kimiko's village or not really didn't matter. The charcoal smoke wafting through the trees told the kunoichi that it was one of the villages that made steel for weapons. The boys weren't buying the lie, but they did at least get the message to lay off the hopeless girl.

"Hey Hisano, did you notice there are no birds or crickets or any noise at all?"

"You didn't notice that because none of you haven't stopped working your mouth all day. You also missed that someone very good has been tracking us for at least an hour. Last year you were saved by a child with a stick. Who is going to save you now?" Benzo, Koan, and Gonji were the worst examples of shinobi in the clan. Disobedient, careless, and clueless, the three of them worried more about the adventure than the mission. If she had done her job, none of them would be here. These were the boys she had grown up with. None of them had the focus that would keep them alive. Now they just stood there, looking around like the amateurs they were as she pushed Kimiko ahead of her. "Relax. If he had wanted you dead, he could have killed us all a dozen times."

It really wasn't much of a village at all. A large building on a small hill was belching the black smoke where they were making steel. Maybe ten, maybe twenty huts were scattered between the few pieces of land flat enough for small gardens. A larger hut, a mansion by this village's standards, was at the other end of what was visible between the trees. Old men, women, and children just stared at them from the fields and openings in the huts with a mix of fear, curiosity, and, strangely, defiance. Some of them pointed to a small mound near a sign she could not read. Ahead, a little girl and an old man waited along the path for them.

"This is weird. These are really creepy people, Hisano. Maybe we should just look for a different village or sleep in the woods. We're way south of the middle road, anyway. We aren't supposed to be here." Gonji nervously fingered his newly won sword as Hisano rolled her eyes at the thought that these brave boys could be afraid of peasants.

"Quiet. You're embarrassing me."

The wrinkled old man had a pleasant smile. Beside him was a cute child of eight or nine, perhaps, with wide eyes that betrayed no fear. Hisano and Kimiko politely bowed as the old man held the little girl close.

"My name is Gendo. I make swords, and this village makes the best steel in Kumi. This is my granddaughter Aki. Please forgive Aki. She recently lost both of her parents to raiders and no longer speaks to anyone. Can we help you?"

"Hai. My name is Hisano, and we are trying to help Kimiko find her village. We mean no harm, and you have nothing to fear from us. We are also looking for the man they call the Mountain Samurai. Maybe you have heard of him."

"Koga, then. You are among friends. What is your business with my Master?"

"He is walking into a trap. General Satake is entering the middle road from the lake side with horse, but he has already arranged a trap with infantry from the eastern side. The two girls

Satake has are nothing more than pleasure girls from the inn. He must not attack."

The old man thought for a moment before arranging for food and sleep for the boys. Signaling for Kimiko and Hisano to follow him, he led the pair to the larger house away from the village center. Motioning for the women to enter, old Gendo remained outside.

The scraggly, middle-aged figure at the end of the hall sat with his legs crossed opposite old Fusa, who was making tea. Everyone exchanged greetings and respects—without introductions, as none were required—followed by a quick report about Satake's plans, minus a few details.

"Fusa reports that the two women were with the column of horse. Her quick thinking permits us to get ahead of them. The horses will be trapped once they reach the canyon. This is our opportunity to kill Satake and possibly rescue important prisoners. It would be helpful if we knew who they were."

"Lady O-Kin and her daughter Yumi. But they were dressed as peasants, and those two girls are probably through the North Road Pass by now. The girls wearing the kimonos are Suni and Kinu, two pleasure girls from the inn. They aren't worth a single Koga life."

"Master Kawachi, this can't be true. I saw them leave the town."

"You saw what they wanted you to see. It was a show for the whole town. The real women left before midnight. Then they were going to kill Kimiko and me. It is strange that they picked us, the only two Koga in town?"

"Kimiko?"

"Hai. What Hisano-san said is true. Then a Samurai made us carry heavy jars of sake, and when he tried to kill us, Hisano pushed me down the hill, and she fought him." The complete explanation sounded heroic indeed and might have gone on half the evening had Master Kawachi, head of the Koga clan, not stopped it.

Kawachi seemed stunned at first. Stun turned to anger, and he closed his eyes while deciding exactly whom to be angry at. "I don't believe it."

"I do."

A young man's soft but firm voice came from behind. Hisano didn't know when he had entered or how much he had heard, yet she had seen him in her village before. And he was no stranger to Master Kawachi, who must have seen him come in. Challenging the head of a shinobi clan was normally a dangerous move. The thin yet well-built young man carried the two swords of a Samurai, yet he seemed too young to have earned the honor that those two swords granted him. Still, the Koga Master assassin at the head of the room didn't question the boy's judgment. The simple brown cloth of his hakama had been patched repeatedly. It also carried a forbidden symbol, the clan crest of the Yorisada, on his right chest. It was when Hisano looked into the boy's dark eyes that she knew who he was.

"With respect, Master Kawachi. I've been tracking Satake's army most of the day. They've been moving very slowly, stupid even for Satake. Why would an army on horse take the middle way? I saw several Iga with him. The Iga village near the lake is almost empty. If the woman Hisano is right, the Iga will lead their soldiers coming from the east to a place above the best ambush point in the canyon, above where the Koga would be. My father and your people will not stand a chance. The reason they are moving so slow is to give my father time to get into position with your people. Please warn my father and move the clan east toward Hino, away from the canyon. Attack Satake near the lake with the forest at our back. I've already asked jonin Saburo to set traps behind the column as he marches."

The boy had thought it out, except there wasn't a reason in the world for Satake to return to Hino. Who was he to give orders to a shinobi jonin, much less tactical advice to the head of the Koga clan? "Forgive me, how do you know that Satake will go back to Hino? That makes no sense at all."

"Silence. Taka-san is right." Kawachi was swallowing his pride. The boy behind her and the chief of her clan clearly respected each other. "How DO you plan on getting Satake to turn around?"

He was as clueless as she was, yet a smile might be seen as disrespect.

"I am going to take the girls and embarrass Satake."

"But Master Taka, they're just peasant girls. They don't matter."

"They matter to me."

"There are hundreds of soldiers. You'll be killed. You are one of the people Satake wants dead the most."

"There were 123. Not counting the servants, only ninety-nine. Not that many, and they have to get off their horses to follow me. Someone sank the boat, so the best soldiers didn't cross. We only want to kill a few of them so Satake doesn't get hurt. We don't want him replaced, so we can't defeat him too much."

"Taka-san was my student. He is very good at estimates."

"Hai, it must run in the family." Apparently so did his sense of what constituted a fair fight, just like his sister.

"What was that?" Kawachi had been caught by surprise.

A question she couldn't answer with Fusa and Taka in the room. It was a foolish slip. "Master Kawachi, why not kill them all, including Satake?"

"Taka?" Kawachi was proud of his student. He was now suspicious of her.

"Because Satake thinks with his pride. If I embarrass him, he'll abandon his plan and come after me. Anyone they replace him with won't be as stupid and arrogant. That will draw Koga that we can't get the message to away from the ambush in the canyon."

The boy has Miki's ability to plan. Does he also have Miki's ability to survive? He certainly could track and remain hidden. Kawachi wasn't happy with her; the head of the Koga clan was a poor choice of enemies. The boy was very smart; had he caught her mistake? If Taka had, he wasn't letting on. "Master Kawachi, may we speak alone? This is clan business."

With a bow and a wave of Kawachi's hand, the boy excused himself, taking the exhausted Kimiko with him. Fusa sat politely, eyes on the floor, embarrassed by her now-rejected report.

"Speak."

"Master. My friend Fusa should go and find the boys from my village. Benzo and the others will no doubt be happy to see her."

"As you said, Fusa correctly reported what she saw. I trust her. You may speak freely."

The next words out of her mouth would be the hardest of her life. She had known her childhood friend since the day she was born. In the world of shinobi, trust was life itself. Hisano hesitated just a bit, watching her friend's face harden. "Master Kawachi, I'm sorry, but I don't."

Chapter 15 - Taka

into the fire
secrets, suspicions, and lies
miki rides a horse

"Hey, Hisano, what did you say to Fusa? She's really mad at you."
It had been a rough evening, and Fusa's dismissal at Hisano's
insistence hadn't been the worst of it. The sun was now up, and
Benzo stared down at her as she wiped the sleep from her eyes.
Gonji and Koan were in the corner, characteristically stuffing
food into their mouths. "I guess now we go home."

"No. We can't go home. Where is Fusa?" Hisano was almost
surprised that she had been allowed to live through the night,
expecting a visit from her skilled companion Fusa or an assassin
more deserving of Kawachi's trust. No reason to run; if that were
her clan's judgment, escape would be impossible.

"She left with Master Kawachi's people this morning. It's
just us and that kid Samurai guy. You know that dirt mound the
creepy old people pointed at. They say it's twenty heads that kid
took in a fair fight. Personally I don't believe it. He looks kinda
scrawny and weak to me."

Koan, the swordsman of the group, practiced his draw in
the tight hut, nearly dropping his sword before getting it into its
saya. "I bet I can take him. Who is he, anyway?" Competent or
not, Koan at least had his self-confidence.

"He is Lord Oto's son and Master Kawachi's best student. He
tracked us all day yesterday, and you never knew. Ask your father

who he is. He led the fight at the temple a couple of springs ago."
Hisano took the bowl Gonji offered, eating potatoes and the
charred remains of whatever animal Gonji had roasted the night
before.

"So what are we doing today?"

"We are going to help that kid Samurai commit suicide by sin-
glehandedly attacking Satake's army and then rescue two worthless pleasure girls. Then we are going to get 123 really angry soldiers to chase us all the way back to Hino, where we hope to kill
just a few of them. Whatever you do, don't kill Satake. Master
Kawachi wants him to live."

"That's funny. That's what I was telling Gonji and Benzo we
should do today. No, really, what are we doing now?" Koan had
never seen this new Hisano, the one with the sense of humor.

"Get your stuff ready." Stuffing her bag with miscooked foodstuffs, Hisano tossed her sword over her shoulder. They would
get the joke soon enough.

"Guys, I don't think Hisano is joking. She's as mad as Fusa
was last night." She'd never thought of Gonji as the smart one.

"Do we get to keep the girls?" At least Benzo was seeing the
bright side.

"And let me guess: then we have to go find Miki and try to
keep her alive."

"Now THAT would be the hard job! I can handle the soldiers
myself. You take care of Miki."

Pushing her way outside into the morning mist, Hisano wondered how hard they would be laughing when they met their new
jonin. It was hard to ignore the eyes of the peasants watching her
pass. Outside a shinobi village, a woman her age was seldom not
part of a family, and never armed.

There the boy stood with two taller and very fit Koga companions at the edge of the village with no name, at least a name that
anyone called it by. The boy named Taka had probably saved
her life the previous evening by confirming her story. Both of the
boy's companions were older and taller, and each had a long-
bow, an unusual weapon for shinobi because it was impossible
to hide.

"Hisano-san. I thank you for your report yesterday. You saved
the lives of many Koga, and my father's life, too. Master Kawachi

was impressed, and I am grateful." The young Samurai greeted her first, not the expected protocol. He seemed genuine, human even. His silent companions, Koga like her, were less so in charcoal black clothing with their faces covered. Impressed wasn't the impression her clan's leader had left her with. "Did you tell your friends the plan?"

Her companions were less impressive as they arrived to stand behind her, dirty, ragged, undisciplined, and very surprised to see the young man. "Hai, Master Taka. They figured it out on their own. We are eager to serve you and your father."

"That's great. We are going to move fast, so keep up." He nodded to his companion, and they started a jog, one behind the other, as scouts. The boy Samurai picked up the pace, third in the line.

"Ahhh, Hisano? What part did we figure out?"

"All of it. Please don't embarrass me. Gonji, you're next, me, then you, and you."

"Miki, too?"

"All of it." The look was worth the moment. Somehow, the joke wasn't as funny.

"Master Rennyo, I do not need an escort. All of these weapons will frighten the townspeople. I can take care of myself." Behind her stood a ten-man escort, complete with white cowls, naginata, and horses.

"You can take care of yourself? The Temple Master has asked me to provide you an escort. The Governor and his son Uji would like to meet you today, and you need to look your best. It would not do to be covered in dust and dirt when you see Governor Mitsuhide, so today you will ride." Normally fearless, the girl seemed terrified of the small pony, making the animal a bit skittish. Rennyo could not remember a single instance when Little Monkey had ever questioned an order or showed fear.

"Why would the Governor's son want to meet me? Is he ill?" *Why are they smiling at me?* This was her day for treating the villagers, and they would be expecting her to be in town for most of the day.

Little Monkey was no longer the scrawny, malnourished child who had entered the temple almost two years earlier. She had grown into a young woman—and a beautiful one at that, thought Monk Rennyo. The only one who could not see what the child had become, it seemed, was the young woman herself. Master Arikuni had finally been forced to allow the Governor's request to have the woman who had once been an orphan girl meet his son Uji. "After you finish today, we will take you to the Governor's Mansion. He wishes to thank you for all that you have done for his people. You will spend the night there."

Picking her up before she could protest, Rennyo plopped the girl on the saddle and signaled for the troop to mount. It would be an interesting day for his little Ama, he thought as she grabbed the horse's mane. Watching the girl being led away, Rennyo wondered if Little Monkey had ever noticed the inordinate attention the young men paid her.

It was nearly noon on this clear, warm day as Hisano watched well-camouflaged shinobi from maybe six or seven different villages and families make their way east toward the lake through the dark woods. Apparently Taka had given her credit for the warning about the trap, as a few of them had politely thanked the tall girl as they passed.

"They move fast. What's the plan?" Benzo collapsed beside the equally exhausted Hisano next to a boulder overlooking the forested trail known as the middle road.

"They took out the Iga scouts. We have maybe ten bowmen on this side. When Taka-san stops the column, they take out every soldier near the girls, and then we run in, knock the girls off the horses, and take them north as fast as we can." As fit as she thought her team was, they had fallen behind Taka-san and his companions. Running into the well-prepared shinobi from Kawachi's village, Hisano had received her orders. This position put her team where the middle of the column should stop, and in forest too thick for men on horse to follow.

"That's suicide. Why us?" Apparently the joke was wearing a bit thin on Koan.

"We're the only ones without bows. The girls know me."

"We get to keep the girls?" At least Benzo was staying focused on the objective. At least his objective. "Where is the Samurai kid?"

"He's standing alone in the middle of the trail ahead where it gets narrow and rocky, as if he's gonna take them all on." Gonji had arrived first, and Master Taka had sought him out. The two boys were similar in age and size, but the topic of the conversation had bothered Hisano.

"Who does that remind you of?"

"Kinda looks like Miki, too. Did you see how dark his eyes are?"

Even as dense as Gonji and the other boys could be, unless she focused their attention elsewhere, even Gonji might add it up. "Silence. Satake is coming. When I signal, I want Benzo and Gonji to grab the girl farthest away. You grab the other one with me and run straight across the trail, and don't stop for anything. Hand signals from now on." The last thing she needed was for one of these boys to figure out a secret worth their lives.

Most of the column was on foot, leading their horses. The girls were not in the middle of the column as expected, but near the front, which was a problem as it left her team out of position. Signaling for the movement, Hisano and team slipped silently back and along the forest bordering the rocky trail. Several of the bowmen took the hint and shifted position with her and her team. It wouldn't be all the support that she had counted on, but maybe they had a trick or two in that bag of Gonji's. He had grown fond of Miki, but even fonder of the girl's tricks of the trade. A touch to her eye and his bag had produced two remaining little bundles, not terribly destructive, but good noisemakers. Normally a spark would be required, but her friend Miki had figured out how to make them self-detonate, now a cherished clan secret in the village her friend had once called home.

Horses wouldn't like noise, nor did they like the smell of the boy blocking their path as the lead soldiers lost control of their mounts when the boy stepped forward, accompanied by a rather large wolf. Wolves terrified Hisano. Wolves terrified everyone living in the mountain villages—all except Miki.

"Where is the coward Satake? Is he so ugly that he has to steal girls from the inn? Suni and Kinu want to go home. After I take them I'm going after the others. Maybe my father already has them. He's already behind you, moving fast." The young, ragged Samurai's head tilted forward. His left hand was on the saya, ready to draw, his conical straw hat hiding his face. He was smaller than any possible opponent, three of whom slowly approached him with swords drawn, working to each side and his front.

The boy had used the information well. It made going forward a waste of time and threatened Satake's primary objective. The wolf made the use of horses in this fight impossible. Satake sat astride his large mount well ahead of the still-hooded girls.

The nervous men attacked as Taka's blade flew out of its home, cutting the man to the left nearly in half. Ignoring the attacker to his front and dodging the wolf racing past him, the boy flipped the blade in a move that all of them had seen before, thrusting the sharp blade into the chest of the man who was nearly behind him now. He stepped forward and went to a single knee as his opponent's blade slid down the boy's katana, opening the hole that allowed Taka to gut the man as he walked past, ready for the next set of challengers.

This was the moment, as every eye was on the fight ahead and Satake as the vicious animal smacked into the General's chest, knocking him off the panicking horse that had already lost its footing. Four men fell as rapid-fire arrows left the clueless women alone on leaderless horses. Moving at a dead run, Hisano caught one of the falling girls, nearly knocking her down as well. Two loud explosions with sparks and hissing made all of the nearby horses uncontrollable as Koan grabbed the other screaming, terrified woman. Benzo grabbed hers, the strong young man easily tossing the squirming girl over his shoulder as he climbed the small slope on the other side of the trail.

The operation had taken not even a minute. Getting as deep into the woods and away from the ambush was now their only thought. Shouting and sounds of horses faded as the four shinobi pushed two confused girls north, away from the battle.

"We got lucky. Did you see that kid? His sword moved so fast I couldn't even see it."

"And we get to keep the girls. Can we keep them, Hisano?"

They had done well. None of them knew what was happening behind them, and it didn't matter because they had done their part and lived another day. All she could do was smile while the boys kidded and played as they always did with each other as they moved through the forest, boasting and enjoying the moment.

The next mission would be more difficult.

"We are looking for a little girl who was left at the temple a couple of years ago. Her name was Miki. She was plain and very scrawny. She liked to help people." Hisano looked at the older woman running the shop attached to the large warehouse. This woman had two daughters, and if anyone would know about her lost friend, these people would. "I am from her village and was curious if she had been adopted."

"I don't remember any child named Miki. I can ask Ama Little Monkey or Ama Tomoe. They live at the temple, and they would know. I will ask Ama Little Monkey to speak with you." Shuffling through the small doorway, she made her way into the back part of the warehouse that the Ama used as school and as a place to treat the sick. On this day, however, it was being used as a school for the town's younger children.

"Ama Little Monkey? Please forgive the interruption. Have you ever heard of a little girl named Miki? A woman out front is asking."

"Miki? That is a name I have almost forgotten. Miki was an orphan girl who was abandoned at my temple two years ago. Miki was a very sad and very angry little girl and very afraid. She died that day at the temple because all her friends had left her, and in her misery, she could not go on. Miki was reborn and now is much happier. I should speak to your customer."

Old Tomoe had a funny feeling about this sudden interest in a dead child. "No. You need to continue your lessons with the children. I will speak to her." Tomoe and Orin headed toward the shop to leave Little Monkey alone with the children.

As Tomoe and Orin entered the shop, Hisano signaled to Benzo wait outside.

Orin took the coins Hisano offered in exchange for some of the candies and a small cooking pot. "I've spoken to Ama Little Monkey, and she remembers the girl you speak of. She says that this girl named Miki died that very same night that she arrived at the temple of great sorrow because all her friends had abandoned her, and was reborn."

Thanking the woman and bowing to the Ama, Hisano made her way into the street, handing the candies to Benzo. "We're too late. Miki is dead. I didn't think anything could kill that girl, but I was wrong. I shouldn't have left her here after all."

"So what do we do now? What do we tell Gonji?"

"Fusa is a servant at the Yoshida mansion now. I think it's time to become yakuza in the River District. We may need to kill Lady O-Kin and maybe that crybaby Yumi to keep them from being used by the Hamatsu. But, for now, let's just get back to the boat."

Tomoe watched the tall, brownish-haired woman leave and wondered about their true purpose. Making her way back into the warehouse, she watched Little Monkey go through each brush stroke in the symbol for mountain. Little Monkey watched each of the fifteen children make the character in the air before allowing brush to hit the paper, the sweet, young Ama giving each whatever praise and help she could. This was a happy time for all. "Ama Little Monkey, you said that the child Miki was reborn. What was she reborn as?"

"A little monkey, of course. What did they want, Ama Tomoe?"

"Nothing. Just curiosity about a story they heard."

Chapter 16 - Uji

spring, a time for love
impossible destiny
brief moments of joy

The two old men faced each other over tea, engaged in the duel of words that both had come to enjoy. The late afternoon sun sat low on the horizon to the west, its light carried in by the gentle, steady breeze that found its way through the large, second-floor windows. For the last several months, the topic had been the same. The older woman pouring the tea dismissed herself with a bow, leaving the warriors to continue the verbal battle.

"Monk Arikuni. Surely you can see the effect the girl has had on the townspeople. Officer Mitsuo tells me there is no more crime, and his officers are bored. Carrying my drunk son Uji home seems to be their only remaining job. Your Little Monkey is educated, intelligent, and very popular with the people. I believe she would prove a useful wife for Uji, and it would be a great opportunity for Little Monkey." The governor sipped his tea and stared into the face of that bald-headed old statue with his polite smile. "Little Monkey will need a new name."

"It's the name she took when she became Ama in my temple. In the temple where she grew up, they called her Amanojaku;[13] that would hardly be better. Uji is what, nineteen? No two people

---

13 Amanojaku – Imp from heaven, commonly used to describe someone who is contrary.

could be so different. You may find that Little Monkey can be a handful. It is unlikely that they will like each other, at least at first. The young man is a problem that I do not believe that even my capable little Ama can solve. He is restless, arrogant, and, like too many young men, in search of undefined glory." Still, to have a former Ama as the wife of a Daimyo would be useful for the Ikko order, thought Arikuni.

"Uji will do as he is told. He will marry a woman who can be useful. Uji will learn to take his duties seriously. All he ever thinks about is his own pleasure and his skill with the katana. He is a father's nightmare. Uji is unfocused, undisciplined, and lazy. No Samurai family will allow their daughter to marry him."

"Simply getting the boy a wife will not change this. Little Monkey has no family, no history at all. If Uji indeed becomes the heir to the clan, Little Monkey's missing past will be a serious problem." And the past that he knew of might prove a serious liability. The old Temple Master could see his friend struggle with his options.

"Little Monkey must have a family somewhere. If she is truly an orphan, then you can make the decision for her. She will obey you. We can give the girl a past."

"She will, but it would destroy my Little Monkey. The temple is her home, and she thinks of the other monks as her family. This is a decision she will have to make herself. Perhaps a different strategy is called for. We should let nature do this work for us."

"What are you saying?"

"Let Little Monkey instruct the boy in religion and Chinese strategy. You have already told me how impressed you were by her knowledge. Uji could instruct the girl in the katana. Monk Rennyo tells me that the girl already has some talent. She is a master with the staff and teaches the naginata to the other Ama. Every third day we will put Uji and Little Monkey together and wait. She is pretty, and he is a good-looking young man when he is not drunk." His Little Monkey needed time, and Arikuni watched the Governor consider the wisdom of his words as he finished his tea.

They heard the soft sound of a woman's foot on the stairs, followed by the polite announcement that both his son and the young woman, a favorite visitor in the Mitsuhide household, had arrived.

"We will see them downstairs at once. Also, see to Ama Little Monkey; she must be hungry and will be spending the night. Tell Uji that I require his presence immediately. It seems that Monk Arikuni will allow Ama Little Monkey to instruct your brother Uji." The excited acknowledgement told Governor Mitsuhide that this was going to be a pleasing edict, at least for the rest of the family, including all three of his daughters. Uji would be a different story.

"Ama Little Monkey, I thought that you were going to teach Master Uji today." The merchant had allowed her to use a portion of the large warehouse for her work. His wife, Orin, enjoyed working as her assistant, especially on days when Little Monkey treated the sick.

"Hai. I waited, but he did not come. So I decided to teach instead. All of the children have learned so much and worked so hard! I am so proud of them all. Even your two wonderful daughters. I need to leave soon, or I will not be able to reach the temple before dark. Master Arikuni gets so upset."

"I don't see why you insist on teaching girls, too. They need to be helping their mothers at home. Still, they do so love learning from you."

Answering the knock at the door revealed one of the girls from the Honeypig Inn, bleeding from a cut on her face and what would become a serious black eye.

"What happened? Who did this to you? Sit down here and let me take care of that."

The girl was crying so hard it was hard to understand her. "The Governor's son and his friends are drunk, and they are mean. Kao was going to get married next week, but who will want her after Benkei and Mitsu have had her?"

"Where are the officers?"

"Gone. Chasing thieves."

"I will take care of this. Please take care of her, Orin-san."

"No Ama, no! They'll hurt you too."

Grabbing her staff, Little Monkey ignored their protests. The Governor had given her a responsibility, and Uji's first lesson would be respect and discipline. Making her way down the street and through the curtain that hung over the door of the town's largest drinking and gambling den, the smell of sake, sweat, and men nearly overpowered her. In the corner was Master Uji, drunk, struggling with a girl he had pulled onto his lap. Three other Samurai were engaged in mischief, each with a tavern girl and bottle.

"Master Uji. Your father the Governor has assigned me the task of teaching you philosophy and the words of Buddha. I would not think that hygiene would need to be our first lesson, but if you insist."

"Ama, no! He's the Governor's son."

"And I am his teacher. Master Uji needs to leave now. Go home, Kao. I am told that you will be married soon." Little Monkey watched the thin, twenty-year-old farm girl old pull away from the confused, besotted man, pushing through the curtain to her escape. As Uji struggled to focus on his petite instructor through the sake haze, Little Monkey continued the lecture. "It is customary to bow before one's lesson."

THWACK! The bamboo staff found its mark on his topknot, sending the boy reeling. "And which of you brave men is responsible for the girl with the black eye in my school?"

"What are you? Who do you think you are? I am Benkei!" There were three of them, and one on the floor. A room full of drunk and enraged Samurai being a poor place to be, all of the girls took the opportunity to be elsewhere.

The crowd gathered outside, concerned for the welfare of their little Ama, entertained by the description of the fight inside. A staff to the throat followed by one to the groin, shouts, shattered porcelain, threats, all described for a cheering crowd.

"What's going on here?"

"Officer Mitsuo. Ama Little Monkey is fighting four Samurai. Well, only two now. But they have swords."

"I'll put a stop to this."

"In the forty-three years I have been in charge of this temple, not once has a monk been brought before me by an officer for an act of violence. Stop biting your lip and look at me. You are a sixteen-year-old, Ama! What were you trying to do?"

"Teach Master Uji about respect."

"Sir Uji was involved? He saw this?"

"Hai. But he was drunk. I do not know how much he will remember. He was mostly unconscious."

"You fought Master Uji? Officer Mitsuo?"

"Ama Little Monkey was defending the honor of the girls in the inn. One of the girls was beaten badly. The Ama had defeated two of the men, who were unconscious, and the other two were begging for mercy. The townspeople have paid for the damages, and the men are too embarrassed to report it. I consider the matter closed. It was quite a sight."

"Thank you, Officer Mitsuo. Ama Little Monkey, I will consider the matter. Until I make my decision, you will not leave the temple grounds. Now go." Arikuni watched the small young woman shuffle off into the waiting arms of Ama Tomoe, who would counsel the girl further.

"Master Arikuni. I consider the girl's actions honorable but ill-advised. She will need protection."

"But certainly no more training. Monk Rennyo may be proud of his student, but this girl makes as many enemies as friends. I am very fond of her, but Little Monkey will be the death of me someday."

"Does Ama Tomoe need to be here?" The old woman just stared at him from the corner, Little Monkey's bag and staff beside her.

Uji wondered how long she could go without blinking, moving, or smiling. Did the creepy old Ama ever smile at all?

"She is here to make sure that I behave. Master Arikuni will not let me carry my staff anymore around you." Little Monkey was always so formal and focused, polite and proper. That was, of course, except for the time the little demon had gone berserk in the Honeypig Inn. Never did she look him in the face. Not once had those dark eyes ever been allowed to meet his, except at the moment in the inn when her staff had made its point.

"So he thinks I need protection from a girl half my size. I find that insulting." Did she know how beautiful she was, he wondered.

"Let us begin. About a thousand years ago, there lived a Chinese General named Sun Tzu, who wrote a book about strategy." Why was he staring at her so intently? This was the first time she had seen the man without the smell of sake and sweat. He was clean for once.

"Was he a Samurai?" Little Monkey ignored his stare. *Does she ever think about anything but work?*

"No, Master Uji. Samurai are Japanese." *How can he not know that much?*

"So why do I care?" She was biting her lower lip. *Is she getting frustrated?*

"Some day you may lead a great army in battle. You are the nephew to Lord Suwa, Daimyo of Yugumi Province. He has no other heir, and your father wants me to prepare you. You need to know about things like formations and strategy if you are to take your rightful place." There it was in her voice, just the faintest twinge of defiance. This was not where she wanted to be. The old oni in the corner heard it also and cast the young girl a disapproving glance that Little Monkey understood. Still, no apology. He was beginning to like this girl.

"That's why I have Generals. What is your name?" He was probing.

"Ama Little Monkey. Sun Tzu wrote that..."

"Your real name. The one your father gave you."

"I had no father. Sun Tzu wrote that if you know your enemy and you know yourself that in a thousand battles you will never be..."

"Everyone has a father. Then what did your mother call you?"

"I barely remember my mother. Never be in peril. In his first book he speaks of five laws. The first is the Moral Law. That is the Law that makes the people in harmony with their leader, and that is our first lesson."

"You were raised by someone. They had to call you something."

"Pay attention, please, Master Uji. My old temple called me Amanojaku. My name is Little Monkey now. My name does not matter. I do not matter. You do."

"I don't like that name. Is it true that you were a Koga shinobi?"

"Women are called kunoichi. Choose another name if you like. Maybe the best way to learn about the Moral Law is to learn about the people. We can do that best in town. Come to town with me. I have patients to visit. We can speak while we walk and I work." He was not paying attention. At least she would be able to see her friends. Ama Tomoe handed her the medical bag but declined her the staff. *What does she think I will do with it?*

Evening brought a cool breeze, foreshadowing rain from the darkening sky. Little Monkey had visited a dozen homes, greeted warmly in each as though a member of the family. "You have been working all morning and afternoon for strangers. Why?"

"None of them are strangers. I know them all. Even if I did not, they would still be friends."

"None of them paid you."

"I am Ama; they donate to the temple when they can. They also fed us."

"You did not eat."

"I am Ama; I do not eat after noon." The knock at the door brought in two familiar faces, the black-and-blue face of the girl from the Honeypig Inn and Kao, the Uji's favorite serving girl. Both stared at the floor, made uncomfortable by Master Uji's presence. "Please let me see that eye. It is going to get worse before it gets better. Your face may even turn a bit green in spots. How is your vision?"

The skin was still tender and the whole area black-and-blue. She glared at Uji as Little Monkey probed and cleaned her face. "Thank you for helping us a few days ago. I'm glad you hit that monster Benkei really hard. He still walks funny."

Uji watched Little Monkey's gentle hands redress the wound while her patient shot hatred at him with every glance. "I did not hit you."

"But you did nothing to help her, and that was worse. Sir Benkei was an animal. Our lesson today was Sun Tzu's moral law, the law that binds its people to its leaders. People expect that their leaders will protect them. That is why those of your class enjoy the privilege and luxury that you do. Misa here expected just a small bit of compassion. Poor Kao just wanted to be pure for her new husband. Did you earn their respect? Did you earn their loyalty? Why would an invader not be greeted rather than opposed? In what way did you serve your father, and Lord Suwa, in securing the loyalty of their people?"

They loved the girl, and now the young man could see why. Little Monkey had risked death for them. By every right, the Ama's head should have been forfeit, and if not for the support of an angry crowd, it might have been. Watching the women leave with a bow, Uji wondered if Little Monkey had planned their encounter. She certainly had made her point. Little Monkey had done that day what he should have. Perhaps the pretty Ama knew more about what it meant to be Samurai than he did.

"That is enough for today. I will return in to the mansion in four days. Our lesson will be Sun Tzu's principles of heaven and earth."

"It has been three months since Little Monkey has been seeing Master Uji. Has the girl spoken about the boy at all? According to Governor, his son Uji talks about nothing else but Little Monkey." The old monk sipped his tea, surrounded by his brush and paper. This evening belonged to Ama Tomoe, who had been given the task of escorting the pair in their visits.

"Not a word to me or anyone else. It is as if he does not exist at all. She speaks of the people she treats, the Governor's daughters, and the children in her school, but never Master Uji. I wonder if Little Monkey sees the boy as someone she cannot have."

"And the boy?"

"He watches her constantly and works hard to please her. But every time he tries to open a door for the child, Little Monkey becomes more formal, more polite, more focused on her lesson of the day. If she does not begin to respond to the boy soon, he will begin to lose interest in her."

Was it that she just did not like Uji, the old man wondered, or was it something else? "I think that for the next meeting, it will be safe for Little Monkey to go alone. She knows that you and I speak often. Perhaps that knowledge keeps the girl from behaving naturally in front of you."

"Do we want her behaving naturally? I am there for Little Monkey's protection. She has many friends, but it is her enemies, particularly that Benkei and Mitsu that Uji hangs around with, who worry me."

"The girl took on four Samurai. It is not Little Monkey I am worried about protecting. No, let us watch what she does when she thinks that no one can see. Let's give Uji an opportunity to show Little Monkey who he is. She is Ama. What kind of trouble can she possibly get into?"

"I will inform her, then."

The trip without the old woman was faster, and she had arrived at the mansion very early. The early arrival had given Little Monkey a chance to speak with several of the Governor's advisors about all sorts of interesting things, from irrigation techniques in use in China to bridges that moved out of the way of boats.

Late as usual, Uji was his normal, pleasant self. "Where is stoneface?"

"Ama Tomoe is very tired today. We will have to learn without her. Today's lesson will be the eightfold noble path. I had been concentrating on military strategy to please your father, but..."

"No."

"Then you do not wish me to be here. I will go."

"I did not say that. You have been teaching me. It is time you spent time in my world. Take a day off."

"Ama Tomoe would not..."

"Ama Tomoe is a stone-faced old oni and is not here. What would Little Monkey like to do? Let us have some fun today."

"I can not. They would disapprove."

"And you always do what they want."

"Hai. Hai. If I did not, then..."

"What? What would happen if Little Monkey just had fun? How do you do it?"

"I do not understand."

"Hai, you do. Why? is my other question. Who is Little Monkey, really? How does Little Monkey live up to everyone's expectations all the time? Why does Little Monkey try so hard?"

"You cannot understand."

"I am the nephew of the Daimyo, a great warrior. I am probably the next heir, and everyone expects me to be everything you are, only a man, and I am tired of it. How can you always live up to everyone's expectations?"

Maybe he did understand. "It is hard. Sometimes I am so tired. If I do not, they will not want me. If I do not, I will die. I am trouble because many people want me dead, and I do not know why. I am just an orphan from a small village." Uji was Samurai, from a great family. It had never occurred to her that he might be feeling the same pressure she was. "I am afraid of being alone. I am afraid of never belonging anywhere. I was banished from my village, from my own mother. I was banished from the North Road Temple and my Koga clan. I do not know why. I am afraid that I will be banished again. I have nowhere else to go. Who wants a homely little peasant girl?"

Why would anyone want to kill her? How many peasants could read and write and teach military strategy to Samurai and cure disease? The tears in the young woman's eyes told her that he had hit his target. "You are not a homely little girl. I do not think that you ever were. Walk with me."

The short trip into town came with a side trip through the peach orchard with its small Shinto shrine. Questions and answers, the life of a Samurai and life in a Buddhist Temple. Lives of rules, restrictions, duties, and special codes of honor, different only in their particulars. Now, for a day, they were free of the expectations both had come to find uncomfortable, burdensome. Most interesting to the young man were Little Monkey's descriptions of her training as kunoichi. They were exciting and revealing, a look into a world that no one outside those mountain villages could possibly understand.

Little Monkey showed the young Samurai her shortcut over the rocky hill that cut between town and the temple, including her favorite spot, where she could see both. She showed him rocks where she practiced balance and even where bandits and shinobi might choose to launch an ambush and how they might do it. Afternoon turned into evening as they made their way back into town.

"I cannot let you go back to the temple in the dark. I forbid it. Spend the night in the mansion. You have your medicine bag there, anyway."

She was exhausted, and the boy was being protective, the first time he seemed to actually care about anything beyond himself. Still, it had been wonderful day, and the long trip back to the temple not inviting. This time, Little Monkey would have to let the boy win.

"I am hungry, and I know you must be also. Let us stop by the Honeypig. You have never seen it after dark. It gets more exciting, and you have more Samurai to beat up." Now he was playing with her. Still, neither of them had eaten all day, and she was thirsty also. If she was to serve her people, maybe this was a side of life that she needed to see.

The inn was crowded and the clientèle rougher than she had ever seen. In the corner a group of men sat on tatami mats playing some sort of game with dice. The smell of men was overpowering. "Master Uji, I have no money."

"You are my guest. Do not worry about it."

The meal was unique. Spicy and tasty in an awful sort of way, it was nothing like the simple meals of the temple. As bad as the food was, although it didn't seem to matter to Uji, the water was worse.

"Try this. Sake. Just a taste. They are out of plum wine."

"Tea, then?"

"Sorry." It would be interesting to see the little woman drunk. One or two cups would at least help her to relax. It was unlikely that anyone had ever seen an Ama in a gambling and pleasure den, and she seemed nervous, on edge. Shouting and the usual disagreements from the other side of the room had caught her attention, and the scene of two men beating up one of the gamblers, a farmer, sent the indignant little Ama to her now-shaky legs. Uji had never seen that little sake have so much of an effect on anyone. Whatever the girl's strengths, holding her sake was not one of them.

"I'm tinking, thinking, that that isn't, is not, very nice. I teach his son and he, what's your name, is a very, very, very good father. Please do not hurt my friend here."

The sight of the drunk little Ama using her staff to stay on her feet amused the men, who dropped the bloody-faced farmer on the floorboards. "Your friend bet with money he didn't have."

"We kill men for that."

"Can I play the game? What is it called?"

The greasy men looked at one another and laughed.

"Do you have any money?"

"No, but Master Uji-san does. He is a great Samurai, and he is my friend. Uji, can I borrow some money?" These were not the sort of men you trifled with. The wiser move might have been to get her out, abandoning her farmer friend to his well-deserved fate. It would be fun to see what she did with a few ryo.

"The game is *cho-han*. You have to guess if the dice will be even or odd. If you guess exactly what the dice show also, you win all the money and don't have to share it with the others who guess like you. But since this is your first time, you will play against the dealer, which means that if you guess the numbers exactly, you win double. If you don't guess correctly, you lose, and we beat your farmer friend to death and take your money."

"And all I have to guess what the number on the little wooden blocks have on them? That's easy. Buddha will help me." Little Monkey placed one of the oblong coins on the mat in front of her, trying to sit up as straight as she could in front of the half-naked man with the cup and dice. Displaying the dice, he tossed them into the cup and slapped the cup onto the mat.

"Cho or han? Even or odd?"

"It is two and three, han. You have beautiful tattoos." He was covered from his neck down to his waist in colorful dragon tattoos. Uji closed his eyes. It was stupid for the girl to try to guess exactly.

"A winner. Does Buddha get a cut?" The dealer revealed the dice and glanced over at the boss sitting at the small table in the corner.

"Does that pay farmer-san's debt?"

"No. He bet with money he didn't have. I'm doubling what he owes us. Take your money and leave. Consider it a donation to the temple."

"If you kill the farmer, little Benyo will be an orphan like me. We will go again." Putting all of the money on the table in front of her, the foolish, drunk little girl smiled as the naked man with the pretty dragon tattoos performed his ritual again, slapping the cup onto the mat.

There were three rho on the table, the one she started with and the two she had won. Uji knew that she could not guess exactly right again. "Little Monkey, listen to me. Just guess even or odd. Don't try to guess exactly."

"Do not worry. It is nine, a three and a six. Can't you hear it?" Uji couldn't believe Little Monkey's stupidity. This would be the last round.

"The Ama wins again, a three and a six. Odd seems Buddha's favorite." Another glance at the boss at the end of the mat.

Uji could see the boss of the gang getting concerned. Other people were beginning to take an interest in Little Monkey's run of luck. "Let the farmer go. His debt is paid. Keep the money, all of it. Little Monkey, it is time for you to go home. "

"Except for your coin, Uji-san. I have to pay you back."

"Not so fast. No one guesses that right. How did you do it? How did you cheat?"

"Your dice, your dealer. Ama Little Monkey never touched the dice."

The greasy, middle-aged boss considered Uji's words. It was bad luck to kill an Ama, and the Samurai was armed. Either way, he ended up with the money. No need to irritate the Governor by fighting with his son.

"Let the farmer go. But you still have one ryo on the table. Care to go again?"

"No. The Ama has to leave."

"Hai, cho-han is fun." The girl belched once and smiled. All Uji could do was let her throw the coin back onto the table.

Once again the tattooed man performed the ritual and slapped the cup onto the table. "Cho or han? You have done well with han so far, little Ama."

"Except that when you just switched the dice, the new dice only had even spots. Since it is impossible to have odds with only even spots, cho, a pair of fours. The other dice were under your thumb. You tossed them under your ankles."

Uji reached for his sword as all of the patrons reached for whatever weapon was handy. How many farmers, merchants, and Samurai had been taken by these crooked fools he could not know. He himself had lost many ryo over the last year. Cheating was the only unforgivable crime, and Little Monkey had caught them cold.

"Never in the forty-three years I have been in charge of this temple has an officer had to bring one of my monks before me for an act of violence."

"There was once." Little Monkey knew at once that this was the wrong thing to say. Her head pounded like a sword maker beating out his creation. *Is this what men go through when they get drunk? Why do they do it to themselves?*

"Silence! Gambling? Drinking? Officer Mitsuo tells me that he found you fighting in the street surrounded by maybe ten yakuza? You were fortunate not to be killed. You were supposed to be here, sleeping! Governor Mitsuhide will be here today. What do I tell him? I can no longer trust you to teach Master Uji. I no longer trust you to represent this temple in town. Now I have to decide if I can trust you to wear those robes at all." Master Arikuni trembled with those last words, almost as hard as his terrified little Ama. "Ama Tomoe is waiting outside. Go with her."

"Master, there were reasons." The last two years since her arrival had been the best of her life. This was tearing the man she respected the most apart. The shame was unbearable.

"Go."

She turned, and the door slid open, leaving the little Ama face to face with Uji and Governor Mitsuhide waiting to see Master Arikuni, as the grim Ama Tomoe was motioned for her to come. Facing the other Monks and Ama would be worse than death.

"Governor. I cannot begin to express my sorrow..."

"For what? My son Uji told me of the girl's heroism. It would be best for Uji to explain."

"Master Arikuni. Little Monkey wanted to return to the temple before dark, but I ordered her not to. The trip to the Honeypig Inn was my idea, and she was obeying me. Little Monkey only had one cup of sake because they did not have anything else to drink, and I told her to. I never saw anyone get drunk on only one cup. I did not think it possible. She is cute when she is drunk."

"Little Monkey is very small."

"Hai. The gambling was to save another man's life. She called him Benyo's father. I gave her the money, and she was amazing. It really was not gambling the way Little Monkey did it. The fight did not start until she caught the dealer cheating and exposed him. And the fight in the inn and in the street, she was trying to protect me. None of this was Little Monkey's fault. It was mine. She saved my life." Uji looked into the old monk's eyes and thought about the wreck of a woman who had just pushed past him a few moments earlier. Never had he considered the consequences to Little Monkey. "This temple is Little Monkey's life. She has honored you and this temple with her conduct. I beg you to let her stay."

The old monk considered the boy's words. To his knowledge, Uji had never taken responsibility for anything before.

One thing was clear: Uji the man cared about Little Monkey the woman. "I need to speak with your father first. Please bring Ama Little Monkey here."

Uji bowed and left to seek out his partner in crime, leaving the two old men alone.

Matsuhide sat beside Arikuni, who had been looking for a way out of dismissing his best student. "There is something very different about that young woman. Did you notice that Little Monkey and Uji fought together against terrible odds? Did you see how he just fought for her now? My friend Arikuni, your plan to get them to love each other is working better than I could have hoped for. The men they fought were gangsters, and we are running them all out of the fief now. Once again she has done Yugumi a great service."

"What are you suggesting?"

"Let Little Monkey believe that Uji's words saved her. It will bind them closer. I will offer her a chance to relax at the mansion. The walk from the temple is too long for an Ama with enemies, anyway. Let her wear her robes and work in the town. My advisors are asking for time with Little Monkey. This is a good excuse."

"So be it."

"Look at the snow, Ama Little Monkey! It is so beautiful." Twelve-year-old Edako bounced on the balls of her feet as her friend made her way out of the Crane room. The meeting had lasted all morning, and poor Little Monkey had been the center of attention for all of it. Now, nearly noon, it had adjourned to give the woman a chance to eat, as she could not do so afterward.

"It is far too early in the season for this. This snow is wet, and it may cause buildings to collapse. I should go into town and help the people."

Lord Mitsuhide, following the other ministers and advisors out of the room and overhearing this, instructed the child to have the servants prepare a meal for his youngest advisor. "Ama, I thank you. Your work over this past season has saved lives and increased our treasury. Your drawing of a bridge that can move has Minister Toyotomi very excited, but it is very unpleasant outside and quite dangerous. I must insist that you stay here today."

"Respectfully, my Lord, my place is with the people. Even Master Uji is in town helping to keep the snow from damaging the rice storage. People will be hurt, and they will need a healer. They expect me and depend on me. Please, my Lord. It is who I am, what I am."

Mitsuhide could feel the girl's desperation to be of value. She was immensely popular with the people, and his support for her had translated to a very happy and productive fief and a very happy older brother. And it placed Uji in an excellent position to be named heir to the clan. Still, he felt concerned that the girl could not see herself as anything more than a servant. "Very well. I will send Benkei and Mitsu with you. But nothing dangerous. If you get hurt, Monk Arikuni will curse my family, and Uji would never forgive me."

It wasn't a walk to the town as much as a wallow through the wet, heavy snow. By evening the temperature would drop, and it would be pure ice. Days of snow and ice had created a horrible mix that had killed the unprotected and made travel impossible. Benkei and Mitsu seemed particularly unhappy that they had been given the task of escorting the woman whom they had learned to hate the most through this misery.

"Tell me again, little girl, why is it that you want to leave a warm house to be out here freezing to death?"

"Sir Benkei, I grew up in the high mountains of Kumi. This is an early spring day there. People need my help."

"And tell me why do we help the baishun and peasants and eta? They are servants. They work in the dirt and shovel ox poop."

"I am eta. I have cleaned stables and collected night waste."

"Something I keep reminding Uji of. But you are his little pet, and he is fond of you. What kind of magic did you use on Uji, you little witch?" Mitsu wanted his friend back. "If Governor Mitsuhide did not like you so much, we might have some fun with you. Uji thinks that you are some kind of shinobi or something. Maybe we should see how well you fight."

"I am Ama. Violence is forbidden to me. Even to teach an arrogant *naga* like you a lesson." Her last punishment had had her cleaning out the stables for more than a month whenever she was in the temple. It was as if they wanted her to ask to go to the mansion, a satisfaction they never got. "I never heard anyone whine and complain as much as you and Sir Benkei. Our Koga women are tougher than you."

Had they not already arrived in the village with its many witnesses, it is unlikely that she would have arrived at all. Uji's friends or not, their last encounter in the Honeypig Inn had humiliated the two men. It was a fight that their friends would not let them live down. Why men did this to one another was beyond her, but for men whose lives were driven by status and prestige, being beaten by a woman, an Ama at that, was particularly embarrassing. One thing was certain: if she had not enjoyed the protection of the Governor and Uji, these men would be very dangerous. Being Ama would not save her.

Several houses had collapsed, and a few roofs were in danger. Directing some of the men to get logs and rope, Little Monkey fashioned a device for men on either side of a building to pull the logs back and forth along the roofs to cause the accumulated ice and heavy snow to be pulled off. The shingle maker, outside of town, would do well in the spring, thought Little Monkey.

"Go inside, Ama Little Monkey, and let the men finish. You are turning blue and are soaked to the skin. Let us feed you, too. You are shaking too hard. Get out of those clothes, too." The women of the town greeted her inside, forcing her to remove her dull orange robes. Gentle hands helped as the little Ama found that she could not control her own fingers. Warm tea and hot soup and noodles brought back feeling to her limbs. Even without her, the women had turned the warehouse into a hospital and a shelter for those whose homes had succumbed. Around her were a few patients with broken bones, frostbite, minor cuts, and rope burns. She could feel the scraping of the logs and boards on the roof above and the shouts of men outside. Then there was a sound she did not expect. Sensing what was happening, she grabbed several of the children hardly smaller than herself and threw herself on top of them.

——————— ❀ ———————

"Sir Uji, come quick! The merchant's warehouse roof has collapsed! The men were using horses to pull the logs Little Monkey made and knocked out the top support." The old, scruffy peasant stood in the door of the Honeypig, allowing the wind to whip through behind him.

"Uji, this is a matter for the townspeople to deal with, not Samurai. Let us go back to the mansion. It's getting dark, and they have been stuffing people in there all day. It serves them right." Benkei had managed to avoid anything that looked like work for most of the afternoon. Mitsu had been not quite as useless, helping to preserve the storage barns for the town's rice supply.

"Where is Mitsu?"

"It was Sir Mitsu's idea to use the horses. Ama Little Monkey told us not to. She said it would damage the roofs too much." The peasant held his hat, desperate for a response. "Ama Little Monkey was inside. My children were, also."

"You said she had gone back to the mansion!"

"I thought she had. She was working in the street all afternoon. When she was not there I assumed..."

"YOU CALL THAT TAKING CARE OF HER! If she is dead, I will kill you myself." Uji pushed past the old peasant and rushed to the scene of confusion. Mitsu was shouting contrary orders, women were screaming, and horses were in a state of panic. Meanwhile, under the snow and ice, wood and tile, was Ama Little Monkey and an unknown number of the people whom she loved, people whom, because of Little Monkey, he had come to know also.

Too many people were doing too much. He had to do what Little Monkey would do and restore order. Taking charge, Uji called for rope and ordered Mitsu and Benkei, the only men still in town who knew how to handle horses, to pull some of the roof debris off, the danger being collapsing the other three walls. It would be a long, miserable night, as the snow was starting again. What was wet would be frozen soon. Time was not on their side—or for anyone under the snow, wood, and shingles.

She had a headache. Little Monkey tried to move, but nothing moved without pain. She was warm, the bedding soft. Light was coming from somewhere, but every time she tried to look, sleep took over. Voices were around her, and gentle hands cared for her, it seemed. *Am I dead? Is this what death is?* She could feel herself bouncing along, and then more of the same. And then, one morning, "Ama Tomoe, where am I?"

"She's awake! COME QUICKLY, Little Monkey is awake!" The old woman flapped her arms excitedly, shuffling out the door to alert the others before returning with Master Arikuni and a few other Ama.

"Welcome home. We were about ready to give up on you. I imagine that you are hungry, little one. Ama Tomoe, send for the boy if you would. He needs to be here."

"Master Arikuni, what happened? My head really hurts. I was in the warehouse, and I heard a sound. There were three children."

"All fine. You took a nasty blow to the head, though. It's been ten days. You should know that Master Uji worked most of the night to get to you out. It seems that you were on the bottom, and you were not wearing your robes. He carried you to the mansion himself. He visits you every day. The whole town is concerned about you."

"He carried me?"

"He loves you, if you have not figured that out. He is a bit angry with his friends who were supposed to be watching over you. Uji has been here every day, sitting with you. He was here this morning holding your hand, talking to you. Do you remember anything at all?"

"Only a little. I should get up. I have neglected my duties for far too long. If Master Uji is coming, I should make myself presentable. I should thank him properly."

"Sleep until he gets here. We can wait a few more days for you to get stronger. For now, get your strength back. I imagine that you two have much to talk about."

The clear, bright day was warmer than normal. Soon it would be spring, and farmers would be planting, reducing the size of the class by the number of children living on the surrounding farms. For the first time since the late fall snows that had nearly killed her, there was no snow visible on the ground anywhere except for the mountaintops in the distance.

Uji had been very helpful. The new roof over the warehouse was temporary at best, but it allowed Little Monkey a chance to resume her service that seemed so important to her. She was walking normally, even managing a cartwheel for the children she taught. Now early afternoon, it was time to send the mixed multitude of boys and girls home, nearly thirty in all, before it started turning cool. Today was special. It was the first time since the collapse of the warehouse roof that Little Monkey would spend the night in the Governor's mansion. A special meal had been prepared, and Master Arikuni had given approval for her to eat after noon, out of respect for the Ministers and dignitaries who would be present.

"I do not know how you do it. So many children. Since you will not ride a horse, I have asked my father to send his palanquin. It is a short trip to the mansion, and it will give you a chance to rest before this evening. You even get to watch me fight. We will be having matches in the sandpit. Just for fun."

"But Master Uji, I can..."

"You are riding. That is final."

"What am I supposed to do in..."

"Nothing. Absolutely nothing. Just enjoy the ride. You will have an escort to make sure you make it all the way in the palanquin."

"But then we cannot talk. Walking beside you when you ride, we can..."

"Enough. It's coming. Just get in. Besides, there is just something about you that makes horses nervous. I have never seen anything like it."

The two men put the ornate box on the road in front of her. Somehow this felt wrong; no Ama and certainly no one of her class should enjoy such luxury! Something else felt wrong, also. Someone was watching. It was a feeling that nagged her all day. Glancing down the street, she saw a dark figure looking at her, staring at her from the corner of the Honeypig Inn from behind some boxes. Female, and somehow familiar. Too small to be Hisano; besides, the hair was jet black, like Fusa. Like Fusa, staring into her eyes. She turned to walk toward the figure, but a set of hands pointed her toward the opening in the side of the small, ornate box that almost terrified her more than the horses. Uji's hand on her head pushed down to get the reluctant girl inside. What a stupid way to travel, she thought, like a crate of cucumbers or a prisoner in a cage.

Chapter 17 – Destiny

destinies collide
death, her constant companion
a loss far too great

"The winter has been harsh this year, little one. Perhaps Master Uji isn't able to make it this time." The girl had been staring out the window off and on for hours. Little Monkey had been up early, and with the help of some of the other women was especially pretty this day. "You must miss the young man greatly. You have done none of your chores this morning, and I detected your impatience during meditation. Never have I seen you squirm so."

Arikuni stood beside his young Ama as if to help her watch for her student. "I apologize, Master. I fear that he is losing patience with my teaching. He pretends to be interested, but I know that he would rather be practicing with his swords."

"And yet his father tells me that he has been neglecting his practice. He even caught Uji reading the scrolls you lent him. He must like you very much to want to impress you that much. My deal with the Governor was more than for you to teach him reading and philosophy. As I recall, he was to show you how to use a sword."

The door swung open on the gate below for the small column of Samurai horses escorting the Governor's palanquin, Uji in the lead on his magnificent black stallion. Biting her lower lip, Little Monkey watched Master Rennyo emerge from the temple to greet the governor as he disembarked from the ornate box, Uji-san with his soldiers following one of the sohei to the stable with the horses.

"Master Arikuni. How do I teach the way of peace with a weapon in my hand? Master Uji is a real Samurai; I'm just a small peasant girl."

"You have seen Uji practice?"

"Hai."

"You have seen real battle. You have trained with real warriors, both shinobi and Samurai. How long do you think Uji would last in a real fight if he continues in his reckless behavior against an experienced opponent?"

Why did he ask her that question? He had to know the answer already. Uji was as good as most, but his arrogance and overconfidence would kill him in seconds. Even the little boy Taka she had taught at the last temple would cut her Uji in half in a real fight. Miki looked around, but there was no way to avoid the question or her temple master.

"I thought so. Then it seems that you have one more lesson to teach Master Uji in the way of peace, and that lesson will be with a weapon in your hand."

Arikuni had done it to her again. What he was asking would embarrass the boy, and given Uji's prideful nature, end her time with the him and the Mitsuhide family. The Governor's arrival ended any further discussion as polite greetings were followed by equally polite dismissals. *There has to be a way out of this!*

Making her way out of the temple, Miki looked toward the kitchen building. Perhaps they needed her help. The last place she needed to be was the school, where Rennyo had no doubt taken Uji-san. They were monks and would forgive her, maybe. One thing was certain: Uji would not if she hurt his magnificent pride.

"Ama Little Monkey, Monk Rennyo is waiting for the two of us. My father will join us as soon as he speaks with the temple master. Please walk with me; we have much to discuss." Uji had found her first. How did she think she would escape? He was supremely confident, as always. Surrounded by his cronies who used his friendship to have access to the Governor, Uji had no reason to question the lies his companions showered him with.

If she did what Temple Master Arikuni wanted, for the very first time her Uji would. Her Uji? How arrogant, how foolish that thought was. He was high-born Samurai; she was eta. No one, especially Governor Mitsuhide, could allow such a union.

Following the strutting young man, Miki felt more like a convict being led to an execution, a feeling she knew all too well. To allow Uji to believe in himself would kill him, not save him. *Do I love him enough to lose what can never be mine anyway?*

At the end of the school on the raised platform were several seats, no doubt for Governor Mitsuhide and Master Arikuni. It would be quite a show, planned without her knowledge. Ten of the girls she had drilled with the naginata had been invited, so this festival of arms would most certainly involve her. Rennyo stood on his stage, motioning to his Little Monkey to join the other women sitting near the left hand wall, their cased naginata by their sides. *I am not dressed for this! What are these men thinking?*

The governor's arrival with the temple master started the formalities. First up were the Sohei with their long naginata; apparently this would be in the Governor's report to the Daimyo. Master Rennyo followed with demonstrations of katana among the very best swordsman, to the delight of the Governor and the Samurai who had accompanied him. Perhaps she would escape this display after all.

"My Lord. It is my hope that you might report to our Daimyo that the Ikki temple stands ready to serve his will. But perhaps there is another demonstration that you might want to see. Ama Little Monkey is the commander of the women of the temple's guard. With your permission." No, she was not getting out of it. This was unrehearsed. Miki was not even aware that she had a title. The standard drill would have to do. All of the women, all older than she, seemed a bit nervous as they filed out into assigned positions, awaiting the girl who was the smallest of all of them to lead.

None of the women were ever comfortable with the long-bladed naginata, but today they were at their very best. Even Seiko-san, who always let the blade drop a bit too much, was nearly perfect. Miki's dress was not ideal but was loose enough to be serviceable. There were several changes of formation while they marched up and down the rough wooden floor, and within minutes, two ranks of five tired girls stood facing her and the Governor's seat. They bowed to Governor Mitsuhide, which was followed by his profuse praise. The Governor dismissed the girls, who stacked their arms while filing out of the school, their part finished.

"Ama Little Monkey, please remain. I was most impressed by the performance of your women. Master Rennyo tells me that you are a full master with the staff. This I believe, as I have seen you teach my daughters and, as I understand it, a few of my Samurai. But he also tells me that you have some skill with the katana. Perhaps a short demonstration." This was it, the setup. This was what Master Rennyo had told the Governor to expect. Why had they not mentioned it to her? Why the surprise?

Taking the offered sword, a bit smaller and lighter than what the men used, Miki cleared her mind and controlled her breathing before allowing her right hand to seize the handle of her sword. This would be the Dance of Death, the form taught to her by a scrawny, little, dark-eyed boy in a temple so far away, so long ago. It was the one she knew best, and the one everyone seemed to recognize, particularly its distinctive move toward the end. It exercised attacks and defense from all angles, and it was her specialty.

He was not smiling, but Governor Mitsuhide was intensely interested. "I have seen series of moves before, but never done with such grace. I would like to see a match. Perhaps with someone you know and trust, with bokken, like Uji? Uji, please be gentle." Here it was, her nightmare. As Ama, if she never held another weapon again as long as she lived, it would be too soon. To do this in front of a crowd, and to embarrass the young man she liked so very much, maybe loved, made her ill.

"My Lord, I am a small woman and no match for a real Samurai like Master Uji."

"And yet your martial skill is evident, like that of a trained Samurai. Your humility hides a secret. No one expects you to win. Just try. My son Uji has grown fond of you these many months, and he will not hurt you. There is no reason to be afraid." The smile on the boy's face told her that this was a game he had asked for. He had a mean streak and liked to embarrass her from time to time. What was Rennyo after, though? Master Arikuni simply smiled as the boy stood in front of her, bragging to his friends and offering her words of encouragement.

"Governor Matsuhide. If this is a test of my skill, may I ask that Master Uji ask for his friends to help? If Sir Mitsu and Sir Benkei would be so kind. I have never fought just one Samurai before." The request startled all of them. Rennyo conferred with the Temple Master Arikuni as the Governor sat stunned. The request was not a boast. It was an admission that this was a game that she had played before, for real. She expected no quarter and would give none. It was a huge gamble, but less than those men knew. These three boys were clumsy, and they would get in one another's way. Losing would cost her nothing, but if she won, it might take the sting out of losing to a peasant girl if Uji had company.

"This is something that I would like to see. Proceed." The Governor motioned to each of the three young men, who reluctantly accepted the wooden swords being offered. Without an audience, it might be fun to tease the tiny girl, but honor was now on the line. For Uji, the realization that combat wasn't a game and that death comes too fast might be the knowledge that would save his life. The question was, did she love him enough to hurt him?

She closed her eyes, and her mind reached out through all of her senses. These boys were not Koga; silence was a weapon they did not understand as they gave each other instructions and encouragement, identifying their position and range to the experienced kunoichi. Miki could feel them breathing hard as they let excitement get in the way as they shifted to the sides.

Benkei yelled as he wasted the time to lift his sword to attack and opened up the hole for Miki to shove the bokken into his chest, knocking the breathless man onto his back. Mitsu froze in midattack as Miki's motion carried the tip of her blade into the back of the man's hand. He dropped his bokken in pain as Miki dragged the false edge of her wooden sword across Mitsu's chest to complete the kill.

Now there was one left. Uji had watched her dispatch his friends in seconds, and he was breathing hard, the prideful pronouncements and playful showing off gone. Looking into her expressionless face, into her dark penetrating eyes, unnerved the boy as the small girl brought her weapon into a guard position, awaiting his move.

Miki's full skirt hid the motions of her feet, an advantage as he shifted back and forth looking for a hole that never appeared. As she realized that he would not attack, Miki brought her sword behind her in a lower guard, shifting her weight imperceptibly to the rear foot for Uji's next and last move. Lowering her eyes, she waited as he lifted his bokken above his head without realizing his foolishness, and both the Governor and Master Rennyo winced at the inevitability of the next exchange.

"Enough! I have seen enough."

"Father. We should continue. I can win."

"I have never seen anything as predictable as this fight. Ama Little Monkey, I will be sharing a meal with Temple Master Arikuni this evening. I expect both you and Uji to be present."

"Hai, my Lord. I apologize for hurting Sir Benkei and Sir Mitsu. I was unprepared for the encounter."

The old man gazed at this beautiful young woman, head lowered before him. Who was she? What was she? Three years ago, a malnourished child appeared in a temple, capable of reading and writing, guarded, according to Arikuni, by a strange Koga girl. Fluent in literature, medicines, and agriculture, and skilled in arts that should have taken a lifetime to master, Little Monkey was indeed a puzzle, and for the people of his province, a gift of compassion and peace. But this day he had been shown a different Little Monkey, a woman whose experience included the Samurai arts. This was the child of a great warrior, and he now had a clue as to which one.

Even in the winter, the garden was a place of peace for her. This would be a chilly evening of a day that had gone nothing like the way she had planned. Tomorrow was her day ministering to the people in the town and teaching the children. Of all the things she did, it was teaching the children that was most satisfying. Little Benyo, the farmer boy whose appendix she had removed a year earlier, was her very best student. All of this weapon stuff was a distraction. Tomorrow she would ask permission to put away the sword forever. To never again lift an instrument of death that Little Monkey the Ama had come to hate so passionately. Miki the warrior, the kunoichi, would die forever, and no one would mourn her passing, least of all the woman named Little Monkey.

The branches on the peach trees were bare, yet Little Monkey could feel the life within, sleeping, waiting for the spring that would follow. Life, not death. Compassion, not revenge. She took a deep breath and felt a slight shiver. Duty had defined her life, and now the woman named Little Monkey felt a prayer that all of the men who defined her duty would understand her decision to be happy. The sound of male feet told her that she was no longer alone.

"Mitsu and Benkei are furious with you! They say that you were a demon. You do not think that you could have actually beaten me, do you?" The boy had learned nothing. The worst possible result was to stop the fight to save Uji's pride. Now, the exercise was wasted.

"Hai, Uji-san. Your father had already foreseen the outcome. I am very sorry. Please believe me that none of this was my idea. All I want to be is a simple Ama. I hate weapons. I hate the death they bring."

"I am Samurai. It is the glory of an honorable death that is my destiny."

"Uji-san, there is no honor in death. There is no glory. It is pain and waste and suffering for the dead as well as for the living. I have seen the tears of the mothers and sons and daughters. I have looked into the eyes of men in their last agony. All that you believe is a lie, and I have seen that lie too many times. I want no more part of it."

"Father is expecting you. You are late. Both of us are. That is an opinion that you need to keep to yourself."

The walk back to the main temple building was a slow one. The walks were clear of ice and snow, yet the dread of what awaited held her back despite Uji's calls for haste. The boy wanted to tell her something but was afraid, reluctant to speak with her. Was he still angry about the demonstration earlier, or was it something else?

Several of the other Ama met her at the door to help her be more presentable. Why did it matter? It did not matter at all when she had been asked to perform in combat in her very nicest clothing. *Is it that men simply do not understand?* Miki smiled as she realized that not long ago, the very concept that a woman was that different was new to her as well. In her little Koga village, she dressed the same and trained the same. Hisano had even earned the right to be jonin, the leader of a team of warriors. What would these men think of that?

Fussing over her appearance was followed by instructions in protocol and good wishes. What did her sister Ama know that she did not? Most of these women had run away to the temple to escape bad husbands. They had treated her like a little sister, teaching her all of the skills that Koga life simply did not permit for her, from mending and making clothing to arranging flowers in a pleasing way. Even the art of making tea and sweets that no one in her village or temple had ever shown her. What were they preparing her for? She was Ama, healer and teacher.

Before pushing her through the sliding door, Ama Tomoe, the gray-haired matron of the temple, had one more word of advice for her Little Monkey: "Oh, and be sure to act surprised when they ask for your consent. Do not agree too quickly. Eat very little. Well, you do anyway. We can feed you later. Men like to think that women are stupid. Try not to be too smart. I know that will be hard for you. All of us are excited for you. Now go."

What? Consent? Multiple hands pushed the now-confused Ama through the sliding door into the second-floor meeting room. All eyes were now on her, the only woman in the room, although Miki was sure that more than one set of female ears was listening through the thin walls. Unsure as to where to go or what to do, all she could do was to bow in place until one of the senior monks directed her to a spot in the center of the room in front of a small table beside Master Uji, facing Governor Mitsuhide and Temple Master Arikuni.

"Welcome. I almost did not think that you wanted to join us. I warn you against lateness in the future."

"Hai, my Lord. I apologize. I did not understand that I was required. My duties would normally be elsewhere." This was not the time to irritate the Governor.

"Monk Arikuni tells me that you work very hard here. He tells me that you are a skilled cook and that many of the monks in this room wear robes made by your hands. You still find time to teach children in the town and heal our sick. Minister Sasama tells me that your suggestions have increased our crop yields by almost a fifth and that your plans for irrigation and the water lifts were brilliant. Our Lord Suwa, Daimyo, has given me the credit for this miracle, and my other advisors are all calling on me for your help. I have a real problem now. What am I to do with you?"

"I am sorry, my Lord. I did not intend to cause problems for you. I just did not want anyone to be hungry." *Is he angry? He sounds angry.* Maybe she should have kept her suggestions to herself, but Minister Sasama seemed so pleasant when she repaired his back. He even seemed grateful for her ideas and drawings. She could feel herself begin to shake, but protocol would mean that the tear was on its own. "I was only trying to help."

"And today you embarrassed my three best young swordsman in a magnificent display of skill. Had it been a real fight, you would have killed all three and a dozen more had you needed to. Your knowledge of strategy that you have taught my son Uji and your ability to lead others has frightened my commanders, who tell me that they would be eager for you to train their own soldiers. There is even a rumor that you broke up a fight in the HoneyPig Inn to protect the virtue of the pleasure girls there. You were lucky that none of those men involved would admit that they had been beaten up by a tiny Ama."

To strike a member of the Samurai class was a crime punishable by death for a peasant. *Was this what he is angry about? It was so long ago.* She could no longer control the shaking as she peered down at her lap to hide her wet face. *Why do this here, in front of my fellow Monks? Are they in trouble also?* Ten Monks on ten poles flashed through her mind. *Am I to become the reason for more suffering?*

"But it seems that my wife and all of my daughters have become very fond of you. And when you are away with your duties at the temple, poor Uji can think of nothing else but you. He is nearly useless to me now."

Being useless seemed to be Uji's full time occupation, even before she began teaching him. *Why am I being blamed for this?*

"Monk Arikuni and I have discussed our mutual problem of Little Monkey, and I believe that we have arrived at a solution. Ama Little Monkey, have you ever wondered what it would be like to leave the temple, to live like other women?"

It was hard to speak, and her voice cracked. "This temple is my home, my Lord. I have nowhere else to go. I cannot go back to Kumi or to my village or the North Road Temple. I am so sorry." *But for what? What have I done wrong?*

"It seems that I have another problem. My son Uji needs a wife. As his wife you would become my daughter and a cherished member of my family. Everything would have to be forgiven. My advisors would be thrilled, and I would become even more popular with my Lord and my people. Think about poor Uji, who would be devastated if you say no."

Wife? Was that the reason for all of this? She was Ama, a servant for Buddha. "My Lord, I am a peasant girl from a mountain village. I am a Koga woman, an eta, and unworthy of marriage."

"Twenty years ago I was a young Samurai facing battle against General Shigenori and the army of Kumi. The men I led attacked along the river against a position being held by just a few enemy Samurai, one of them Monk Rennyo's father. Their leader was a swordsman of extraordinary talent and alone killed maybe ten or twenty men. To break their resistance, I sent a dozen more with myself included to kill this one man. I watched him cut through us all, and as I looked into his cool, dark eyes, I felt a fear that I have never felt since, until this morning when I looked into your eyes, and I saw those same eyes and felt that same fear. I watched you fight, and I saw him fight. No mountain peasant girl could ever do all that you have done. Monk Arikuni tells me that the Koga girl who brought you here said that you had a destiny, and that is why her people protected you. Ama Little Monkey, this is that destiny."

Little Monkey opened her mouth, but no words would come out. Was this her destiny? For more than two years, she had been happy, she had saved lives. Would it be different if she were the wife of a Samurai, part of a powerful family? Another man would make her decisions for her—yet his father valued her judgment, her good works. They all seemed to see that this had taken her by surprise. Tomorrow they would want an answer. Somehow she could not eat, and as the evening proceeded, she welcomed her dismissal. Her Ama sisters met her.

"Are you telling me that you had no idea that the Governor was going to ask you to marry Uji? Why do you think that he has forced you to be with that dreadful man for the last year, although you have worked a miracle with him? I ran away from a better man." Ama Tomoe held the still-shaking, teary-eyed girl as she put her head on the old woman's shoulders. "How can anyone so smart be so stupid? You could do worse. Another man would be better, but you will be part of a great family. You will always have us in the temple."

Standing up, Ama Tomoe directed the other women to make sure that Little Monkey got to bed, wondering how anyone seeming so strong could be so fragile. This would not do! These men treated this event like a game, and she wondered if even now they realized just how much damage had been done. Heading up the stairs, she decided a word to Temple Master Arikuni was in order.

"Ahhh, Ama Tomoe, how is my Little Monkey? She did not react as I might have expected this evening. I know that she loves the boy. But..."

"Arikuni-san, how dare you. Little Monkey was terrified. What kind of life has that beautiful child had to believe that she could be executed for the things she heard this evening? She was most afraid that something that she had done might cause the Governor to have you or another monk suffer also. It is my fault also. I did not realize that the only one who did not know what was happening was Little Monkey herself. All of us just assumed."

The stern-faced old woman was as angry as he had ever seen her in the long years they had known each other. The girl's truth had been kept hidden, but perhaps a woman's understanding might help. "Executed? Is that what she thought? Please sit down, my old friend. Your question is one that deserves an answer."

"Tell me again, Hisano, why we're living in a warehouse full of stinky fish. The boat was better." Koan peeked out at the workmen below through the cracks in the rough wooden walls of the second-floor room built for making deals and hiding contraband.

"And it had a couple of girls, too."

"Because Fusa knows about the boat, and you interfere with paying customers that Kinu and Suni need to survive."

Gonji, sharpening his blade, prepared to take his watch protecting the street of broken dreams and providing what little protection Hisano's little gang of yakuza could for the peasants living in this backwater slum. "Why are we afraid of Fusa? Fusa is one of us."

"Because Fusa is a maid in the Yoshida mansion. Two other Koga spies were caught and tortured there. If they catch Fusa, then they will come after us. Suni and Kinu don't need that." If that were all, it would be enough. But very little useful information was coming out of Fusa, and nothing that had happened in the last year had altered her suspicions about her friend. Hisano had insisted that Gonzo be Fusa's sole contact and that even he not know where her team was. With Miki dead, Princess Yumi was the only remaining legitimate female member of the Yorisada clan. With Satake in the mountains searching for Lord Oto, and especially his son Taka, soon it could be too late to save her clan from either the Hamatsu or the Iga.

A knock at the ladder leading to the corner of the room sent hands to weapons, but the threat turned out to be Kinu with a pot of stew. She and Benzo had developed a relationship that the boy had used to his advantage, repeatedly. Still, the stew was good, and to be honest, the girl's information gleaned from drunk customers in the throes of ecstasy as useful as anything Fusa had provided.

"Hai, hai, Hisano-san, business has been very good this week. Here is your share." For whatever reason, Kinu and Suni had adopted her as boss, probably out of gratitude, maybe out of respect, as she led the gang that had rescued them, and most certainly because they saw Hisano as protection from the gang inside the pleasure district. As cover stories went, being a Yakuza boss wasn't ideal but certainly preferable to being known as shinobi.

Hisano let them keep most of the money, as running the floating whorehouse did involve some expense. The money Kinu and

Suni earned made them the wealthiest among the eta on the street of broken dreams and for the first time provided enough so that no one was going hungry. The boys had proven useful in preventing interference from the other yakuza.

"Thank you. I especially thank you for the food. It has been wonderful. And by the way, Benzo is not the quality inspector, and you shouldn't let him take advantage of you."

"Hisano-san, last night after my last customer fell asleep, a man came looking for you. He said he wants to hire your gang for a job at a temple up north. I told him that I would deliver a message to you. Have you ever heard of a girl named Little Miki?"

Choking on a piece of fish, Hisano put the bowl on the floor as Koan took the opportunity to slap her hard on the back, dislodging the soft-boned chunk. Breathing for a few seconds, Hisano noted that she was not the only one stunned by the question. "Hai. But Little Miki died a couple of years ago."

"It can't be the same girl, then. The other people on the street tell me about a wonderful little child who could cure all sorts of illnesses, and all the people loved her. And then one night General Satake found out and became very angry, and the little girl had to run away, but General Satake chased her and was furious that he could not catch her. They say that because of her goodness, the Buddha protected her that night and took her with him. According to the legend, he gave her great wisdom and beauty and named her Little Monkey after the Kami of the mountains, where they say she came from. Buddha himself delivered Little Monkey in the form of a tall girl to the Ikki temple in Fujiwara for protection. At least that is the story. I gave some money so that the people can build a shrine at the end of the street to her. I hope you don't mind."

"Nice going, Buddha! At least with the shrine we'll have something to remember Miki by."

"Shut up! All of you shut up and be quiet. I have to think." Why did none of this come from Fusa? Why had she not heard these stories?

"I hope that they get her scraggly hair right, and her eyes. They can paint the eyes black."

"That's funny, Benzo-san. All of the people on the street said that Little Miki had dark, beautiful eyes that could even see into your soul. That is how the girl from Governor Yoshida's mansion could tell it was her. Anjoe, Suni's customer last night, said that Little Monkey always has an escort of sohei so that they couldn't get close to her. He said that that they were looking for real shinobi to kill her before she could marry the Daimyo's son or something. I don't know; it's just what he said, but he was drunk. Personally I don't think that shinobi even really exist. They are just stories to frighten bad children. Why are you laughing so hard?"

What else was there to do? Gonzo had missed his last two meetings. She hadn't heard from Fusa in more than a week. The only information that she had was secondhand gossip from drunk soldiers as relayed by clueless whores. "What else can go wrong?"

"Oh, by the way. Suni said to stay off the streets of Isawa. General Satake is staying at the Governor's mansion. He might be mad that you rescued us."

"You asked."

"Kinu, tell him I will meet him in the inn at the end of the street tonight, but to come alone. We will know if he isn't. Ask the innkeeper to keep the corner table free for us. We need details for work so far away." Indeed, in the more than a year since they had arrived, Hisano's gang had established a complex set of signals and a system to track anyone in the river district who wasn't a resident. The thugs, thieves, and hooligans who had preyed on the poor and weak were gone, unable to match the focused, disciplined, and highly trained gangsters, shinobi in disguise; they had found other places to be. With the support of the people, nothing happened in the river district that Hisano didn't know about. And, with crime gone, business was up, and the officers patrolling the rest of Isawa gave her and her well-mannered gang free reign in the place that they had always feared to tread.

Matsuhide peered out toward the mountains in the east, the sun cresting the rise just southeast toward the province that had once been Kumi. It would be a busy day. Lord Suwa would arrive within a few days to meet this miracle that he had heard about. Turning, he was greeted by his youngest daughter, Edako.

"Where is Little Monkey?"

"She is in there, working on plans for a bridge that can move out of the way of boats. It's amazing what she built. Minister Toyotomi will be pleased. Father, I am worried about Little Monkey. She has trouble sleeping and has bad dreams. Last night was the worst. She screamed and cried. She only sleeps for a little bit at a time. Father, I have never seen her so, and it has been getting worse every night. She has visions, but Little Monkey will not tell us what they are."

"And your brother Uji?"

"He went to town. Little Monkey asked permission to go and teach children today, but he forbade her to leave until she learned her duties here. Father, what more can she do? Little Monkey already works every moment of the day. She also has trouble eating. Uji is being so mean." Little Monkey was her friend. Watching her come apart trying to meet everyone's expectations was killing the girl.

"Speak of this to no one. Tell Minister Toyotomi that Little Monkey is ill and will see him tomorrow. The girl needs rest, and I must speak to her first."

Sliding the door open, Little Monkey bowed, wiping the tears off of her face. Behind her was a model of a bridge made of rope and bamboo. Longer than a man, it had pulleys and wheels to allow men or horses to move the central span to the side, pivoting to allow boats to pass. It would be Toyotomi's greatest challenge to build, but here was the proof that it could be done.

"The work that you have done here is impressive, Little Monkey. Where did you learn to design bridges and water lifts? All of my advisors are begging for you to look at their departments. I can see that you are exhausted and upset. Young Edako tells me that you are having problems sleeping. I heard you scream last night myself. You are working far too hard. We have servants in this house who will care for you if you let them. Today you will rest."

"My Lord, Minister Toyotomi is expecting this bridge. I made a promise..."

"That clearly you have kept. I did not ask Master Arikuni for you to be a servant or builder of bridges, but a wife and a woman and a mother. You are killing yourself."

"Hai, my Lord."

"Edako tells me that you have been having terrible dreams every night. She called them visions. As I understood, you were raised Ama, not miko. Have you ever had visions before?"

"Hai."

"And have your visions ever come to pass?"

"Hai, my Lord."

"You are Ama, not miko. How did you end up in the temple?"

"I had a vision when I was a child of six. Old Iyo was a miko who lived in our village. When Iyo told them that I was telling the truth and that I would be a miko like her, they banished both of us from the village. Iyo tried to take me to the shrine, but the scarfaced Samurai almost killed her. She took me to the North Road Temple instead."

"Why did Old Iyo the miko think that you were miko, too?"

"Because as a small child I could speak to the wolves in the mountains. They protect me there. Old Iyo told me that I had a destiny. She died that night in the temple, and the monks adopted me."

"And have your visions ever come to pass? Can you still speak to wolves?"

"Hai."

This is the most that he had gotten from Little Monkey since the girl had moved to the walled mansion several weeks earlier. The monks had mentioned none of it, if in fact they even knew. Now the question was whether Little Monkey was an asset or a liability. "I do not understand your reluctance to marry Uji. Has he said something to you? Hurt you in some way?"

"Oh, no, my Lord. Uji-san has been much nicer than usual. Everyone is very nice to me. It's just that I miss the temple and the children and treating all of the people. All of my life I have lived in a temple or served others, except for my time with the Koga when the soldiers would not let me go home." She had agreed to marry Uji as her duty to the temple. "There is so much that I do not know about the life outside the temple or the village. All I have ever wanted to be is Ama. There is so much that

Uji-san does not know about me. There is so much I must not talk about."

Secrets. Matsuhide looked down at the girl who worked so hard to stay busy with those petite hands and that brilliant mind. What was missing was her smile, and it was clear that Little Monkey was not as happy as a young woman about to be married should be. Her secrets were what bothered the old Samurai the most. It was not that the little Ama was an extraordinary woman, but that she was an impossible one. No problem escaped resolution once presented to Little Monkey; no suffering escaped her attention. Smart beyond comprehension, the girl seemed unaware that no one else could see the things that she could, or that she had any value beyond being a mere servant.

"Perhaps we should discuss your past. Have you thought about a name yet?" It was at this point in the conversation where the girl always froze up. Not even the Chinese could build the wall Little Monkey had built to protect her past.

"Master Uji has chosen one for me. I am not sure that I like it."

"You must have had a name before Little Monkey. They gave you that name at this temple. You bite your lip when you are upset. Why are you upset now?"

"I am afraid, my Lord. My being here places all of you in danger. No shinobi would ever enter a temple to kill, and even General Satake would not risk a war with Yugumi and the Suwa clan or a fight with Master Rennyo's sohei. But here, they will come. All of you are in danger. I have been selfish."

"There are walls around this mansion. We have soldiers also. Uji will protect you."

"No my Lord, Master Uji cannot protect me. Uji cannot even protect Uji. I love Uji-san, but he will be the first to die. When they come the walls will not matter. The soldiers will not matter. The Iga will kill every woman just to be sure. Uji-san will be the first to die and will never see his assassin. If General Satake comes, he will be stupid. He will use criminals. I have stayed here too long. Hisano was right. I will never be allowed to be happy." So there it was. It was the truth that he had been asking for. It was the vision in her dreams, her nightmare. So clear, so terrible.

"Who are you? What are you? What is your secret, Little Monkey?"

"I do not know."

"Maybe I do. For now it would be best for you to return to the temple. Master Arikuni and I have much to discuss. You will ride with me." Silent tears flowed. She had nothing to be ashamed of, and yet the girl was ashamed. Mitsuhide watched the tiny woman's heart shatter, as though every dream lay bleeding before her. Little Monkey's service to Yugumi would have to be rewarded, but nothing could compensate for the agony ripping her to shreds. None of this was her fault. It was his.

"I should speak with Uji-san first."

"Perhaps later. There will be time later. I will take care of Uji."

Sake flowed freely among the patrons of the inn at the end of the pier in the river district, with the girls working the floor doing well profit-wise. Since Hisano's gang had come to town, the usual abuse had stopped and no one refused to pay, as had been the case so many times before. Gonji would follow her client for the evening through the gates to the river district, and Benzo would take over near the inn. No matter what the man wanted, at least Hisano knew that she would learn more than she knew. The corner was dark, and the back door led down a pier where escape would be easy. Koan was standing by, just in case a distraction became necessary.

Two clicks and a bell, and a hand signal from Benzo told the innkeeper that the next customer would be Boss Hisano-san's, but that he was someone more dangerous than expected. Just how dangerous became obvious as the scarfaced Satake with his missing ear made his way into the room. A motion with the eyes told the innkeeper to direct the ugly monster to her table.

His appearance would seem to fit right in on the street had not every single resident on the street of broken dreams not had a reason to see him painfully dead. Satake stood over the gangster boss woman as though he expected her to grovel. A flip of her hand signaled for the earless tyrant to sit. He reached for his katana, and the sound of two men, one with a bow, motivated the Samurai to carefully and slowly place the sword beside him. This was a woman who could plan. This was a Yakuza boss who knew her business. She waited, unconcerned, silently, for him to speak.

"This must be done quietly. There is a group of thugs whom I've sent to perform a task for me. They are being guided by a woman. There are several men, but the woman is especially dangerous. Make sure they do not return. Do not kill them until after they have completed their task."

"And if they don't complete their task?"

It was a question he had not considered. Meiko-san's men were thugs, thieves, and filth. The reputation of the River District gang was seasoned, practiced professionals, experts with weapons, and disciplined. So much so that the officers of Yoron had learned to afford them respect as fellow officers. Perhaps, he thought, he had chosen the wrong group to kill the witch. "If they do not kill their target, then I will double what I pay you for you to do it."

"Who is their target?" Had she asked first, he would have balked. Now it was essential to the mission. He could not refuse the answer.

"An Ama. A young girl, maybe sixteen or seventeen. She is unmistakable with her dark eyes. Her name is Little Monkey. Feel free to kill anyone with her. If she suffers, it would be better."

"It is bad karma to kill a monk. But you already know about that, don't you? Fifty for killing Boss Meiko-san's trash. They will probably be caught before they get close to the Fujiwara temple, anyway. For the Ama, a bit more. The Ikko temple has sohei, so it will be difficult. It will require special skills. Two hundred up front now, two hundred in seven days' time here. And we will bring back proof."

"Why should I pay if it is not your mission?"

"Boss Meiko-san is an old whore. She doesn't appreciate the value of these things. You offered each of that trash twenty, only half up front. They aren't worth it. They will get drunk and talk.

This is political and sensitive. Done wrong, Hamatsu will have a war with Yugumi. Neither of us wants that. It's bad for business. My boys know better."

A stack of gold coins slid across the table under a cloth. Taking the stack, Hisano tucked them away in her sleeve.

"You did not count it."

"It's unnecessary. That isn't how business is done. If you cheat us, you will join your Ama friend when we return. For us, walls don't matter."

Watching the demon walk out the door brought Koan and Benzo to her side.

"That was a big stack of coin. Who do we have to kill for that?"

"A stupid little Ama named Little Monkey. Benzo, take this and give it to Suni and Kinu. Tell them to distribute this and all the other money among the people. Get Gonji and our stuff; we have to leave tonight. We won't be coming back."

"Why not? I like it here."

"Because that stupid fool Satake plans on meeting us later to kill us to steal the money back. We have what we came to Yoron for. It's time to go. The people know how to take care of themselves now."

"We aren't really going to kill Miki, are we?"

The old man looked through the barren peach trees of the temple's little orchard for his favorite little Ama. It was late winter, and soon new leaves would peek out of new buds, and the harmony between the beautiful spirit of Little Monkey's compassionate heart and the life that blossomed in abundance wherever she walked would fill the temple. It was as if the earth itself could see in Little Monkey what the child herself could not. The little one was confusing. So willing to give of her own heart but so unwilling to take the love that so many wanted to give her. The old temple master spotted the young woman, lost in thought beside her favorite peach tree.

"Governor Mitsuhide explained your visions. He tells me that your service to Yugumi province was exceptional, and he wants to know if you would continue that service from here in the temple?"

"Hai, Master Arikuni. As you wish." He was angry. Little Monkey had avoided everyone, ashamed by her failure. All of the other Ama were quite disappointed, as if they had placed all of their hopes and dreams in this one great possibility. Hiding among the barren peach trees gave her a moment of peace away from the downcast eyes of her friends. She had failed the temple and embarrassed the man she respected and loved the most.

"I am very sorry that it did not work out with Uji. You have brought so much happiness to so many. All of us wanted you to find happiness for yourself. This is my fault."

"No, Master. It is mine. I had no right to expect happiness for myself."

"Then I have failed you again. Do you think the laws of karma only apply to other people, Little Monkey? I have allowed you to use this temple as a place to hide, and I see that now as a mistake. I was an old man in need of the peace that you have given me. I was selfish. It was my hope that your marriage to Uji-san would bring you the joy you deserve and reward you for all that you have done for so many. Visions and fears without foundation. Is this the way of Buddha?"

"No, Master."

"Was it fear of the future or fear of the past, little one? I cannot even imagine what you have seen in your short life. But you must not be afraid of what can be, because of what was! Even a short life of joy is better than the life of endless misery that you have condemned yourself to."

"It is my destiny."

"Destiny. And who told you what your destiny was? Is it destiny or an excuse, little one? It was the destiny of a farmer's child to die in his father's arms until you changed that destiny. It was your destiny to die until a woman who loved you saved your life and your destiny. Destiny is rewritten with every choice we make. It will be your destiny to live a happy and complete life the moment you choose that destiny for yourself."

"I have seen..."

"One future of many. If you believe it, then prepare for it and rewrite your destiny again, but do not be surprised when your fears are groundless. No one wants to hurt you. Promise me, Little Monkey, that you will give your happiness a chance. There is a young man who wants to see you in the temple. Speak to him. I will no longer permit you to use this temple to hide from the life that you deserve." Was it anger or concern? Uji had tried to see her several times in the week since her dismissal. Everyone had been waiting for her to open up; no one had asked her about it, and she had spoken to no one, to the disappointment of all the Ama and Monks whom she considered family.

As quickly as he had appeared behind her, Temple Master Arikuni was out of sight. She owed Uji-san an explanation. The few times that she had been to town, Uji had either been drunk in the inn or away on whatever business his father had sent him on. Three times he had come looking for her, and she had avoided him. Under Master Arikuni's orders, she could not avoid him again.

As she walked toward the temple, it was clear that the man would not give her the opportunity to do so. Tall, well-built and very proud, his topknot perfectly arranged on his partially shaved head, he walked toward her. There had once been a time when that figure would cause her heart to skip a beat from fear. Now her heart skipped a beat for other reasons. "Little Monkey. Walk with me. Why did you leave the mansion? You will return with me now." He liked to give orders, as though he controlled everything.

"Your father sent me away. I am not allowed to return. I will serve him from here and from the town."

"He tells me that you wished to return to the temple for your health. All of the Ministers are concerned for you, particularly Minister Toyotomi, who respects you greatly. Why would my father send you away?"

"To protect his family and you. You deserve a better wife. Uji-san, I cannot be what you need. I have a past, and when I told your father about it, he sent me away. You need a Samurai woman." He needed a woman whose very life would not get him killed. Even here in the temple, the dreams were getting stronger, more terrible.

"I do not care. Tomorrow I will be going to see my uncle, the Daimyo of Yugumi. I want you to be with me. He will name me as heir. When he dies I will be head of the clan and Daimyo of Yugumi, and then nothing you have ever done will matter. I will execute anyone who mentions it."

"No, Uji. It is not what I have done. It is what I am. I am a Koga kunoichi from a small mountain village, and I have enemies. Those enemies would hurt you to hurt me. No one must ever die for me again!"

"I can protect you."

"Uji-san, you do not know your enemy. No one can protect me. My life does not matter, Uji, but your life does. Someday you will be a great Daimyo and leader of your clan."

"Your life matters to me. It matters to my father and the people, too. It seems that I am fond of you. Tomorrow you will come with me to the mansion. There our Lord Suwa wishes to meet you, to thank you for what you have done. Master Arikuni will be with you in case you get scared. There will be a great celebration in Fujiwara for you. It seems the people wish to thank you also. That is where and when we will announce our marriage and my new position as heir."

Uji was not asking for her consent, but then, did he need to? Two old men had decided for both of them, for the good of the temple and the good of the clan. Did Uji even have a choice, she wondered, although he seemed happy with the decision. She should be happy, but something was very wrong. A celebration meant a crowd, and a crowd meant opportunities for her kind. Her kind. Professional assassins and spies. This was the vision she had seen in all of her nightmares, the impossible confluence of events that would put all the wrong people together. "A celebration? For me? That is impossible! I am Ama, Master Arikuni, please tell Uji-san. Please!"

"There they are, the happy couple. I see that you have resolved your differences." Master Arikuni was waiting for them by the door of the main temple.

"Master Arikuni, we never had any differences. It's just that I am not worthy." The nightmares had continued even here.

"Your simple modesty is your most endearing quality. Who could be more worthy?" Stupid enough to marry Uji, more likely, she thought. This was a political marriage between a temple and the ruling clan of Yugumi Province. It had taken her until this moment to realize it. The lessons, the time together, that tragedy of a weapons demonstration, the time in the mansion, all parts of the plan. It had all escaped her until now. They would not let it fall apart, but in their enthusiasm they had created the means and the motivation for all the misery that would now follow. Secrets had defined her life. She truly was a child of shadow. "And after your meeting with Lord Suwa, we will prepare..."

Temple Master Arikuni and Lord Mitsuhide had it all planned. The other Ama knew, Uji's family knew. Uji was standing in front of her; he had to have known. Everyone but stupid, stupid, trusting Little Monkey had figured it out or knew. Arikuni continued to speak, but she could not hear him. Why did everyone have a choice in this but her? Uji was looking at her, wanting something from her, waiting for Uji to speak. What did he want to hear from her?

This was too much. She loved Uji, but she loved the temple more. It was her work in town with the people that she would miss, the children, the simple people who needed her most. One more time the rich and powerful would take what they wanted, and Little Monkey would find herself locked away in a castle making sons for Samurai families, being the perfect little wife.

They were staring at her. Arikuni had stopped speaking, and she had missed it, lost in thought. Now they were waiting for her to say something, anything, but she did not even know what she had been asked. "Hai. Hai. Please forgive me, please." With a bow she darted into the main temple room. She needed to be alone.

Little Monkey closed her eyes, trying to focus as she sat, realizing that she had not even removed her sandals as she entered the building. She had to think; there had to be a way out of this for everyone. If they would all just leave her alone. Sliding feet on the polished wooden floor behind her was Ama Tomoe.

"Master Arikuni said that your behavior today was abominable. Poor Master Uji is very angry, and that will cause a problem tomorrow. Why are you so afraid, child?" Old Ama Tomoe had watched over her for the last week since her return, probing for answers, feelings. Tomoe was Master Arikuni's spy when he did not understand her. "This is so unlike you. You will be the wife of a powerful Lord some day. You did not expect to live your entire life in this temple, did you?"

"Hai, that is what I wanted. Can I stop this? I have never consented to this. Master Uji should choose a better woman."

"Oh my! You are serious. I did not realize." Sitting beside her facing the large stone Buddha made Little Monkey realize that this would be a long talk. "No, child. It cannot be stopped. Tomorrow you must go with Master Uji and the Governor and ask Lord Suwa for permission to marry. It would humiliate Master Arikuni, the boy, and the Governor if you do not. Master Uji is outside. You must apologize to Uji-san. We all have our duties. I have given Uji-san your things. Please do not make this hard. You will learn to love the boy someday."

"No, Ama Tomoe. I do love Master Uji. I just do not want to be the reason for his death. I am Ama."

"Not anymore, child. Not anymore."

The road below wound around the hill they were on. One side overlooked the mighty Fujiwara temple itself, while the other side overlooked the only trees from which an amateur might plan an ambush. Plopping down beside the kunoichi jonin, Gonji took a swig of water from the gourd, letting it drip down his chin. Corking the gourd, he wiped his face to wet it down.

"Hisano, Boss Mieko-san's guys are on both sides of the road. Stupid position, too. No woman with them. There is a group of acrobats like us who look like they could be Iga who went into Fujiwara last night. The people in the town said that a big, important Samurai guy is on his way. About twenty *sohie* on horse went up the road a while ago. I can't believe they didn't see Mieko-san's boys. Something important is happening."

It was midmorning, and whatever would happen would happen soon. "Any word from Benzo?"

"He's in love. Three Samurai on horse are getting ready to leave the temple with a really beautiful woman. He hasn't seen

Miki yet. He wants to know if we can keep her if we rescue her."
With Benzo tracking whatever came out of the temple and Koan
in town, it was just Gonji and she.

"No. How many did you count?" What worried her was the
sohie cavalry. They weren't stupid, and they also didn't ride out
without purpose. Never had she seen Miki ever walk into a trap;
it was as though the girl had the instincts and senses of a wolf.
It remained to be seen if living in the temple had dulled those
senses.

"Six and Stinky. Seven if you count Stinky as human. We can
take them if we need to. No way they are taking three real Samurai in a fair fight. We aren't going to really kill Miki, are we?"

Interesting question. Just what was she going to do with Miki?
If the girl really was going to marry someone important, then
why interfere at all? A Koga woman in the ruling family of the
Yugumi province would serve as well there as in Kumi. Better,
in fact. "No. We are here to protect Miki, no matter what. Don't
interfere and don't get involved. I'll tell Benzo. Go to Fujiwara
and find Koan and get ready for a show. I will take care of Miki.
Take my sword. I don't want to be caught with it."

"The ambush?"

"Let the sohie take them. Miki has already figured it out."
Had she? It was a huge gamble. Did Miki still trust her? Three
years was a long time. How much had her friend changed? It was
time to find out.

"Master Arikuni?"

"I will be walking into town with you. Ama Tomoe will be
coming also."

"Then she should ride the horse, not me."

"No my Little Monkey, today you are the important one. A
bride needs to look her best when she sees the Daimyo of Yagumi.
I will stay with my friend."

"Forgive me, Master. I have made this walk for two years to
serve the people. Please let me be Ama for one more day. I beg

of you, do not make me ride the horse. Besides, I cannot use my staff from the back of a horse."

Uji winced at the thought that she might need a weapon while under his protection. Little Monkey's intransigence was wearing his patience a bit thin, and her stilted, halfhearted apology the previous day had done nothing to help his anger. "GET ON THE HORSE, OR I WILL MAKE YOU WALK!"

"Hai. I will walk." Perhaps in his anger, he had chosen his words poorly. Still, old Tomoe seemed important to Little Monkey, and having her on the horse would make the trip faster.

Arikuni mouthed an apology to the stern-faced boy. This had started poorly, and a test of wills between the girl and the man who would be her husband would make it a disaster. Holding it together, at least until the pig-headed young woman had actually consented to the request for marriage in front of the head of the clan, was proving difficult.

All in readiness, with the wave of a hand the great gate opened, and three Samurai, four horses, two Ama, and a Monk made their way out.

"In a few days, you will not be living at the temple. You will be my wife. Who will you obey then?" What had he done? A week ago she had been loving and respectful. This was a different woman. Something had happened.

"I will do my duty, as I always have." Where had the spirited, gentle, loving Little Monkey gone? This was not the woman he had learned to love. Mitsu had gone ahead to clear the path ahead. Now he returned.

"Two people ahead. A man and a woman. By the side of the road. She claims to be a merchant with a bodyguard. He has a straight sword, but the woman is unarmed. Harmless, I think." Mitsu turned his horse and proceeded down the road at a canter. Soon they came to the woman and man, who stood bowing beside a triumphant Sir Mitsu—Samurai warrior and conqueror with sword drawn.

Ama Tomoe had been nearly silent until now. "Congratulations. You've captured an unarmed peasant woman and servant. Yugumi is safe now."

"Silence. Where are you from?"

"Yoron. I heard about a celebration in Fujiwara. I came to see. I have a border pass. I am a merchant in the River District."

"I know them." Little Monkey walked forward to face the tall woman with the large, round hat. "Once, when I was wet and cold and scared and all alone in the middle of a thunderstorm, they took me in. They fed me and gave me clothes. They hid me from the men who were trying to kill me, and they were kind to me. This one held me close to keep me warm. Please walk with me to the town of Fujiwara. I would be honored."

Miki could have killed them both with a word, but that would not have been Miki. But this was a different little Miki. It wasn't little Miki at all. A glance and a few facial expressions were answered by a slight bow of the head. Miki still understood.

"My name is Ama Little Monkey. Benzo, why are you staring?"

"You're beautiful. You've grown so much."

"You have, too. It is good to see you again. My friends were acrobats. There will be other acrobats in town."

"If you know my wife to be Little Monkey, you must know her name. It seems that she has forgotten it." This was an opportunity to crack they mystery that was Little Monkey.

"We called her the Imp. At the temple they called her Amanojaku. It seemed appropriate." Hisano didn't know why Miki hadn't shared her name, but it was a good idea. Little Monkey also seemed appropriate somehow. This Miki wasn't scared, wasn't so eager to please. This Miki was confident and beautiful and in control. But she still had Miki's magnificent smile. She still had Miki's dark, penetrating eyes.

So much needed to be said, but not with a Samurai audience. As they moved around the bend, led by a fuming Uji, they were met by Monk Rennyo and some of his cavalry. Behind them were several whimpering, bound men.

"It seems that Little Monkey's dreams were accurate. There were seven of them. One we chased toward town. She was fast and good. Shinobi, I believe. These were hired thugs; they each had five ryo on them. Two are dead." Five ryo.

The cheap bastard Satake didn't even pay them well. Either that or Boss Meiko-san had kept the difference, thought Hisano.

"What kind of coins did you find on these two? Little Monkey's, or should I say the Imp's friends, Mitsu?"

"No gold. About a hundred *zini,* copper and a few silver. Reasonable for a merchant." Leaving the gold behind had just saved their life. Hisano breathed a bit lighter. The last thing she needed was to lose Miki's trust.

"You are clearly not shinobi. These thugs would have robbed you. You should thank Little Monkey for sending her sohie companions."

"Hai, thank you Ama Little Monkey. Oh look, the crowd in town. They are waiting for you." Little Monkey seemed a bit apprehensive. Friendly greetings and a crowd of children were all that she could want. This was a perversion, a public show for the private benefit of the Governor and his son. Rennyo's sohie were in attendance, supplementing the few officers this town needed. Too many people, too much noise. There would be no way to see anything coming. This happy place was now a death trap. Hisano faced her old friend as Uji pushed his horse through the crowd, and it became clear that he now needed Little Monkey's full attention. Protecting Miki might be impossible in this town today. "Ama Little Monkey, it is best if you are not so trusting. Boss Meiko-san's thugs aren't the only danger. I heard that there was a kunoichi who escaped. There might be more shinobi."

"If a kunoichi wanted me dead, I would be so already. If you can, please see me later, Hisano san. It may be difficult."

Drums, a few acrobats and street entertainers, some local, including a couple who weren't so local whom Little Monkey recognized, made her smile. Perhaps she was wrong after all; maybe there was a reason for joy. Maybe, just maybe, there was a reason for hope. But Hisano's presence disturbed her. She knew about the thugs. What else could her Koga friend not say? Master Arikuni knew who Hisano was also, and the significance was not lost on him.

Dances of the children and all of the people whose lives had given hers value surrounded her. Compassion was the heart of her service, and joy its result. Behind her stood Uji, watching her receive the thanks and enjoy the simple gifts of food and combs and the labors of craftsmen given from the heart, and he wondered what it would be like to be loved so much instead of being feared. This was what he would be taking away from the girl he had learned to love, but could he ever have Little Monkey's loyalty by locking her away? Is this what Little Monkey was afraid of? Perhaps this beautiful woman could never really belong to him. Little Monkey drew her life from their love. Maybe a life of privilege and power would never suit this young woman who would be ripped away from those who loved her and needed her more than he ever could. Locking her away in the mansion for ten days had nearly killed Little Monkey, causing his father to send her home. How long would she last as his wife?

The evening would be chilly, but for many the celebration would go on. Uji watched the young woman's tearful goodbyes to all those she had cared for over the last several years, fighting to not let it touch his own heart. On this day Little Monkey had been Ama one last time. Tomorrow would she be a dutiful and loyal wife or a joyless prisoner cringing at his touch, longing for escape? Worse, would he be loved by the people of his province or hated for what he had stolen from them?

Making her way down the street as the light faded toward the Governor's mansion, flanked by Temple Master Arikuni and Ama Tomoe, she walked like a condemned man who had accepted his fate, occasionally stopping to say good-bye or to gaze at a happy memory that would be no more the instant the sword fell. Closing his eyes, Uji knew his duty to his clan and father and could now see the conflict that was tearing his Little Monkey apart.

Mitsu and Benkei followed behind the trio of monks to protect the girl as much to prevent her escape. Little Monkey had been right about the thugs on the road. What else was she right about?

Edeko watched her friend wash her face and comb her hair slowly. "You have chosen to appear before our Lord as Ama?"

"Hai. I an Ama until Lord Suwa gives his consent. I have nothing else that is mine."

"You can wear one of my kimonos."

"I thank you, but I do not have time now. Besides, Temple Master Arikuni and Ama Tomoe will be there also. They are already getting impatient with me."

"Why do you not want to live with us?" The question had been bothering her since Little Monkey had left more than a week ago. "We love you here! Uji does not understand. None of us do."

Little Monkey bit her lip as the thirteen-year-old Edeko pushed for a response. Somehow, a simple "you would not understand" would not suffice. "Every happy moment in my life has been as Ama. I have never dreamed of anything else. I am a peasant girl, and I have done things, been things. Uji deserves better. And my presence here is dangerous to all of you."

Ama Tomoe impatiently slid the door open. "Child, it is well past time. You still are dressed that way? You will embarrass us all. No more delays. Lord Suwa can have your head for this. You should be ashamed of yourself."

"Hai, Ama Tomoe." Edeko's question would have to wait.

The meeting room was one Little Monkey knew well, having built a model of a bridge that moved there. Lord Suwa was an old man but somehow seemed familiar. His dark silk kimono had very little design, and his light blue over jacket bore the embroidered clan seal on both sides. Behind him were two guards with naginata in their light, bright-red armor. Uji was already there, as was Temple Master Arikuni and Governor Mitsuhide. Everyone, it seemed, but her. Master Arikuni's stern glance signaled his displeasure. There would be no forgiveness on this day.

Greetings, bows, platitudes, and a short speech about punctuality later, Little Monkey sat, hands on her lap, wishing she were anywhere else.

"Today I walked among the people and could see for myself the work that you have done. No woman is capable of all that they say that you are, and yet the bridge that you designed is nearing completion, and the coffers of my province are full, and my ministers beg for your services. The people of the town gave you many gifts today, but you wear none of them. Sitting there in the simplest of rags, biting your lip like a guilty child, you try my patience. Yet I see in you profound beauty and a powerful mind tempered by compassion and wisdom. I confess myself jealous by the way the people respond to you. Master Uji even tells me that you defeated three warriors in combat recently, he being one of them. It is strange that you do not feel yourself worthy."

"I am a mere peasant girl from a mountain village, my Lord."

"Do you think that all of my Generals were born Samurai? My best three were farmers whose courage and intelligence I learned to respect. They earned their positions. You are the youngest Ama anyone has ever seen, yet Master Arikuni and Governor Mitsuhide tell me that you are a master with a number of weapons, praise he does not give easily, and the commander of a unit of naginata. A healer, an engineer, accomplished in the Samurai arts, even, I am told, skilled in *ninjutsu*. How did you meet Master Uji?"

"I was asked to instruct Uji-san in military strategy and philosophy. This included poetry and writing, estimates, and the wisdom of Buddha."

"That is what you were asked to do, and you have done it well. But that is not how you met my nephew. He tells a different story."

"Hai, my Lord."

"Biting your lip again: I was told about that. It seems that Uji and his friends were behaving badly, and you reasoned with him as you explained it to him."

"Hai."

"Four of them. Drunk was his excuse. So why are you here, my mysterious Ama Little Monkey, looking so guilty, with Master Uji sitting beside you?"

"I have come to ask permission to marry Master Uji. To be his wife and to serve in his house."

"To serve in his house. And why do you wish to serve in his house? You must know that Uji will someday become Daimyo. Is it power that you seek?"

"Oh, no, my Lord. It would be better if Uji-san were a farmer! I have seen what men do with power." They were the wrong words spoken to the wrong man, and Little Monkey knew it at once.

"Have you, now? You disapprove of power. Or is it the men who have power that you disapprove of?"

Her mind raced, but nothing came. He was angry, and she had no answers.

"So why DO you want to marry my nephew Uji?"

It was the question she feared most. "I love Uji-san, but I must not marry him. My love will cost Master Uji his life. My enemies have found me, and neither the Iga nor General Satake of the Hamatsu will give up until I am dead. Everyone around me always dies. They are already in the mansion, I can feel them."

"Check the compound. Get her out of here."

Uji grabbed her by the arm, forcing Little Monkey to her feet and out the door. Uji was furious, as were Temple Master Arikuni and Ama Tomoe, who followed as the angry man pulled the tiny Ama out the building and into the courtyard.

"I told you that Little Monkey would not consent. She sees enemies everywhere."

"She saw them on the road."

"Thugs, ordinary thieves. WHY? The life I would have given you. WHAT DO YOU WANT? Get away from me. Leave my sight forever." Uji was feeling hurt, rejected. This is not what she had intended, but what did she expect? "If I see you again, I will take your head myself."

Getting close to the gate, the enraged young Samurai shoved her toward it, making her fall into the dirt. What was to be a day of joy was ruined. There were no guards at the door. Not even the Hatamoto, the Daimyo's guard. "UJI, where are the guards? Protect our Lord. Protect your father. Send your sister into the town." The boy was dumbstruck. She was right.

Shadows in the darkness; the lanterns had been extinguished. Why had he not noticed this before? Noise from the mansion, screams, shouting, the clash of steel. There was a fight going on. "Stay here and be safe. I will show you that I can protect you."

"Uji, give me your sword. They do not fight fair."

The shadows made their way closer, out of the darkness. Four black, hooded figures. Probably one more out of sight; she knew that shinobi never reveal everything. This was it, the nightmare. All the people she loved the most, trapped with her.

A tall, hooded man dressed in black held his sword down and to the side. He was reading Uji correctly. "Save the woman for last. They want her head as proof. Little Miki is yours." There was a kunoichi beside him, staring at her, only the eyes visible from under the hood she wore, as the other two shinobi fanned out to surround her. "Little Miki is one of us; make it fast."

"UJI!" The boy threw himself forward, striking downward as the tall shinobi easily cut across his belly, ducking out of the way. "UJI!" The dark kunoichi drew her ninto, motioning to the two men, who moved toward Master Arikuni and Ama Tomoe as they struggled to open the gate. One brief opportunity for her as Uji's killer made his one mistake and stepped forward, allowing her to dive forward. Grabbing Uji's katana, she blocked the tall man's blow while kicking hard into the man's crotch, sending the tall man to his knees. Little Monkey screamed as she shoved the sharp blade into man's heart.

Tomoe had managed to get the gate open, and Rennyo's sohie were pouring into the courtyard. The kunoichi who was to kill her had disappeared into the darkness, but the other two shinobi lay squirming on the ground, cut to pieces by angry, armed monks. Naginata penetrated the tall shinobi's back through to his chest, completing what Uji's sword had begun.

Rolling Uji over, Little Monkey prayed that he was still alive. Uji was breathing, but bleeding hard from the long slit across his stomach, bowels visible as they spilled out. It would not be long, as she worked to stem the flow with her shaking hands. If she could just keep him alive long enough.

Uji coughed blood and labored to breathe. "Little Miki. He called you Little Miki. You are right, death hurts. It is not glorious at all. I really do love you." As she held his head, he grabbed her arm for a moment or two before she felt his hand go weak.

One more time death had followed her. Agony gripped her heart as hands pulled her away from Uji. Warm blood soaked through her clothing as she fought to get back to the boy who might have been her husband had fate allowed it. Temple Master Arikuni was being carried into the mansion, as was the Ama Tomoe. Maybe she could help them.

Pushing into the mansion, Little Monkey wept as she tried to comprehend that this was her doing, her fault. In this scene from hell, Uji, Tomoe and Arikuni were all dead or dying. The Daimyo had survived, but sweet little Edako was slain. Soldiers, servants, and a few shinobi were scattered about in pools of blood amid the devastation.

Governor Mitsuhide and Rennyo stood beside Master Arikuni, motioning for her to come. She moved toward his bloody form, and the old temple master seized her hand. "Closer." Seizing the back of her head, he pulled her face close to his. "You have become more than the animals I saw tonight. You must not take revenge. Be Little Monkey. No one else should die for this."

Rennyo passed her bag of medicines to Little Monkey. "Can you do anything for him?"

"I will try, but the Iga poison their weapons. How did you know to come?"

"The girl who brought you to us came to the temple and told me that you needed our help. She counted perhaps twenty Iga. When I told her of your visions, she convinced me that you are never wrong. Hisano is a merchant in Yoron now, and she would like to talk to you when you are finished."

The Governor stood in the shattered door, watching the young woman who would have been his daughter pray for his oldest friend. "You did all that you could do. I grieve for the loss of your master and my friend." The sun peeked over the mountains to the east. It had been a long, terrible night for all. "Our Lord is returning to his castle this morning. You are welcome to go with him. He feels that you can still be of great service to Yugumi."

"Thank you. I have duties here first, Lord Mitsuhide. I am very sorry about Uji-san."

"How did my son die?"

"Bravely. He fought the jonin, the largest and strongest of them, to protect me. It was Uji's sword that penetrated the man's heart." That knowledge seemed to satisfy the man who had been so kind to her. Walking into the mansion, he had two children to ready for burial.

"It was Uji's sword, but not Uji's hands. I was first through the gate." A familiar voice. Hisano.

"Thank you for getting Rennyo. I could not make him believe."

"You were almost a Princess today. I really wanted you to be happy. What will you do now? You should come home with us."

"I have matters to attend to."

"How many more people have to die to keep Little Monkey safe? How many more monks need to die because you won't accept who and what you are? Last night you killed for the first time. How many Ama can say that?" Hisano sat beside the bloodstained Little Monkey and watched her words take effect. "It might surprise you to know that after you told Lady O-Sho about Teruko, she ordered Satake to kidnap another Princess, Lady O-Kin, wife Lord Shigenori, the rightful Daimyo of Kumi, and her daughter Yumi. Poor, poor little Yumi, Princess Yumi, will be forced to marry Yoshida or maybe even Satake because some girl named Miki failed to kill her target as ordered. That was the time Toko died, as you might recall. I wonder what he would think if he knew that bringing you along would mean the death of Kumi province. You see, once Lady O-Kin marries Nobunaga, the Emperor will probably have to recognize the Hamatsu takeover of Kumi as soon as Shigenori is dead. They are no doubt working on that now. You did valuable work for Hamatsu that day."

"Where are Lady O-Kin and Yumi now?"

"Unreachable. In Hamatsu castle, I would expect. So are you going to go with Lord Suwa and be his personal advisor or go back to the temple so that more monks can die for their Little Monkey? You can serve the Koga clan by being an advisor to Lord Suwa. Who knows, you might even find a General to marry. Or, you can come home with me. Kumi needs a princess, it seems."

"I have matters to attend to."

"Miki, we are your family."

"This must end. All of it. The death, the running, all of it. The evil must stop."

"And with our help, it will. We can help. We are at the inn in town. I will wait for you there. Take the time you need."

Watching Hisano walk through the mansion gate, Little Monkey knew what had to be done. She was no longer a child, but a woman who had nearly been married to a Samurai. As a child, she could run. Now she had a duty—to Kumi, to Uji, and to the monks who had given her everything. There would be no more running. She had matters to attend to. The damage that the child Little Miki had caused, the woman Miki would have to fix.

Seeing Uji's friends Benkei and Mitsu in the courtyard, she called to them. It was time to grow up.

Koan stared out at the activity on the street below through the windows of the inn. Women were wailing, men were angry, soldiers and officers were keeping order. The Iga attack on the mansion had come close to killing the Daimyo of Yugumi Province and had killed the heir.

"It's been two days since the fight in the mansion. Miki isn't coming."

"Are you sure she didn't go with Lord Suwa?" Hisano stood and grabbed her hat as the tall boy shook his head in response. *Is Miki still in the mansion?* the tall kunoichi wondered. Little Monkey was too well known to sneak anywhere. Sliding the partition door open, she greeted Gonji on his way up the steps.

"I'm going to find Miki. She has had long enough to grow up."

"Haven't you heard? Miki, I mean Little Monkey, is dead. Why didn't you tell us that she was wounded in the fight? They say that Uji and Miki, I mean Little Monkey, fought together and killed dozens of shinobi defending Lord Suwa."

"Where did you hear that? I spoke to Miki the morning after the fight. She was fine."

"It's all over the street. Master Uji and his wife Little Monkey were buried in the family shrine near the mansion's garden. They say that Little Monkey, I mean Miki, loved that garden."

It wasn't possible. She had seen the girl, spoken with her. Pushing the boy aside, Hisano nearly tripped getting down the steep stairs. Rushing out of the building, she could hear the sorrow and anger of the townspeople, some claiming to have seen the girl's body lying there in her beautiful white wedding kimono. Soldiers were everywhere.

The garden sat behind the mansion bordering a peach orchard. Groups of mourners, monks, sohie, townspeople, and Samurai offered their condolences to all those who had known the star-crossed pair of lovers. Most impressive was the number of children near the new graves. Wherever Miki went she made a difference, and for a moment, the kunoichi wished that her friend had been permitted to live the life of joy and giving that she had wanted so badly. Little Monkey, Miki, always made a difference.

"Hisano-san, is that you?"

"Monk Rennyo."

"My deepest sorrow over the loss of your friend. She told me about the two of you growing up together. Please come with me. This should not be done in the open."

As Hisano followed the well-built monk through the gate into the mansion, nothing about this felt phony. The grief was real, the tears were real. The damage inside the mansion was severe. A terrible fight had taken place here. But how had she died? How, and when?

Stopping, Rennyo asked one of the servant girls for something. The girl retrieved a small package with a letter that the monk now handed to her. "These are Little Monkey's blood-soaked robes. This letter is addressed to Monk Akaki at the North Road temple. Little Monkey could no longer live with the pain that she felt at the loss of Uji. She asks that you deliver these as you return home. Little Monkey was my friend as well as yours. I have never known a more beautiful spirit and a more compassionate woman. I shall miss her greatly."

Hisano peeked inside the paper surrounding the robes. Had she misjudged the girl that badly? Kumi had two Princesses; one was in Hamatsu Castle and unreachable, the other lay buried in the garden outside and she—Hisano—had lost them both. The game was over. Nothing stopped them from returning home now. Nothing at all.

Chapter 18 – A Princess Saved

terrible revenge
a purpose rediscovered
miki is reborn

The trip back to Yoron was a quiet one for Gonji, Koan, and Hisano. One of their own was dead, and no one wanted to talk about it. Benzo had gotten a job at the mansion cleaning up after the attack, so he would be along later.

Gonji tossed the sword onto the sack he used for a pillow near the corner of the small loft area that had become headquarters for the Hisano gang. "I thought you said that we weren't coming back here, not that I mind at all. I know Benzo will be glad to see the girls again. What are we going to do with Miki's stuff?"

"I have to let Gonzo know what happened. He may send us home; he may send us to Hamatsu. Miki's robe is worth two hundred ryo to the people outside if Satake doesn't kill us before he pays. Have you seen Benzo yet?"

"No. But he should be here today. He was watching the road out of Fujiwara in case Miki went with Lord Suwa. He helped bury Miki, I think. Are you crying?"

"No, of course not. It's the smell of the fish. I've grown use to fresh air."

"Me, too. Miki was different. When I was sick, she sat with me all night, as she did with everybody. I always wondered why all of us had to be killers. Miki never was. I really liked her. Hisano? Since it doesn't matter anymore, she really was Lord Oto's daughter, wasn't she? Do you think the Mountain Samurai or that Taka guy knew?"

"No. You aren't supposed to know, either. What I can't believe is that Miki never did. How a girl could be so smart and so stupid at the same time was amazing." Hiding the secret seemed pointless now. The Iga knew, Satake knew, the only people it seemed who didn't were a brother and her father.

"Did you see the shrine they built down the street? What makes it so great is that it was paid for by Satake's gold. Didn't do badly with the face, but they made the eyes a bit big. Too bad she didn't know."

"They loved the stupid imp in Fujiwara, too. I wonder if she gets a shrine there. Where is Koan?"

"Praying at the shrine, I think."

"Oh for the Buddha's sake! She was eta, like us! People die. People like us die faster. Stupid girls like Miki who can't stay hidden and won't lie and won't run away die really young! She was lucky not to be dead until now." Enough was enough! Hisano thought back to all the times that her life had been ruled by the need to babysit the child. At least for now, she was free to be herself. Getting up, she swung on the ladder that took her down into the room where they cured and pickled the fish. Pushing the door that led to the street, she saw that the evening crowd was starting to show up for the inn and girls on the boats. If she never smelled another fish or saw another filthy river, it would be too soon.

"Hisano-san! Benzo's back! He's been with Suni all afternoon."

"Has he now? I'll just go in and say hello." Why hadn't he seen her first! All of the boys had grown a bit too independent, but Benzo was worst, as the boy did all of his thinking with the head between his legs. Hisano climbed onto the boat, and a happy Suni met her.

"Benzo-san is back! He's very tired, so I'm going to get him more sake."

"Don't bother. He'll be too busy." Pushing past Suni, Hisano glared at the worthless, half-naked, lazy excuse for a man nursing an empty cup.

"Hey Suni, get me some more sake, too. I'm thirsty. And keep my being back a secret. You know how nasty Hisano gets."

As shinobi go, no one on her team could be considered extraordinary. Adequate would be nice, even mediocre occasionally all right. Being worthless was becoming tiresome, however, and now she wondered if she was leading this team or merely walking in front of it. Looking around, she saw a bucket of what was probably water. "Drink this, you stinking swine. You haven't seen bitchy yet, you asshole!"

"Hey!"

The water, or whatever, was followed by the bucket and anything else the enraged Hisano could grab. In all the years that they had known each other, had trained and worked together, had risked their lives together, never had she been this hurt, this angry. She pulled her dagger. Maybe it was time for the animal to lose the part that kept him distracted from his duty. "DON'T RUN! If cutting it off is the..." THUD!

Her head hurt. Koan and Gonji were beside her as she opened her eyes. Hisano wondered who her attacker was, a question answered by Benzo's personal little whore, Suni, who offered her sweet, heartfelt apologies. Benzo stood nervously by the door, ready for a quick escape if need be.

"Why did you have to get so mad? I was just helping Suni and Kinu. Suni was happy to see me."

"Happier than I am. Why didn't you see me first? Where was the respect you owed me? What about your duty to your clan and to this team and to me?"

"I'm sorry. I was tired and wanted to relax. Suni saw me first and, well, you know. It's not like Fusa is with us anymore, and you...well you...and Miki turned into a really beautiful woman, but she isn't with us anymore. Now I guess one of us wouldn't be good enough anymore. Miki likes Samurai now."

"Miki is dead."

"How did that happen? She was alive when I talked to her, and when I saw her sneak out of the mansion with those two Samurai."

"Didn't you help bury her?"

"Hai, but that wasn't Miki. They called her Miki, but it was a kid named Edeko, the Governor's daughter. The Iga split her face down the middle, and she was about Miki's size and all, and missing her face looked like Miki, who still had her face when she slipped out with her face all covered, as if that would fool me."

"Miki was alive?"

"After you talked to her, she went in to see Lord Suwa and Governor Mitsuhide for the longest time. She took those two Samurai with her. I decided to listen in from underneath, and Miki told them everything about Lady Teruko. She asked for Uji-san's sword and promised to get revenge on the Iga and Satake by rescuing Lady O-Kin and her daughter Yumi. That's when they decided to bury the kid Edeko in her place."

No. NO! Miki had done it to her again! If she was angry with Benzo, how she felt about Miki was beyond measure. "I want the whole story. NOW!"

"After the meeting I saw Miki, who asked me about Yumi and O-Kin, so I told her everything, including the part about Satake paying us to kill her. She said goodbye, which I thought was weird. Later on I saw her sneak away with two Samurai and a few extra horses."

"And you didn't think that I needed to know that right away? Miki has a five-day head start on us, and she is on a horse."

"We don't know where she is going, or why."

"Hai, we do. If anyone else were being chased by Iga or Hamatsu soldiers sent from Hamatsu castle, they would run away from it. Not Miki. Oh no, not our dear, sweet Miki. Little stupid monkey will wade into the middle of every bit of trouble she can find until everyone around her has cheerfully died to save her noble ass. It's our turn again."

"Why us? Why do we even care? Miki is eta like us. Why are we always chasing that girl? I like living." Benzo glanced at Suni, the girl who had no right to actually be in the room, or listening to the conversation of a team of shinobi.

"Benzo, you stay and take care of business here. Suni, there is a package in our room, covered in paper with string. Deliver it to General Satake at Lord Yoshida's mansion and ask for payment. Only speak with Satake! He knows what he owes us. Tell him that we are watching."

"You don't want me with you?"

"No. Someone has to tell Gonzo what is happening. If it looks like Satake will betray you, take the girls and the money and go to Yugumi and start a new life running a pleasure house. You'll be good at that. At least one of us should live through this. Koan, get us ready to leave. Gonji, make sure we have rope. Miki is coming home whether she likes it or not."

"What about O-Kin and the girl Yumi?"

"We shall see."

The large Samurai Benkei stared at the castle building atop its stone base. Twice the size of the castle in Yugumi, it was probably as large as any in all of Nippon. Thousands of guards and soldiers were in the area. The main keep housed maybe a hundred or more servants, and, of course, the Lord Nobunaga's Hatamoto, his personal bodyguard.

Also within those walls, according to Little Monkey, were about a dozen Iga warriors serving Teruko. Those were by far the most dangerous if the tiny woman was to be believed.

"That's a big castle. Well guarded, too. Tell me again, Little Monkey, why do we need you? And why the haste? We have time. If what you claim is true, why not simply go in and expose the woman Lady Teruko as an impostor? I am her older brother; they would believe me." Taking orders from a woman was bad enough, but taking direction from this excuse for a woman was worse. Benkei sat behind the tree where he had been sitting before first light. What the girl was doing escaped him.

"Ama Little Monkey died in the courtyard with Master Uji and Master Arikuni and Ama Tomoe. My name is Miki, and I am a Koga kunoichi. You wouldn't live long enough to expose anything. Teruko has maybe twenty Iga inside with her. You can't get inside the castle. I am kunoichi; those walls mean nothing to me. There is another group of shinobi on their way to free Lady O-Kin and her daughter. We must move before they arrive."

"Why is it that no one can see these Iga but you, you little witch? Why is that?"

"You saw them the night Uji died. By the time you recognize one for what he is, you will already be dead. They killed twenty guards before even I realized that they were in the mansion. We lost over forty people, and we only counted six Iga dead, three in the courtyard with me. Over two hundred men searched for a day and never found any of the survivors. Had Monk Rennyo not arrived, all of us would have been killed. I need you to see for yourself and then live long enough to tell Lord Suwa the truth."

"Why not just let the other shinobi rescue her? Are they not like you?"

"Shinobi protect secrets the way you breathe. They will preserve the Iga secret because it is something that they can use later on. Also I think that Lord Suwa and Governor Mitsuhide will protect Lady O-Kin and her daughter Yumi as a matter of honor, returning them to their family. The Koga will bargain with them, use them, keep them until an advantage is gained by revealing them. To protect those secrets, they will kill you. Maybe they will kill me also. I am nothing but an eta and unimportant. They would not touch me as Ama. No Koga would ever harm a monk."

"So why are we watching the castle? It has not moved all day, and I am getting hungry."

"We aren't watching the castle. We are watching the shrine on the side. The Iga teach their kunoichi to be miko to carry messages. It's one of the few ways a woman can travel unnoticed. I traveled as a street acrobat. By now they should be getting reports back from their attack on the Governor's Mansion. Sir Mitsu is watching the woods on the other side, but I think that there is a tunnel between the castle and the shrine. I can go up the wall to get in, but I need to get Lady O-Kin and Yumi out somehow. That tunnel would work."

"If it exists."

"How many people have gone in since this morning?"

"I was not watching. Why does it matter?"

"Twelve. Only eight have come out, all senior Samurai. Not counting the people who live there, two were women, mikos, and two were lower-class *ashigaru*. Why would a common soldier ever enter a shrine? That shrine is for Samurai and the senior members of the clan. The mikos might spend the night, but not the ashigaru. I remembered one of them. He was part of the group that took your sister."

"Why did you not tell me?"

"Because you would act the way you are acting now. He would remember me. He was the ugly, hairy one who was told to take me into the woods to kill me. He made the mistake of letting me keep my staff. That move that I used on you works on shinobi, also."

"I remember. We will talk about that later. What now?"

"You go get Mitsu-san and have fun with the girls at the inn. You know how to do that. I'll wait for darkness, and then I go to work. Meet me at the Temple on the other side of the town tomorrow morning. Speak to no one."

"If I were not Samurai, you would frighten me."

It was a relief to be free of the unhappy Benkei's constant griping as Miki settled down for a few hours' sleep before what could either be a very long, or a tragically short, night. Alone for the first time in recent memory, she felt strange. Totally alone in a hostile land, living the life that Hisano would have cherished. In the temple she had been constantly surrounded by monks, and in town the constant center of attention. Even in the mansion and with Uji, loneliness had never stood with her. Now, at the edge of a woods in a land where death would quickly follow discovery, loneliness was welcome.

She had missed the sound of the insects, the nearly imperceptible motion of nocturnal animals hunting or avoiding becoming a meal. In the mountains there would be wolves to protect her, but not here. Nothing would protect her here. The night was turning cold, the light wind bringing the smell of incense from the shrine, the smell of dirt, the odor and shouting people from the nearby town pursuing their pleasures. All these things she had missed over the last three years in her life surrounded by people. Life no longer mattered. All that she had loved was gone. Uji, Master Arikuni, Ama Tomoe lay buried because of her. Ama no more, forever, but not quite kunoichi. What was she? Miki, the child who had grown up in the shadows, truly belonging nowhere, without clan or family. Out of friends, nowhere to go when it was over. So what did it matter if she lived? A child of shadow has nothing to lose, and nothing to gain in a world of people who will use her but never accept her as one of their own. Her mind wandered as she drifted in and out of sleep on the cold earth in the center of the woods. Ama Little Monkey was truly dead; Miki was reborn.

An owl startled Miki into full consciousness. A look at the stars told her that it was well past midnight and time to go into motion. Her approach could not be through the open grassy area in front of the temple, as that would take far too long to do right. From woods to rock to back wall would be the path. Mitsu and Benkei would get in the way, make too much noise, would get her killed. This was work for shinobi.

A check of the stars told her that she had to move fast. Priests were like monks and typically up before dawn to get ready for prayers and the day's labors. This was reconnaissance only. Any human contact, anything left behind would be a disaster. No trees were close enough to use to get over the wall. The door was locked from inside and might have a bell on it in any case. It would have to be the hard way: over the wall.

The wall was not terribly high, about twice her height; this was a small shrine and not a castle. Getting over should not be hard. Getting the rope ready, she would need to catch either the wooden lip on the other side or the crossbeam on top or the wall. If this were a shinobi mission, she would have claws, and then she could use the wooden support, but neither Samurai nor monks used such things. Testing the rope, Miki took a deep breath before the quick climb to the top. She recoiled the improvised hook; it would not do to have it found, and she might need it for an escape. A nearby storage building gave the nimble kunoichi a way down as she positioned a patch over one eye. Inside there might be lights, and retaining her night vision might be the difference between life and death.

All her senses were in play. Every noise, every smell, even the movement of the wind or the vibration of the wooden floorboards told her a story. She went to ground as a man made his way out of the small building in the back and walked toward the smaller building along the wall. Pressing her face against the ground, the last thing she needed was to have one of the temple's priests trip over her. A few minutes later, the man made the return trip, rushing to get out of the cool night air. He would certainly be awake for a while. Best to lie on the ground for a few more moments even though she was starting to shiver.

Getting up slowly, she made her way though the unlocked back door to the shrine. *Why lock a door for a place that has nothing to steal and is surrounded by walls?* The entrance, if she was right, had to be hidden—perhaps a sliding door or a floor panel. What was curious was that the pedestal for the brass shrine itself backed up to a wall. Normally they stood alone to make it easy to clean and polish. Perhaps there was an entrance behind the wall? Maybe it slides forward, she thought. Lifting the mat in front revealed a small hole with a cord. She pulled it, and the side panel on the pedestal popped open slightly. One side of the tunnel! So far, all had gone well.

Whispers and the sound of the back door opening sent her heart to her throat. She had nowhere to hide—or did she? It was also curious that the only light in the shrine came from starlight through its small, high windows. Why no lanterns? Why no candles in the shrine? Touching the black eyepiece over her right eye made her realize that this was how Iga shinobi came and left through the castle. Eliminating the lights allowed the shinobi on missions to retain their night vision, as she was doing with the patch. Dropping the mat, she slipped through the panel as her foot found the ladder. An audible click told her that the lock had engaged. Voices on the other side made escape through the panel impossible for now.

Moving the patch to the other eye didn't seem to help, as there were no sources of light at all. There was a rail on one side to guide someone through the dank, moldy tunnel, which seemed to continue forever until she could make out the faint light around what appeared to be a small wooden door. Feeling around revealed a latch—nothing too complicated, all too easy. Way too easy. Slipping through the door put her into a large room full of boxes and weapons. She was under the castle somewhere, but where? Somehow she would have to get two women, one only seventeen, to this spot to get them out. Only seventeen. Miki snickered as she realized that she herself was only seventeen. By seventeen most women were married and mothers.

Looking around, she saw a larger door that would lead into the castle proper somewhere.

"First time here?"

Spinning around, Miki drew her sword, facing the voice in the dark. It was female, young, and quite sweet. "Hai. I am here to see Lady Teruko with a message. I also have a message for General Satake and Lady O-Sho."

"From Yoron?"

"Fujiwara. I worked at the temple there."

Lighting a lantern, the young miko examined the small kunoichi, sword in hand. Unconcerned, the young woman began to get dressed in the traditional red-and-white hakama and keikogi of a Shinto Shrine Maiden, a miko. "You can't wander the halls like that. Teruko, I mean Gozen, would have a fit. Use that kimono over there. My, my, you are a small one. First mission? What are you, fourteen?"

"I'm older than I look."

"Sure you are. I am getting too old to be a miko, so they want me to go to find some guy named Katsu to get close to. Oh, stay away from the ugly, hairy one named Yabu. He can't keep his hands off of any of the girls, even though Gozen told him to stop. Imagine, too old at twenty-two."

"I know about Yabu. He pulled me into the woods once." *To kill me.*

"Poor girl. That explains why they didn't send you out as miko. They wanted us to be virgins, not that I am now. You do what you have to."

"Nice to meet you. Oh, out that door and up two flights of steps. The first room is guarded; that is Lord Nobunaga's special secret prisoner. Avoid her and her whiny crybaby daughter. She is supposed to be Sir Yoshida's new wife. It's all part of the plan. Imagine being a Princess and that unhappy all the time. But then, Lady O-Sho beats her silly for everything. Teruko is with Nobunaga now, two more flights up. Bye!" Slipping through the door to the tunnel, the miko disappeared as she closed the door behind her. The bedding indicated that this was the official quarters of Teruko's personal messengers. *I didn't even have to ask any questions. This is too easy.*

Making her way up the stairs, she could see the door. A pin held the door closed, but no was guard in sight. Why guard a prisoner locked in a room? She opened the door. Now was the time to find out if her information was correct. "Lady O-Kin. Get up, come with me now!"

"Momma." Yumi, most likely, thought Miki. The girl was terrified for her mother.

"It will be all right. Lord Nobunaga needs us alive. In a few days you will be married and too valuable to kill. You are a Samurai woman and the daughter of the rightful Daimyo of Kumi. Be strong."

"I do not want to be married. I have never met Sir Yoshida." O-Kin pressed her fingers over her daughter's lips before getting up and putting on a simple kimono. Following Miki out the door, she seemed surprised when the strange girl pointed down the stairs.

"What does Nobunaga want now?"

"It is not about what Nobunaga wants. It is about what you want."

"Is he going to execute me?"

"That isn't part of my plan." Miki pushed the soft, middle-aged woman into the storage room where they could talk out of sight. Even if she could get Yumi and O-Kin out through the tunnel now, they would be tracked down and captured before they could reach Yugumi. The Samurai Benkei and Mitsu needed to get them out on fast horses. It would be her job to give Mitsu and Benkei the head start they needed. With any luck, Rennyo and his cavalry would meet them across the ridgeline separating the two provinces. "Do you want to escape? Do you want to get Princess Yumi home?"

"What? Who are you?"

"I am Koga kunoichi. See that small door over there? It leads to a Shinto temple. When I come for you tomorrow, we will have control of both ends of that tunnel. You will go with the Samurai at the other end of the tunnel, and they will take you to Yugumi by horse. So, do you want to escape?"

"Hai. Very much, but not for myself. I cannot go home. But if you could help Yumi." Lifting the lantern that Miki carried, the surprised woman stared into Miki's eyes. "Oto?"

"I have met him and his son. Say nothing to anyone. Anyone at all, do you understand? Be ready. I have a plan, but we do not have much time. Listen carefully..."

"Those two Samurai have been in front of the temple since mid-morning. Do you think that they are the ones who left with Miki?" Gonji shoved another one of Suni's rice cakes into his mouth. The small shop down the road from the temple provided a good view of the front of the temple.

"Hai. The large, tubby one is Benkei, and the muscular, smaller one is Mitsu. The question is Miki. Where is she?" Hisano grabbed a rice cake also. They had moved fast and light, but money wasn't a problem. The tall kunoichi wondered if it might be wiser to quit the shinobi business and stick with crime. It paid well and was less dangerous. Her instinct that Miki would always choose a temple as a meeting place seemed correct with the presence of two Samurai and confirmed as she spied a small woman in a simple kimono, face hidden by a large hat, marching down the road from the town with Miki's usual deliberateness. "Get back and stay out of sight. Sneaking up on that girl is impossible. Track the Samurai instead. That will tell us what Miki is up to."

Watching Miki speak to the men was revealing. Angry at first, the men grew very interested in what she had to say. Within moments the girl was pointing toward the castle, giving directions. Whatever was happening, it was Miki's plan, and that made her far more dangerous. As the meeting broke up, the men moved slowly toward town. Miki disappeared quickly behind a wall going in the opposite direction, emerging from neither side. Directing Gonji out the back door with a quick glance, she returned to watch the men stop and argue right in front of the door of their hideout. Listening in, it was as if they were arguing about nothing in particular.

"Hisano, I found Miki." And indeed he had! Gonji backed into the room, the point of Miki's katana at his throat.

"You look good for a corpse."

"How did you figure it out?"

"Benzo, who didn't bother to tell me for five days. Miki, you can't do this! No one can get into that fortress. The attempt is suicide. We taught you better."

"I found a way in last night and talked to Lady O-Kin. She is expecting me tonight. These men? These men are under my protection. MY protection. I have a plan, and I don't need you."

Benkei and Mitsu made their way through the cloth guarding the door. "We are under YOUR protection?"

"The little witch did figure out we were being watched. So far she has been pretty good. What do you want to do with these two?" Mitsu held the saya of his katana in preparation. More frightening was a seriously disturbed former Ama, whose eyes had darkened even more than normal. As she held her sword at Gonji's throat, Hisano could hear the resentment and anger in the girl's shaky voice. For the first time the boy was speechless, terrified at saying something that could trigger an attack from a girl he thought he knew.

"You have a lot to learn, Mitsu-san. Shinobi never show you everything. Where is Benzo? Fusa? Gonzo? Koan? I know you sent Fusa into town to spy on me before the attack. Why? If you knew, why didn't you warn me? You let them kill Uji? YOU LET THEM KILL MASTER ARIKUNI AND AMA TOMOE! WHY? "

"I didn't send Fusa. I haven't seen Fusa in a year. Gonzo said that she was working at the Yoshida mansion as a servant. Miki, that is blood running down Gonji's chest. Please back off. We thought you were dead. We came looking for you, but an old lady we thought was Ama Little Monkey told us that the girl Miki died the night she arrived at the temple. Gonzo didn't send me. It's just Koan, Gonji, and me."

"Satake hired you to kill me."

"We are yakuza. That is who you go to when you want someone killed. We didn't figure out that you were alive until Satake paid us to kill you. Our mission was to bring you home, alive and willingly. When Rennyo asked me about your visions, I told him to believe you. One more thing—and this one hurts. I don't think

Fusa is on our side anymore. I haven't seen Gonzo in a month, and I am afraid that he is dead. We have no permission to be here. We are on our own."

"Miki, please. Hisano is telling the truth." The bundle of rage hadn't lowered the blade a bit. This was a very different Little Miki than the one he had grown to like. This new Miki was a demon, so much like the brother she did not know about.

"Miki, think before you act! Think! Having a Koga woman as the wife of a Daimyo is what WE wanted. That was what the Iga were afraid of. We wanted Uji alive, not dead. That is why Satake sent Meiko-san's gang after you and why we were sent to kill that gang—to keep his secret. Miki, you condemned Uji to death the moment you caught his eye. Not us." Hisano had to get through to her friend before poor Gonji either bled to death or did something stupid. Watching Miki lower her blade, but not her pitch black eyes, she knew that she was reaching her.

"You should leave. I have already accepted my destiny. You don't need to die, too."

It was what Hisano had feared most. This was Miki the Samurai, not Miki the kunoichi. "There is no reason for anyone to die. If you want revenge, we can help you get it. Did you actually get into the castle? Let us help, please. We will follow your orders, but not if all you want to do is die. I won't help you do that."

"We could use the help. Can you trust them, Little Monkey?"

"We will find out."

"Lady Teruko, where is the new girl? She had the prettiest, darkest eyes I have ever seen. A bit small and young, though. Really, really fast with a katana."

"What new girl?"

"The girl who came through the tunnel last night. She knew everything, all about you and O-Kin and the brat. She even told me that she knew Yabu, and how he pulled her into the woods once."

"She knew my name?" *It cannot be. The Koga named Miki is dead.* But then, how many times had the little demon had been reported dead before? She had escaped execution with the monks in the mountains. The officers in Isawa had supposedly executed her. Yabu himself had told her that he had killed the little oni after pleasuring himself with her. And at the cost of ten Iga shinobi, the little Ama had died in the governor's mansion. Witnesses had seen her body, had watched her be buried with her husband. Miki simply could not still be alive. "What else?"

"And about O-Sho and Satake and Lord Yoshida. She said that she had a message for them, and you."

"It cannot be. No, it cannot be! She had dark eyes? She knows about the tunnel? What else does she know, I wonder. What does it take to kill this girl? IN THIS CASTLE, LAST NIGHT!" The elegant woman was stunned. The single most pursued woman in Nippon had simply walked into its largest, best-guarded castle as though she owned it. "It seems that our friend Fusa is correct. Little Miki is very resourceful. She may be even more dangerous than her troublesome brother and father. Get Yabu in here NOW! She has to be still in the castle. Don't let the Hamatsu guards know, but have our people search for her. We have to find her first." Teruko could feel the shiver up her spine. *How bold, how daring, to slip into the heart of Hamatsu province and enter its most guarded fortress! I must not underestimate this girl again.*

"Forgive me, Teruko-san; who is this girl?"

"Her name is Miki. The daughter of Lord Yorisada no Oto and a Koga miko whore. She is Taka's older sister. You know how much trouble Oto and Taka are. Miki is a trained kunoichi, more skilled than I was led to believe. She looks so small and helpless, but nothing can be further from the truth. She fooled me several years ago when I thought her a filthy little peasant child. Nothing, and I mean nothing, is more important than capturing that girl alive. Killing her seems to be a waste of time."

"Lady O-Sho. It is pleasant to see you again this afternoon. Shall I get Yumi?"

"Lady O-Kin. I doubt very much that you want to see me. I will not be teaching Yumi today. The child is as ready as she will be ever be. Sister, you must not do what you are planning to do. You do not understand what is at stake. If you are caught, you will be executed, and then Teruko will marry our Lord Nobunaga. Please! Kumi is dead. Lord Shigenori will never accept you back. He would force you to commit *jigai*.[14] My son will be a good husband to Yumi, and her son will some day be the heir to Hamatsu and Kumi. But if you do what you are planning, it will all be ruined! Please, sister."

"And what am I planning?"

"When I arrived at the castle today, I noticed a small, young woman with a very large hat leaving the main gate. I did not believe my eyes. Do you remember the young child I told you about, the one whom I met at the temple?"

"The little Ama? The brave one who was nearly executed?"

"She was the girl I saw. I am sure of it. Little Miki was taken in by the Koga, who taught her their magic. Little Miki was the one who told me who Teruko really was. The boy who helped my Little Miki get into my son's mansion was tortured and killed by Lady Teruko and her guards. He was there to collect night waste. If she was here, it was because of you, because I brought you here. I heard a rumor that she was Ama at the Fujiwara temple. I so wanted to believe that my dear, sweet girl had found happiness."

"She had. Until Teruko sent her Iga to kill her and the man she was to marry. The boy was heir to the province of Yugumi. She is here to put an end to her misery, not to rescue me. She knows that I cannot go home. I knew that once that dirty animal touched me, Shigenori could never take me back. I want to die. If the young girl is who you say she is, and who I think she is, even if she does not know herself, Yumi will live. Death will be welcome, my sister."

---

14 Jigai – A female form of seppeku that involves cutting the jugular vein.

"Ah, Yabu. I need to speak with you about a visitor the castle had last night. Someone I think both of us have already met." Teruko looked at the ugly, disgusting, lying piece of filth who stood in front of her. Usable for his cruelty alone, Yabu was not the sort of man you could trust alone with any woman. Somehow he had earned her father's trust, but only her status as the daughter of head of the Iga clan had saved her from his attention as she grew up, unlike so many of her friends. Standing up, she faced the brutal, scarred-up, hairy animal, smiling as she looked into his shifty eyes. "The little peasant child I asked you ever so nicely to kill three years ago. You remember her? The fleas? The pretty dark eyes? Tell us again how you made her moan and how she begged for death as you enjoyed yourself."

Reaching into her long sleeve, Teruko glanced at her other guards, Iga shinobi all, as they shifted position in obedience to her eye movement. The elegant woman stepped behind the smirking, middle-aged toad, swiftly slitting the animal's throat from ear to ear. Standing back as the writhing man struggled on the floor, she passed the blade to the miko, who had given her the welcome news of Miki's visitation.

"Sadao, please take our companion Yabu to the woods behind the castle. I want our guest to find him so that little Miki can see how sorry we are about our prior disrespect. Our Koga sister deserves this before we take her this evening. Then take eight men and guard the north road into Yugumi. Our little Ama will no doubt try to meet the Monk Rennyo's Sohie Cavalry across the border. I want nothing to interfere with her getting into the castle this evening."

"But Gozen, why not kill her in the castle?"

"And how would you explain that to the Hamatsu? No. We are going to let her rescue that little whelp Yumi and O-Kin. She only has two Samurai with her, no shinobi. Her own people think that Miki is dead. We will take them in the shrine's courtyard. Kill the Samurai first. Leave Miki alive; she will be useful. Yumi and O-Kin? Nobunaga will have them both executed, and the path will be clear for me to become his wife. We will use the little Ama's plan against her. You six will be in the shrine with me to take the women. This should be easy."

Crickets chirped and owls hooted in the darkness of the woods near the shrine to the east of the largest castle anyone had ever seen. Three shinobi, including the tall Hisano, waited for Miki and her guardians, if that is what they were. Somewhere in her three years in the Fujiwara temple, her friend had changed. Maybe, the tall kunoichi wondered, Miki was becoming who she really was.

"Hisano, I don't like Miki anymore. Gonzo didn't tell us to be here. We need to go home." The cool late evening wind whistled through the trees opposite the shrine that Miki had identified. It was where several women would make their escape if Miki was right. But something was wrong. There had been almost no traffic into or out of the temple most of the afternoon. One or two Samurai, one with a woman, all of whom left within a few moments.

The tall Koan readied the equipment that Miki had requested. He bound the claws, the hooks, and the saw together, wrapping them with soft rope. "Come on, how scary could Miki be? It's Miki. Small and cute."

"Gonji is right. There was nothing small and cute about the girl I saw this morning. It's not the Miki we know. This one was ready to kill one of her own. She was eager to kill and too willing to die. Has the cut stopped bleeding yet? Koan, please help change Gonji's bandage, if you would. If we get the chance, we take Miki by force and abandon this stupidity. If she does get the women out, take the young one and leave the older one to the Samurai. Koan, it will be your job to take her south and get her to the old woman I told you about. By splitting the pair, I'm hoping we can get at least one of them out of Hamatsu. The one we keep will be our piece in the game. Let the head of the clan, Master Kawachi, decide what to do with her." Hisano watched the miserable Gonji stare into the woods, focused on nothing. Leading these men into suicide was not her intention. Lady O-Kin and her daughter Yumi would be difficult enough to get out, but they would at least be cooperative. Miki was the problem. Assuming that Miki and her crazy plan survived the night, she had to get the girl to think like a shinobi again and abandon a woman's revenge. There would be time enough for that later.

A noise in the bush told the shinobi that the Samurai had arrived. A quick glance sent hands to swords, but Miki would expect a trick, so best not to provoke the girl, thought Hisano. At least pretend to go along for now. A wolf call was answered from behind, not the direction of the Samurai. Trust was something that Miki seemed to have forgotten. Miki had managed to crawl almost into the camp unspotted by trained shinobi. At least that skill had not deserted her.

"Koan. You and Sir Mitsu will enter the castle with me. I see that you have what we need. Once we secure Lady O-Kin and Princess Yumi, Sir Mitsu will escort them out of the tunnel with you. There is a rope that pops the door on the left near the top of the ladder. Don't try to leave until Hisano signals. The tunnel is under the shrine statue on the left; the rope is under the mat. Give Lady O-Kin to Sir Benkei and let him go north as you planned. Mitsu will take Yumi south with Gonji. Don't leave the woods until you see my signal. Escape east with O-Kin and protect her if you can."

"Your signal? Where will you be?"

"Drawing the Iga away from you and the shrine."

Why do all of Miki's plans involve suicidal acts of Samurai-like bravery? "Why should the Iga be guarding the Shrine?"

"Because they know I was in the castle last night. We found a body of a man named Yabu on the other side of the castle near where we are holding the horses. Yabu was the man who was ordered to kill me the day the real Lady Teruko was taken. Also, Lady O-Sho may have seen me when I was leaving. She said nothing."

"We are going home. All of us, even you. This is crazy! You are crazy!"

"Then go, and stay out of my way. Benkei, the woman leading the Iga will be Lady Teruko, your sister, or an impostor named Gozen. You decide. When Sir Mitsu brings the women through, ride south, then east, not north. They must know about Rennyo's sohie cavalry, and you would never make it. Take them directly to Ikido and to Lord Shigenori. Do not harm the priests, but do kill the mikos. They are Iga assassins."

"You will die." Hisano could not believe her ears—Miki giving orders for Samurai to kill women. This Miki wasn't deferential, not a shred of doubt about her path or plan. This Miki was powerful, confident, and competent. This was a plan she had thought through with all its consequences. Given the girl's continued survival, she stood a chance.

"I am already dead. I am buried next to Sir Uji, heir to the Suwa clan as his wife. Tonight, he will rest peacefully. I counted eight Iga soldiers on the road north. That leaves four, plus the miko and any of the servants that are Iga. Those four, maybe six, will be in the shrine to capture me. Our odds are excellent. It also gives Teruko an excuse to have the Yorisada women executed, and if she implicates Lady O-Sho, it will get rid of any obstacle to marriage with Lord Nobunaga. Teruko is kunoichi, so she will not involve the Hamatsu. Too many questions."

"Why do you need Koan?"

"Koan is strong and can climb and is well trained, thanks to you. Benkei is too large to get through any of the windows, and I need a man who can look like a Samurai and sound like a Samurai. That means I need Sir Mitsu. You need a Samurai who knows how to handle horses. Koga shinobi cannot do that. You need Benkei for his katana. I also need for Benkei to see Teruko to be able to report the truth back to the Suwa clan. Kumi and Lord Oto need allies."

"How are you getting out?"

"Koan and Mitsu-san will bring Yumi out through the tunnel."

"How are you getting out?"

"Lady O-Kin will be helping me. It is not her plan to escape. Do not tell Yumi this."

"How are YOU getting out?"

"That depends on Teruko and the Iga."

"Escape is not in your plan?"

"I intend to escape the way I did from Fujiwara."

"I understand."

"Koan, the Iga will not follow you through the tunnel. I promise that. Hisano, remember to wait for the signal. Wait to give Teruko time to return through the tunnel."

"What is the signal?"

"You will know."

Watching Miki disappear into the night with Koan and the thin Samurai named Mitsu, Hisano tried to imagine a signal that could be seen or heard from the shrine.

"Little Monkey is very brave. In her chest beats the heart of a Samurai warrior."

"You have no idea how true that is. Benkei-san, we need to get both Yumi and Miki out of Hamatsu. There is something about Miki's heritage that even Miki doesn't know. It would seem that Kumi has two Princesses. Koan does not know this. Monk Rennyo suspects this, but now you know. Take Yumi and O-Kin, but we need Miki. I have a plan, but I need your help. We are here to protect Miki, but I need her cooperation to get her home. Miki must believe that both Yumi and her mother are dead. Miki can't be allowed to sacrifice herself to save them."

"Little Monkey was correct. You people keep secrets the way we breathe. Once we have Yumi, I will help you save Little Monkey's life. I owe that to Uji. But you underestimate the woman's intelligence. She will see through all of your secrets."

"That's my biggest fear. Thank you. Rest now. It will take Miki a while to do whatever it is that Miki is planning to do."

"She did not tell me what her signal was. How will we know?"

"Miki is very good with things that burn, explode, and make noise. We'll know, Benkei-san. We'll know."

There was no moon, and with the clouds, not even stars to lighten the pitch black air.

"So where do you want to make the climb? I'm thinking that corner on the inside away from the shrine. It's dark, and the shadows are deep. Lots of wood for the claws. No more than a few moments to get up the rock base, and it looks as if the windows on the second floor are wooden slates."

"They are. You and I can make the climb. Sir Mitsu isn't trained and would get us both killed."

"Then how did you plan on getting me in?"

"I wandered around the castle for half the night last night. See that wooden block in the back? It's where they send women out to get water in that stream over there. It is guarded by one Hamatsu guard, but he sleeps until someone wakes him to go out or come in. They knock twice to get back in, but sometimes the guard doesn't put the timber across the door because it is very heavy. That is how we will enter."

"Then why the claws? We can use the rope to get down."

"To complete the illusion. They will be found in O-Kin's room. The rope will be out the window."

"But we won't be leaving that way."

"No."

"Then why do you need me?"

"My friend Koan cannot look or act like a Samurai. From your topknot to the way you walk, to the way you speak and give orders, you are Samurai. They are looking for someone like my friend Koan, not you, Mitsu-san. You do not stand out like a peasant would."

"Then why do you need me?"

"Because you know how to use our tools, and you can do what is necessary. Shinobi follow no rules except those that bring us success. Remember?"

"Us?" An exchange of smiles followed by hand signals saw Miki take the lead, moving toward the far corner of the imposing castle. The danger would be moving around the inside; even at night there would be guards, and the Iga knew they were coming. Miki handed the sword to Mitsu at the edge of the woods before proceeding to the back door alone, stopping along the river to fill a bucket in the dark.

"Do all shinobi let their women lead?" Mitsu looked at the lanky kid they called Koan and wondered just who, or what, his new companion was.

"No. Hisano is the only one. She's the best at planning, spying, and killing. Really good at killing. Mostly Samurai. That's all Samurai are good for."

"And Little Monkey?"

"Because Hisano said so. And curiosity. I've seen that girl do some crazy, unbelievable stuff. She's cute when she isn't trying to get us killed, like now."

"You do not like Samurai?" The boy stared into inklike night toward the small shadow, watching the tiny figure slip through the door crack.

"Not much. Good for killing. When Hisano says so, I'll kill you." The boy was honest, at least.

"You think you can beat me with the sword?"

"No. I'm not stupid enough to try. I'll stab you in the back or slit your throat, or poison you or bash your head in when you're sleeping. Killing is what we do best. We're pretty good at stealing, spying, and destroying stuff, too. Look, Miki is signaling."

"You go first."

The boy Koan moved fast, as though he could see in the dark. Sloshing through the brook, Mitsu tripped over a branch, going into the water on one knee. How did the boy move so silently, he wondered. *Is he walking on water?* Mitsu could see the boy slip through the cracked door as the small figure, highlighted by lantern light, signaled for him to hurry up the stairs.

"I sent Soun the guard upstairs to tell Lady Teruko that an Ama named Little Monkey has a message for her. I told him that Lady Teruko is probably in the Shrine waiting for her, but the Little Monkey will not be there. The Ama's revenge will be here, waiting for her. Why are you wet?"

"Some Samurai you are. You can't even walk on water."

"Didn't you tell him about the walking stones?"

"Must have forgot."

"You know the plan. Let's go."

Closing the door and locking it with the timber hiding a pyrotechnic surprise for later, the girl quickly signaled for haste. Mitsu would carry the lantern, as he needed to be as obvious as possible to hide the girl moving through the shadows in the halls behind him. Distraction was the key to deception, letting them see what you want, calling attention to it. Mitsu was impossible to hide, which made him perfect to hide behind. Koan would provide other distractions as well as prepare the way.

The halls and rooms would be confusing for the Samurai if it were not for the clicks and creaks the girl made that kept him on course. She was there, behind him, in the shadows somewhere. Heard, but not seen. Women passed him, ignoring him except for the polite greeting or bow. He was a Samurai; he was supposed to be there, but behind him was a girl no one saw. Was she even there, he wondered, as before him stood a sleepy guard and a thin, flimsy door held shut with a pin.

"Get awake! Now! Intruders have been spotted outside the walls. Check on Lady O-Kin and then warn our Lords Hatamoto. Move!" Mitsu watched the young man struggle a bit with the sliding door, forgetting for a moment that the pin held it shut. Little Monkey was right: act as if you belong, and they will believe it. Walking into the room, he held the light high to ruin the night vision of the guard, according to the girl they called Miki. The two women scrambled to their feet, only one appearing surprised. "They appear well. Warn our Lord's guards now. To make sure that Lady O-Kin remains here, I will take Yumi-san with me."

Grabbing the shocked girl by the arm, he dragged her out the door following the guard and headed down the stairs as instructed, as the guard continued on. A dark shape that Mitsu assumed was his companion Koan pulled the whimpering girl out of his hands and stuffed her under a cloth behind a few boxes. Explosions, yelling, and confusion were elsewhere; confusion was everywhere as he made his way back up the narrow, steep stairs past the soldiers who were now running to guard Lord Nobunaga.

Working his way into the now-unguarded little room, he saw the body of a larger girl in hakama, a miko lying still in her own blood. Little Monkey, now in a blood-soaked white kimono that Lady O-Kin had handed her, tied off the rope, threw the length out the now-open window, and turned to drop the climbing claws on the floor. O-Kin sat on her heels with what appeared to be a sharp knife. She held the blade against the side of her neck, and a quick draw down sent a spurt of blood soaking the white kimono that she had been sleeping in. Little Monkey watched with tears in her eyes.

"Sir Mitsu, please make the announcement. Get Yumi to safety. Nothing else matters. I have given my word and Lady O-Kin her life." Miki lay beside O-Kin, pulling the mother's arm over her, taking her place beside the mother she wished were her own. She could only hope that the young woman named Yumi could understand her mother's gift, and hers. Miki knew that when Teruko came in to see the carnage, she would have just one opportunity to kill the Iga bitch. Lying in the pool of blood, she knew that patience was her one hope for Uji's revenge.

"GUARDS! Lady O-Kin and Yumi are dead. Send soldiers outside. I saw someone leave through the window." Mitsu remembered standing with the small woman with Lord Suwa and Uji's father as the brave girl had sworn revenge, that promise having brought the determined girl to this moment. No Samurai had ever fought harder, and now he regretted the disrespect that he had shown the courageous woman. He uttered an apology as he made his way down the stairs toward the secret tunnel entrance. Someday he would tell the Princess Yumi just who had saved her and how. This he owed to the Ama called Little Monkey.

Miki lay there in the dark, her face coated in blood, her head under the breasts of Lady O-Kin. There would be one perfect moment, one opportunity to shove the blade that she held in her right hand into the bowels of Teruko. For an instant before Teruko's guards killed her, she would have the opportunity to watch the evil woman's face contort in agony as she died, the same horrified look in Teruko's eyes that she had seen in Uji's.

Voices, panic, as the rooms were searched for the remaining shinobi invaders. The fire that she had started in the storeroom would be tough to put out. The powder that she had included burned more viciously when wet. Women were being herded out of the castle as men passed buckets and turned the castle inside out looking for the army of shinobi that had done so much damage. Rumors, lies, tears, and eventually silence.

She had not slept for nearly two full days, and even with the pain of lying under Lady O-Kin, Miki felt the tug of sleep. She was dead and could not move. Muscles ached, and the cramp in her leg was excruciating, more so as time passed. She heard Lord Nobunaga's voice above her as his worthless toadies described the shadows that they had seen and the battles they had fought that evening. If she could move, she would laugh in their faces.

The sun peeked through the broken window. If only she could shift her position. No Teruko. Lord Nobunaga had not gotten close enough for her to get past the Hatamato Guards. What if she was discovered by a servant girl? Who would she kill then? Voices, familiar voices. Peasants? Servants? No, undertakers. She could feel the weight of Lady O-Kin being removed, but before she could act, the weight of a man's leg held her down as a very familiar voice whispered into her ear to remain dead or all of them would be. Hisano. Why, how? She felt herself being lifted and shoved into a sitting position in a barrel as she bounced back up and down in the darkness. It was now that she could smell herself and the filth she was covered in. She bit her lip as they dropped the barrel, turning her upside down onto some sort of wagon. She adjusted what she could inside the bumpy, dark coffin.

Would they bury her? Hisano must know that she was still alive. Once away from the castle, she could hear a transaction of some type. Startled by a slap on the outside of the barrel, she knew that she was now alone with her friends, if they were her friends. What had happened to Yumi, Mitsu, and Benkei, she wondered? Soon she would know. Nothing mattered more than Princess Yumi. Killing Teruko was what she really wanted, though.

Light peeked through the shattered wooden slates of the room. Behind the elegant woman were servants scrubbing the smooth wooden floor of the blood that had soaked through the tatami mats. The amount of blood had shocked even the experienced kunoichi, now called Lady Teruko. The night had not gone as planned. The girl Miki had seen through every trap and killed her best kunoichi assassin. The Ama's rage had been as impressive as her skill. This was an enemy that no one could have foreseen.

The old minister shuffled into the room, nervously moving past the girls who were weeping as they worked. "Lady Teruko, I am happy that you are safe. It appears that Lord Shigenori has resorted to shinobi to continue the illusion that he is still worthy of being the Daimyo of Kumi. Never could I have believed that he would order the death of his own wife and daughter. We still have no way to determine the number of attackers. The attack was vicious. The miko that you assigned to attend Lady O-Kin was murdered, and it appears that Lady O-Kin committed jigai after young Yumi was killed. Lord Nobunaga is furious. Fortunately the attackers did not get past the Lord's Guards. I see that your guards were successful protecting you. Did you have any casualties?"

"A guard named Yabu. I knew his family, and his brave death is quite upsetting. Minister, I do not believe that Lord Shigenori was behind this attack. I do not even believe that Lord Oto was responsible. This was the work of an Ama. An evil, little dark-eyed Ama from the Fujiwara temple named Little Monkey. I hear that she was trained in the Koga arts. The little oni has been reported dead so many times I have to wonder if she is even human."

"Why would an Ama want to kill Lady O-Kin and her daughter?"

"Revenge. It seems that my family may have opposed her marriage to Suwa no Uji, heir to Lord Suwa. I believe she killed my dear Yumi and Lady O-Kin to hurt me. I pray that my brother Benkei survived the Koga attack on the Governor's mansion. I believe that you had only one attacker."

"One attacker? An Ama? We will track her down. She will pay, I promise."

"Minister, you should not kill the girl. Capture her instead. She has been reported dead so many times before that I am not sure that she can be killed." The old, gray-haired fat man had earned his position as Chief Minister by his obsequious support for every foolish, brutal, and psychotic idea that found its way into Lord Nobunaga's mind and escaped his vile lips. She hated the man, and yet his weak mind made him useful. "Minister, I think I know which way they are going. I should discuss this with our Lord at once, if you could make the arrangements."

Dismissing the maids left her alone with her friend and fellow kunoichi. "We need to speed up the plan. That little demon has done us one favor. Killing the two Yorisada women has cleared the path for us."

"Maybe. But what I don't understand is why she killed our sisters and our brother in the shrine? She had two Samurai with her, but the Priests said that the girl that they had was scared and crying. That doesn't sound like the kunoichi you described." A doubt half-formed in Teruko's mind. *But it sure sounds like that crybaby Princess Yumi. It cannot be! Not one more time!*

"Where are the bodies? Nobunaga would not let me see them."

"Picked up by the undertakers very early this morning. Both of then were placed in coffins and taken away. I thought that it was a bit convenient that there were undertakers right outside the castle."

"Who identified the bodies?"

"There was a Samurai that no one seemed to know giving orders last night. You don't suppose?..."

The two women stared at each other for a few moments before the epiphany caught hold. "Catch those undertakers. NOW! I will ask the Hatamoto for every horseman they have. I hate that woman. AHHHHHH!"

"I think that we should leave her in the barrel. She's easier to control that way."

Gonji had a point. If they were not being chased, it might even be worth the delay to move her that way. It would be safer, also, as the unhappy girl, screaming for release, had refused to relinquish the dagger that she had planned to kill Lady Teruko with. "Let her out, but watch for that dagger. We have to get her cleaned up fast. She's covered head to toe in blood. Gonji, you know what to do."

Koan removed the top of the barrel, stepping back as the angry Ama popped up armed, wielding the sharp blade with serious intent. Gonji, sensing that Miki was going to be less than reasonable about the whole thing, pushed the barrel over, spilling Miki into the grass and knocking the blade out of her hand, providing Koan the opportunity to dive on top of the squirming girl and control her, with Gonji's help.

"My, my, my. Are you that disappointed that you aren't dead? Tie her until she calms down. The Hamatsu aren't stupid, and Teruko will have figured it out by now. Wouldn't you like to get out of that clothing? Miki, it was a brilliant plan. Too bad you're worth more to us alive than Teruko is worth dead. We will have another chance to kill her. I promise that. I will help you do it. Miki, it's time to go home, but we need your help."

"I GAVE MY WORD THAT I WOULD GET REVENGE!!!"

"And you have. Your plan was brilliant, and Princess Yumi is free. Your Samurai friends have her, and with Benkei's help, Kumi now has an ally. I promise the time will come when you see Teruko and Satake dead. But for now, it's time to go home and let Teruko squirm. Miki, please! Think about what you have accomplished. Help me get Gonji and Koan home. We owe them that." Hisano watched the girl calm down a bit, although she still vibrated with unfulfilled rage. One Princess had rescued another. It was time to protect both.

Chapter 19 – One More Chance

escape, but to what
plans, treachery and deceit
missions incomplete

Somehow they had done it. Hisano stood outside Master Kawachi's hut in the south village, and the merc fact that she was alive surprised her. To have made it with both Gonji and Koan was the work of the Kami. Miki roamed the village behind her—looking for what? Hisano wondered. Escape? She had had her chance on the trek home, and with winter already in evidence on the ground, travel would become difficult. Besides, as Miki herself had pointed out, where could she go?

A girl about twenty, dressed like a warrior, motioned Hisano inside the crude hut. She took her leave as the tall kunoichi took her place in front of the head of her clan. Bows followed by the offering of drink seemed more cordial than their last meeting.

"Hisano-san, it is pleasing to see you again. Gonzo has told me of your success rescuing both Princess Yumi and our sister Little Miki. I would like to hear it in your own words."

"Master Kawachi. I am honored that you would want to see me again. Little Miki is not quite so little anymore."

"Are her skills as great as Gonzo describes? The Iga are as terrified of her as they are of her brother. Satake has posted a large reward on her head. It seems that Gozen has asked her father to make killing Miki his priority."

"Hai. It isn't her skill that worries me. Miki is still the Ama. She is more a Samurai than shinobi. If she ever learns of her heritage, we would have to kill her to stop her." Hisano looked at the gaunt man with the thin, scruffy, graying hair; somehow he seemed more trusting than before. "Miki thinks five moves ahead of her enemies, and there are times that she thinks of us as the enemy. If she knew that Lord Oto was her father, or that Taka was her brother, we couldn't stop her. What of Princess Yumi?"

"We intercepted the Samurai Benkei and Mitsu before they got into Ikido. The girl Yumi is in our hands now. The plan is to hide her as a servant girl in the inn on the south road. We need to keep Miki well away from her brother and father and Yumi. The Iga have sent a kunoichi to find Prince Katsu. That will be your next mission. Do you still mistrust Fusa?"

"Hai. Miki confirmed that Fusa is working for either Satake or Gozen. It was Fusa who identified Little Monkey as Miki and set up the attack on the Governor's mansion, although Miki blames me for sending Fusa." It was good sake. Far too good to waste on a woman, even a kunoichi. There was something he wasn't saying, something he needed. "Master, what do you need of me?"

"The head of your village, Master Ryuzoji, is dead, killed by poison. His wife Sakai was blamed, and I was told that she took her own life by knife when she was accused. The village selected Fusa's father Ogura as the new village chief."

"Master Kawachi, I can't believe that. Sakai would never hurt Master Ryuzoji. Ogura? He's a swine."

"I don't believe it, either. Your actions could have destroyed this clan had you failed. Your success and judgment have earned my trust. Your mission is to watch Fusa and her father and report back to me. Kimiko will be your contact. You may trust Gonzo, but no one else with this, particularly Miki. You must protect Miki no matter the price. You have my permission to disobey Ogura's orders to do it. No mission is worth Miki's life. I will watch over Yumi, and Gendo, the old sword maker, will keep Taka away from Miki."

"So Gendo-san knows."

"It's Gendo's plan. He's also working with Sir Mitsu and Sir Benkei to buy arms for Kumi's army. He knows that I trust you. The problem is Lord Shigenori. Next spring we will be ready, but he just won't cross the border from Ikido. Reports are his son Katsu has been banished in the east near the sea because his own father fears him. We want Lord Oto to be Daimyo, not Shigenori. We don't know Katsu at all." The old man had just laid out the whole thing. He needed an ally, and Hisano knew that she wanted to be that ally. This man would have her loyalty.

"Master Kawachi, I have a plan to force Lord Shigenori to act. It may not be possible this spring. We can use Fusa and her father to feed information to the Iga. Let her succeed a few times so that they trust her. When we have the weapons and when Lord Oto has trained his army, then we use Fusa to suggest a plan to draw Katsu in to Kumi. If Shigenori is as jealous as all the other Samurai, he will need to act or lose the opportunity for power." She could see the idea interested the man. "Miki has taught me how Samurai think. At the right time, use Taka to kill Ogura. Monk Akaki will see that he knows. I ask permission to be the one to kill Fusa myself."

"And your plan to get Katsu into Kumi?"

"False orders in Teruko's handwriting. Miki could do it if Teruko can't be fooled into it. Miki never forgets anything, and it was Teruko, I mean Gozen, who wrote the secret code that Miki figured out. If he is as arrogant as his father, he will jump at the chance to be the hero. The trick is to convince Teruko that it is her idea. Princess Yumi might recognize Teruko's handwriting. Who is Gozen, anyway?"

"Daughter of the head of the Iga Clan. She has been prepared for this role from birth, it seems. Now, tell me about your mission. Tell me about the girl named Miki."

"Hai. Miki is small, but her heart is limitless and open. I once thought that my friend was cursed by the Kami, but now I see that she was their gift to us. I once thought that the girl's kindness was weakness. Now I see it as her power, her strength. Miki touches the innocent heart as a soft rain would the tongue of a man dying of thirst. She is wise but impulsive. Miki is very smart but terribly naïve. She is gentle but ferocious, terrified but fearless. I have known her from my earliest memory, but I am just now starting to understand her."

"I am told that her eyes are dark, like her brother's. Like her father's."

"Hai. I have seen them both. She can see right through you, as though your heart were as clear as water, and move in the night as if it were day. She remembers everything, forgets nothing. She speaks to wolves, just as her brother does. Miki can see the future. Sometimes, even I am afraid of my Ama friend."

The old man's back straightened as he considered Hisano's words. "Miki is the other side of the same coin. This is an omen. Tell me about your rescue of Yumi."

"The plan itself was entirely Miki's. It started when General Satake..."

The elegant woman stood gazing out at the first snow of the year in her blue-and-silver kimono, her straight, black hair reaching her waist. Snow had come early this year for the plains of Hamatsu. She heard a knock at the door followed by a voice she recognized.

"Lady Teruko, we have word from our spy in the north Koga village. The village chief was disposed of as you suggested. His wife was blamed after they slit her throat. Neither Miki nor Princess Yumi have arrived there. Fusa reports that her father Ogura is the new chief, just as she promised. She expects that Miki will show up with Yumi soon. Miki has nowhere else to go."

"No. Our spy in the south village tells me that Miki is there, or was ten days ago. The head of the Koga clan was furious when he first heard about the operation. Everything the evil little oni did was her own idea. She planned to lie under Lady O-Kin and kill me when I got close. It was lucky that the undertakers took her out when they did or the daughter of a whore might have succeeded."

"The crybaby Yumi?"

"No one knows. The Samurai with the dark-eyed demon probably have her in Ikido or Yugumi by now. She is lost to us."

"Maybe. But our Lord Nobunaga has decided to marry you instead. Hasn't the Ama Miki done us a favor by getting rid of O-Kin and Yumi for us?"

"Unless she plans to kill me before I marry him. Everything she did was with precision. We will see her again. She will try to keep her promise."

"Her promise?"

"She carved it on the inside lid of her coffin. It said, 'When I return, you will die.' I have not slept a full night since. Nobunaga is convinced that he was her target. The coward will not go outside without a hundred-man escort anymore."

"When will she return?"

"That the Little Monkey did not say."

"Ouch! Are you trying to kill me?" Gonji squirmed as the sullen, dark-eyed girl straddling his chest trimmed a bit of skin, tugging the silk to close the wound.

"Stop being a baby. If you had let me treat you before, it wouldn't have become infected. The sake will help."

"Then let me drink it instead of pouring it on my chest."

"It doesn't help that way."

The women in the large, rough wooden hut went about their chores, the oldest one handing Miki a warm, wet cloth to clean her unhappy patient's wound. Finishing up, Miki stood, letting the taller boy escape. The rough wooden door slid open behind her briefly, letting in the bitingly cold wind as Hisano slipped in.

"Miki, it's time. Master Kawachi wants to see you."

"I need to leave while it's still possible to get through the middle pass by morning."

"Master Kawachi is the head of the Koga clan. You won't be permitted to leave without his permission. Besides, the Hamatsu have thousands of men looking for you, and the Iga would love to catch you, too. You have a unique way of making enemies, Miki. Do you really need the Koga after you, too?" Hisano watched the girl's mind work for a moment before conceding the point. For the first time in recent memory, Miki had no argument. Straightening her clothing, the immaculate girl in her black hakama followed her into the evening wind.

Standing outside Master Kawachi's hut, the second largest building, the largest being the training school in the central part of the village, the two women waited for the invitation to enter. Hisano looked over at her friend, noticing that the girl had shoved her sword, which should have been left in the other hut, into her wide obi, Samurai style. Before she had the opportunity to correct Miki, the door slid open, and the determined Miki entered ahead of her.

Inside were two old men, the graying, gaunt Kawachi and a still older man whose thin, white hair surrounded the bald patch on the top. Miki didn't recognize this man, who sat on Kawachi's right. Going to her knees, Miki snapped the hakama out of the way as a Samurai might before placing her hands on the rough wooden floor and bowing low enough to place her forehead on the ground. Startled by this unexpected act of respect, Kawachi glanced over to the man on his right for guidance. The girl was clearly waiting for some signal.

"Sit up. Master Kawachi, this woman is well trained." The older man was either Samurai or trained in the household protocols, thought Miki.

"Master Kawachi, this humble woman begs for permission to be allowed to leave so that she may complete her mission. If she leaves now, she could be through the middle pass by dawn."

"You have never been through the middle pass this time of the year. Even on a clear day, it takes two days. It's also heavily guarded right now. It seems as though they are looking for a small woman who tried to kill Lord Nobunaga, or so they think. Why are you wearing that sword that way?"

"Master, please forgive this girl. This is the katana of Sir Suwa no Uji, and she has been sworn to revenge his death. Only the necessity of rescuing Princess Yumi and the misguided interference of your servant Hisano has prevented this simple Ama from accomplishing her promised task. She begs to be allowed to return to Hamatsu Castle and to end the misery caused by an Iga woman named Gozen pretending to be of a noble Samurai family." Bowing low, she had said what she came to say. She had asked politely; her motives were clear. Whether the man consented or not, she had tried.

"Misguided interference? We saved your life, you silly imp."
What's Miki doing? Is she crazy? A quick glance from Kawachi
silenced her, for now. Miki would hear from her later.

"Miki, Hisano has told me of your determination to kill Teruko and Satake. No one has a right to revenge more than you,
but no woman has the right to give her life away without the consent of her master. I am the head of your clan, and I understand
your anger, but you are far too useful to be wasted in this way. I
can't allow you to sacrifice your valuable life. You have skills that
we don't. You have knowledge we need. No."

"Master Kawachi, a girl was banished from this clan. A girl
was adopted by the monks of the Fujiwara temple and was to be
adopted by the Suwa clan before she died. She walks on this world
to bring those who killed her back to hell with her. The unworthy girl's master was Monk Arikuni, a holy man who showed her
kindness and taught her compassion. This simple girl is responsible for that holy man's death and the death of a Samurai who
offered this ungrateful baishun his love. She has accepted her
destiny. This girl's unhappy life is not yours to save. Her life is
already lost, promised to the man who would have been her
father."

The two old men looked at each other, unsure of what to say.
Miki's anger complicated everything. "If you wait until we are
ready, we will help you with your revenge. Things are in motion,
but your premature actions would cost a great many innocent
lives and destroy the future of Kumi. You will not leave this village."

"Then this girl is a captive?"

"If that's what Miki chooses to be. What I want is for Miki to
learn the skills that this village offers and teach us what she has
learned. The time will come when all of us will taste revenge for
what they have done to the Koga people. When that time comes,
Miki will have her revenge, the Yorisada will have Kumi, and
you will have your destiny. This I promise. For now, be one of us
again. We need you."

To be continued in the book *Three Yorisada*

Chapter 20 - The Beach

3 yorisada
a family united
power and revenge

It had been more than two years since the last time she had entered Hamatsu. So much misery, so much joy had passed through her life. Beside her was the man who would now be her husband, lying on the sandy floor of a fisherman's hut under the leaky roof by the river that separated Kumi from Hamatsu. The vicious beating that Satake had given her had left her body scarred, and yet the man called Katsu didn't care. Turning, she touched his whiskered cheek, hugging him as much to assure herself that he was real and not an illusion as for warmth. This was happiness that the girl named Miki had never known. This was a man who would never leave her, never abandon her, who had fought for her and with her. He had come for her, as had Taka, as had Yumi.

First light peeked through the many holes that perforated this hopeless shack, and through the miserable excuse for a door, she could see the thick morning fog. The sound of the water lapping up on shore reminded the kunoichi that they were already supposed to have crossed, as Hisano and Taka had done the previous night.

It would not do for her new husband, the Samurai named Yorisada no Katsu, heir to the province of Kumi, to cross the river unfed. Miki slipped away from the muscular, well-defined man and checked the bags as well as the fish that they had cooked the previous evening. The meal was certainly not going to be fit for a high-born Samurai, but it was all they had.

"What am I supposed to do? The wood and kindling is wet."

"No time, anyway. Taka and your friend Hisano have to be wondering where we are. We will eat in Hamatsu on the march. Get this stuff ready." How long had he been awake?

"Katsu-san. You need to eat. Let me..."

"No time."

"Hai, Katsu-san." *One does not disobey one's husband on the very first morning. Besides, he is right.* She watched the man stand and stretch, pushing out the door. *I should be ashamed of myself. This man deserves better.* Shoving the small pot into the Katsu's bag, Miki placed the dried fish inside. She would make it up to the man, somehow.

Voices. Not Taka or Hisano, either. Soldiers! The sound and smell of horses. *HOW STUPID CAN I BE! I'm killing this man JUST AS I DID UJI! Not this time. NOT THIS TIME!* Grabbing Taka's katana, Miki cut a few of the cords holding the boards on the back wall and slipped through the opening. This time would be different. It had to be!

The thick morning fog hid her quick crawl to the woods. The sound behind her wasn't a soldier. Hisano! Making her way through the edge of woods bordering the river's edge, the tall kunoichi touched her eyes, and with a few head gestures and hand motions let Miki know that Taka would be arriving on the opposite side of the fight. A quick and silent reply told Hisano to take the horses. There would no doubt be a single horse holder.

The scene from the corner of the shack was not particularly encouraging. There were at least six men, one heading toward the shack.

"We are looking for a woman."

"Have you tried the pleasure district?" Katsu was at least staying calm, although the soldiers were not enjoying his humor. The experienced man stayed close to water's edge to avoid being surrounded on all sides. Katsu, the sword master of Ikido, wasn't the inexperienced boy named Uji. Katsu at least stood a chance.

"This one was short and young. Scars and bruises on her face and body. There is a reward for this woman." Satake! He knew about the scars and bruises because he had taken great joy in giving them to her. He had helped kill Uji and Arikuni and Tomoe. He had tortured and murdered ten monks and tried to kill her more times than she could count. *It is time for this man to die.*

"What has this woman done to warrant this sort of manhunt?" The conversation was fooling no one. Katsu was trapped against the water, surrounded and seemingly without escape. This could only end in blood. Why men felt the need for verbal sparring before a fight had always confused her. "I may have seen the woman. What did you say the reward was?"

"She murdered two retainers and stole an item that Lord Yoshida would like returned. Have you seen her? Do I know you? We are also looking for a man who was seen near here named Kiyotaka. A vile, murdering coward. Perhaps you should come with us." Every hand was filled, waiting for that moment.

"I can assure you that I am not Taka-san the demon."

"And why would I believe you?"

"Would you believe me?" All heads turned to the ghostly figure emerging from the fog on the opposite side from her, his wet clothing hanging off his thin frame, giving the boy who had adopted her a frightening, ghastly appearance. Taka stared up at the soldiers from underneath his large round hat like a wolf sizing up his prey, a look Miki knew well. This was the moment!

"It was four retainers, not two. Sent to kill me in spite of a deal that your master made. I WANT THAT MAN! He tortured me all night. He didn't even ask me any questions. He did it just to hurt me! He enjoyed hurting me!" She could feel the rage building inside her. Rage for the woman who had died in her place, the innocent monks he had executed, the old man whose only crime was compassion, and the boy Uji, who had died because he loved her. Nothing mattered but killing this man. The evil had to end here.

One of the soldiers bolted for the horses; Hisano would get him. The soldier closest to her was in her way and deflected her blow. She blocked his response, but the large man was very strong and pushed the blade into her scalp before she could drop to a knee and let his blade slide off of hers, cutting the man's leg nearly off. The ease with which this blade cut surprised even the experienced kunoichi. Feeding her anger, she continued to strike until the beach was red with blood. Looking up, Katsu was still facing two men, including Satake. That was the fight she wanted. His head would be hers this morning.

Katsu glanced at her, moving between her and his only remaining opponent, the scarfaced Satake. *What's he thinking? Get out of the way!* Was he protecting her?

"You seem to have me at a disadvantage. We have met before, have we not?"

"I apologize for your ear. As I recall, I was not as kind to you as I should have been."

The men had met before. No matter, Satake needed to die. Painfully.

"Let her go. Then it will be just you and I."

"I cannot. She is my wife."

Katsu had acknowledged her. He was protecting her. *Get out of my way! The bastard won't take you away from me as he did Uji!* The two men clashed, Katsu taking the man's hand off at the wrist. Now out of the way, it was her chance.

Miki's first blow cleaved Satake's head open. She slashed as rapidly as she could, delivering the misery and rage of a lifetime's worth of suffering blow by blow until exhaustion and blood let the blade slip from her hand. Katsu was alive! Kicking the blade away from her, she could feel Katsu's arms around her as she collapsed beside the mutilated body and wept. She could feel the water washing up the beach and onto her legs, taking Satake's lifeblood away.

Now there was only one more. In a large castle that she had visited before, she would once again save the Princess Yumi. This time the Iga kunoichi Gozen would be exposed as a fraud. This time Gozen would die, and Benkei's sister Teruko would be avenged. This time, she would keep her promise to Governor Matsuhide, Uji's father.

Glossary

Ama - Buddhist nun.

Amanojaku - Literally "imp from heaven." Used as a diminutive for one who is contrary or who has a contrary nature.

Aruki Miko - Shinto female shaman whose gifts include speaking for the dead.

Buddhism - An Asian philosophy of compassion, ethics, and truth.

Daisho - A combination of katana (long) and wakizashi short sword that together is a privilege of and symbol for those of the Samurai class.

Genin - Primary spy or operative in a Shinobi or Ninja organization.

Hai - The word meaning "yes."

Hakama - Loose skirt or pants normally worn by a swordsman because it hides the motion of the feet.

Jigai - A female form of ritual suicide that involves using a tonto or small blade to cut the jugular vein in the neck.

Jonin - Head man in a shinobi ryu, or school.

Katana - A curved, two-handed sword about forty inches in length. Light, fast, and extremely sharp, it is the soul of the Samurai.

Keikogi - A long top normally worn by a swordsman, warrior, or miko. Tucked into hakama.

Koi - A large decorative fish used in landscaped ponds.

Kunoichi - A female ninja or shinobi. Trained in a different way than her male counterpart to make use of her gender.

Miko - A Priestess, Shamaness, or Maiden of the Shinto religion. The traditional costume is a white keikogi (top) and a red hakama (bottom).

Naginata - Essentially a sword blade on a pole, commonly used by foot soldiers, ashigaru, and retainers.

Ninja - More a Hollywood term, the art is ninjutsu; hence, "ninja."

Ninjutsu - Art of being a Ninja.

Shinobi - One of seventy-three clans that practice ninjutsu. A Ninja.

Shinto - The native Japanese religion or spirituality that teaches that everything has an essence or spirit.

Shrine - A Shinto place of worship, frequently smaller than a Buddhist temple. There are many small roadside shrines throughout Japan.

Sohei – A Warrior Monk, frequently of the Ikko order. There are no Zen Warrior Monks.

Temple - A Buddhist place of worship. Buddhist temples frequently have Shinto shrines on the grounds.

Tonto - A short blade used as a symbol of status for a female of the Samurai class. Used to commit suicide when required.

Torinawa - Arresting rope used by police officers of the day to snare the prisoner's weapon and person during the arrest.

Yamabudo - Mountain grapes.